THE WRONG GANG

One by one, they stepped under a pool of light from one of the streetlamps. Their eyes were lined with smudged mascara and their lips were bright with red lipstick. The flesh-tone bandages some of them had on their faces stood out like dark patches. They wore tank tops with brassieres underneath, leather pants and black riding boots, and they carried an assortment of weapons—including a smoking gun—in their immaculately manicured hands.

Nancy Boys.

I swallowed, remembering Ferman's words of warning.

"This just isn't your night," laughed one of them.

It was futile, but I turned and started to run. I heard a crack and waited for the pain of something biting into me but it never came. There was a whoop from behind and the sound of running. I pumped my legs hard, but fear was getting to me and I could feel myself weakening. What strength that remained ebbed, and I collapsed in the middle of the street.

I had closed my eyes and was waiting to die when something grabbed the collar of my coat and lifted me off the ground.

"We'll be taking it from here, Mister Boddekker."

And then, for better or worse, I knew that Ferman's Devils had come to save me. . . .

Also by Joe Clifford Faust

Old Loves Die Hard (Play)

A Death of Honor

The Company Man

Angel's Luck:
Desperate Measures
Precious Cargo
The Essence of Evil

Pembroke Hall:
Ferman's Devils
Boddekker's Demons (forthcoming)

FERMAN'S DEVILS

JOE
CLIFFORD
FAUST

BANTAM BOOKS
NEW YORK TORONTO LONDON SYDNEY AUCKLAND

FERMAN'S DEVILS

A Bantam Spectra Book / December 1996

SPECTRA and the portrayal of a boxed ''s'' are trademarks of Bantam
Books, a division of Bantam Doubleday Dell Publishing Group, Inc.
''Spit in Your Food,'' by Jodie Falco Stroff, © Poke in the Eye Music
Ltd., administered internationally by Pembroke Hall Music Rights
Distribution and Licensing Agency (PHMRDLA). Lyrics reprinted with
permission. All rights reserved.

ISBN 0-553-57621-6

Published simultaneously in the United States and Canada

Bantam Books are published by Bantam Books, a division of Bantam
Doubleday Dell Publishing Group, Inc. Its trademark, consisting of the
words ''Bantam Books'' and the portrayal of a rooster, is Registered in
U.S. Patent and Trademark Office and in other countries. Marca
Registrada. Bantam Books, 1540 Broadway, New York, New York 10036.

PRINTED IN THE UNITED STATES OF AMERICA

OPM 0 9 8 7 6 5 4 3 2 1

For Joshua Bilmes:
who played extra innings for Francis and the boys . . .

FERMAN'S DEVILS

The destiny of Western civilization turns on the issue of our struggle with all that Madison Avenue stands for.

—Arnold Toynbee

PEMBROKE, HALL, PANGBORN, LEVINE, AND HARRIS

"Selling you to the world since 1969"

Offices in Principal Cities: New York - Montreal - Toronto - Sydney - London - Tokyo - Moskva - Beijing - Chicago - Oslo - Philadelphia - Amarillo

CLIENT: »International Pharmaceutics		PRODUCT: »Daily Jones Line
WRITER: »Boddekker	TIME: »:60	MEDIA: »Audio
TITLE: »*Give Us This Day Our Daily Jones*		
PRODUCTION ORDERS:	»Use no music or backgrounds unless indicated	

MAN: Our Father Who art in Heaven, hallowed be Thy name. Give us this day our daily jones—

ANNOUNCER: Do you find that you're always praying for the quality and purity of *your* daily fix?

MAN: May it be pure and may the measure be true—

ANNOUNCER: Are you tired of shoddy quality-controlled procedures that mean you lose time from work due to toxic buildup or lack of a precisely measured dose?

MAN: May it bring the release I seek—

ANNOUNCER: Have you had it with cheap synthetic substitutes that promise you the bang but only take your bucks?

MAN: May it sustain me.

ANNOUNCER: Then you need to switch to the *Daily Jones Line* of pharmaceuticals! The *Daily Jones Line* is made right here in the United States, according to the strictest standards set by the DEA! Whether you're smoking, snorting, or mainlining, you can rest assured in knowing that only *Daily Jones* goes the extra mile to ensure that the dose you get is accurate, pure, and packs the punch you need!

MAN: And please, Lord, don't make me have to knock over that market on the corner—

ANNOUNCER: *Plus* . . . you'll find that a *Daily Jones* fix is competitively priced, while remaining well within FTC guidelines!

MAN: Amen!

ANNOUNCER: The *Daily Jones Line* . . . because something *that* important should be the *best*.

ONE

Deep, Deep in Enemy Territory

When I heard the voice behind me, I knew I'd made another stupid mistake. I'd made more than my share of them over the last couple of days, but this one was far different from the others.

This one was going to be fatal.

It hadn't been long since I'd stepped out of a place called Ogilvy's and started walking in the first direction to catch my eye.

I was down. I did that a lot, letting myself get depressed over little, stupid things. But in retrospect I can say that this time the depression was not my fault.

I had caught it from everyone else.

Part of it was Hotchkiss and his problems. Not that Hotchkiss's problems have ever affected me in any way, but this time it looked like he was telling the truth when he said that the world was coming to an end. I had tried to blame it on the fact that he'd recently broken up with Dansiger, but that strange way of comforting myself didn't last.

Especially when one of the old men got up in front of the whole company and said that the end of the world was coming. Of course, according to the old men there was always a way out of the end—but this time it would mean the end of an era, and only the strong were going to survive.

So at that point in my life, as I walked down the wet NYC streets, I wasn't sure of anything, let alone how strong I was.

I wasn't strong enough to tell Bainbridge to get lost. Or perhaps I didn't want her to get lost. Maybe I wanted her around, although the way she tended to fawn over me made me feel uneasy. She was pleasant company, and she was handy to take along when the agency had a function, but that was it as far as I was concerned. That bothered me. It was wrong to use her like that—although she certainly didn't complain about it. Maybe she believed that someday she would make the great conversion, and I would be forever hers.

On the other hand, maybe I'd end up with Honniker In Accounting. In reality, the chances of that were roughly equivalent to winning the Grand Jackpot in the Beijing Lottery. Every male at the agency, married or un, considered himself her suitor, and Honniker In Accounting somehow managed to remain oblivious to their attentions. The agency was rife with speculation on how she was able to ignore us, and the theories ranged from outlandish to obscene.

But Honniker In Accounting liked creative types, of which I was one. There were a hundred or so others at the agency, true, but none of them had had the privilege of talking to her twice in one day. True, once had been all business, and I'd made a complete fool of myself when it had happened.

Still, I wouldn't forget that second time—at Ogilvy's, when she made a most deliberate attempt to get me into a snake dance. I replayed the moment and smiled. "Come and shake it," she had said. It would be one of those moments in my life that I would file away and haul out to replay when I was feeling miserable. After all, how many guys at Pembroke Hall could say that Honniker In Accounting had asked him to grab her hips and dance?

Reminded of Ogilvy's, I began to wonder about the woman with no future; the one who sat by the juke, pumping in money and playing every song by the least-talented acts of the last century. She had told Ogilvy that this was her last night on Earth. What was that all about?

Then there was the Smilin' Guy and his roses and the problems I had coming up with something for the Boston Harbor account and all the excitement over World Nanotechnologies, Ltd., and what had happened to poor old Pangborn.

First and foremost there was that house in Princeton. The solid, beautiful house that I couldn't have.

I stopped walking for a moment and exhaled. My breath steamed.

Yes. Going to Princeton and believing that I could outwit the conventions of the real estate business had been my first major mistake.

The light turned. I walked across the street and down the next block.

Definitely it was the house in Princeton. It had been the focus of my life for the last sixty hours or so. I had become obsessed with it, and it had consumed everything. It had thrown my life into chaos on a day that would have enough chaos of its own.

A mistake, the house. A big mistake, like getting drunk and not calling Bainbridge, like going to work still hungover, like buying that rose from the Smilin' Guy, like listening to Hotchkiss when he was depressed. It was a mistake to not pay attention in the big meeting, which meant I acted like an idiot when Honniker In Accounting approached me. On top of all that, I was sure that my meeting with the old man was a mistake, too.

I had to say yes when Hotchkiss asked me to come to Ogilvy's, and I had to let him buy me a couple of drinks. And I had to let myself get hooked into staring at the woman with no future until I had fallen in love with her eyes.

I should have gone to her. Or I should have danced with Honniker In Accounting. Instead, I stepped outside for a walk.

That proved to be the biggest mistake of all. I often wonder how things might have turned out if I had shaken it with Honniker In Accounting or gone to comfort Mez No Future instead of letting the overload take me outside for a walk.

Now I was at the end of a block, somewhere deep on the island, waiting on a street with no traffic for the WALK icon to flash.

I flexed my fingers in my pockets and watched my breath steam again. Why, I thought, am I waiting for a light when there was no traffic? That should have told me something right there, but I went on, crossing the street.

As I neared the other side I saw the reason why the icon never flashed.

It had been broken out.

I tried to exhale, but couldn't. A growing feeling of dread trapped the air in my lungs.

I looked around. It was obvious now that I wasn't pondering my run of mistakes.

The stores on this street all had electrosnap bars across the windows and photo-ID security systems behind the burgproof glass. Trash baskets were overflowing. New subway entrances were sealed shut—it looked as if they'd never even opened. Most of the streetlights were out. At best, only one on each block was working. It was too quiet, and as I shuffled in a tight circle, I could see something spray-painted in reflective red NightOpt on a building across the street. It was a crude portrait of a man with a goatee and a toothy grin, a bent nose, fiery eyes, a widow's peak, pointed ears, and horns. Below the visage in NightOpt blue was the word *Devals* and then a NightOpt orange symbol indicating that the Devals were members of the Manhattan Street Gang Cooperative Association.

And there I was on a street that had been co-opted to them. I punched myself in the thigh and cursed, then looked up at the street sign to find out how far I'd gone from Ogilvy's.

I was at Sixty-second and Amsterdam. It was a long way from Madison Avenue, from Ogilvy's, from anywhere that would feel safe. Worse yet, the straightest line between the two points would take me right through The Park.

The darkness made me shiver, but then, like in the commercial I'd written, I began to beam from a mental ray of light. *You might be in trouble and you might be in the thick of it, but have no fear! Because no matter your situation, help is always as close as . . .*

My right hand crossed to touch my left wrist. My watch wasn't there. I closed my eyes and for a brief instant I could see it sitting on my desk. I'd forgotten to put it back on before leaving work.

No problem. All it meant was that I couldn't put in a lifesaving call to Emergency Central.

Thanks, Boddekker, I told myself.

For a moment I stood frozen, trying to control my breathing. It was the only sound I heard, the streets were that quiet. My lips started to turn up in a smile. *Well, isn't this in keeping with the way the day has gone!*

I had to think out my options. My best bet was to head back the way I came—whatever that was. The problem was, I wasn't sure how I'd gotten there, and I wasn't sure how many gang territories I had gone through to get where I was.

It looked like a case of eat or be eaten. I wondered how I would look with a fat apple stuffed in my mouth.

I turned back to head south on Amsterdam, but my eye caught a fleeting shadow about a block from where I was.

Great. Now I was cut off.

There was always the nonchalant approach. I stuffed my hands back in my pockets and started down Sixty-second toward The Park.

"I don't think you want to go that way."

I wasn't sure if I heard it, or if it was Reason speaking from my subconscious. All I knew is that it made my pulse race, and I fought the urge to let my legs run wild.

When I got to Columbus I turned south, but it looked like the shadow had trailed me from a block away. It rounded the corner and came toward me. I stopped and looked down the street toward The Park.

No. I'd rather die first. And that looked like my option no matter what course I took. If I must die, I thought, I'll do it on my terms. I spun on my heels and ran back up Sixty-second toward Amsterdam, going straight up the middle of the street.

"Smart choice."

I *had* heard that. It came from behind me, and the speaker started to run at a maddeningly casual pace, like he had all the time in the world to catch up with me. Yes, there it was. Add to the list of stupid things the act of running away from a gang member on his own hallowed ground. Let that be my epitaph, then: "Here lies Boddekker, dead at twenty-eight, of chronic stupidity."

If that's the way it was going to be, then at least earn your executioner's respect. I crossed from the middle of the street to the opposite side and slowed to a walk, bending over to look like I was winded. My shadow's footfalls increased in pace. I feigned a stagger, and with both hands, leaned on an overflowing trash basket.

As soon as I saw him in the corner of my eye, I spun, shifting the basket between us. He danced around the junk spilling out under his feet, a wild look in his eye. I threw the barrel. It rolled toward him and he jumped. His foot caught one edge, tangled, and he went down, end over end. I stepped back. He grunted and threw the barrel aside. I kicked him in the stomach and ran.

At the intersection, I aimed for the middle of the street and swerved as if I were going to run north on Amsterdam. Then I stopped, turned south, and ran as hard as I could. As I came back to the intersection, someone jumped at me, arms flailing. I ducked and hit him a glancing blow with my shoulder. The impact knocked him down and sent me staggering toward the west side of the street.

I looked back. There had been two of them, and they were now standing on the corner watching me, bent over in various stages of pain. My fists clenched in triumph and more adrenaline dumped into my blood. Legs pumping, I was certain to hit light speed by the end of the block.

I lifted my head to see where I was going and screamed. There was a big, *big* black guy right in front of me. His face showed no emotion as he held his arm straight out, exactly level with my throat.

When the exploding lights and ringing in my ears began to fade, I was flat on my back. Something blunt was experimentally jabbing my side.

"You kill him, Jet?" asked a thin, nasal voice.

"Naw." Another prod. "He ain't dead yet."

"I really hate it when you do that."

"You want him to get away?" asked the voice called Jet. "After he nailed the two of you?"

"Stop it." This voice was low and malevolent and sent a chill up my spine, adding to the cold from the pavement. I fought the urge to shiver and laid as still as I could. Maybe they'd go through my pockets and leave me for dead. That I could handle.

"We going to kill him, Ferm?" asked the nasal voice.

"Don't know," said the low voice. "He's a civilian."

"What's he doin' here at this hour?" asked Jet. "I thought he was a Nancy Boy. Thought maybe we could squeeze him out good."

"Technically, yes," said a voice as warm as the voice called Ferm was cold. "We could kill him because he's in our zone. To be here at this hour, wandering unprotected, he must be completely suicidal."

I hadn't thought of that.

"Or completely stupid," said Ferm.

Sadly, that was more accurate.

"I'm with Jimmy Jazz," said the nasal voice. "Let's spill some."

"I didn't say we *should* kill him," corrected Jimmy Jazz. "I was merely stating that killing him would be within our rights."

"Seems a shame," said Jet. "He put up a pretty good fight. For a civilian."

"Speak for yourself," said the nasal voice. "He fought like a Nancy Boy."

"He fought *better* than a Nancy Boy," said Ferm. "He put you away, didn't he, Nose?" There was a slap and the nasal voice grunted.

"He nailed Rover, too."

"Rover don't know any better. You do." There was another whack.

"What do we do, Ferman?" asked Jet.

"We pull out his liver and feed it to Rover," said Nose.

Still another whack. "I think," Ferman said—and then there was another jab in my side. "I think we should find out what this guy's story is."

Nose swore in disappointment.

"Then we pull out his liver and give it to Rover."

Great, I thought. There I was, destined to be dinner for some animal, and I'd never handled a dog food account in my life.

"Wake up, Snow White." Another poke in the side.

"Jet killed him," Nose pouted.

"No," Ferman said. "He's playing dead. He's hoping that we go through his pockets, take his wallet, and leave him here." Hands grabbed my lapels and pulled my head off the pavement. Odor breathed into my nose, garlic, tobacco, cayenne, and the sourness of someone due for their daily jones. "Isn't that right?"

I kept my head relaxed and let it roll as if I were unconscious.

At close range, Ferman sighed, driving that awful breath up my nose. "All right. If you don't knock it off, I'm going to have Nose whack off your 'nads, and we'll have us a little street barbecue."

I straightened my head and my eyes popped open. "You've got a way with words, Ferman."

He let go and my head hit the street, starting a nice throb. I opened my eyes for a look around. There were five of them, standing on all sides of me, looking down with much the same dismay that I was using to look up. I recognized the one called

Nose first. He was dirty faced with a large nose, an earring poked through one side. He had been the one I had tripped up with the trash barrel. The one I had identified as Jet was large and muscular; he was the one who had stiff-armed my flight. There were three others there, but I hadn't yet matched them with a voice; a tall, relatively clean-cut boy who wore glasses and looked up and down the street nervously; another with eyes hidden behind a mane of tangled, shoulder-length hair, and lips that betrayed a facial tic; and the shortest of all of them, with hair shorn away to a soft fuzz, revealing a network of scars across his skull—and a scraggly growth of hair under his lip and chin that told me that he would never be able to grow a mustache or beard. They all wore heavy snow camouflage flak jackets that were surplus from the Norwegian war and each jacket was cluttered with buttons and marks and stains. Over the right breast of each was scratched the word *Devals*—with the exception of the boy with the glasses, who had the word spelled correctly, and poor Nose, who didn't have a *Deval* at all. I shivered and wondered where their dog was.

The one with the close-shorn head opened his mouth and spoke in Ferman's voice. "So, you going to tell us what you're all about? Or do we have the street barbecue so Nose can get his badge?"

"I'd rather have it off one of the Nancy Boys," Nose whined.

"You'd rather *have* one of the Nancy Boys," Jet said, making a gesture with his hands to leave no question as to what he meant.

"*Stop it!*" Ferman said icily, and then looked down into my eyes. "Let our guest talk."

I didn't say anything. I was calculating what my best move would be.

"Well?"

I calculated that a show of bravado might work. Maybe I could bluster my way out of this situation and gain a little respect in the process. I said, "What exactly am I supposed to say, Ferman?" I pushed my elbows against the asphalt and sat up. "Is this one of those stupid truth-or-dare situations, like you're the cannibal chief and you're going to eat me unless I ask a question that confounds you?"

"What are you talking about?" asked Jet.

"If anyone does any eating tonight," leered Nose, "it's going to be me."

Ferman tossed his hands up as if the situation were hopeless. "I guess we're going to have to kill him, boys."

The clean-cut boy looked up and down the street, shifting his weight from foot to foot. "I don't think we want to do that, do we?" he asked in the voice of Jimmy Jazz. "I mean, he's a *civilian.*"

"Tell me something I don't know," Ferman said, crossing his arms impatiently. "I think he should give us a reason for not killing him."

"Oh, that's right," I sneered, "play this stupid, macho game where you rob someone of every last shred of human dignity before you torture and kill them like some sadistic—"

Nose snapped out his foot. It struck me in the side of the head with enough impact to knock me back down.

"You talk too much," he said.

So much for bravado.

That was all I had time to think, for suddenly they were all over me, kicking and kneeing. I tried to curl into a fetal position, but they attacked my kidneys. When I rolled on my back, they went for the stomach and ribs. I remember having the strange thought, *Hey, these guys are real pros.*

Then it stopped. I had the feeling that the attack had been a warning. Then Ferman told me it was only a warning, and he dug deep into his Norwegian war surplus flak jacket and pulled out a long bone handle.

"Awright!" Nose cried. *"Eats!"*

"You got to understand something here," Ferman told me. "What we are availing you—" He looked troubled and then looked over at Jimmy Jazz. "Did I use that word right?"

Jimmy Jazz nodded.

Ferman smiled, obviously pleased with himself. "What we are availing you, sir, is the opportunity to save your own stinking life. Which right now isn't worth a whole lot, because you're in enemy territory. So maybe you want to tell me something that will make us not want to kill you."

I wheezed, "I get it."

"So whaddya got for us? Remember, it's got to be the truth, or we'll *really* get mad."

I coughed.

"Well?"

To save my life I couldn't think of a thing to tell them.

"Man," Jet groaned, "he ain't no fun."

"Come on," said Jimmy Jazz. He was pale, as if he weren't up to killing that night. "Isn't there *something*?"

I shrugged.

"You have a wife? Kids?"

I laughed. If I'd had a wife and kids, I certainly wouldn't have been in this fix. If only they'd known.

"I know," offered Jet. "You're some big doctor who is doing important research to rid the world of Creeping Chlamydia."

"Sorry," I wheezed.

"I got it," Nose said happily, as if this were some sort of game. "His poor old momma is dying in the hospital and she's waiting for him to come see her."

It was nice, but my mother was not in the hospital. She was living with some gentleman who was making a fortune salvaging records from sunken buildings in LA and San Francisco. My grandmother, however, was in the Woodstock Memorial Alternate Lifestyle Extended Care Facility, and I did visit her regularly, but the Devils didn't need to know that. I shook my head.

Ferman circled around, scratching his semibald head. "You got no wife and kids. You're not a big important doctor, and you don't have any close relatives who are about to croak it. Then what good are you? I mean, do you have a life? Just what *do* you do, pal?"

It was time for the inevitable. Confess and let them take my wallet and get it over with.

"I work in advertising," I said.

"You one of them guys who sells door to door?" Jet scowled.

"No," I said quickly. "I write commercials."

"The ones that get into my computer?" asked Jimmy Jazz.

"Someone else in my group does that." It was sort of a lie, but under the circumstances, totally warranted. "I handle audio and vid." That was true, mostly.

Jimmy Jazz shrugged. "That's a good reason not to kill him."

"Not good enough," said Ferman.

"Which agency do you work for?" asked Jimmy Jazz.

"Pembroke, Hall, Pangborn, Levine, and Harris."

"Yeah!" he said, then looked at the others. "Guys, Pembroke Hall, they have a group label."

"You handle any groups?" Nose asked quickly.

"As a matter of fact," I said, "I was given one today." They all looked at me, eyes full of anticipation. "The, uh, SOBs."

The one with the tangled hair turned away and spit on the sidewalk. The faces of the others soured.

"Not *those* old SOBs," Jet said, scowling.

I rolled my eyes. There were some things that there was no getting away from.

"What about Hateful?" Jimmy Jazz stared hard at me. In retrospect, I see that he was trying to tell me something. At the time I was simply too scared to notice.

"No, uh, someone else handles them."

"How about Killer Without A Conscience?" Jet asked. And then they all started snapping their fingers in cadence, singing, "Gonna spit, spit, spit, spit in my hands . . . gonna spit in your food."

This was too much. I wanted to stop them, but decided to take the initiative while they were busy. I rolled to my side and kicked the wild-looking one square in the groin. He folded and pitched forward. I curled and rolled, hitting Jet in the legs and pitching him over. The others cried out and tried to catch their falling comrades. By the time they realized what was happening, I was on my feet and running down Amsterdam.

"Stop him!" Ferman shouted.

I got to Sixtieth and turned toward Columbus when something caught my arm and pushed me toward the sidewalk. I tripped on the curb and flattened a trash can, spraying the street with debris.

"Trust me," a voice whispered in my ear, "and I'll get you out of this."

I started to look up and saw Ferman rounding the corner. The grip on my arm suddenly went from benevolent to malevolent.

Ferman stopped, looked at me, put his hands on his hips and laughed. "Well," he said, "I see you found out why Jimmy Jazz is the master of the shortcut."

Sure enough, it was the clean-cut kid who had the grip on my arm.

"Sorry," he whispered through clenched teeth.

Nose appeared from behind Jimmy Jazz, and Jet joined Ferman. The wild-looking one was nowhere to be seen.

"I should break every bone in your body," Ferman said. "You racked up Rover pretty good. You better hope he's not dead. He was the best dog we ever had."

Rover. The wild boy. Now it made sense.

"You've spoiled our fun," Ferman continued, fingering the bone handle. "And since you don't have any reason to stay alive—" He shook the handle and a bright silver blade popped out of the end. Closing in, he brought it to my throat and that awful mixture of scents filled my nostrils. "What do you think of that?"

So this was it. Almost at the prime of life, about to be cut down by a franchised street gang. I kept waiting for my life to flash before my eyes, but it never came. All I got was a melancholy commercial that I would never write for an insurance company that wasn't even my creative group's account.

> *It showed a little kid playing with blocks saying, "My daddy was stupid and stayed out after dark. He got killed by bad guys.*
>
> *"But what was really stupid"—pan back to reveal the mother now talking, and we see that they're living in a hovel, not a nice house in Princeton—"was that his insurance didn't have a street gang rider."*
>
> *Cut back to the little kid. "So we're stuck here in hell," he says.*
>
> *Smash cut to black, with the insurance company name in white letters, and an announcer says—*
>
> *"I can put you in a commercial."*

Of course. It was brilliant. Why else did kids join gangs? Ego. Self-aggrandizement. It was perfect. It also popped out of my mouth before I realized what I'd said. Judging from the look on Ferman's face, I could see it had had the same effect on him.

He said, "What?"

"I can put you in a commercial. A vid commercial, for a major product. We're talking a multimarket timeshare buy, a virtual all on the big ten cablenets, with maybe a dozen of the minors to pad out the demographics. Your face will be all over the place, in every city in the world."

"Me?" asked Ferman.

"And your gang." I started pointing. "Jimmy Jazz, Jet, Nose"—I noticed a limping latecomer—"and Rover."

"Will we get paid?" asked Jet.

"Of course," I nodded. "Union scale. Nothing to sneeze at."

Ferman lowered the blade. "I don't know about this. How do I know you're not giving me a line?"

"He's not," Jimmy Jazz said quickly.

"I'm a creative group leader," I said. "I'll be the one writing the spots. I'll be supervising the shoot. I'll insist that you guys appear in it, put a rider on the contract."

"What product?" Nose looked at me suspiciously. "Not something to make fun of my face."

"No. Not at all. To tell you the truth, I don't know what product yet, but I swear I can do it."

"No hemorrhoid commercials," said Jet.

"And none of them 'don't sleep around and you won't catch the creeping crud' ads, either," Ferman warned.

"No hemorrhoids, no PSAs, no problem."

Ferman shook his head. "I still don't know. It'd be a lot easier to kill you."

"Come on, Ferm," said Nose. "This sounds like fun."

Jimmy Jazz gave me a concerned look, then his face brightened. "Think of the girls, Ferm."

Jet liked that prospect, too. "Yeah."

"You can get us girls?" Ferman asked.

"To be honest, no guarantees on Nose or Rover," I said, "but once you've been on the vid, you probably won't have to go looking."

Jimmy Jazz gave me a slight nod.

"But all you'd have to do," I continued, "is mention to some girl, 'Yeah, I was in the Compound Casualty Insurance Company spot,' and anything you do to prevent the creeping whatsis is up to you."

Ferman looked at the others. The consensus was in favor of accepting the offer. He gave me a wry smile, then quickly brought the knife back up to my throat. "You'd better not be lying to us."

I fumbled in my pockets and brought out a piece of plastic. I held it out to Jimmy Jazz.

"It's his phone card, Ferm."

"What's his name?"

Jimmy Jazz started to butcher it. I stepped in with the correct pronunciation.

"Boddekker," Ferman smiled. "Well, we've got your number

now.'' He turned to Jimmy Jazz. ''Is it from . . . from whatever agency he said he was with?''

''Pembroke, Hall, Pangborn, Levine, and Harris,'' read Jimmy Jazz.

''You're not giving me a line, are you, Jimmy? I always suspected you of being soft.''

''Check it for yourself,'' I whispered.

Ferman scowled at me. ''No,'' he said bluntly. ''I'm going to trust you.'' He let the blade touch my neck. It was cold. ''And if you do jack us, we know where you work. We'll come back and break every bone in your body. Got that?''

He lowered the knife so I could nod.

''Jet,'' he barked. ''See our new friend here out of our territory.''

''Can I go with?'' asked Jimmy Jazz.

Ferman shook his head. ''Need you to look at Rover's unit, make sure he wasn't damaged.''

Jimmy Jazz rolled his eyes. ''Right,'' he said, disappointed.

I heaved a huge sigh of relief and swallowed to send something down my dry throat. ''Thanks.''

''Be careful heading back,'' Ferman warned. ''The Pinheads have got the Parkway to Eighth, from Fifty-ninth to Fifty-fifth. The Sluts run from Fifty-fifth to Fifty-second between Amsterdam and Seventh, and they'll really do a number if they catch you, whack your unit right off. You should be safe once you get to Broadway.''

''And watch out for the Nancy Boys,'' Nose warned.

Ferman spat on the ground. ''Nancy Boys are ranking amateurs.'' He looked at me. ''Don't worry about them. They aren't even co-opted yet. They're parasites.''

''Right.''

I let myself give in to the shakes as Jet started down Sixtieth. I fell into step behind him, keeping him a good ten feet ahead of me the whole time, until he left me with a nod at the corner where Broadway meets The Park.

From there I got far enough down Broadway to get a bikeshaw, where I trembled until we were back at Ogilvy's. I had the driver run in and buy a bottle of scotch, and I uncapped it as he took me home, taking desperate, sloppy gulps, trying to relax enough to enjoy the fact that I'd outwitted a bunch of hoodlums.

But it wouldn't take. Even when I was in the locked confines of my apartment, wrapped in a blanket with the vid set blaring the weather for noise, I couldn't get what had happened out of my head.

It was a chain reaction. A line of falling dominoes. Nobody could possibly know for certain when it all would end, but I knew without a doubt when it all started.

It all started with that house in Princeton.

PEMBROKE, HALL, PANGBORN, LEVINE, AND HARRIS

"Selling you to the world since 1969"

Offices in Principal Cities: New York - Montreal - Toronto - Sydney - London - Tokyo - Moskva - Beijing - Chicago - Oslo - Philadelphia - Amarillo

CLIENT: »A.N.S. Products		PRODUCT: »Toidy Nuke
WRITER: »Boddekker	TIME: »:60	MEDIA: »Audio
TITLE: »*Nuke It #71*		
PRODUCTION ORDERS:	»Use standard Toidy Nuke jingle #3a, instrumental, w/sing at end	

ANNOUNCER: Once upon a time, keeping your bathroom or bidet clean was as simple as applying corrosive chemicals. But in this era of ecological overmindedness and hardline antipol laws, a clean toilet bowl could get you thirty to life. So how do you deal with post-UV diseases like Retro-Parvo Simplex IV, Lyme's Variant, HIV 12, Creeping Chlamydia, and others? The same way we cleaned out the frozen fjords of Norway! [*SFX: Nuke explodes.*] With a high-intensity burst of cleansing gamma-type radiation from *Toidy Nuke*! Just drop a *Toidy Nuke* in your toilet bowl and leave the house for an hour. You won't have to worry about diseased relatives contaminating *your* loved ones anymore! Remember, if it ain't clean, it's time for tactical nuclear intervention with *Toidy Nuke*! *Toidy Nuke*, now available without a prescription!

TWO

A House Not a Zone

It had been love at first sight.

The house was ninety minutes out of NYC if you were on a zep, less by rail if you could get your hands on a rail pass. I had gotten there by rail, but it was a Sunday afternoon.

At the rail station I flagged down a bikeshaw and some surly, underemployed Appalachian type pedaled me the rest of the way into Princeton. I got out my notebook and brought up the map the agent had zapped, taking great delight in telling this guy where to go.

In spite of my instructions, we arrived at a nice middle-class Princeton neighborhood. By my watch it would be a full fifteen minutes before my contact from the agency arrived, so I told the driver to wait. That made him real happy. He likely couldn't read the sign stuck between the rocks in the front yard, but it was clear to him why I was there. The place obviously wasn't a Quarantine House—it had to be for sale. So the driver hunkered down in the passenger seat of the bikeshaw, pulled a Qube from his satchel and started watching the Houston Glads play the Chitown Philistines.

I couldn't wait. I walked up the sidewalk to the house, going slowly, looking across the yard. The place had synthetic hedges and trees bordering the front of the yard, and ground level was done up in very nice stone, the smooth on all sides kind that you find on seashores and lakesides. There were big rocks, too, none smaller than my fist. A nice size to keep the local kids from picking them up and throwing them at each other.

I saw that the place was deserted as I went up the sidewalk. Even though the agent had told me the house was empty, I was pleased to see that it looked well kept. There's something about an empty house—it seems to decompose when there's nobody to live in it. I'd seen my share of houses over the last eighteen months, and some of them weren't fit for anything but razing to recycle.

This place was nice, a warm terra-cotta color of stucco, the kind of look that got its start in the Southwest. There were no curtains over the windows, so I stepped up to peek through the window. On close examination, I saw that the house didn't need curtains. The windows had the familiar tint of the Opti-Block process. The agency had left them in Full-Open mode to tempt people like me into scrutinizing the interior. Some agencies would have left the windows on Full-Block so you'd have to endure a sales pitch when you went to see the house. But this agency had a rep for taking a soft-sell approach, something I sought, coming from my line of work.

Beyond, I could see the empty living room. It had extended-life carpet whose color I couldn't determine from the glare on the window, and there were plenty of outlets—one every meter, it looked like, with extra ports for phone/modem and cable access and uninet basing. A brick fireplace stood in one corner, with its License for Use prominently displayed. Farther back I could see a small dining area, with light falling in from a large opening that had to lead to the kitchen. Right in front of the door was a flight of stairs with an Old-Wood banister. At the top, the railing hooked to the right and vanished behind a wall.

The bedrooms would be there. Three of them and a full bath upstairs, the zap had said. Downstairs, the living room, kitchen, dining room, laundry/pantry, and a three-quarters bath.

At that point, I didn't really need any more convincing. After seeing so many houses that did nothing for me, I was starting to fall for this place. It was crying momma, as Bainbridge liked to say. I smiled and I backed away from the window, then hurried to check out the back of the house and consummate the affair.

As I went back, I checked out the outside finish, the gutters, the windows, the sidewalk. The place was in shape, there was no doubt about that. The former owners had cared, and more important, this agency had cared enough to make sure that the house stayed in prime shape. The stucco finish looked new, although the zap said it had been done over thirty years ago. Maybe a visionary had built it, using one of the now-mandatory acid-resistant finishing formulas. It wasn't faded; it wasn't scratched. Look at that! The sidewalks were fading but the siding wasn't! After years of abuse by the weather, *it still held its original color and texture!*

I stopped short, my hand on my chest. I was doing it again. I took a deep breath and chastised myself. I wasn't at work, and while I was falling, I wasn't supposed to be in love yet. That should wait for a few minutes at least. Besides, I was supposed to save my best licks for work. I continued.

The backyard was marvelous. A deck. A solar grill, with batteries to run the thing when the sun count was low. The backyard was nonfading AstroTurf, and as I stepped onto it my feet sank, just a little. Extra padding underneath! The previous owners must have had children and had taken the extra step to protect their precious little hides.

Oh, yeah, this was a great place to raise a family. If it ever came to that.

I looked back at the house. The roof was lined with Solar Plus paneling. I ran up to one of the windows, cupped my hands around my eyes, and looked into the kitchen. There were plenty of outlets here, too, and it was equipped with the low-draw, high-tech appliances that were coming out when I was getting out of high school. Great. The house would cost more because of that, but the savings would be made up when the power draw bill came along.

I let my eyes wander, imagining that I was inside, wandering through, opening the fridge, checking out the nuke and macrowave, cranking the handles to see if the water flowed, palming light switches, opening cupboards, running a finger along the counter, scuffing a foot across the patterned polyvinyl: *Grabbing a beer from the fridge along with a dri-pak of White China Noo-*

dle Snax; opening the beer; the smell filling the kitchen, and taking a long, yeasty sip; then pulling the top of the dri-pak open and tapping in a little water; covering it and throwing it into the nuke for three or four minutes; and drinking beer as the smell of cilantro or tarragon or paprika or cayenne filled the kitchen . . .

Now the house was starting to arouse me in much the same way, I suppose, as walking into a motel room. I sensed ultimate privacy here, no walls for amorous shouts to go through, no neighbors peering through spy holes to wonder about movements in and out, no landlords to appease. A quiet place where 'Turf and rock and plain air separate you from your neighbors and you're friends enough to borrow power tools and maybe watch some sporting event over a couple of beers.

Yes, it was definitely this house. Through the opening from the kitchen to the dining area I could see the fireplace, and I could see myself wandering over to it on a cold winter night with two hot cups of the latest from Boston Harbor, and sitting down on a thick synthetic rug with someone like Honniker In Accounting before a crackling fire, then drinking and talking and laughing until the words ran out and all we could hear was the sound of fire and wetness as large, white flakes of snow slowly tumbled to the ground outside. Yes, these are the moments. Those golden moments that you enjoy, you treasure. And because you want those moments to be right—oh, so right, that's when you rely on—

I abruptly drew away from the window, shaking my head. Enough of that. Save the licks for work. Boston Harbor would love something like that, so hold the thought.

"This place," I said, grinning, "is—"

"A steal."

My heart bounced and I turned with a yelp. The agent whooped and took a step backward, slapping her hand to her mouth.

"Oh!" she exclaimed. "Mr. Boddekker. I'm so sorry."

"Oh," I exclaimed back. The blood rushing back into my head made me dizzy. "You must be Jean?" I offered her my shaking hand. "Hello. I wasn't expecting you quite yet."

"I'm late," she said, taking my hand for a single shake, cradling a case against her chest with the other. "I apologize. I had a closing run late, and I ended up with a 'shaw driver who was kicked out of the Neanderthals for stupidity."

"Late?" I laughed and looked at my watch. Half an hour had passed. I had been raptured. "Oh. It's no—"

"And I feel bad that you had to start without me. Really."

"Don't worry about it," I said. "It's nothing. I've been looking around the outside, and I didn't notice—"

"My boss is a stickler for these things. I do hope I haven't made a mess of it. I really am sorry."

It looked like there was going to be no way to staunch the flow, so I took her by the arm and led her away from the window, saying, "Look, Jean, I'm loaded with questions about this place. Why don't you show me around the inside?" I asked her how old the roof was as I led her around the side of the house I hadn't seen yet. She fumbled in her case for her notebook and had started to punch the request in by the time we got to the front door, so I stood politely and waited for her to answer, resisting the urge to say, *You're new at this, aren't you?*

After a moment of keying and rekeying figures, she looked up at me. "The roof was redone with acid-resistant materials thirty-two years ago."

"Fine," I nodded. Not bad, but not great, either. Some work would have to be done, but nothing that I couldn't afford. I had the credit. In fact, I had the money on hand, enough to reroof the place where it stood, but I was saving it as my trump card for the Moment of Glory.

I smiled at Jean, and it finally occurred to her that we were there to go inside the house. She scrambled in her case for the key and worked at the door while I looked out toward the street. Her 'shaw driver had pulled in behind mine, and had joined my driver in sharing a drink and the Glads game on the Qube.

The door finally opened and I turned to follow Jean inside. I took a deep breath.

Jean looked at me nervously. "It's not right, is it?"

"No," I said. "I'm smelling the air."

She cocked her head.

"It's all right, really. It smells like an empty house."

The woman gave an apologetic shrug. "It really hasn't been on the market that long, Mr. Boddekker. If it would make it easier for you to look at, uh, I could have a cleaning crew come out, and, uh, well—we could set up another appointment for next weekend. Uh—I think my calendar's open." She started to poke at her notebook.

I knew her agency prided itself on not giving the hard sell to clients, prospective or otherwise, but this was ridiculous. "Jean," I said, taking her arm and pulling her into the house. "Why don't you tell me about the appliances in the kitchen?"

She wandered off, still poking her notebook. I followed slowly, stopping in front of the fireplace. Yes, that would be it. Honniker In Accounting, a warm rug, a few huge throw pillows, some Boston Harbor tea, or if we didn't feel obligated, some really great wine . . .

Jean's voice came from the kitchen in a mumble, so I caught up with her and let her tell me about the ages of the kitchen appliances. I opened the fridge as she did. It was off—there was no electricity anywhere in the house—and there was a lone can of beer sitting inside. I thought of the Neanderthal 'shaw drivers outside.

From there, Jean started to warm up, and I followed her through the house, checking the types and locations of outlets and letting her tell me about the living room, the dining room, the three-quarters bath. A door off the kitchen led to what at one time had been a garage, but had been converted. There was now a small hallway that connected to a sizable pantry, a laundry room, the small bathroom right off of the back door, and the battery room for the solar works.

"Do you want to power up the house?" she asked, tapping the notebook. "Everything should work."

I shook my head. "I believe you." That part didn't matter. If anything around here didn't work, it could be fixed by myself or a hired professional.

The fact that I didn't want to put the electric to the test seemed to relieve her, probably because the activation sequence couldn't be found on her notebook. We went back to the living room and headed up the stairs, Jean in the lead. She seemed oddly distracted, as if there were something important on her tiny computer that she couldn't find or didn't want to mention. I knew what it was. Her creditline program had probably flagged my marital status as a stumbling block. It didn't worry me. I had saved, and I was ready for the Moment of Glory.

"Three, uh . . . three bedrooms up here," she said, turning the corner from the top of the stairs to the hallway. "And a bath. And, uh . . . access to an attic."

She stood rooted, so I gently stepped around her and looked in on the first of the bedrooms. Nothing too huge, but roomy. Roomy enough for everything I had—and all the right inlets and outlets. Across the hall, the bathroom was *nice.* Garden tub; separate shower; a toilet and a bidet; nice, high sinks—two of them— ample closets; warm lighting; and a fog-free mirror.

"You'll find this place has a very nice bathroom," Jean said, in almost a monotone. Then she tried a joke: "And with two sinks and plenty of fixtures, it's Divorce Preventative."

"Great," I smiled, ignoring a statement that was clearly meant to make me prematurely divulge my marital status. It was a game. She knew it, I knew she knew it, but she had to make me say it. But I wouldn't until the time was right. "Nice idea," I said, and continued.

Straight ahead, at the end of the hall, was a linen closet. Above it, the pull-down door to the attic. To the left and right, two more bedrooms. Checking them, I saw that the place had a nice view of the neighborhood, plenty of room, inlets and outlets—I needed to quit worrying about those now as the place had plenty—and lots of potential. I could feel it, standing at the window and looking down on the street at the houses, the yards, at the two 'shaw drivers bouncing up and down with their fists in the air at the spectacle on the Qube.

This place was *it.* It was a safe place. It had a sense of community. It had history. Stately Princeton. A fine university, and site of a very important first contact—not quite a hundred years ago, when humans first got a glimpse at our own spiritual frailty against the most powerful weapon we'd ever know. What a great place for an ad man. My first priority after moving in would be a pilgrimage to Grover's Mill.

"This is it," I said, emerging from my inspection. "I love this place."

"All right," Jean smiled. Her eyes flickered to the notebook. "How, uh, what will you be doing with the bedrooms?"

Part of the pitch, I knew. I indulged her. "The one across from the bathroom has 'office' written all over it. The big one facing the street will be the bedroom. The last one . . ." I glanced into it. "It'll be a playroom."

"For children?" she asked. Nice move. I'd give her credit for that one.

"For sex," I said bluntly. Jean gave me a blank look, and I thought, *touché.*

"Just kidding," I said. "I don't know what I'll do with it yet." I put my arm on her shoulder, and she shuddered, probably thinking I wanted to make her my first playmate. "Let's go downstairs and work out the details."

We walked down to the kitchen and Jean set her notebook on the counter. She set up a small uplink dish, and it rotated until it located its datasat. The notebook flickered.

"Okay, uh," she said. "The going rate for this house is, uh, twenty-six."

I nodded. She was right, it was a steal.

"The current prime rate is thirty-eight percent." She paused to stab a key. "What kind of a down payment were you looking at, Mr. Boddekker?"

Here it was. The build up to the Moment of Glory. I held out my hand, fingers spread apart. I hoped she'd be impressed, but I couldn't tell if she was.

"Five," she said, and then her eyes widened. "Uh."

Yes. She was impressed.

"Five. Uh, five. Very good. All right . . . with insurances, taxes, liability rates, and mandatory options, your monthly payment would come to thirty-three thousand, six hundred forty-one dollars, seventeen cents, and twenty-eight mills."

"Right on budget," I said, "Although I don't know where I'll come up with the seventeen and twenty-eight."

"Huh?" She looked at me with a cocked head.

"A joke," I said, "and not a very good one at that. Do go on."

"I'll need to see your verification and references."

I gave Jean my name, five major credit cards, my citizen's ID, a work history card, work verification ID, and proof of recent residence. She ran them through a slot on the notebook, the information fed to the screen, and she nodded. I leaned back against the kitchen cabinet and stared into the living room. "Is that license for the fireplace current?"

Jean nodded without taking her eyes from the notebook. "Uh, yes. Yes it is. If you'll give me a moment, Mr. Boddekker, I should have . . ." She looked up for a moment. "Well, I should think we'd have an approval."

Back to the fireplace, with a smile. There'd be properly chilled wine and two glasses, and Honniker In Accounting would be there, wearing nothing but the glow of a real wood fire. Or maybe a simulated wood fire. But a real *fire,* that was the key, and a real glow, not a simulated one. With Honniker In Accounting, that was important. I reached out to touch one of her glowing breasts and—

Honk!

"A problem?" I said, startled.

Jean's notebook made the noise again and she stabbed a key to silence it. "This thing . . ." I could see a problem in her eyes. That noise was standing between her and the sale and the bonus commission she'd get on such a large down payment. "I'm sorry," she said. "Sometimes this net gets bogged down with stupid details. I need to confirm a couple of things."

I had expected this, but it was no problem. Let her ask the questions. The Moment of Glory was coming. "Go ahead."

"Are you married?"

"No."

She stabbed one key. "Do you have any children, and if so, how many?"

The killer question, but my answer shouldn't matter. "No. No children."

She stabbed the same key. She waited. I wanted to look back at that fireplace to see if Honniker In Accounting was still waiting, but I didn't dare.

Jean frowned at the notebook.

"Problems?" I asked.

A slight nod.

"Credit?"

"Familial," she sighed. "You don't have one."

Take a neutral position. Make her explain it. "My parents and sibs would be very disappointed if they heard you say that."

"That's a backline family, Mr. Boddekker." Jean's tone was at once disappointed and very businesslike. The change in her was almost chilling. "You have no line-plus family. No children, and since you're not married, there doesn't seem to be potential for them at this time."

"They're going to drop my credit because of that? That's an awfully minor detail."

"Not from the mortgage company's point of view, Mr. Boddekker. You've got a twenty-six-million-dollar house financed over a period of a hundred years. They want to be sure that someone's going to be around to pay it off.''

"Let's be realistic about this, Jean. I'm putting five million dollars down on this place. I make a hundred thirty thousand dollars a month. I'm a creative group leader in a company where there's no place to go but up, and I'm only twenty-eight. I've got sixty more working years before I retire—probably as a full partner in the company, in which case my monthly stipend will be more than the cost of this house. Who are they kidding? Do they actually think that someone's kids are going to make payments on their parents' house after they're gone?''

"You've got a compelling argument, Mr. Boddekker, but the way the mortgage company sees it, longevity isn't the issue. Even if it was, you're still past the prime age for that, because at twenty-eight, it means that there'll still be a decade's worth of payments left after you're gone.''

"Even with the down payment?''

"Even with the down payment. The problem is getting through life. You don't know when you're going to overdo your jones and end up in a mental ward, or as a frozen corpse in the sewers. You don't know if you're going to get called to the heavenly zone in the next terrorist attack. You could be the next statistic on a chart of a product liability case—'next we have the case of a Mr. Boddekker, who depilated himself to death with your product. Unfortunately, his case will have to speak for itself as he has no family to speak for him.' You can see how it looks.''

"Yes,'' I said. "The company has to have its money.''

"That is why we're in business.''

"Look, isn't there some kind of insurance I can get that will see that the company recovers its investment in the event of my death?''

Jean looked at me like I was crazy.

"Forget it. It was a stupid question, I know.''

She flicked a switch on her notebook and started to fold the screen down.

"All right,'' I said as the notebook clicked shut with a blunt finality. "What would it take for me to get into this house?''

"Getting a family would be the easiest way, Mr. Boddekker.''

"Sure. Tell you what. Marry me. We can adopt, and then call it off. You get the kids, I get . . .''

Her eyes started to raise above what she was doing in a cold glare. They told me that I wasn't funny. Worse yet, they told me she'd heard the gag before. On many occasions.

"All right. Besides that."

"A bigger down payment might do it."

"How much of a bigger down payment?"

She shrugged. "I'm no math-in-your-head wizard, but another five million might bring the finance price down enough to put it in your range."

"Five million dollars for another *maybe*?"

She nodded.

I stood for a moment. The roaring in my ears was my Moment of Glory, diving straight to the ground in flames. I hated her. If only she'd known how long it had taken, the deprivation I'd put myself through, in order to get what I had. "This isn't over. Not for anything."

"There's no reason to develop an attitude problem over this. It's only a house."

"Maybe to you," I said, "but not to me. I *want* this house. And I'm going to find a way to get it."

"That's fine," Jean said, tucking the notebook in her case. "Just make sure you do it fast. A house at this price won't sit here forever."

No, not forever, I thought. But at least part of forever. It certainly hadn't been put on the market yesterday, and it certainly hadn't been snapped up in the months it was sitting here vacant. There would be time. I would think of something.

"Mr. Boddekker?"

I looked up. Jean was putting away the uplink.

"I have to go. You'll need to leave so I can lock up."

"Right." I looked back at the fireplace. Honniker In Accounting looked glumly back. She'd have to finish the wine on her own.

"There are other ways of approaching this, Mr. Boddekker. If you can put fifty percent down, you may be able to significantly reduce the terms of the mortgage."

Sure. Like I was going to take out a career indenturement loan and stay at Pembroke Hall for the rest of my life when other agencies would surely be coming after me. "Or," I said cynically, "I could pay for the house outright."

"You could," she smiled, "although I should warn you that with closing and taxes and other added costs, the one-time price would be significantly higher than the financiable amount of twenty-six million.''

I didn't say anything.

''Or you could always wait a few years to see if the President's antihyperinflational measures do any good. That might bring the price down. Whatever the case, if I can be of any further, uh, assistance, let me know. I've got a line on some nice apartments and townhouses you can get into with only a year's rent deposit—''

I glared at her.

''Yes. Well. If you happen to get married in the near future, that would be your easiest course of action. I know children would guarantee your approval, but with your credit and the potential rating upgrade you'd get from being married, well—'' She turned to lock the door.

''Thank you, Jean,'' I said, and walked down the sidewalk to my waiting bikeshaw, too stung to look back. I slapped my hand on the vehicle's edge to get my driver's attention. He snapped off the Qube and Jean's driver scrambled out.

''Well, sir,'' he said brightly, hopping over the seat to mount the bike. ''Get yourself a zone?''

''Take me to the station,'' I said, picking up the Qube, flicking it on, and watching the Gladiators and the Philistines murder each other. It suited my mood.

It was one of those times. One of those bad times. A time when life had dealt you a fecal sandwich and expected you to eat it without catsup. A time when you knew the world was out to get you no matter which way you turned. And as fate smiles and you realize that you don't even have a napkin, all you want to do is go out and get righteously drunk. Well, friends, you've come to the right beer! You've come to—

I'd had enough. All of that traveling, only to be deprived of my Moment of Glory. I didn't even feel like saving that last good lick for any beer campaigns that might be coming my way—but it did give me a good idea.

''Stop at the first bar you see,'' I told the driver, ''and I'll buy you a drink.''

He gave me a sincere grunt of thanks and kept pedaling.

I was relaxed by the time I got to the rail station. The bar car was open, so I was numb by the time we pulled into NYC. I went back to my cramped apartment and proceeded to get royally hammered.

I spent all of Sunday with a blissful hangover, one that I savored. I would be grateful to go back to work tomorrow, although I couldn't shake the feeling that there was something important I had forgotten to do.

PEMBROKE, HALL, PANGBORN, LEVINE, AND HARRIS

"Selling you to the world since 1969"

Offices in Principal Cities: New York - Montreal - Toronto - Sydney - London -
Tokyo - Moskva - Beijing - Chicago - Oslo - Philadelphia - Amarillo

CLIENT: »TransMind Technologies		PRODUCT: »Gender Preference Reorientation
WRITER: »Boddekker	TIME: »:60	MEDIA: »Audio
TITLE: »*Homer*		
PRODUCTION ORDERS:	»Full digital storage & datasat uplink of completed spot ASAP pending approval	

[SFX: *Footsteps down busy Manhattan street.*]

MAN #1: [*Sounds like a real tough.*] Hey, Bill, whaddya know, here comes our ol' friend Homer!

MAN #2: [*Ditto.*] Yeah . . . *Homer Sexual!*

[SFX: *The two toughs guffaw heartily as UP MUSIC.*]

ANNOUNCER: Let's face it—homosexuality is not only passé . . . it's downright *embarrassing!* Well, you no longer have to live with the consequences of misaligned neuroconnectors! At a TransMind Sexual Reorientation Center, you'll find *only the very latest* in Electrocranial Recircuiting hardware, technicians who are trained *on the cutting edge* of this exacting new science, a pleasant atmosphere, courteous staff, and as always—*they're discreet!* TransMind Technologies was *first* in Reorientation, so they're the best—and, TransMind is the *only* company that offers you a one-hundred-eighty-day guarantee! That's right—if you revert to your old sexual habits *within six months* of your final treatment, TransMind will refund your money or treat you until *you're just the way you want to be!* TransMind has clinics in all major metro areas and will accept payment from all major creditlink nets, so there's no more excuse to live with impaired gender preference!

MAN #3: [*Sounds like one of the boys.*] Let's go have a *beer*, fellas!

ANNOUNCER: *Call* TransMind Technologies *today!*

[*SFX: TransMind Technologies sonic logo.*]

VOICE OF TRANSMIND: At TransMind Technologies . . . we *know* how the brain works!

THREE

A Rose to Last Forever

On the Monday morning subway ride, Jean's words about my financial situation burned my stomach along with the last of my hangover. I rode with my notebook on my lap, unable and unwilling to read the new disc I'd bought at the end of last week— *Remodeling Your Flat in Nothing Flat.* It was too depressing.

I stared out the window at the darkness, at nothing, head bobbing as we made stop after stop. A nauseous feeling was welling up inside of me, and I couldn't tell if it was from depression, my weekend binge, or the rocking of the subway cars. I glanced at my watch. Fifteen more minutes of this, providing things went well.

The train lurched and I fiddled with the buttons on my timepiece until it brought up the phone number of Jean's real estate agency. I hovered a finger over one of the keys on the watch face, debating whether or not I should delete the number. After all, it didn't seem like I would be doing business with them, not with the way Jean had been talking. Still, the challenge steeled my resolve. If there was a way to get into that house, I was going to find it. I was going to write the killer campaign, I was going to become a partner in the firm, I was going to marry Honniker In Accounting.

This last thought really brought things home. I didn't stand a chance of getting into that house. I might as well drop a thousand bucks on a Beijing Lotto ticket and face odds approaching those in favor of my spontaneously combusting during the subway ride.

Still, I wasn't going to let it get to me. I wasn't going to indenture myself to Pembroke Hall, nor would it force me into living the next nine decades in a tiny, miserable apartment. In fact, I wouldn't sit still for that, even for a decade. Playing it safe took too long, and I was on an emotional timetable.

The choice was between getting into a house—the one in Princeton, in particular—or picking a jones and getting into it so heavily that I no longer cared where I lived. I had a definite aversion to joneses, even though a lot of the Pembroke Hall gang had them, insisting that regulation had made them safe. None of them had my background. My grandparents were into the jones stuff back when they were kids—back before it was all legal. It had inspired them to name my mother Yellow Sunshine. Legal or not, the jones business didn't do my grandparents any good, and it certainly didn't help my mother. Whenever my eyelid starts twitching uncontrollably or my mind wanders off, stacking phrase upon phrase for an advert that'll never be heard, I wonder if I'm reaping the genetic legacy of a decades-old struggle that turned a generation of revolutionaries into stock brokers with massive guilt complexes.

My finger hovered over the watch face and punched a button that brought the time back. Jean's agency was safe for now, until I could think of a way to get into that house. The train pulled into my station. I set my resolve, grabbed my notebook, and made my way out.

Fifteen minutes later I walked into the Madison Avenue building that was home to Pembroke Hall—a big glass-faced thing that looked like all the other buildings built in the last century. The lobby was massive, with lots of tile and marble. It was one of those places where the dropping of a pin was as loud as the rending of metal, and with the Monday-morning crowds filing in, the din was almost unbearable. Pausing for a moment to look at the building traffic monitor, I decided to take one of the executive express elevators to floor thirty and walk the remaining seven flights to my office. I turned, heading for the nearest line, when a familiar voice called out.

"Hey, Mr. Boddekker! *Mr. Boddekker!*"

I knew before I looked that it was Smilin' Guy. I wasn't disappointed by the sight. Smilin' Guy had at least a three-day growth of beard *(Forget to shave this morning?),* was wearing a spring coat over a flannel shirt and denims *(Still a little cold to dress like that, isn't it?),* and a fistful of carefully crafted . . . it looked like some kind of flowers *(What have you got for me this morning?).* And, of course, he wore the trademark smile that was frozen on his face, day in and day out, rain or shine, every time I saw him. Some people's grandparents, it seems, had been more daring and experimental during that lost revolution.

"Hey, Guy," I said. Guy wasn't his real name. I don't think anyone in the building knew what it was, or even if he had one, and most of us at Pembroke Hall referred to him as the Smilin' Guy. I pointed at him. "Forget to shave this morning?"

Smilin' Guy reached up to touch his face with the hand filled with what looked like flowers. He poked himself in the cheek with one, then brought up the other hand, recoiling as he felt his chin. "Oh," he said, and I wasn't sure if he was surprised or horrified. "Yeah. I guess I did." He shrugged and laughed.

"Still a little cold to dress like that, isn't it?" I said, nodding at his attire.

The smile didn't budge, not a millimeter. It was one of those things that unnerved you and then wired you right back together. It was so a sincere . . .

"It's s'posed to get warmer today, and the boss, he wants me to do some stuff around the outside of the building today. 'Planting bulbs,' he said, and running around, that always gets me all sweaty, you know, 'so I said, 'Well, I oughta be ready for that!' "

"And what do you have for me this morning?"

Smilin' Guy's gaze fell to the floor and he kicked the side of his left foot with his right toe. "Boy, you don't miss a thing, do you, Mr. Boddekker? These, they're flowers. Made them after some pictures I saw in a book, they're called roses." He held them out for my inspection. They were delicately carved and mounted on some kind of stiff green wire. "Only these roses, they won't stick you like the real ones."

I touched one of the petals with a finger. It made a scratching sound that set my teeth on edge. "It doesn't stick your finger, anyway," I said, shivering. "What's it made of?"

"A plate," Smilin' Guy said proudly. "This real light stuff that I dug up at my brother's salvage place. There were lots of them there, crunchy stuff you could break with a finger, but tough, too, you know?"

He was waiting for me to catch up with him, so I nodded.

"My brother says they used to make plates and cups out of this stuff and then they'd throw it away. But the joke was on them because it lasted longer than they did. Some of this has been buried fifty years, my brother said. So I brought a bunch of the plates home and made some roses that would last a pretty long time."

"If not forever." I looked over the ersatz bouquet in his hand. His work was immaculate. "How much?"

"Uh," he said. Smilin' Guy always stumbled with me. Anyone else, he would have blurted the price right out. "Five. Five hundred. But for you, Mr. Boddekker—"

"Nonsense," I said, pulling quickcash from my pocket. "This is one of the finest things you've ever made, and you'll not take a dollar less."

"All right." He fumbled the quickcash into his pocket transactor, then handed it back, offering the fistful of roses. "What color do you like?"

"Red looks good." I pulled one from his hand, and he nodded excitedly.

"Thanks, Mr. Boddekker, I hope—I mean, I know you'll really like it, because, you know, you like all of my stuff."

"This really is the best," I said, and I caught myself, unconsciously, waving the rose below my nostrils to catch the scent. "You've really made something wonderful here."

"Well," Smilin' Guy smiled, "I got to get back to my work." He waved and wandered back to a marble column, where he'd left a skinny broom and a dustpan at the end of a pole. He wandered toward the elevator lines, sweeping up imaginary pieces of debris.

A hand clamped to my shoulder. "Come on, dreamer. The big meeting's this morning."

It was Hotchkiss, another Pembroke Hall copywriter, a skinny geek of a guy with constant sinus problems and a year's worth of seniority over me that he never let me forget.

"Meeting," I said, and then I looked through the fog of my

hangover to what I thought I'd forgotten over the weekend—the agency-wide creative meeting. The old men wanted to address us all at once. Something was up. "No, that's not it."

Hotchkiss started to muscle me toward one of the opening elevators.

Instinct kicked in. I looked back at Smilin' Guy. "I need another rose." Although I couldn't explain why, I knew the reason would become clear in a matter of minutes.

"We can't keep the old men waiting," Hotchkiss said, shoving me into the waiting car, which immediately started to pull us up. "What do you think it is?"

I gave Hotchkiss a blank look. My weekend of excess was catching up with me, and I was in no mood to try and read someone's mind. Especially not Hotchkiss's.

"Define *it*."

"The meeting, Boddekker. Something hot, rumor has it. Me, I think it's the end of the world."

"Then they don't need the media creatives for it," I said. "Once the EBS Burst comes over the wire, the adverts go out the door."

"Lighten up," Hotchkiss said. "You should be in a brighter mood. What's wrong? Didn't you find a zone of your own?"

"A zone," I said. "I found this zone, it was beautiful, Hotchkiss. It was in Pr—it was in Jersey. It was everything I was looking for."

"Your use of the past tense bodes ill, Boddekker."

The elevator lurched. Doors opened and we spilled out. I started for the stairs, but Hotchkiss grabbed me again, pulled me toward an elevator that looked as if it hadn't been used since the last century.

"No," I said uncomfortably.

Hotchkiss dangled a key, grinning stupidly. "I got Ride of the Week."

"What else is new?"

He dragged me to the direct-access elevator and keyed into it. The car lurched hard—some reward, I thought, for meritorious service—and Hotchkiss's eyes drilled into mine. Then he spoke in low tones, his deepest conspiratorial voice.

"I suspect," he said, "that we're all going to be using the past tense a lot more. I've been thinking about this, Boddekker. What we're doing, it can't last much longer. Something has to change—

something has to give. If the old men are smart, they'll see it coming, too, and they'll do something about it."

"About what?" I asked.

"Never mind," he blurted, as the elevator began to slow. "So. Did you get the zone for your own?"

"Trying to change the subject, are you?" The elevator opened. We stepped out.

"You were making such a big deal of it on Friday. I expected you to come in a lordly land baron this morning, complete with a case of ego. What of it, Boddekker?"

"I'm working on it," I sighed. "These things take time. What about your weekend? Tell me the sordid details about what you and Dansiger did this weekend. I want to know shapes, sizes—"

"Now *you're* trying to change the subject," Hotchkiss said quickly. We turned a corner, pushed through a set of double glass doors, and were in the reception area of Pembroke, Hall, Pangborn, Levine, and Harris. Hotchkiss and I took turns greeting the secretaries as we walked through, and my interrogation continued when we were out of earshot.

"You don't give up, do you?" he said.

"Come on, Hotchkiss." My elbow sank into his ribs.

"If you must know," he said with a resigned sigh, "nothing happened."

"Oh. Yes. Right." I nodded sternly. "And next you're going to sell me a prorated percentage of the Moon Treaty."

Hotchkiss stopped dead in the hall. "I took her out of my watch, okay?"

I stared. "I'm sorry. I, uh, didn't know it was that serious."

"Not serious." He was almost too loud. "Over. All right?"

"Sorry. I didn't know."

"Nobody does. You know, I hated the thought of coming in this morning. I'm going to have to explain it now, to everyone."

"I feel for you." Although I was sure he didn't believe me, I really did. I faced a similar situation. I had left on Friday, swearing to bring feudalism to the twenty-first century. Hotchkiss had promised to bring tales of erotic excess from his weekend.

"If it weren't for this meeting," he was saying, "I probably would've hung the whole matter and slept in."

I had thought about that, too, although Hotchkiss certainly wouldn't believe me.

We split apart at the end of the hall. I went to my office and

began to weed through the messages that had accumulated on my
mainframe. One had been stylused in big, looping handwriting:
"Don't forget!" Then I saw its author coming down the hall. It
brought a sudden attack of memory; the memory of what I had
forgotten, the memory of why I needed another rose, the memory
that had been lost while I was absorbed in my own problems.

"Boddekker," she said. "Hey, Boddekker." She was short
and chubby faced, her hair long and tangled brown. Her eyes
could be deep when she wanted them to be—not at this particular
instant, of course—and the gentle voice I had known to be hers
was currently lost in a grating whine. "Didn't you get my note?"

It was Bainbridge. She was a senior in college, working as an
intern with my group. She was interested in linguistics and
wanted to work for an agency, making sure that adverts made
smooth transitions into other languages, mores, and cultures. She
expected to be hired by Pembroke Hall when she graduated. She
was, I think, mistaken.

"I—" I held my hand up, pointing at the screen.

"I left it Friday so you wouldn't forget," she said. "All I
wanted was for you to call me." She stood in front of my desk,
her notebook held like a shield between us.

"Look," I said, "I'm sorry. This weekend—" A throb told
me that my hangover was making a triumphant return.

"You didn't call me," she said. "You told me you'd call,
Boddekker, you *promised*. But you didn't call. You never call me.
Never. What does it take to get a call from you?"

I eased back in my chair. "Bainbridge, it was pure irresponsi-
bility on my part. The weekend didn't go quite the way I had
hoped—" I thought, do I tell her the truth? Do I tell her that I had
spent my weekend drunk, sick, and hungover rather than live up to
my social obligations? I didn't think it would go over.

But, then, neither did standing there with my mouth hanging
open. Bainbridge shook her head in disgust.

"Honestly, Boddekker, I don't know where this relationship is
going. I really don't. Can I count on you? Can I depend on you?
Are we supposed to be friends or what? I can't take this! I mean,
you won't even call."

I suppose I could have called her when I was stone drunk, and
she surely would have taken it badly. Or I could have done it
Sunday and suffered while she played Florence Nightingale, nurs-
ing me back to health from whatever virus I could convince her

that I had. I wouldn't have been pleasant company, either, not with the way I felt, and certainly not with the way she tended to chatter like a magpie about things that meant nothing.

"Well?" Her hands went to her hips. If she'd known she'd done that, she would have hated herself.

Nothing came out of my mouth.

"Don't you have something you want to say to me, Boddekker?"

I nodded. I knew she wanted an apology, and I swear it left my brain that way. But on the way it mutated, and it left my lips as something I regretted the minute my ears heard it.

I said, "Bainbridge, would you marry me?"

Some other place and time in the universe it would have been funny.

Bainbridge said, in outrage, *"What?"*

Now I was stranded. The gag hadn't gone over any better than it had with Jean. Worse yet, Bainbridge wasn't privy to what had happened in Princeton, so any further conversation involving matrimony and children would probably do nothing for her self-esteem. Ultimately, I said nothing, for Bainbridge took it upon herself to get righteously indignant.

"I don't understand it. I really don't. You don't call me. You treat me like dirt. Then you pull something like this. You don't like me very much, do you, Boddekker?"

No, I didn't, if the truth was to be known. In fact, she had attached herself to me over the last couple of months, and the kindly act of acknowledging her existence had become a nightmare. It was my fault for not sitting down with her and saying "Bainbridge, it's not that I don't love you anymore . . . I never loved you." Why couldn't people be friends and leave it at that?

"Honestly," Bainbridge continued. "You love me. You love me not. What are you doing, pulling petals off of a flower?"

My eyes flickered to the rose. I knew I was dead then, betrayed by a stray glance. Bainbridge's eyes followed mine like a hawk, and when she saw the flower she melted.

"Boddekker," she said, reaching for it. "You shouldn't have."

I didn't, I thought. *You were a subconscious afterthought that I didn't get to act on.*

She started to pet the thing like it was some kind of fuzzy

mammal. "Oh, it's beautiful," she said. "It cries momma, it really does. Oh, and it's red, for love!"

"Red for love?" I swallowed.

"Haven't you ever heard that? Red for love, yellow for . . . well, yellow for something. And white for something else." She saw I was totally confused. "Never mind. Where did you get this?"

"Uh, the Smilin' Guy who works maintenance in the lobby made them."

"It's so lovely," she said. "You were so thoughtful. And I was so horrible to you. Oh, Boddekker, apology accepted."

There I was, left in an "ah, well, uh" situation. Bainbridge was apologizing for my ill behavior and I was getting praised by my victim. All I could do was stand with a stupid look on my face, saying, "Ah, well, uh . . ." while trying to think of a graceful way out.

Then Bainbridge said, "I've got to watch myself, because I've never allowed myself to get into a serious relationship with someone else, you know? I mean, I'm finishing college, and there are boys there, but you know how they are at college age, these awful, hormonal animals. Heavens, I'm sure you know because you were there yourself, but Boddekker, you've got this maturity about you, it's like you're over all of that, so I know you can appreciate how I feel—"

It was torture to have to listen to this, and it did nothing for my train of thought. As it turned out, I needn't have worried about getting out of it. About the time Bainbridge's monologue started to get serious, my creative group's account executive stuck his head into my cubicle and said, "Come on, gang, the meeting's in five."

"Thanks, Griswold," I said, and meant it. Then I looked at Bainbridge and said, "We'd better go."

I ushered her out without touching her, which was an enormous task since Smilin' Guy's rose had reoriented her emotions and her eyes were begging for the reassurance of physical contact. On the way out, I saw Griswold rousing Hotchkiss, who was sitting at his desk, staring glumly at his watch. Finally he responded to Griswold's call to action and said, "Right. Got to be there for the end of the world."

The four of us headed to the stairs with the others, then down to thirty-five and the multitiered conference room. We were among the last to arrive. Two of the three remaining old men, Levine and Harris, were at the table at the bottom of the small amphitheater. With them were Finney and Spenner, the two senior partners and heirs apparent to having their names added to the Pembroke Hall masthead. I let Bainbridge in ahead of me, and she took the last seat at a table two tiers down from the door. Realizing what she'd done, she gave me a helpless look, the rose still in her hand. I shrugged and stayed at the top. Griswold followed me in and we took places at a table with the Church Brothers. Hotchkiss stayed by the door, standing in spite of the fact that there were vacant seats. I felt bad. I hadn't meant to drain him of his bravado. It apparently had been a bad weekend for everyone.

"If this is it," said Finney in a naturally loud voice, "we'll bring this meeting to order."

My hangover burned. I wasn't in the mood for this.

"I wonder where Pangborn is," Upchurch said, elbowing me in the ribs.

He was right. Old man Pangborn wasn't down with the others.

"Probably off buying bird seed," said Churchill.

"Incontinence pants," countered Upchurch.

"Colostomy supplies," amended Churchill.

"Another treatment at TransMind," stated Upchurch.

My head throbbed. I wasn't in the mood for the antics of the Church Brothers, either.

"Quiet," Griswold barked, and the Church Brothers gave him a withering look. It didn't bother him. Nothing bothered good old Griswold. "Those of us who are serious about our careers would like to hear this."

That offended the Church Brothers' pseudo-professional attitude enough to quiet them.

". . . dispose of the usual amenities," Finney was saying. "Instead, the creative groups will report to their group leaders, who will report to lower management, who in return will report—"

There were murmurs as Finney introduced old man Levine. Skipping the individual reports meant a short meeting, and a short meeting usually meant that something out of the ordinary was happening. My stomach gurgled. I leaned back in my seat and shot a glance at Hotchkiss, who mouthed the words "It's the end of the world." I turned back as Levine started his speech.

". . . years, and it's been good to Pembroke Hall. And since the Decade Of Collapse, it's been incredible to us. Whole new markets opened up that had heretofore been closed, a fact that younger members of our staff know only as questions on a Retrohistory exam. There was potential to be exploited. Entire races of people had to be taught capitalism, had to learn the value of a dollar and how to buy what the rest of the world was selling.

"This resulted in some of the finest hours of our company. The opening of Poland. The German reunification. The commercialization of the Arab Emirates. Opening the Confederation of Baltic States, and Volga, and Beloruskaja, and after the beginning of the century, the Empire of China. A golden age for those of us in this liar's trade, a golden age that gave us the opportunity to sell to the world. And what a golden time it was . . ."

A chill went up my spine. I was remembering what Hotchkiss had said about use of tense, and here was Levine, witnessing the company's history and doing it in the past tense. I knew Hotchkiss's eyes were boring into the back of my head but I didn't dare look back. All I could do was hope he was also right about the old men rising to meet whatever crisis was looming.

"But now," Levine continued, "that is all about to end." Disturbed murmurs from the crowd. The old man held up both hands. "Not the end of the world as we know it, my children, but merely the end of an era—the golden age of advertising. Pembroke Hall has ridden high, and it will be up to us to determine whether we continue or fall by the wayside, another in a series of capitalistic casualties.

"Nor should you be mass zapping résumés all over the world, my friends, for we know what the writing on the wall will say before it is written—"

"It has raised its middle finger," said Upchurch, who had the best Levine voice this side of Levine himself. "And it is shaking that finger at us."

"You're mixing your metaphors," complained Churchill. "The old man's prescient, don't you see—"

Griswold gave them one of his "can't shake me" glares, and they fell silent again.

". . . figures show a slight decline in Western product sales. Some of this is to be expected, as industry begins to gear up, but these trend out beyond the normal fall-off for Eastern industrialization. These figures show that the fall-off is not only in durable tangibles like pots and pans, micro- and macrowaves, pocket cookers and solar panels and bicycles and railhead controllers and the other products a successful nation of industry needs and can produce. Indeed, we have encouraged these new and struggling nations to help fill their own need as we profited from it.''

The Church Brothers started to act up again, but then Levine said, ''Ladies and gentlemen, what my people in Data have shown me is the beginning of a decline in the market for Western kitsch goods.'' Instantly the Brothers were shocked into silence, along with the rest of us. You could have heard someone draw breath— had anyone dared to do it. ''Brothers and sisters of the advertising world, I am talking about bubblechip collections of country and western music. I am talking about nograv simushoes and orthodontic jewelry and roboerotic playmates and nutricheese in pump cans.

''Thirty-one percent of the films made in Beloruskaja last year were made in English. Three of these films were nominated for, and I don't have to tell you which one swept, the Academy Awards. The Union of Mongol States is now the world's largest producer of novelty figures made from lacquered animal droppings, and last year's biggest seller was the Elephant Dumpty from India. This is the year that Vladimir Jones was named the Country Music Association's Best New Artist. Couscous Critters cracked the top ten of world snack foods, and France's EZ Brie blew away everything else in the topping category. Wisconsin Wonders almost went under, and the state had to go back to putting cheese whey on icy roads to keep them afloat. I don't have to tell you about the latest news in professional wrestling, or where the latest rash of Ronald Reagan sightings has been. And if I see another one of those Beijing Buddy's Rice 'n' Run places on another street corner, I swear I'm going to slit my wrists.'' There was a smattering of polite laughter. Levine paused, then went on.

''Now we of the Western civilizations have a noble and grand tradition. We call it consumption. And those of us in this noblest of professions have remade it into something else again. We have made it *conspicuous consumption.* Soft drinks haven't always come in sixty-four-ounce cups and the seventy-two-ounce GigaGulps. There was a time when a child would be perfectly happy with eight ounces of drink. Can you imagine that? *Eight measly ounces!*'' He stopped to laugh for a moment. ''I don't know of a single child—and I'd bet my position that none of you do, either—who is happy with anything less than a thirty-two-ounce KiddieSip." Laughter rippled through the crowd and Levine waited it out. "My friends, we of the West taught ourselves to consume. And in the years since, we have taught the rest of the human zoo to consume and consume and *consume*!

"And what has been the result? We have Westernized the world until the world itself is Western. These new, burgeoning markets are developing capitalist personalities of their own, and now they're going to sell them to us. This is fine. It keeps humankind fresh and lively. But something much darker than that is at the heart of all this. People, we are quickly reaching the saturation point. How many more imitations of Couscous Critters will the market bear? How many more canned gourmet cheeses can the shelves hold? How much of a stomach will we maintain for Rice 'n' Run, and the inevitable army of imitators?"

"The companies that pay us to spread the word about their products expect results. They expect sales, and they expect those sales to increase. Need I remind you of all the cast-off product lines that were revitalized at the beginning of the century—because while we'd had our fill, the new Orients and the Mongols and the Poles and the Slavs and the Ukrainians and the White Russians and the Balticans all wanted their share. They now had a right to buy paintings on black velvet and reissued music anthologies from fifth-generation masters, and stupid, useless things that were supposed to peel potatoes and make bread and boil soup and purify the air and electrically charge their drinking water. And they wanted them. They wanted them right away. It was our responsibility, it was our bread and butter, to see that the other four-fifths of the world had their chance to buy hydrosuspension sneakers.

"Never forget that the UMS market is the one that kept Sony from going under after the debacle with holovision. Bless those people, they embraced it like it was brought straight off the mountaintop by Moses. Ninety-eight percent of the world's holovision broadcasts are made from the Mongol States, and virtually every holo repair shop in the world is within their borders. They embraced a technology that nobody else wanted. They weren't the only ones. We emptied out warehouses full of bamboo steamers, waffle makers, borscht cookers, carbon steel knives, tummy tuckers, thigh busters, pocket televisions, two-way wrist radios, home laser shows, Love Slave Robottes, and we prospered. Four-fifths of the world wanted what we already had, and we made a killing from selling it to them. Eighty-nine percent of all the world's billionaires since the beginning of time have been made since the beginning of this century.

"And now, my family, it is all over. The golden age is done. The world has had its fill of kitsch goods. And our clients, the companies that are still manufacturing them by the metric ton, are going to find the words *market saturation* a rather feeble excuse for why their product is gathering dust in warehouses throughout the globe.

"We find ourselves now on the precipice, looking out over a brave new advertising world. It is now no longer enough merely to tell people about the product and advise them where to get it. We must now make them desire that product, make them burn with lust for it. We must *sell* these things to them. And if they already have it, we must sell it to them again. We must sell them another pair of hydrosuspension sneakers, another bamboo steamer, another oil-on-velvet painting, another dispenser can of gourmet cheese. And they must desire *our* products, and not their own, homegrown versions of the same.

"Our responsibility will lie as follows. First and foremost, we must persuade our target markets to buy the particular product. Second, as the saturation point on the market becomes critical, we must persuade these same people that they must buy another of these products for themselves. This will be easier with things like return trips to the Rice 'n' Run, or the multimegavitamin styrettes, harder with items like the electrostatic water chargers or mood-sharing plasma balls, where one per household is the sensible maximum. Third, we must persuade these people to buy the same product yet again to give to a friend, or to have them in turn persuade their friend to buy. Fourth, we must persuade them to buy yet another and leave it unopened for whatever reason you can concoct—time capsule storage, for barter during some future holocaust, for their children's children—whatever. And if we cannot accomplish any of these, then we must sell them on the product merely on the fact that our commercials for these things are lovely things to behold and highly entertaining, so they'll invest in the product to keep the announcements on the air.

"You must be bright and scintillating and stimulating and highly creative. You must grab their attention and give them a jones for the product or for the pitch itself. This will of course necessitate rethinking of our creative processes, but it should be something we can all work on and adapt to as soon as it's possible. Our projections show that the critical saturation break point of fifty percent of world product lines is eighteen to twenty months away. That's plenty of time to implement new programs—but in the face of time's march, it is not much time at all.

"True, the prospect is frightening, but you are all my children in the creative sense, and I know we will come through this standing strong." Levine gave a bow with a flourish of his hands. "Bless you," he added, then took his seat.

The air was so thick with tension that nobody moved, nobody spoke, nobody even dared draw breath. Everyone was waiting, I think, for Levine to say, "And if you all believe that, I'd like to sell you some Electromagnetic Pulse Insurance" or "April Fool!" But he didn't.

I was quite ill now, and I wondered if it wasn't round two of the supreme hangover. Or maybe it was the bad news from Levine. To check, I glanced back at Hotchkiss, who was slowly nodding his head. In an instant, my mind drew a mental picture of that Princeton house with the wings of a gull, flying unoccupied into the sunset.

On the floor, there was some shuffling at the table where the old men sat, and then Spenner stood.

"Well," he started. "That is certainly some interesting food for thought."

"Yeah," said Upchurch—or maybe it was Churchill—"a happy little cupcake lightly dusted with cyanide."

"Fortunately," Spenner continued, oblivious to the derision floating about the upper tiers of the room, "as Mr. Levine has pointed out, there is plenty of time for us to prepare for this and be ready when things go market critical. To whet your appetites for the new work ahead, here's an exciting project for something that won't saturate the market for a long time. In fact, it may never saturate the market. World Nanotechnologies, Ltd. is going to be introducing a new product within the next few months. Since this is something very different from anything they've done thus far, they've decided not to go with their regular agency, which specializes in corporate imagery. They've asked for campaign submissions from all the major agencies for something called—"

My head began to throb with renewed arrogance and my stomach felt heavy. Whatever it was, I was taking it badly. I felt light-headed, and cold sweat dotted my back.

I closed my eyes and let my mind wander back to Princeton, back to the bikeshaw ride from the station, back to the house, that wonderful piece of real estate with three bedrooms and the licensed fireplace. What are the nice things about a home—your home? You can always go back there and you can leave your shoes wherever you want. Your home protects you from things that you want to keep out. But while your home is protecting you, what protects your home, watches over your mortgage, and covers your homeowner's liabilities? The answer is simple—

I snapped out of it. Our homeowner's insurance account was handled by another creative group; but, more important, I could see the answer, and I wasn't sure that I liked it. It involved losing hold, and that vision of a crackling fire, pull back to reveal a fireplace with a Prominently Displayed License, pull back farther to reveal a living room, big, spacious, nice, while a man speaks in *basso profundo* tones about homeowner's insurance—it would never exist because of what was happening in the world market.

All of my options involved my becoming the resident genius at Pembroke Hall. That was simple enough. It could be done in a matter of weeks by pulling the right strings. But now things had changed. There was going to be a vicious, competitive edge to everything. Hotchkiss had known that part of it, or maybe he'd only felt it as an instinct that he couldn't define. He was thinking on a global scale, in terms of what it would mean to the industry as a whole, seeing only its ultimate impact on him. The end of the world as he knew it.

On the other hand, as Levine had spoken, I'd seen the immediate impact. Excellence would suddenly matter. Brainless nattering over semantic context of translating phrases like *cleans like a demon* into Croatian would no longer matter. An edge was coming to Pembroke Hall, which would gradually surface as everyone realized you could no longer sell product merely because it was available. What was going to matter was pushing product into the hands of customers, the product of our clients and not the product of someone else. From here on out, it was going to be hard sell.

This was it, the time of your life when it all comes down to one thing. And now that you've done your job and gotten it right, there's only one thing on your mind—putting yourself in front of a big steaming mug of Boston Harbor . . .

I suddenly realized that people around me were talking and standing and leaving the room. The Church Brothers were on their way out, one of them saying in mocking tones, "Nannaclean? What kind of name is Nannaclean? Sounds like something you'd use to wash off your grandmother." Griswold was absorbed in pecking entries into his notebook. I took a long glance through the amphitheater and read the faces of those who were leaving. Whatever Spenner had said hadn't done much for the mood of the audience in particular or the morale at Pembroke Hall in general.

"Another one of those wonderfully upbeat tail chewings," I said to Griswold.

"Um?" he grunted, looking up from his notebook.

"They're so wonderful at motivating us here."

"I'm sorry," Griswold said, eyes falling back down to his notebook. "It's this NanoKleen thing. It's going to be a challenge. Everyone's going to want to discuss it, and I want to have a jump on it." He hammered at his notebook's keys using one finger from each hand.

I made my way over to Hotchkiss, who was filing out with the rest of the stunned crowd.

"It's the end of the world," he told me.

"So I've heard. I congratulate you on your insight."

"You know," he said, "maybe this is for the best. I'm thinking that we were getting too complacent. This'll really sharpen things. Redefine them. Make things like they were before the walls came down."

"A giant step backward," I said.

"Beats plunging off of a cliff." Hotchkiss shrugged. "If you'll excuse me, I've got some thinking to do."

I caught his arm. "Hotchkiss, what's the big deal? I mean, you and Dansiger are through, but you've gotten an elevator key for the third time this year, you're in pretty good shape. It's the end of the world, but you saw it coming before everyone else. You've got a future here."

"But I didn't see it soon enough, Boddekker. That's the problem."

I dropped my grip, and Hotchkiss vanished, muttering to himself. I looked to the table where Bainbridge had been, but she had apparently gone straight back to our department, sparing me a line of stupid questions that I wouldn't be able to answer.

Market critical. Nobody liked to hear those words. Not when

they applied to one product and especially not when they applied to everything. Everyone had been stricken by Levine's pronouncement of doom.

"Well," I said to no one in particular. "Might as well go and face the end." I stepped in line to leave.

"Boddekker?"

I kept walking. I wanted to put off dealing with Bainbridge as long as I could.

"Boddekker!"

I took another step and then the scent hit me, something so intoxicating that I knew it could only be the one person at Pembroke Hall who didn't have to resort to hallucinogenic perfumes because they couldn't match the effect of her own pheromones. I stopped. I turned.

Honniker In Accounting was coming toward me.

I know that when I looked at her, my face said that I'd been waiting all of my life for her approach. Why couldn't the Church Brothers have been here to see this?

"You're Boddekker, right?"

My ego instantly deflated. Honniker In Accounting was being all business, and I hated myself for those smug, prurient thoughts I'd entertained. It embarrasses me to this day to look back on that moment. "Yeah," I said, forcing myself to pull my gaze away from those fabulous dark eyes, the color of which was known to change at a moment's notice.

"All right." Her voice was soft and smooth, even in business mode. It distracted me long enough to wonder what that voice could do to someone in front of a crackling fireplace. "I'm supposed to tell you that the old man wants to see you."

My mouth hung open for a long moment. I wasn't sure if it was from the proximity of Honniker In Accounting or what she had said. Finally, the message sank in.

"The old man," I said. "Pangborn?"

She shook her head. Her earrings chimed melodically. "Levine."

"Oh," I said stupidly. "Right. Thank you."

Honniker In Accounting turned and was gone, her pheromones burning in my brain. I stood, tired, confused, and hungover, trying to make sense out of what had happened.

A hand landed hard between my shoulder blades and I took a

step forward to check my balance. Norbert, an overly handsome man who was also a creative group leader, leered at me.

"Called in by the old man, eh, Boddekker? Tough break. But then, it is the end of the world, isn't it?"

I'm sure I tried to give a typically witty response, but the hangover slowed me and he was out of earshot by the time it had passed my lips. Nobody near me at the time had the context with which to appreciate it.

Called in to see the old man.

Yeah. Well.

Hotchkiss had seen it coming, but not soon enough. At least he had seen it.

Falling into line once more, I cursed my luck and wondered why I seemed to be the only one at the agency who hadn't had some form of Monday-morning prescience.

Pembroke, Hall, Pangborn, Levine, and Harris

"Selling you to the world since 1969"

Offices in Principal Cities: New York - Montreal - Toronto - Sydney - London - Tokyo - Moskva - Beijing - Chicago - Oslo - Philadelphia - Amarillo

CLIENT: »The Witkins-Marrs Company		PRODUCT: »Corporate Image
WRITER: »Boddekker	TIME: »:60	MEDIA: »Audio
TITLE: »*Image #21*		
PRODUCTION ORDERS:	»Use Witkins-Marrs music bed #14a ("Variant")	

ANNOUNCER: [*In slow and even tones.*] Sometimes it's a feeling you get—sometimes it's something that nags you but you can't put your finger on it, although you can sense it's there, you *know* it's there, and you've got this sensation that the feeling knows you know. And sometimes it can be overwhelming, it can be so much that you don't know how you can face it, and other times it's so dim that it's almost gone, and you find yourself missing it. It can be the presence that keeps you company while you're walking down a rain-soaked city street on a night when the sky is dark with clouds and only a third of the street lamps are working. It's the unnerving feeling when you're lying in bed in the middle of the night and you realize that something is keeping you awake, something sinister, something right there just beyond the edge of the bed, and then suddenly it's *in bed with you* and *it's become a part of you*— then with a sigh, you understand that it was the ringing in your own two ears. And that's us. That's why we're here. We're like the ringing in your own two ears.

FOUR

Some Time Spent with the Old Man

Maybe it's human nature or maybe it's only my nature, but when confronted with the prospect of facing something unpleasant, I become a master of burning time to delay the inevitable. Maybe it's immaturity. My nephew, who is ten, is gifted at it, too. It could be hereditary.

Even though I knew it would not be in my best interests to tarry, when Honniker In Accounting told me that Levine wanted to talk to me *in his office,* I automatically switched into slow motion. I straightened out my desktop. After all, if I was going to suddenly depart, I would have to leave it looking neat. By doing it now, I wouldn't have to come back to do it.

I activated my terminal, intending to forward anything personal to my datatrap at home, along with copies of all the best work I'd done for Pembroke Hall. There was a beep and the terminal winked, which was normal enough, but then came the voice.

"Hello, Mr. Boddekker! *Hello* Mr. *Boddekker!* You know, it's lucky that I'm not a virus or a transcode, or your datasys would be in really big trouble right now!"

I groaned. Not another one.

"For example," the program continued, "if I were typical of the Munich series of viruses, I would have already wiped out your files for A.N.S. Products, including that lovely work you've done for Toidy Nuke! After all, a polluter is still a polluter, even *with* our hard-core antipol laws . . ."

From the way it tapped into personal files and used your own writing against you, I guessed that the spot had come from Mauldin and Kress, one of our biggest competitors in the interactives field. I sighed in disgust and called for my ferret.

"I might have *butchered* all those notes you've downloaded on the Boston Harbor account. I might have tapped out your feed line of petty cash, some three thousand two hundred sixty-one dollars seventy-one cents and—"

I was impressed. I hadn't looked in my petty cash feed for quite a while, and had buried it in a basement subdirectory. The virus had to work for that one. I called for my ferret again.

"—malevolent, I would have wiped out your datebook and you would have forgotten to call Mez Bainbridge on Saturday night! But I didn't. Now, call me compassionate, call me a weakling . . . but it goes to show you that there's still a need for a truly *great* preventative access program, one that goes beyond your common ferrets, and stops the intrusives *before* they make systems access! That's where my creators at Erehwon Programming come in! With their new—"

"What's all this about a common ferret?" blurted another voice.

"Ferret," I said, almost shouting. "Is that you?"

"Yessir, Mr. Boddekker, sir. Sorry I'm late, but this fjordhead virus blocked all the input access bits and I had to reconfigure—"

"Don't give me excuses. Just run a purge."

"Yessir"

"And ferret," I added. "Get me a source authorship on that one. It's a nice piece of work."

"Will, do, Mr. Boddekker, sir! All right, virus—"

"Surely, you jest, Mr. Boddekker," said the intruding program. "You don't think this miserable save of software is going to get rid of something like me. That's why you need Erehwon Programming's new—"

"I most certainly *do* think ferret will get rid of you," I told the virus. "If not, then your agency is in direct violation of FTC rules and regs."

"Prepare to meet thy doom, fiend!" said the ferret.

"Go run a self-check." The virus made a yawning sound.

"Out," demanded the ferret.

There was a loud whistle. "You're pretty good," the virus admitted. Then it yelped. "You've got root/source interference management backups!" It sounded truly shocked. "How did you hide that from me?"

"Version twelve-two update," the ferret bragged. "Now get out of here."

That would have been it, except the virus's programmers wrote in one last detail that made the thing stick in my mind. It let out a bloodcurdling scream.

"Finished," the ferret said proudly. "And it really wasn't that hard."

"Thank you, ferret."

"Source agency is Mauldin and Kress. Personality development and copy was by Ben Walters and the programmer was Pascal Clark."

"Thank you, ferret. You may go."

There was a pop and the ferret was gone. I had the strange feeling that someone had left the room—and I was left alone with the prospect of having to go and talk to the old man.

I quickly made a note in the private section of my notebook about Mauldin and Kress and found myself laughing over the intruder. Only, I thought, I didn't need a virus to make me forget about a date with Bainbridge. My own stupidity could take care of that quite nicely.

Finishing the note about the virus, I flipped into the company datanet and started loading farewell messages. At the last minute I decided not to dump them, telling myself that I was overreacting. Perhaps Levine was merely supposed to break the news that one of my spots had won an award. At Pembroke Hall, my attitude toward them was whispered about in the halls and discussed in private circles, so I suppose the old men knew about them. If I had won something, they'd have to call me in and sweet-talk me into accepting it. That wouldn't be so bad, compared to what it could be. Then it occurred to me that I didn't have anything up for an award this quarter.

No, it couldn't be anything good. It was Hotchkiss's end of the world, and mine was going to be the first to end. It was almost enough to make me dump the farewell messages, but I balked again. With the exception of Bainbridge, the people I wanted to say good-bye to I should see in person.

I sighed and took one last look around my office, then walked out, past reception to the elevators, punched up the local access cars and took the first one to the thirty-ninth floor.

Floor thirty-nine is administrative, the old men and their assorted assistants and underlings and vice presidents. It's all very plush and airy and nice, and you can't get there from the main floor unless you have a key similar to the one Hotchkiss had— Ride of the Week, the Month, the Year. For the most part, you have to get there through a gauntlet consisting of the rest of the company, from main reception down on thirty-five to a transitional reception area on thirty-seven, and finally, the administrative reception area where I now stood.

Below the main desk were two holoplates of Pembroke and Hall, the two founders who were too old to be helped when longevity technology boomed. Each plate rested on a motorized swivel that slowly turned, animating the holo etched onto it. Pembroke, who to me always looked like the friendlier of the two, started with the palms of his hands flat together. Then his arms spread out, and as his hands swept by, an image of the revolving Earth appeared. Hall, who looked to me like someone you'd see on a street corner hawking Electromagnetic Pulse Insurance, held a can of something in his left hand. He pointed at it with his right, then swung his arm out and shook a thumbs-up at you, winking as he did. The plate would come full circle, and Pembroke and Hall would start all over again. It made for a nice display. It was too bad you had to die to get on it.

The receptionist finally acknowledged my existence, and I told her that I was here to see Levine. She didn't look up. She didn't even check her notebook to see if I had an appointment.

"You're Boddekker."

"Yes."

"Go on in."

I stood there for a moment, frozen.

The receptionist made a directional shake of her head. "He's waiting."

I walked around the desk and down the hall, past the offices of vice presidents and senior partners, down toward where light came in from windows overlooking Madison Avenue, to an open door on the right with a brass plate mounted on it, into which had been pounded the name *Levine*. I stepped through and Levine's personal secretary, the last person in the gauntlet, stopped me.

"You are?"

She would make me say it. "Boddekker."

She raised a finger. "Fifteen seconds."

Ten seconds later, the door to Levine's inner sanctum opened, and a beat later a handsome-looking woman longevically preserved at age fifty stepped out. It was one of the old men, Harris. She smiled and nodded at me.

"You're from Creative, aren't you?"

"Boddekker," I nodded.

"Yes," she smiled, picking up my hand and shaking it. "Boddekker. You're the one of those Witkins-Marrs audio spots, aren't you?"

"Well, it was my creative group—"

"But you're the broadcast media expert in that group, aren't you? Aud and vid?"

"Yes," I said, "and my group."

"A wonderful job with those," she said. "Very attention getting. The Witkins-Marrs campaign is my favorite for the quarter. You must keep it up."

"Thank you," I said. My gaze started to drop to the floor, but Harris had released my hand and was talking to Levine's secretary about ordering a large floral arrangement.

I turned and walked up to Levine's door. Levine was seated behind his monster of a desk, talking to someone I didn't recognize. Levine saw me and smiled.

"Come in," he called. "Come in. Please."

I eased into the office. The person Levine was talking to was on his way out, their conversation drawing to an end. Levine gestured at a chair in front of his desk, so I walked over and sat.

"So anyway, I spent, like six hours at the police station," said Levine's guest, "going over that build-a-face software and working with their support officers. And I finally got what I thought was a good construct of the guy who did this." The guest turned slightly, emphasizing something for Levine's benefit but not mine. I had enough of a view to see that his eyes had been blackened and his nose was taped. "So they tapped it into something they called a PerpNet, kind of a rogues gallery, I suppose. And what do you suppose the search found, Levine? Just what do you suppose it found?''

Levine didn't say anything, which was good, because after half a second, the guest continued.

"It found someone, a gang leader, they said, one of the Times Square packs. Yes, yes, I'm telling them, that's where it all happened, so they do a download of the match, and I'm looking at it on the screen and saying yes, yes, that's the one who did all this, and they said . . . they said . . ."

The guest smiled sadly, like imparting the punch line to a long joke that wasn't worth telling.

"They told me the guy was dead, Levine. Killed in a gang battle for possession of a block with a Rice 'n' Run on it, something."

"Justice, then," Levine said.

"That's just it. There is no justice to it—"

"Justice is a relative thing," Levine said. "If your assailant is dead, then no matter what the circumstance, the end has been served."

"Levine, they told me this guy had been dead for *two weeks*. There was no way he could have been on Times Square the same time as I was. I couldn't deal with it anymore. I put my hands in the air and said, 'Well I don't know, maybe he has an evil twin brother' and the support officer looks at me and says, 'Mr. Robenstine, if this guy has an evil twin, he's working in Washington, DC.' Irreverent so and so's. *Uffda.* There is no justice, none, not anymore."

"The police—" Levine started.

"No!" said Robenstine, shaking his head. "I don't even want to talk—not even to think!—about them! No, it's out of hand! Yes, they're understaffed. Yes, the gang problem is the worst it has ever been. *Yes,* the police level of technic is escalating, faster now than the ability of evil to wield it for its own purposes, but what's the difference? What is it to you and me? It means a Citizen Affectation Rate of one hundred thirty-four percent! It means that you—and me—and us, too—are going to be victimized by someone in this decaying heap one and a third times in our life. Guaranteed. And that's the *national* rate. The NYC rate is higher. It's nonnegotiable, Levine!''

"It's what we get for living here," Levine said, trying to sound wise.

"*Uffda.*" Robenstine shook his head, then rolled it to look upward. "These blind, accepting fools." His head pivoted back to stare at Levine. "Wait until it happens to you, Levine. You wait until one of those young hoodlums gets to you. We'll see what you think of your *police*!" Robenstine turned and slowly walked out of the office, leaving me alone at last with the old man.

"That was Robenstine," Levine told me. "He's one of the senior partners that we've had running the Oslo office. I've temporarily brought him back to take care of a few things." He rearranged the items on his desk, then glanced out the door to make sure his subject was now out of earshot. "A funny thing about him. He's very cinematic. Larger than life. And when I watch him, when he's going on and on, I get this feeling that he's not talking to me. He's *emoting*. And I feel like I'm not listening to him like someone in a conversation, but I'm watching a performance, as deliberate and filmed as one of our commercials, only less entertaining. I call it the Silver Screen effect. A strange feeling when it happens."

"I'm sure," I said politely. What he said didn't mean that much to me. I'd heard that Levine made a hobby of watching old vids on room-sized screens the way people used to. I think that was the context of his analysis.

"What poor Robenstine doesn't realize is that I *have* been victimized by gang members. Twice in the last year. And while I was able to run positive identifications each time on the PerpNet, none of my assailants was caught. But does that bother me?"

He said nothing else. That was my cue, I realized. "Apparently not," I said.

"And you're right, of course. Do you know why? Because there *is* justice. I've just zapped the draft of a bill that I had our R and D department research and test with the public. This bill would by law prevent any criminal or any proven member of a gang from ever being able to purchase longevity products. Imagine that, living only long enough to realize your body was going to fall apart, and only then you'd die. There is justice. There is. But poor Robenstine feels that he has to complain about it. He was in the Norwegian War, you know. The Oslo campaign, in fact. Highly decorated. I suspect he still carries small bits of metal inside of his brain."

"Surprising," I said, "that a veteran would let himself take that kind of treatment from a gang member."

"Ah, well. People must complain about one thing or another." Levine unfolded his hands and sat back in his chair. "Now, onto business. You are . . . ?"

"Boddekker," I said. "Uh, Boddekker in Creative."

"Very good," Levine smiled and typed into his notebook. "And the reason you're here, Boddekker?"

"You called for me. Uh, actually, Honniker In Accounting said that you wanted to see me."

Levine squinted at his notebook, looked confused for a moment, then nodded. "Ah, yes. I did. Forgive me, Boddekker. As you can see, it's been quite a morning." He entered something else.

"That was quite a speech you gave," I offered, then wished that I hadn't.

"Yes, well, it was something that needed saying, and better to say it before you reach the end of the world, right?"

"Right." I looked down at my lap. I had clasped my hands so tightly that my knuckles were white. For the moment, Levine was doing nothing but staring at his notebook and rapping his fingers on the desktop. I realized he was waiting for something to come up on the screen, so I tried to relax and conceal the fact that I was shivering from nerves.

"Yes," Levine said finally. "Boddekker. I've got it now. You're a writer and group leader for Griswold's creative group, is that right?"

"I'm a writer-specialist, sir. Broadcast media, audio and vid. Our group has special writers for intrusive software and subliminals."

"Yes," Levine nodded. "Yes, yes. You then, Boddekker, are the one who wrote the Lovejoy Specialties end-of-the-year clearance spots on their Exxtasy Robotette line."

I shifted in my seat. Those spots hadn't been written in one of my better moments. I'd broken up with someone significant, largely due to Bainbridge's untimely attentions, and I'd been tempted to go out and buy one of those Robotettes for myself. "Yes."

"And you—" Levine stopped to clear his throat. "You wrote the line, 'For a limited time, Lovejoy Specialties has marked down their most popular models—you'll save up to fifty-five percent and more.' ''

I gave a slight shrug, filled with the memory of the darkest hour of my career. ''Yes.''

Levine's lips parted into a smile. ''I *loved* that line, Boddekker.''

''Sir you have to understand that when—'' I cut myself off. *''What?''*

Levine gave an animated nod. ''I heard that in transit,'' he said. ''I keep my radio to the Wall Street Satlink. I heard that spot, and that line—oh, that precious line, and I made note to myself to call the man who wrote that spot, no matter who sh/he worked for, and say how valuable that was. Imagine my delight when I found out that Lovejoy was our account and that the line had been written by one of my own people!''

''But Mr. Levine, that line was an accident, and there wasn't time to correct it.''

''Now don't be modest, Boddekker, my son! Let's look at it for what it was! It was a twofold implication, contingent on the listener's state of mind. First, to a normal listener with a middling to low IQ, you simply stated the fact that Lovejoy wanted us to convey, which was that they had marked some models down by fifty-five percent. To them you implied that they'd get *more* out of the deal, which had direct sexual connotations, which the Lovejoy people loved once I pointed it out to them. And when you consider that some of the Lovejoy models are real tigers—or tigresses in this case—once you get them properly charged—well, that made a bright addition to the sales pitch.

''And then there are the folks who picked up on that piece of subtlety. You snookered them with that line, too, Boddekker! I did some testing among first-time buyers who had previously fallen into the Interested Skeptic category when it came to Lovejoy's products. You know what they told me about that line? They said they thought an idiot had written the copy and was trying to pull one over on them—and they figured if Lovejoy was stupid enough to actually run that copy, they might be stupid enough to undercut the fifty-five percent mark. Of course, Lovejoy dealers *didn't* offer any further incentive. In fact, they started their on-floor discounts at forty percent with authorization to go as low as fifty-five, so the ad played right into their strategy. So people going in thought they were getting fifty-five cut to seventy, when they were actually getting forty cut to fifty-five. It couldn't have worked out better if Lovejoy had actually told us what sales strategy they'd had in mind!

"That was a wonderful piece of writing, Boddekker! In fact, dare I say your copy for Lovejoy brings home to me what advertising is all about."

I swallowed. "It certainly brings it home to me." By then I was calm enough to manage a toothy smile.

"There was another one, Boddekker, another one I heard, only I knew it was one of our accounts, but I had again told myself to get in touch with the writer on that one, and imagine my surprise when it turned out to be you again." He tapped a key on his notebook. I found myself hoping that it was one of my better spots this time.

"Ah. The Witkins-Marrs Company. You did an image spot for them about . . ." He stared at the screen. "Just a minute," he said, tapping. "I'll bring that script up."

I squirmed but he didn't see it.

"Here it is. Witkins-Marrs Image spot number twenty-one." He squinted at the screen and frowned. "Let's see . . . a feeling you get . . . overwhelming . . . walking down a city street . . . ringing in your ears. Well, I don't know *what* this spot is about, Boddekker, but I did like it, and it happened to be a fine piece of writing on your part. You should feel proud of the work you've done for us."

I thanked him for the thought, but I wasn't proud. He caught it right away. I was doomed.

"When you say it, mean it, boy," he said. "This is a proud profession we work in. We're keeping the world economy afloat by keeping the gold circulating. We sell those Robotettes to savage Brazilian men. We use the money to eat lunch at one of those accursed Rice 'n' Run places. The Japanese take it and buy out carbon expulsion rights from some little place on the African continent, and they send it back to us for CDs of Akiro Yakamoto's Twenty-five Greatest Country Hits. We send the royalties to Osaka . . . the cycle continues.

"Let me tell you, Boddekker. You've got something. You may not even know what it is, but I can tell it. It's in your writing, and it goes out to the whole world. It's in your personnel file, and it shows up every time we try to talk you into accepting an award. You're going to go places, Boddekker, and I hope to thunder that when you do, you're going to be taking Pembroke Hall with you.''

For an instant I thought that I could ask for more money—something that would get me into that Princeton house—but common sense prevailed and I offered a meek word of thanks instead.

''I wish you'd been around when I first joined this company, Boddekker, I'll tell you that. With your way of words, you would have been great at print ads. Outdoor ads, too. That was back when billboards were outdoor signs, Boddekker. You learned about those in school, didn't you?''

I nodded.

''Advertising was so much simpler then. You didn't have to have all these experts on individual fields and then put them with other spoiled creative types into groups where they had to get along with one another. It's a nuisance, son. We've got to have the art director get along with the linguist who gets along with the programmer and the software personality consultant and the musical director and the broadcast media expert and the account executives, and they're all a bunch of prissy prima donnas who think they're the only right ones in the bunch. Ah.'' He took a moment to look at me. ''Present company excepted, though. I don't think you're a prissy prima donna, Boddekker. Your attitude file shows me that. No, I think you're a different breed, and that's why I brought you in here.''

''Sir?''

''We've got some big things coming up. Big. Everyone's going to be working on that NanoKleen thing, blowing out their brain cells on that one. I expect you to come up with the miracle on that one, too, son. But don't completely burn out because I've got a pet project that I'd like you to work with. Interested?''

I cleared my throat. ''To be honest, sir, it depends on what it is.''

Levine smiled. ''Good. Very good. I like you. Yes, I knew that. Well.'' He leaned back in his seat and stretched. ''Boddekker, since you've got this talent and since you're affiliated with broadcast media, I want to expand your horizons a little bit. One of the musical groups that we own is wanting to make another comeback, and I'd like you to come up with something brilliant for it.''

''One of the music groups?''

''Now you won't have to deal with the music rights or the management end of it. That'll fall to another department. I want you to take this case to your creative group, and I want you personally to handle all aspects of making the public aware of them again.''

''Who would that be, sir?''

''The SOBs,'' Levine said, as if it couldn't be anyone else.

I suddenly felt lightheaded. The SOBs weren't anything special. They'd been around longer than anyone cared to remember, and the last thing the world needed was for them to come back—*again.* What struck me about Levine's proposal was the fact that the SOBs were one of a handful of acts that was still handled by one of the other old men—one who still insisted on writing their copy himself.

''Well, sir,'' I said carefully. ''I'm really honored that you want me to handle them, but—''

''You hate them, and you despise the thought of them making another comeback.''

''No.'' I stopped to shake my head in spite of the truth in Levine's statement. ''I mean, I *do* despise them, but I'm a professional, sir, and I think I can rise above personal taste to do a campaign for them. It's that''—I looked out the door into the lobby as if I were asking about a personal dark secret—''Aren't the SOBs one of Mr. Pangborn's pet projects?''

Levine nodded. ''All the more reason why they should get to work with some new blood here at the agency, Boddekker. You recall our last big act, the Dry Heaves?''

''Yes, sir.'' There was a group I wouldn't mind working with, a kind of postpop retropunk outfit that was extremely popular.

''And do you recall the key line to Mr. Pangborn's campaign for them?''

Who could forget it? Every stand-up comic from Moskva to Montreal had picked up on it. '' 'Now you can have the Dry Heaves anytime you want.' ''

Levine nodded. ''Now Boddekker, you're a creative type. You understand what can happen when a person runs out of ideas—how their work can develop an alarming sameness to it. Don't you?''

''Yes sir.''

''That's what I thought. And that's why I want you to take a wild, stupid guess off the top of that fertile mind of yours—what Mr. Pangborn's proposed key line was for the SOBs.''

I sat back and thought about it for a moment. I tried to think alarming sameness, and I tried to combine it with the idea that perhaps even dear Mr. Pangborn must be getting tired of comeback attempts by these guys.

"Not these old SOBs again," I said.

"Close," Levine told me. "Very close. He wrote 'These old SOBs are back again.' That is the reason why we need some new blood on this, Boddekker."

I felt myself squirm. While I certainly wouldn't have minded taking the account, I didn't think my skills would extend to writing a great campaign for a bunch of old guys trying to cash in on the names of their fathers by playing hopelessly outdated music. There was someone I could think of, however, who could bring the right attitude to the project. "How about Hotchkiss, sir? He's—"

"Bah," grunted Levine. "Hotchkiss is a bottom feeder. He's got plenty of in-house awards, but that's only because he's great at politicking. If he spent half the time being a great creative man that he does sucking up to people, he might be a great creative man. As it stands, all he's good at is recycling ideas. We need a fresh approach to this, Boddekker, and from what I've seen of your work, you're the one to bring it to some of Mr. Pangborn's accounts."

I pondered this for a moment, and suddenly the cash registers rang in my head. An idea began to form, and it was taking the shape of that house in Princeton.

"You know," I told Levine, "I don't think I'd mind doing that at all."

"Very good. If you do a good job with the SOBs, you might find yourself with a case of the Dry Heaves." Levine chuckled at his own joke.

"You know, it might be good for me as a copywriter to branch out like this. Perhaps I could spend some time working on this with Mr. Pangborn."

Levine shook his head. "I'm sorry, Boddekker. As much as I'd love to set you up, I'm afraid it would be quite impossible. You see, another reason we're looking to farm out these accounts is because Mr. Pangborn is dead."

"What?" Come to think of it, I hadn't seen him at the meeting, but it hadn't registered.

Levine gave a grave nod. "This weekend. Saturday, I think. He went into a pet store to buy some seed for his canary and the place was bombed while he was there. A couple of extremist groups are taking responsibility for it—Animal Rights Front, Animal Liberation Political Organization, Animals 'R' Sentient Equals—one of those crackpot groups that believe chickens can work crossword puzzles.''

I looked down at the floor, not knowing what to say. ''It's a tragedy,'' I said, ''that an innocent bystander should get in the way like that. But sir, why didn't you announce that at the meeting this morning?''

Levine shrugged. ''It wasn't on the agenda. Besides, Boddekker, it no longer matters to Mr. Pangborn whether the world ends or not. Correct?''

''Correct.''

''Good. We have business to do. Not to worry, though. An announcement will be made at the appropriate time—preferably when we've got the NanoKleen account nailed down.''

I raised my head and my eyes found my wrist. ''Well,'' I sighed, ''I suppose I should take him out of my watch.''

''Let's not get too hasty,'' Levine advised. ''Give him a proper period of mourning first.''

''Of course,'' I said.

''Now then, young Boddekker. You'll be handling the writing for the SOBs. Mr. Pangborn had accumulated some information on what they want to accomplish and left it in the general filing system, so you can send your ferret after it.''

I nodded.

''Any other complications with this account, take them to your group, let them work it out. Don't let your musical director get too involved, though. You know how independent musicians can be. They get resentful if some professional from an agency tries to tell them what to do.''

''Yes, sir.''

''Now, do you have any other accounts that might be interfered with by your working on the SOBs?''

''Not right now. I'm doing some work on the Boston Harbor Tea account, but that's a fairly simple sell.''

''If you have any troubles, tell me. I can get your workload eased up. This SOBs thing is important. Not that they're going to go burning up the charts with new music, but we're expecting another resurgence of nostalgia, and I think we can use them to turn a tidy profit. Five years from now, we can discard the act and let one of the lesser agencies milk them until the principals start to die off, but by then you'll have moved up in the company."

"Thank you, sir," I said, and meant it. I stood, leaned down toward Levine and shook his hand, then started out of his office. Before I reached the door, however, he called my name.

"Yes, sir?"

"Boddekker, when do you think you can have something for me on the NanoKleen account?"

NanoKleen. My mind was blank. "I'm sorry?"

"The World Nanotechnologies, Ltd. account?"

Of course. The big whatever-it-was that I had ignored during the meeting. Apparently I had underestimated its bigness relative to Pembroke Hall. "Well," I said, trying to carefully choose my words, "this is something that you can't rush creatively. Not when it's this important. I should have something for you by deadline, no problem."

Levine folded his hands and smiled. "Outstanding. Well, I know you're going to have your hands full with everything else you do. I'll let you go now—but let me leave you with one final word."

I waited for a moment. Nothing. "Sir?"

"I can tell from the way you work that you're a team player. I couldn't ask for more than that from anyone who works here, but you, Boddekker—you're good. That makes me happy. I want you to know that we expect great things out of you."

I thanked him again and backed out of the office, thoughts racing. I wasn't sure what to make of all this. I had survived a trip to see one of the old men. Better still, I had been called in by an old man to be told that I did good work and that I was being given an account from one of the other old men. Granted, the other old man was dead, and the account was hardly what one would describe as glamorous, but it was a start, and I might certainly be able to parlay some of this goodwill into a large sum of cash with which to buy down the price of the house in Princeton.

In the meantime, I made mental calculations as I walked back out to the lobby. There were things I would have to learn about the SOBs, and I needed information on the World Nanotechnologies account. Both of these I could accomplish easily enough.

In the lobby I went to a secretarial desk and asked to use the system. The secretary relented and disappeared, probably happy to have an excuse to get away. When I was sure I was alone and that nobody else was listening, I called my ferret.

"Boddekker!" it said. "What are you doing on floor thirty-nine? You didn't get in some kind of trouble, did you? I know. It was that spot you did for the Love Slave Robotettes."

"Stop," I ordered. The ferret quit chattering. "Look, I need you to dig up something for me. Old man Pangborn had some information he was putting together on the SOBs. I need you to get anything he had in direct access and bring it into my office memory. Any other tidbits you can find loose in the net you can bring along. It might help."

"Is that it?"

"I need the text of the speech that Spenner gave to the combined groups this morning, highlight and key into World Nanotechnologies, Ltd. There may be some stray databits floating around on the net, so anything extra you might pick up would be appreciated."

"There's a lot there," the ferret said, matter-of-factly. "A lot of people in Creative are starting their own closed files on the subject. I could obtain some of this for you."

"No," I said. "I work clean, ferret, I've told you that."

"But it wouldn't hurt you. It would improve your competitive edge."

"If you load any dirty info into my memory, ferret, I'll tell Software that you let an Erehwon Virus into the system."

"Very well. An order is an order."

"Ferret," I said. "I'd better not find out that you've been supplying some of the others with loose bits from my files or it'll be the reformat program for you."

There was a beat of silence. "Anything else?" it said, very businesslike now.

"Nothing further."

"Very well." With a pop, the ferret was gone.

I stood for a moment, not quite knowing what to do next. Downstairs, I realized. Downstairs. The day wasn't even half over. The rest, I was sure, was going to be torture.

I decided to take the stairs. What was left of my hangover was about gone, and for the first time in twenty-four hours I felt coherent. A jog down the stairs would purge whatever poisons were left in my body.

Besides, I needed time to think.

It didn't last long. Three flights down I ran into Churchill, who was carrying something up to the art department for production. I smiled and gave him a friendly nod, all the while holding my breath to see if anything would happen.

Nothing did. Any kind of response would have implied some kind of friendliness on Churchill's part, and Churchill wasn't made of that kind of stuff—especially when his big brother Upchurch was watching over this wet-behind-the-ears kid.

It was too bad, really. I had worked with Churchill when he had been an intern, before he had become one of the Church Brothers. He had been nice enough then—but times change.

He continued past me on the stairwell, and I thanked my luck. If I could get through the remainder of the day without anything else happening, then things would be all right. I would be a good boy from then on. I'd even be nicer to Bainbridge.

But as fate had it, things didn't happen exactly that way.

PEMBROKE, HALL, PANGBORN, LEVINE, AND HARRIS

"Selling you to the world since 1969"

Offices in Principal Cities: New York - Montreal - Toronto - Sydney - London -
Tokyo - Moskva - Beijing - Chicago - Oslo - Philadelphia - Amarillo

CLIENT: »Azerbadzhan Appetizers		PRODUCT: »Couscous Critters
WRITER: »Boddekker	TIME: » ∞	MEDIA: »Subliminal
TITLE: »*It's Never Enough (Wanting and Emptiness Variant)*		
PRODUCTION ORDERS:	»Insert on actual musical tracks of *Young and Stupid* by Hateful (release date to be determined later)	

. . . you are listening you are listening you are listening to this music you are listening to this music but it's not enough you are listening to this music on a player but it isn't enough no it's not enough the music isn't enough and the player isn't enough no they're not enough and you feel empty and you feel a wanting because it's not enough no it's never enough and you have money probably you have money and that's how you got the music and that's how you got the player you bought it with money yes you didn't steal it no you didn't steal it you must not steal it you must never steal it you must never steal anything because stealing is bad stealing is evil do not steal the money do not steal the player do not steal the music even though they're not enough that's right they're not enough you know they're not enough not the money not the music not the player and nothing is ever enough no nothing not the money not the music not the player because you still have that wanting you still have that empty and it makes you ache not the money or the music or the player not even your school not even your parents not even your spouse not even your job no nothing is going to take away that want that empty that feeling that it's not enough only one thing can take it away only one thing can take away that feeling of empty take away that feeling of want take away the fact that the job and the spouse and the school and the parents and the money and the player and the music is never

enough and the sex is never enough and the jones is never enough
and you can be free from that feeling that nothing is ever enough
because something is enough something is enough not sex not jones
not job not spouse not school not parents not job not money not
music not player only one thing are you listening only one thing listen
carefully only one thing is enough to fill the empty only one thing can
fill the want only one thing is enough only one thing satisfies you can
feel them feel them feel them on your teeth now yes you can feel them
on your teeth and it's not the sex jones spouse job school parents
money player music it is Couscous Critters it is Couscous Critters
Couscous Critters satisfy Couscous Critters are enough Couscous
Critters feed the want Couscous Critters fill the empty Couscous Critters from Azerbadzhan Appetizers Couscous Critters from
Azerbadzhan Appetizers Couscous Critters Couscous Critters Couscous Critters fill the empty fill the want it is enough not the sex jones
job spouse parents school money player music but Couscous Critters
from Azerbadzhan Appetizers are you listening are you listening are
you listening . . .

[loop back to start.]

FIVE

The Short List of Possible Outcomes

The rest of the day was a washout, complete and utter. I think everyone else in the company had been demoralized by Levine's pronouncement—but, hopefully, this was the dark cloud that would part to reveal the silver lining of people working far past their capabilities to bring the World Nanotechnologies, Ltd. account to Pembroke Hall. At least, that's what we were all hoping.

After lunch I learned what World Nanotechnologies was all about when the ferret showed up with the data from Spenner's speech. It was something, all right.

Toward the end of the last century, a handful of scientists became intrigued with the idea that they could produce machines of microscopic size. While they all saw the possibilities of Nanotechnology, only one had foresight enough to see the commercial potential.

So he set up World Nanotechnologies, Ltd. in a spare room of his house. It was a loosely organized think tank at first, a network of strangers connected by zaps and modems, all bound by the common goal of coming up with theoretical and practical ways for Nano machines to be used for the betterment of humankind—and their own bank accounts.

By the time Nanotechnics had become a reality, World Nano was ready to go, first with medical applications. Nanos repaired heart valves; removed blood clots; and as they got smarter, excised cancer cells. Then they started on the quality of life. They kept drinking water pure without adding chemicals. They sped up the biodegradability of plastics. They were appointed to keep watch over fragile computer hardware and fiber optics, and heavy industry used them to dismantle insidious molecules of industrial waste.

As practitioners of internal microsurgery and bodily maintenance, Nanos closed potentially lethal cuts for hemophiliacs and opened diseased blood vessels in diabetics. Nanos went on to treat ulcers and hemorrhoids, and some went on to hunt down bacteria like those that caused meningitis. Before long the tiny machines had become environmental watchdogs and had even made it safe to eat bottom feeders from Lake Erie.

If World Nanotechnologies, Ltd. had only those laurels to rest on, that would have guaranteed their place in the history datanets. But the company was set up to *fully realize the potential of Nanotechnology.* Just when everyone thought that Nanotechnics had reached its limit, someone at corporate headquarters opened an archived file and a new application was born.

The newest application would make World Nanotechnologies, Ltd. a household name by bringing this technology into people's everyday lives. It was an area for which Nanos had never been considered.

World Nanotechnologies, Ltd. was about to introduce a new line of laundry soap—one that would take out a stain set in fabric as well as give permanent protection to clothes.

It was called NanoKleen. It was a concentrate form of laundry soap supplied by a major manufacturer. But World Nano would add the secret ingredient—water-activated microscopic creepers. Washing clothes in NanoKleen would impregnate them with Nano machines, which would travel along the cloth fibers each wash day to keep clothes cleaner than anyone imagined possible. Nanos would even recognize when the fiber had been stained and take steps to restore it to its original beauty.

NanoKleen was brilliant, a product that ad men all over the world would slit their wrists to get. Since it was liquid activated, clothes could be washed by merely soaking them in cold water. On a messy liquid spill, NanoKleen would activate and go right to work on the localized area, effectively preventing a stain. The only thing required was to rewash your clothes in the product once every three to six months to impregnate more Nanos. And ecologically it was a dream, since NanoKleen users would cut down drastically on soap consumption.

Best of all, none of the other Nanotech companies had been able to imagine that World would head in such a strictly commercial direction. If the competition suddenly decided to come out with a competing product, it would be three to five years before they'd have something workable on their R and D boards. In that length of time, consumers would give NanoKleen a lock on the market.

World Nanotechnologies, Ltd. was looking for an agency to launch it for them, and launch it *big*. It didn't matter how many people understood what a Nano was or how it could mean cleaner clothes. All that mattered was that the ad lock onto some universal experience and drive home the point that NanoKleen would do laundry better than anything else. Whichever agency had the campaign that did it best would launch NanoKleen.

Pembroke Hall had to capture this one. Levine wanted the account so badly he could taste it, so badly that he was willing to sacrifice the unity and integrity of the agency for a winning campaign. He had opened the project to every creative group in the agency, which meant that back stabbings, walkovers, shutouts, and heaven only knew what else would be rife until World Nanotechnologies, Ltd. chose an agency.

And when the dust cleared, Levine would have his brave new advertising world. The probable cost would be a full quarter of the agency's personnel, but that was his vision. Get rid of the Hotchkisses, and maybe the Boddekkers would survive.

With Pembroke and Hall long gone and Pangborn freshly dead, there was no one to stop him. Levine outranked Harris in tenure, and it was doubtful that she'd try to stop him. She might even share Levine's vision of rebuilding in a bloody aftermath.

It didn't matter. Not really. Not to me, especially. Levine liked me. I was guaranteed a slot as long as I didn't screw up. It wouldn't hurt if I came up with something good for the NanoKleen competition. Certainly, I had the motivation. A house in Princeton was calling my name.

The problem was that the house wasn't calling loudly enough. Or maybe it *was,* but I couldn't hear it over the din of collapsing morale at Pembroke Hall. Perhaps I didn't understand its siren call, still bound by the self-pity of knowing I wasn't going to go home and pack for the Big Move.

I took my watch off and brought up Jean's number, ready to purge it. Then I changed my mind. I put my watch down on the desk and rubbed my wrist.

Maybe if I tried some stream-of-consciousness jotting . . .

That wasn't any good either. I was able to enter only a few stupid and worthless notes about the account on my notebook, and when I tried to do something for Boston Harbor, my creative paralysis became worse. There was that fireplace in Princeton, a scene shot from the glow of a real wood fire with the very undressed Honniker In Accounting, and it was *perfect* for Boston Harbor, but how to translate it into an advertising scenario escaped me.

I tried revising a spot for Daily Jones, but every keystroke only served to make things worse. I was at a dead end and I knew it. My only hope was creative procrastination, which meant looking busy for the remainder of the day while accomplishing nothing. Maybe tomorrow would bring a new creative charge.

So I spent a lot of time at the water cooler and in the bathroom and going through the archives and bugging the researcher and making myself scarce when Bainbridge was around. That got me through the day, and by the time I found myself with a way to revise the Daily Jones spot, Hotchkiss popped his head into my office and flashed the lights to get my attention.

"Hey Boddekker, what are you trying to do, make us all look bad?"

"Huh?" I looked up.

"In case you hadn't noticed, there's an agencywide epidemic of creative constipation. The lows have hit, my friend, and there's only one cure. As someone who claims to be creative, I know you'll want to participate."

I raised an eyebrow. "Ogilvy's?"

Hotchkiss nodded. "Honniker In Accounting is going to be there."

I shrugged. It was her nature to be there. And because she was going, so would half of the guys from Pembroke Hall. It was a nice idea if you could stand the competition. I couldn't.

"Doesn't matter," I said. "But I could use a trip to Ogilvy's."

"I'll count you in."

"Wait. Is Bainbridge going to be there?"

Hotchkiss shook his head. "Left early. Classes or something. Too bad, huh?"

"Yeah. I'll definitely be there."

He smiled. "Philanderer."

"Reorientation freak."

"Bjorn brain."

"Fjord face."

"Ishta."

"Uffda."

"What's all this?" said Upchurch, appearing from behind and throwing an arm around Hotchkiss. "Lover's quarrel?"

"Sparring for the fair hand of Honniker In Accounting, no doubt." Churchill's voice drifted in from the hall.

"Of course," said Upchurch, "they don't have a chance."

"Who does?" I said.

"Ah," said Churchill. "But my friend here is working as we speak on a way to interface hardware with wetware."

"And Honniker In Accounting," embellished Upchurch, "is some piece of wetware."

"Back to realtime," said Hotchkiss. "A bunch of us are going to Ogilvy's for a creative enema. Either of you interested?"

"Certainly," said Upchurch. "Honniker In Accounting or no."

"What about your evil twin brother?" Hotchkiss nodded toward Churchill.

"Yeah," Churchill replied, "but I gotta do a jones check first."

"Right. Likewise." Upchurch nodded at us. "We'll meet you there." The Church Brothers vanished.

"Don't worry," Hotchkiss said. "They don't stand a chance with Honniker In Accounting."

"Who's worried?" I said. "Neither do I."

"You stand a better chance than the Church Brothers. Word has it she doesn't like computer people."

"Churchill isn't computer."

"She doesn't like jonesers, either."

"Thanks," I said, giving Hotchkiss the evil eye. "You're very encouraging."

He laughed.

Ogilvy's was an easy walk from Pembroke Hall, and was on the same block as a subway access. Over the years, the creative people from Pembroke Hall had adopted the place as their own. It was a rustic place with a lot of Old Wood and brass, crammed with all sorts of toys for us to blow off steam—dart and ball tosses, oldvid and holovid games, interactives, even billiards and playing cards. On any weekday night, there was a large handful of creatives from the agency on hand, playful and raucous as ideas and insults bounced from person to person. Few of the noncreatives could stand to be around the place after quitting time, so they went elsewhere—to special bars for number crunchers and hardwireds, places with interactive abstract calculators built into the tables and prints of fractals hanging on the walls.

Tonight, Ogilvy's was packed, mostly with Pembroke Hall people. All of them looked like something heavy was on their minds and their eyes were searching for a way out from under it.

Judging from the noise, they were looking their hardest. The juke was blaring a song by the Infidels, and every game in the place was running.

"Well," Hotchkiss said with a relieved smile. "I'm glad to see we're not alone in our misery."

"Nothing's worse than drinking alone," I said. "Unless it's drinking with someone you don't like."

Hotchkiss made a vulgar gesture. "Who says you have to do that? Look."

I followed his gaze across the room. In one corner of the bar, several tables had been pushed together, and in the middle of the commotion was Honniker In Accounting, a smile on her face and a drink in her hand.

"Who says number crunchers are boring?" I said, noting the presence of some at the table.

"She's got a jones for creatives." Hotchkiss elbowed me in the side.

"What are you pushing me for?" I asked. "If I recall, you once expressed a desire to—"

"I'm in mourning," Hotchkiss yelled. "Or have you forgotten?"

"You need consolation, then."

"Forget it, pal. This is your night. I saw her talking to you after the meeting."

I shook my head. "This *isn't* the night. Not after the day I've had."

"You don't believe me? I'll bet by the end of the evening, you end up in her sweet caress."

"Realtime check, Hotchkiss."

"Well." He looked almost disappointed. "At least let me get you drunk enough to try."

It couldn't be any worse than being a hungover fool like I had been this morning. "That's the best offer I've had all day."

I walked to the bar with Hotchkiss, having forgotten that it was only hours ago that I had recovered from my weekend binge. While Hotchkiss bought the first round I hovered around the bar, grabbing two stools as they were vacated. I took one and pivoted to watch the anarchy, and Hotchkiss returned with two mixed drinks. I complained. I had wanted only beer.

"Live," he said. "The world is coming to an end. You have to have one night that you'll regret." In retrospect, Hotchkiss was right about the regrets, although it was in a way that he never could have imagined.

"I've got enough of those already." I took a careful sip of what he'd brought me, and noticed a leggy blonde hovering over the juke, punching in a song. "Who's she?"

"Who?" Hotchkiss asked, coming up for air. He had already finished his drink.

I pointed at the blonde. "She's not a regular."

Hotchkiss sucked an ice cube. "She's not with the agency."

"Another creative-type joneser?"

Hotchkiss opened his mouth to reply, but at that moment, a familiar and solemn chord came through the speakers, and his face bent into a wince. "No," he said. "Not those old SOBs again."

The woman stepped back from the juke, pleased with her selection. She didn't hear the boos coming from the Pembroke Hall people.

"We know one thing," Hotchkiss pronounced. "She can't have any interest in true creativity." He shook his head and took a mouthful of ice. "Parasites."

I spun my stool to face the bar and flagged down Ogilvy, a

handsome man who in later years had taken to wearing a patch over one eye.

"Boddekker," he said. "Another round?"

I shook my head. "My friend wants to know why you still have 'Hey John' in the juke."

He shrugged, not understanding. "You're all Pembroke Hall people."

"But we don't necessarily listen to Pembroke Hall acts," Hotchkiss said. "Especially *that* one. Those guys are creative carrion eaters."

"Some folks still like to hear that one," Ogilvy said, "That woman in particular. She's been playing it, on and off, all day."

"Who is she?" I asked. "A daytime regular?"

"As of the last few days, yes," Ogilvy said, wiping the bar with a towel. "I'd never laid my eye on her before that."

"You're getting old," Hotchkiss said. "Nobody comes here cold. They've all been introduced. She's got to have a connection. She's with someone here."

"She's here, and she's drinking alone," Ogilvy said. "And I might be getting older, and I might lack some of my original equipment, but what I have left is still tuned to the fineries of the female form. And gentlemen, I would have remembered that woman from the twentieth century."

Hotchkiss and I turned for a second look. Ogilvy was right. The form was there.

"The eyes, boys. Take a look at those eyes."

It would have been one of those wonderful literary moments if she had turned right then, so the two of us were treated to the glory of her eyes, but it didn't happen that way. Hotchkiss and I had to wait six or seven minutes for "Hey John" to end. I exchanged my drink for a beer, and watched a handful of agency people crowd around the juke to keep the woman from programming the SOBs again. It got loud fast. The woman wandered away, then suddenly appeared off to our left for a refill. Hotchkiss and I casually looked her way.

Ogilvy was right. He hadn't lost his appreciation or any of his faculties. The woman's eyes were jewel blue, and so piercingly haunting that it put goose bumps on my arms.

"Wow," whispered Hotchkiss.

"That's an understatement," I said.

The woman turned away with her drink, looking past and

through Hotchkiss and me. If she had noticed either of us there, staring with open mouths, it didn't show. She took her drink and strolled back to her table near the juke, arriving as the agency people wandered off to commit more acts of excess. We shamelessly tracked her with our eyes, and when it looked like we were about to be spotted, we quickly turned to face the bar.

"So," Hotchkiss said to Ogilvy, who was bringing a third refill, "tell us more."

Ogilvy shrugged. "She doesn't say much. She pays for her drinks with a Gold Standard bank card. She only orders drinks that come with something in them like umbrellas or little swords. And she's made me sicker than I ever thought I could get of 'Hey John' and 'Baby Baby Baby Baby Baby.' "

"It's a start," I said.

"Wait a minute," Hotchkiss protested. "I thought this was your night for Honniker In Accounting."

"Let's look at the cold, hard facts," I said, setting my glass down hard. "You saw the way that woman looked through you and me? Honniker In Accounting does that on a daily basis. She doesn't even know us by name."

"She knows you," Hotchkiss said, guzzling.

"Try not to burst a blood vessel, but it was nothing, Hotchkiss. What you saw after the meeting this morning was all business."

Hotchkiss stopped drinking long enough to give me a forlorn look.

"Really," I said. "Listen, you're the one who keeps bringing her up, maybe *you* should be the drunken fool. You're through with Dansiger, so you need Honniker In Accounting more than I do. Why don't you go for it, Hotchkiss? Maybe the Florence Nightingale effect will set in, and you'll end up putting her in your watch."

He slowly put his glass down. He was thinking about it.

"And what are you going to do, Boddekker?"

"Me?" I wiped a bead of moisture off of the mug. "I thought I would wait for an appropriate break in the music, then go over and punch in 'Baby Baby Baby Baby Baby' and see if it gets me into a conversation with Lady Fatal Eyes."

"You're a friend, Boddekker," Hotchkiss said. "A real friend." He slid off of the stool and wandered toward the back of the bar.

"Good luck," I called after him, and then added under my

breath, "You've got about as much chance as I do." And that, of course, was no chance at all.

I stayed on my stool and watched the happy chaos, choreographed to a loud melange of retropop, grind, worldbeat, and old stuff I was surprised to find that people still listened to. Pembroke Hall had overrun Ogilvy's now. The Church Brothers had shown up along with dozens of others, including computer people and number crunchers like Honniker In Accounting. If there had been any nonagency regulars in Ogilvy's at 5 P.M., they had long since retreated to somewhere with a more civilized atmosphere. What was happening now was the celebration of the end of the world.

But the woman with the piercing blue eyes stayed around, too. She kept drinking, slowly and alone, as Ogilvy or one of his hires kept her in drinks, reacting to whatever came out of the juke, but only responding to those old songs that I thought no longer had an audience. She didn't look up, otherwise she would have seen me. She sat in her chair, staring forlornly.

"She's trouble, Boddekker," Ogilvy said from behind me.

"I'm just looking," I said.

"But you're doing that in-depth looking. You watch yourself."

"What does your bartender's intuition tell you this time?"

"Nothing. It's what she told me." He smiled.

"Are you going to tell me or am I going to have to drag it out of you?"

"That last drink she bought? When she paid for it, she told me that this was her last night on Earth."

"She doesn't look sick," I said.

"I wasn't thinking of that," Ogilvy said. "I got the impression that she's waiting for something to pick her up and carry her off."

I spun the stool to face him. "What? A UFO?"

Ogilvy shrugged. "I didn't say that."

"Didn't that Stephen Hawking emulator prove they were mathematically impossible?"

"I'm not saying anything, son, other than think twice before approaching that woman."

I turned back to her. "But I have thought about it twice," I said. "I'm on my third or fourth time."

Leaving my glass on the bar, I slid off the stool and set a slow course for the juke. It was time, I thought, time to play "Baby Baby Baby Baby Baby" and see if it would catalyze a conversation with the mystery woman.

Halfway across the room, Honniker In Accounting suddenly appeared, walking to the middle of the bar, shouting to get everyone's attention. I stopped. It looked like she was coming right toward me, but I had vowed not to make the same mistake twice. She was heading for the juke, only she stopped before she got there and turned a slow circle to see what kind of attention she had gotten from her colleagues. Then she put two fingers of her right hand into her mouth and blew an ear-splitting whistle that instantly silenced the bar.

"What is going on in here?" she demanded, pacing in a tight circle. "We're the number one agency in new concepts. Creatively, there's not another organization that can touch us. And you're all moping around like a bunch of indecisive Reorientation cases because somebody said it's the end of the world.

"Let me tell you something, people. We're going to *get* the World Nanotechnologies, Ltd. account, and we're going to do it by giving them the best campaign we've ever done for anyone. Every agency in the world is going to hate our guts. They're going to be talking us down while they're zapping us their résumés because they're all going to want to be a part of Pembroke Hall."

There was a scattering of applause. Some people had bought it. Most hadn't.

"All right," she said, disgusted. "Morale is a little low. What we need is a fight song. Something to remind us that we're going to march into the halls of World Nano, and march right back out with that contract in our hand. And we're going to do it because *we are Pembroke, Hall, Pangborn, Levine, and Harris!*"

There were murmurs as she went to the juke and coded in a selection. A split second later, a martial-sounding drum beat pounded out of the speakers at an impossibly loud volume.

"This is it, people!" called Honniker In Accounting. "Mark your territory!"

The patrons of the bar were instantly divided into two camps. The smaller one broke away from what they were doing and formed a long conga line behind Honniker In Accounting. They hunched down together and started a bowlegged trot across the floor. The other camp, which included me, simply stared, unsure of what to think as the growing line marched to the beat.

The vocalist chanted about someone being "not not mine, but you will be fine . . . it's only just a matter of time," and the conga line wound through the bar, picking up passengers as it went. Hotchkiss, who had joined early on, was singing, "gonna mark, gotta mark, gonna give you my mark . . . so the world will know where you belong." And the anthem about territoriality went on.

Then Honniker In Accounting raised her fist into the air, shouting, "All right, people, this is it—*sing!*" and the conga line snake dancers drowned out Killer Without A Conscience.

> "Gonna piss on my hands,
> Gonna spit in your food!
> I'll do anything to make you mine!"

A dog should be so clever about marking its territory, I thought. The dance was picking up people right and left, forming a long, dense line that was winding in and out of Ogilvy's obscure corners. My colleagues were firmly in the grip of this hormonal, militaristic song, and the song now belonged to them. They had spit in one another's food. I didn't know if Killer Without A Conscience was a Pembroke Hall act, but if they weren't, some poor agency would be forever kicking themselves for signing them if word got out that the group's only hit had become our fight song.

There were more verses, "gonna write my name all over your life . . . gonna bury my dead in your yard," and there were more choruses. It was all the same. It was war, and we were going to win. Ogilvy, I noticed, had cleared the floor of his people, and they now stood with him behind the bar. They watched as the dance took on a life of its own, heading into a belated middle eight.

> "I'm gonna spit, spit, spit in my hands,
> I'm gonna spit in your food . . ."

It became a chant that went on close to forever. A handful of agency people had not yet joined the line, and those ranks were dissolving fast. Ogilvy was smiling and shaking his head, and the woman with the eyes—my objective in all of this—saw it with the same wide-eyed horror that an ancient missionary might have used on seeing a native fertility rite. She was both fascinated and repulsed by what she was seeing. If there was ever a moment for me to act, this was it, right now.

"I'm gonna spit, spit, spit in my hands—"

My throat tightened. What in the world was I going to say to this person? *Want to go somewhere a little quieter? Forgive my colleagues—they've had a bad day?* Whatever I came up with, I was going to have to do it fast, because this woman's last night on Earth was showing signs of coming to a slam-bang ending.

"Gonna spit in your food . . ."

I looked at the line, winding in and out of Ogilvy's little rooms and around tables, past games, doubling back on itself. The members of Pembroke Hall were all a little bit drunk and a lot sweaty. They were all in a long line, for the most part boy-girl, boy-girl, hanging on to one another's hips as if their lives depended on it, and their eyes all had the same curiously demented gleam. The next few minutes were going to be critical, and the air was heavy with possible outcomes. Inhaling deeply, I could tell that the air was charged. And strangely enough, at that moment of what was clearly a rally from the valley of the shadow of the end of the world for Pembroke Hall, I began to feel scared. But I was convinced that the strange woman would know what to do.

I took a step toward her table and someone brushed against me. It was Honniker In Accounting. The snake dance was making her glow, and it was touched off by the way her dark hair framed her face. Her clothes were clinging to her body. Her lips were moist. She smiled. At me. And with a nod of her head, she made me see that the boy-girl order of things had gotten disrupted, and repairing it would require my hands on her hips.

"Boddekker," she said, laughing. "Come on. Come and shake it."

It was suddenly all too much. It hadn't been that long since I'd shed one hangover, and there I was, cultivating another. The air was stifling but I felt ice cold, and I was trembling. There was a woman with siren eyes that I wanted desperately to get to know, and Honniker In Accounting was standing between us.

A pity it hadn't been Bainbridge. I would have known right then what to do.

But all I could see at the moment was that I was about to be forced into making the worst decision of my entire life. Given that, I did what any other man would do when he found himself about to be torn apart by his own libido.

I took one more breath of the bar's sticky, stale air, ran my glance from the siren to Honniker In Accounting, and with a polite nod to both, walked out the door.

Outside, it had finished raining. The fresh air seemed to clear my head—or so I thought.

I splashed a puddle with my toe, stuck my hands in my pockets, and decided a walk would burn off what remained of the fog that had developed inside Ogilvy's.

I went straight down the street to my meeting with Ferman's Devils.

PEMBROKE, HALL, PANGBORN, LEVINE, AND HARRIS

"Selling you to the world since 1969"

Offices in Principal Cities: New York - Montreal - Toronto - Sydney - London -
Tokyo - Moskva - Beijing - Chicago - Oslo - Philadelphia - Amarillo

CLIENT: »Innovative Chemistry		PRODUCT: »Lover's Mist
WRITER: »Boddekker	TIME: »:60	MEDIA: »Audio
TITLE: »*Listen for the Hisst! (jingle variant #2c*)*		
PRODUCTION ORDERS:	»*Deppe to provide music score*	

SINGERS: Before you and your wetware go back to your wee
   abode,
And before you do a Tango in the horizontal mode,
There's just one slight distraction you should check off on your list,
Just listen [*SFX: two brief bursts of spray in cadence to music.*] for
   the hisst!

Just a squirt upon your privates makes you set for all the night,
Even if you both stay busy till the break of morning's light,
And those calls about your blood test—you won't panic if they're
   missed,
If you listened [*SFX: same as above.*] for the hisst!

[*SAMPLED SOLO (guitar? see Deppe for details).*]

ANNOUNCER: [*Over solo.*] That's right—just two squirts of Lover's
   Mist from *Innovative Chemistry* will protect you from even the
   most virulent sexually transmitted diseases for up to twelve hours!
   That's twice as long as the other leading brands—and there's
   none of the associated numbness or swelling!

SINGERS: So you can smile with confidence and take your partner's
   hand,

For you know that your protection is the finest in the land,
And you know you'll have no problems when you're using Lover's
   Mist,
'Cause you listened [*SFX: as with previous verses.*] for the hisst!

ANNOUNCER: Lover's Mist from *Innovative Chemistry*. Also available in contraceptive formula.

SIX

The Hour of the Wolf

A week went by.

A week went by, and I managed to forget about Ferman's Devils in such a complete manner that it was almost blissful. There were lurking, sinister figures from my school days and old sex partners that I wished I could forget with such impudent completeness. But for this part of my life, I would have to settle for forgetting the Devils like you'd forget an inconvenience that strikes you when you're on the way to somewhere else.

Naturally there were other things that I wanted to forget but couldn't. Like NanoKleen, and the total specter of doom that hung over the agency while we scrambled to come up with a campaign for it. Nothing had been the same between any of the creatives since that night in Ogilvy's. We were all scrambling, caught up in the search for genius-on-demand. Unfortunately, the genius wasn't coming on demand. Not even the announcement of a strict deadline loosened the agency's collective creative spirit— and usually it did wonders. This time there was nothing.

And even though I knew that it was better to stay away from

certain people at times like this, after an uneventful morning spent staring at my terminal and wandering around my floor in the game I call creative procrastination, I walked over to Ogilvy's for a sandwich and ended up sitting at the bar next to Hotchkiss.

The man was a wreck. He was staring blankly into a glass filled with liquid lunch—and I'm not talking about the high-carb neo-protein steroid-enriched liquid lunches that nine out of ten bodybuilders prefer. Hotchkiss's liquid lunch had a white, foamy crown and sat in a clear mug riddled with dots of condensation. It was golden and yeasty and Hotchkiss reeked of the stuff.

I ordered a sandwich. Hotchkiss ignored me. I said, "It's a little early in the day to be starting that, isn't it?"

He took a long sip. "I'm stuck."

"Aren't you trying the wrong cure? That stuff's not going to help—"

"I'm beyond help," Hotchkiss said. "I want to forget."

I reached over and gently pushed the glass away from him. "I think you're forgetting the wrong thing. You're forgetting that we're Pembroke Hall, and whenever we set our sights on a client, we get them."

"No thanks to me," Hotchkiss said sullenly. He reached around me and cradled his beer.

"Give yourself some credit, Hotchkiss. Who gets the key to the elevator all of the time? Who has the wall full of plaques?"

"That doesn't mean a thing," he said.

"Prove it."

"Remember when I broke my leg in the softball game against Mauldin and Kress?"

I nodded.

"They gave me the elevator key then, too. And the day after I broke my leg, I didn't have to come to work."

"Are you telling me that you want to go out and break your leg?"

"I'm telling you that breaking your leg is better than winning those stupid plaques and awards that the old men give out . . . but look who I'm talking to about that." He shrugged and drained his glass, then stabbed his finger on the counter to order a refill.

"You know what my problem is, Boddekker? I don't know a thing about advertising. It's true. Not a thing. The more I look at this Nanotech thing, and the more I try to think of a way to sell it, the more I realize it.

"I've spent my whole career regurgitating what the customer wanted. They'd tell me what they wanted and I'd put it into a script. It didn't have to be good. It didn't have to be clever. It didn't have to tap into something in the collective consciousness. In other words, it didn't have to be good advertising. All I had to do was tell someone where to buy the product. That's all. I never had to sell. I never had to get attention. As long as it translated well and sold to the Mongol hordes, it didn't matter. They were all so hungry that it didn't have to be good.

"All those times I thought I was downloading what I'd written onto script slates, I was actually vomiting. I was just puking on those slates, Boddekker. And now that it's the end of the world, I can't do that anymore. Not when it all has to matter." He smiled sadly as Ogilvy refilled his mug. "I've got the dry heaves."

Mercifully, Ogilvy didn't say anything and I kept my mouth shut, knowing that it would be a mistake to make the obvious joke at this point. It occurred to me that I was making another mistake by listening to Hotchkiss when he was depressed, because it was making me think of everything I had to do, most of which I'd put off so I could creatively procrastinate on doing something for NanoKleen. There was Boston Harbor and the SOBs, raiding Pangborn's old files, and the creative group meeting where I had to come up with some kind of outline so they wouldn't think I was as strapped for an idea as everyone else had been.

The words *creative group meeting* burned me for a moment, until I finally looked at my watch and yelped.

"Is this the wrong order?"

I looked up to see Ogilvy balancing a dish on which was laid a sandwich and chips.

"Box it for me," I said, throwing him my money card. "I've got to be somewhere."

"Me too," Hotchkiss smiled. "But they all know I got nothing on my stomach anymore. So I'm going to blow it off." He sipped and lowered the glass to reveal a mustache of white foam. "Right here."

"Hotchkiss," I said as Ogilvy processed my order. "If you're not going back, can I borrow your elevator key?"

It hit the bar with a loud clank. "It won't pay your rent," he warned.

"Thanks," I said, grabbing the carton that now held my food.

I hopped off the stool and started for the door. "If there's anything I can ever do for you . . ."

Hotchkiss said something about Dansiger, but I was out the door before he finished. Tucking the food under my arm, I set out with as close to a dead run as I could on the crowded street.

Was there never any getting away from it? I suppose everyone had their demon to wrestle with. Hotchkiss had the realization that he was the creative equivalent of a carp. Mine was the fact that I tended to forget—or maybe it was a convenient way of ignoring—things I wanted to avoid. In this case I had gone too far from the agency in search of lunch—and had I eaten, odds are I would have missed the meeting completely.

By the time I got to the lobby, I was beginning to wonder what my hurry was. I was as clueless over NanoKleen as anyone else. I didn't need to bring that home to the rest of my group.

Maybe it was knowing that they depended on me. Maybe it was knowing that Levine was counting on me. No, I decided. It was none of the above. I didn't want them to think that I was stuck. I didn't want them to think that I was like everyone else.

On my way to the elevators, I blew by the Smilin' Guy, shouting a quick apology for not having time to stop and look at whatever he was selling. In Hotchkiss's elevator I checked the time. I couldn't really afford to stop in my office, but I desperately needed to. I would have to be fashionably late for the meeting.

The elevator stopped. I was moving before the door opened and was down the hall like a shot, shouting for the terminal to activate before my foot hit the carpeted surface of my office floor.

"Good afternoon, Mr. Boddekker!" chimed a synthetic voice. "In looking over your portfolio files, I can see that you're drastically underinsured for a man of your position. What would happen to your poor wife Yellow if you were to suddenly fall victim to a retroplague?"

"She's my *mother*!" I growled at the screen. "If you'd bother to check my beneficiary data, you'd know that!" I called for the ferret to remove the intruding software, which it did in slightly less than a second.

"You're slipping, ferret," I said. "You're letting the sloppy ones in."

"The sloppy ones have been upgraded to slip in as handshake coding," it replied. "Sorry. Did you want authorship on that one?"

"It wasn't even smart enough to check my tertiary data files before making its pitch. Forget it."

"Very well. Oh, Mr. Boddekker, I'm supposed to remind you that there's is a creative group meeting this afternoon. You're seven minutes late."

"I know. Look, ferret, I want you to go into my basement; access batch archive 'Rainyday.' "

"I'm there."

"I want you to bring me a file called 'Holiday,' but don't supply it until I call for it. Stand by on our meeting room subcircuit."

"See you there." The ferret left with its trademark pop. As it did, there was another pop from my telephone and another familiar voice came from the intercom.

"Boddekker," said Bainbridge. "Oh, Boddekker! Where are you? We're waiting."

I said nothing, but picked up my sandwich and walked quickly out of the office, leaving behind the voice of Bainbridge.

"—know you're in there. I can hear you moving—"

It was a short walk to our meeting room. As Bainbridge had threatened, everyone was waiting on me—and Bainbridge herself was still on the phone, making further threats against my person.

"—not fooling anyone, Boddekker. I can hear that rattling. You're *eating,* aren't you? Eating, and the rest of us are here waiting for you to come in and show us a little guidance—"

I held out the wrapped sandwich. "Want a bite?" I asked. Bainbridge went deep red and everyone except Dansiger laughed. Dansiger was our group researcher, and we weren't always on the best of terms because of my reliance on the ferret to do legwork for me. And because I had introduced her to the man with whom she had just broken up, I expected that for a time our relationship would be testy at best.

Dansiger didn't disappoint me. She said, "Well. Fearless Leader."

"No applause," I said. "Really."

"None offered," said Harbison, our software personality consultant.

I pulled a chair from under the table and flopped into it. "You're probably wondering why I called you here."

"*I* called the meeting." The complainer was our art director, Sylvester. Sylvester was one of those types whose gender tended to change from week to week. The bills from the Reorientation clinic must have been staggering. On this particular day, Sylvester was male, and he was doing his best to play the part of the curmudgeon. "Everyone but you seems to know about it, and everyone here but you seems to know what it's all about."

Good old Sylvester and his disposable personalities. If this one ever smiled, the face would probably shatter from the stress.

"I'm sure he was joking," Bainbridge offered, too quickly.

Dansiger rolled her eyes and Mortonsen, our AI programmer, shook her head. Mortonsen hated Bainbridge with a passion and saw her attentions toward me as sucking up. As group leader, I had to keep them from killing each other. If you've never been a creative group leader before, take my word; the political permutations between eight people are endless.

"World Nanotechnologies," I said. "NanoKleen. The modern miracle of twenty-first century science that will make dreary washdays truly a thing of the past."

Deppe, our music director, booed. Then, with great production, he gave me a thumbs-down.

"I hope that's not your initial idea," grumbled Sylvester.

I shook my head.

"Let's see it, then," Bainbridge said, her eyes shining a little too brightly. It looked like I was going to have to reinforce the talk I'd had with her about keeping her political preferences to herself.

"There's nothing to see."

"Hear, then," Deppe said, always a quick study—or maybe that was the musician's training.

I folded my hands and slowly looked at them as they surrounded me at the table—Mortonsen, Dansiger, Sylvester, Griswold, Bainbridge, Deppe, and Harbison, who was nervously rattling her fingernails on the synthetic finish of the tabletop. I tried to look dramatic, as if I were about to impart the wisdom of the ages. Actually it was a tactic designed to stall while I gathered my thoughts.

"Well?" asked Sylvester.

"Let's not sell this product short," I said. "This is going to be a major event. We're looking at a ten-kilo box of laundry soap that could last a lifetime."

"I wouldn't be too ecstatic about the initial returns until the

Department of Environmental Accountability has had their say,'' said Harbison.

"It would seem to me they've had their say," said Deppe. "This product is going on the market. That must mean that it's eco-safe."

"I think calling it eco-safe is an understatement," Bainbridge said. Oh, how I hated her for saying that, because it looked like she was doing it to agree with me. But she was right. "How much soap—even the eco-safes—does the average consumer use during the course of a year? Now cut that down to ten kilos in a lifetime—"

"Those are initial baseline figures with no bearing on what the market will actually move," Sylvester said.

"All right," chimed in Harbison. "Let's do a worst-case scenario, shall we? Let's say we've got a real spendthrift who manages to use a kilo a year. Stack *that* up against the amount of a regular eco-safe used over a ten-year period."

"What I want to know," said Mortonsen, "is if some of these Nanos wash off during the cold water washings, and they make their way into the ecosystem, what do they do?"

"They have a secondary and tertiary triggering system," I said, having the data fresh from the ferret's briefing. "Once they make their way in, they'll go on a search-and-destroy mission, hunting non-eco compounds."

"What kind of a life span on these things once they're in the ecosystem?" asked Deppe.

"Not known. The only practical model was the Lake Erie series of Nanos, and they were specifically designed for survival in a harsh ecosystem. The NanoKleen machines may last only a matter of hours once they've washed away."

"But with millions of people using NanoKleen," said Bainbridge, "even a matter of hours will make an impressive difference."

Sylvester set his coffee cup down hard on the table. "People, the whole point of this is millions of people will *not* be using NanoKleen unless someone sells it to them. I prefer, and I know that Mr. Levine and Mez Harris all prefer, that we be the company that sells the product that goes to the house that Jack built. If we're all through discussing the eco-consequences of this product, perhaps we can move toward the work for which we have been hired, which is coming up with a campaign to send upstairs that will get the account and ensure our extended stay here at Pembroke Hall.''

"Consequences are exactly what this is all about," I said. "Forget what it does or doesn't, might or might not do to the ecosystem. What is it going to do for you and me?" They looked at each other. I could see wheels turning, but so far, only Deppe had caught on.

"Harbison, how much time do you spend doing your laundry each week?"

"I don't," she said. "I send it out."

"How about you, Dansiger?"

"I send it out, too."

"Bainbridge?"

"Couple of hours."

"When you could be doing something else?"

"I take something to read. Study."

"What about someone who had no need to study? Maybe someone doesn't like to read. Sylvester?"

"I don't see what the point of all of this is, Boddekker."

"The point is, how much money do Harbison and Dansiger spend on their laundry in a month? How much time and money does Bainbridge lose? What if you could get it all back because all you had to do was throw what you needed clean in a sink full of cold water? We're not talking convenience anymore. We're talking freedom."

"Make it into a campaign," Sylvester challenged.

"Ferret," I said.

The ferret's voice chimed from one of the speakers. "Here, Mr. Boddekker!"

"Please open the file marked 'Holiday' and give us a data reading."

"One moment."

"We're going to engage in the most time-honored and the most proven selling tradition of all time," I said.

"Ready," said the ferret.

"Feed."

"The following is a listing of holidays during a typical calendar year that may be used to stimulate retail sales. Or, as Mr. Boddekker has annotated, a listing of every excuse that has ever been used for trying to sell someone on the idea of giving a gift or a card.

"Listing: New Year's Day. Stephen Hawking Day. War Day. Martin Luther King Jr. Day. The entire month of February, including presidential birthdays for Washington, Lincoln, Reagan, and Smithers; Valentine's Day, Ramadan, the beginning of Orthodox Lent, Ash Wednesday, and Vice President's Day. St. Patrick's Day. Vernal Equinox. Mother-in-Law's Day. Palm Sunday. Norwegian Invasion Day. Good Friday. Passover. Easter Sunday. Easter Monday. Easter Tuesday. Orthodox Easter. Tax Day's Eve. Tax Day. Earth Day. Mother's Week. Armed Forces Day. Victoria Day. Memorial Day. Flag Day."

"What are you trying to prove?" Sylvester grumbled.

I glared and motioned for him to be quiet.

"Father's Day. Summer Solstice. St. Jean Baptiste Day. Children's Day. Canada Day. Independence Day. Eagle's Landing Day. Elvis Day. Civic Holiday. Hiroshima Day. Wall Fall Week. Weird Day. Women's Suffrage Day. Labor Day. Grandparent's Day. Just Because Day. Citizenship Day. Rosh Hashanah. Fall Equinox. Yom Kippur. Mohammed's Birthday. St. Francis of Assissi Day. Columbus Day. United Nations Day. All Hallows Eve. Guy Fawkes Day. Sweetest Day."

"I really *hate* that one," said Mortonsen.

"Election Day. Veteran's Day. Gettysburg Address Day. Kennedy Assassination Day. Thanksgiving Eve. Thanksgiving Day. Pearl Harbor Day. Hanukkah. Winter Solstice. Christmas Eve Day. Christmas Day. Boxing Day. New Year's Eve Day.

"This list is designed to primarily target North American audiences and does not include localized celebrations such as Cantaloupe Day. It also does not include variable dates related directly to a potential customer's private life, such as anniversaries of births, marriages, religious conversions, radical surgeries, or deaths. This concludes the list."

"Boddekker," Dansiger said, rising. "I must protest this use of the ferret. I could have easily compiled this data for you—"

"Calm down," I said, gently motioning with my palms toward her.

"Calm, nothing," Dansiger said. "I get paid to work here. The ferret is just software."

"This was not a research list," I continued. "It was one I gradually accumulated by taking notes off of different calendars. When the time comes to do something with the idea, I'll have you compile a more complete international listing."

"So," Sylvester said. "What's the point of all this?"

"Let's give them a real holiday," I said. "Freedom Day."

"A lot of the eastern nations already have that one," Dansiger said. "We celebrate it here as Wall Fall Week."

"I'm talking about a holiday that will last people for the rest of their lives. I'm talking about the gift of time. Two hours a week on laundry. One hundred four hours a year. How many days does that come to over the course of a lifetime—days that can't be replaced? Days that NanoKleen will give them."

"Not bad," said Deppe. "Maybe you could start with something like, 'Look, your days are numbered.' "

"I'm on it," said Bainbridge. "Follow that up with, 'Why spend all of that time doing the laundry? Let NanoKleen set you free.' " She looked around to see what kind of approval her idea had gotten her. There wasn't much to be had. "Or words to that effect."

"That's not bad," Harbison offered. I think she was trying to be generous.

"It could be better," Mortonsen said evenly.

"Not better," Dansiger said. "Hot. This needs to be *hot*."

"Define *hot*," Bainbridge taunted.

"I can see this," Griswold said, which was a good sign. "I can see where Boddekker is taking this." He looked at me. "Correct me if I'm wrong, but you see this as an antispot, one where you hit people with all of these holidays—bam, there's Hawking's birthday, wham, here's Summer Solstice, boom, here's the Fourth of July. But all of these holidays don't mean as much as the freedom you give yourself when you use NanoKleen."

"Yeah," said Deppe. "Like, 'For every other holiday, you have to buy somebody something—a card or flowers or candy or an expensive gift. With NanoKleen, now you can give yourself the most precious gift of all.' "

"Time," said Bainbridge.

"Better," said Mortonsen. "It's getting better."

"I don't like the direction you've taken this," said Harbison.

"Maybe we could find an open date on the calendar and declare an actual 'Freedom Day' and have it coincide with the day that NanoKleen hits the shelves." Griswold sat back in his seat, obviously pleased with his idea.

"It'd cost a lot to grease that thing through the House and Senate," grumbled Sylvester.

"Forget that," Bainbridge said. "We'll make World Nano pay for it."

Everyone stopped to look at her.

"They're buying the time, aren't they? Who says we have to buy a bill making an official declaration? Boddekker here can write the spots with a real authoritative edge, and we plaster it all over everywhere with a max-saturation multimedia buy, and we declare it as a matter of fact—" She spread her hands out wide, as if to graphically show us the size of the letters I would be writing. *"July nineteenth is freedom day! Wait for it!"*

It was a nice idea, hindered only by the fact that Bainbridge had chosen her birthdate as Freedom Day. Still, the group had taken my notion from a weak idea and had turned it into something viable. Well, some of the group had, anyway. Some of the others were still thinking it over.

"You put it in the public's eye as a holiday," Bainbridge said in a meek postscript. "And let them install it in their lives as one. That way, you let World Nano foot the bill and you bypass having to buy it into law."

Deppe nodded.

Griswold smiled.

"Yeah," I said, and looked at the others for input. It wasn't good.

Harbison shook her head.

Mortonsen frowned.

"No," said Sylvester.

"Why not?" asked Deppe.

"Do you really think we need another stinking holiday to sell this product to someone?" said Sylvester.

"It's a time-honored tradition," I said. Besides, it had long been my secret desire to be one of the few in the industry who would actually create a new holiday. This would be a great chance.

"It's not big enough," said Harbison.

"Big?" Bainbridge said, outraged. "How big do you want it? The return of the prophet Mohammed to endorse NanoKleen for taking the stains out of his jerkin?"

"No!" shouted Sylvester. The room went instantly silent as we all turned to look at him. "That's asking for trouble. You want a *jihad* or a *fatwa*? Look at what happened to Azerbadzhan Appetizers when they came out with Mohammed Munchies."

"That wasn't their fault," Harbison said. "There was an agencywide data glitch. The product was supposed to be called *Mohammed's* Munchies."

"Doesn't matter," Dansiger said. "The munchies were still in the shape of the prophet. That violated Islamic law."

"People," I said, "this is territory we've been over before—"

"But it is relevant," Mortonsen said. "The upshot of all of this is that NanoKleen should have a really sensational launch. But we don't want it to be *too* sensational or we'll overshadow the product."

"But it's a big product," said Griswold.

"It'll only be as big as the advertising makes it," said Sylvester.

"That's why it has to be big," I said. "A monster. A giant. Because that's what World Nano wants it to be. Think about it. They've saved the world a hundred times over. Now they want to make some serious money."

"Careful," Dansiger said. "I smell blood."

Mortonsen and Harbison laughed.

"I suppose you have a better idea," Bainbridge challenged.

"As a matter of fact, I did have something in mind."

Harbison shifted uncomfortably in her seat. "We think that the NanoKleen account needs *education* instead of *sensation.*"

Suddenly I smelled something, and it wasn't blood. There was power at stake here, and it was obvious that Dansiger and Mortonsen and Harbison had been collaborating to seize more for themselves. If Pembroke Hall got the World Nano account, and if our group was the one that brought it in, the three of them could pretty much write their own ticket. If Sylvester was in their pocket, that would give them a deadlock vote, and that would put them in a win-win position. Should the group go with either idea and things worked out, the results would be obvious. But if we went with the holiday idea and things didn't pan out for us or the company, the three of them would have every right to move somewhere else in the company—and my effectiveness as a group leader would be brought into question.

I put on my best sincere smile and looked at Dansiger. "All right. I'm open to suggestions. What do you have?"

"Well, I think you'd get a better grasp of what we're seeking if you were to see a graphic example. Do you mind if I show you some research I've done on the subject?"

"Go right ahead."

She picked up a remote and thumbed a button. A thin screen lowered from the wall, and we adjusted our seats for a better view as the lights dimmed. Static appeared on the screen and Dansiger called for her ferret to run the demonstration she had stored. The ferret answered her with a more businesslike tone than mine, and numbers flickered across the screen, digitally counting backward. Before it reached one, the screen went black, and an image appeared—a computer animation of a caveman washing a skin in a creek and banging on it with a rock. It was detailed enough for me to tell that this sequence was intended to be live action.

I glared at Dansiger. "Wait a minute. Is this what I think it is?"

"Watch," she said.

A voice from the screen said, "It has taken wash day thousands of years to reach a convenient stasis." This was accompanied by quick shots of people doing laundry from different periods of history, ending with the ultramodern washer and dryer of 1950s America.

"And since then, nothing has changed—"

A shot of a modern wash day, where things looked pretty much the same.

"—until now!"

Boom! A box of NanoKleen slammed down hard in front of the modern scene. It was accompanied by the words *Pending Further Info,* which told me that what I saw was a mock-up, based on what the programmer thought a box of NanoKleen would look like. A feminine hand picked the box up, the shot pulled back to reveal a modern woman examining it. She looked right into the camera.

"But this is just a box of *soap!*"

"Ah," said the narrator, "but it's no ordinary soap. *This* is *NanoKleen!*"

"NanoKleen?" asked the woman.

The narrator then went into a big explanation of how NanoKleen worked, complete with computer animation of the Nano machines crawling across the fabric of the shirt, zapping stains and dirt with a tiny laser cannon. The words *Pending Further Info* appeared again. Obviously, this sequence was meant to represent the way the Nanos actually worked, and what was showing was fanciful filler.

The spot cut back to the modern kitchen and modern woman, and the narrator concluded, "The newest in a series of modern miracles from World Nanotechnologies, Ltd. NanoKleen. The modern miracle that will make dreary wash days truly a thing of the past."

Deppe grunted and shook his head.

The screen went dark and the lights came back up. I bolted out of my chair. "That was a cassie of another group's spot," I said. "Where did you get it?"

"You ought to know," Dansiger grinned.

It took less than a half-second of thought. She had instructed her ferret to dig the spot out of Hotchkiss's file. The give-away was the caveman. Hotchkiss loved them and tried to use them whenever he could.

"Dansiger, you can't do this—"

"Boddekker!" snapped Mortonsen. "Let her make her point."

"The point is," I said, "that you could get us into a lot of trouble doing that."

Dansiger threw her head back and laughed. "Really, Boddekker. You think *this* spot is capable of capturing the attentions of the old men, let alone the account for Pembroke Hall? If anyone stands a chance of making a show for the agency, it's you."

"Does Hotchkiss know you did this?"

"Do you think he'd care if he did? He's preoccupied with other things at the moment . . . but seriously, Boddekker, this isn't about my personal life."

"Make your point, then."

"I had my ferret make a representative sampling for content of the spots already on file—"

"Dansiger!"

"Let her finish," said Harbison.

"And eighty-three percent of them hit on an element that is missing from what you want to do with our spot. This is the best example of that element, and there are those of us who feel it belongs in the spot."

She waited for me to take the bait. I said nothing. Finally, Bainbridge couldn't stand the silence and said, "The evolution of wash day."

"Wrong," Dansiger and I said together. Then Dansiger laughed and said, "Hotchkiss was right about you, Boddekker."

I didn't wait to hear what he was right about. I said to Bainbridge, "Instead of making this spot a tease, they want us to tell how the product works."

"Exactly," said Harbison, a little too loudly. Dansiger and Mortonsen shut her up with cruel stares.

"There'll be plenty of time for that later," said Deppe. "All you need to do is promise them something that will work like nothing else before it."

"Then they won't know how special the product is," said Mortonsen.

"Bainbridge," I said quickly. "How does laundry soap work?"

She looked up at me, startled. "Well, uh, you put it in the washer with the clothes, and turn on the machine, it suds up—"

"But how does it work?" I turned. "How does it work, Harbison?"

"If it's anything like dish soap," she said, "when you put dish soap in greasy water, it like, coats the top of the water and the dirt and stuff forms a disgusting ring around the outside of the sink."

"Great," I said. "Now tell me *why* it does that. Tell me the science of how it works. Is it surface tension? Is the soap lighter than water but heavier than the grease? Does it do something at the molecular level?"

Silence. From everyone.

"People don't know how regular soap works. And they're not going to care how this one works, either, as long as it keeps its promise."

"The World Nano people will want them to know how it works," said Dansiger.

"They won't if it's not good advertising," said Griswold. "People already know what Nanos are, they know what they've done for the world. All we have to do is tell them that a miracle is now available for their laundry pile."

"You must consider the client on this one," Mortonsen said.

"Excuse me," I said. "But I thought Griswold was the account executive here." I looked from Dansiger to Harbison to Mortonsen. "Maybe you three have forgotten something, so I'll give you a reminder. Why do we do what we do for the customer? For the money? The product samples? To win awards for our agency? Or do we do our work to make an upward sales curve?"

Dansiger folded her arms. "I told you," she said to Mortonsen and Harbison.

"It's not a bad idea," I said, "but it's too early for it. When this product hits the shelves, you won't hear the people who are flocking to buy it asking for the 'revolutionary Nanotechnological breakthrough for stain removal and fabric maintenance.' They're going to be asking for 'that modern wash day miracle.'"

"You're really sure of that, aren't you?"

I held out my arms. "You think I'm making a mistake? All right, we'll put it to a vote."

Dansiger smiled, and I knew I'd made a mistake. By calling for a vote, I'd excluded myself from the formality to prevent a tie vote. One look at where everyone was sitting—Harbison, then Dansiger, Mortonsen, and Sylvester—and I knew I'd been set up.

I sighed, trying not to show that I knew I'd been suckered. "All right. Those in favor of emphasizing product capabilities as opposed to product technicalities, signify by raising your hand."

Those in favor went right along the party lines—Griswold, Bainbridge, and Deppe.

"Now," I said, trying to conceal my handy defeat, "all those in favor of emphasizing product technicalities as they relate to capabilities."

Dansiger, Harbison, Mortonsen, and—

Sylvester was drumming his fingers on the desk top.

"Sylvester," Dansiger urged.

"How are you voting?" I asked.

"I'm thinking about it," he said.

"Oh!" Harbison growled. "You rotten, castrated old—"

"Not today, I'm not," Sylvester warned, shaking his finger at her. "And that's going to cost you."

"How do you vote, Sylvester?" I asked.

"I abstain," he said, looking away from his cronies.

"But you promised," Harbison said, outraged. "We had a deal—" She withered under glares from her two allies.

"We have a tie vote," I said, "which means that further discussion is necessary."

"Forget it," Dansiger said, folding her notebook up. "You can't trust some people."

"Isn't that the truth," said Bainbridge.

"What do you know, you miserable little sycophant," snipped

Mortonsen. "You get a whiff of the most minute amount of tes-
tosterone, and you lose the ability to think."

Deppe exploded into laughter.

"What are you laughing at?" Bainbridge accused.

He shook his head. "If you had seen Mortie at the New Year's
party, you wouldn't take that from her."

"You're no guardian angel yourself," said Harbison.

I slammed both hands down on the tabletop and shouted for
everyone to be quiet. When I had their attention, I spoke in very
soft tones.

"All right. I understand that the pressure is on to nail this
account down. And the pressure is doubled on this group because
we're so good. I'm as concerned about it as you are—perhaps
more so, because I've got one of the old men breathing down my
neck, expecting my contribution to be the soul and essence of
twenty-first century advertising.

"Don't get me wrong. It's important to me that we get this
account, but it's more important that I keep you together as a
functioning creative unit. And one thing I'm not going to stand
for is to have this group fall apart, because believe it or not"—I
made sure that I looked straight at Dansiger for this—"I owe my
success to you. All of you. And I wouldn't trade any one of you
off." As I said that, I realized that this might compound my
Bainbridge problems, but I went on.

"We all feel very strongly about this spot. Everyone wants it to
work, but the stakes are enormous. So I'll tell you what I'm going
to do. I'm going to take into consideration everything that's been
said here, and I'm going to go sequester myself in my office until
I've written a spot that will make this group happy."

"Can't be done," Sylvester said.

I held up my hand. "*If* I don't succeed we'll have to collabo-
rate. But you've got to let me try first."

The Dansiger gang started to protest.

"Hear me out," I said. "We have to do something. We have to
be represented. If you'll trust me on this, and if heaven and earth
should move and our spot represents the agency, then the glory
will be ours to share. And if it turns out to be a miserable, humili-
ating failure, then each of you will have the right to wash your
hands of it. You can tell the old men and all of your friends that I
was being a prissy prima donna and turned in a spot that had been
taken out of group hands, because I had this stupid vision." I

slowly looked at them all. "You still get your win-win situation," I said to Dansiger. She looked back at me, alarmed that I had read her mind. "There'll be other accounts to deal with, after all. All you have to do is keep the peace between yourselves and cooperate with me when the time comes. Are we agreed?"

Surprisingly, Sylvester was the first one to nod, beating out Bainbridge by a full two seconds. Then came Deppe and Griswold, Mortonsen and Harbison.

"Are we agreed?" I repeated.

"Yes," Dansiger said in a thin voice.

I looked at my watch. It was a little after four. "All right. You've put in a full day. It's time for Ogilvy's."

That put everyone in a festive mood. They rose from their chairs and started down the hall, suddenly all friends and smiles. I caught Deppe on the way out and pulled him to the side.

"I want you to make sure that the first round is put on my tab," I said. "I'll call Ogilvy and square it before you get there."

"What?" Deppe said. "You're not going?"

"Me?" I laughed. "No. I have to go back to my office and start sweating blood."

He started to protest, but I sent him off. Then I slowly walked back to my office to contemplate the grave I had dug for myself.

I called Ogilvy's first thing and told him about the drinks. On terminating the call, I leaned back in my chair and stared at the ceiling, unsure of where to start. I wanted to do something catchy; something that would at least reassure everyone in the group; and most important, something that would sell us to World Nano, and then sell NanoKleen to the world. I rubbed my eyes. Genius on demand was such a headache.

What would sell this product? Perhaps the universal experience of having to do laundry. On the other hand, how many people still did their own laundry? Hadn't Harbison—or maybe it was Mortonsen—mentioned that she sent their laundry out? That was no matter. You wouldn't sell NanoKleen to someone who didn't do laundry. You could, of course, target that audience, but that would come later, after the product had been established.

"Ferret," I said.

"Yes, sir."

"I want you to go into archival research. Somewhere, somebody has done a listing of human experiences and their ranking of universality among Westernized cultures. Would you see if there's a recent update on that and retrieve it for me?''

"Absolutely. Will there be anything else?''

"Yes. Power up my terminal and open a new spot file called 'NanoKleen One, draft one.' Give it the strictest security level you can, and if you catch Dansiger's ferret in my sysfile, you have my permission to burn it out.''

"Burn Dansiger's ferret?''

"You heard me.''

"Yes, sir.''

My terminal winked on and the coding of the new file appeared at the top of the screen.

"Give me a vid script standard form.'' The screen reconfigured itself. "All right. Client is World Nanotechnologies, Ltd. Product is NanoKleen, spelling, capital n, a, n, o, capital k, l, double e, n. Identify writer by voice, sixty seconds, media is vid. Special instructions as follows: full copies to Sylvester, Mortonsen, and Deppe for creation of a full cassie, pending acceptance.'' I waited for a moment as the form filled itself out. I stared at the screen, and inspiration struck. "Video. Instructions. Open with a side-tracking shot of people—dozens of people—all doing laundry, and they all look bored out of their minds. Audio. Announcer. Wash day drudgery is something that affects—''

The desk phone rang, driving the next word from my mind. I swore, loudly.

The phone rang again. I hadn't thought to lock it out. I had assumed that with everyone from my creative group gone, I wouldn't be bothered.

"Answer,'' I said to the phone.

"Mr. Boddekker?'' said the ferret. "I have an unidentified male on the line who says it's a matter of life and death that he talk to you.''

It always was. Probably some student I'd talked to on career day, now on the verge of graduating, and wanting to know if I could get their résumé to one of the old men.

"Do you want me to terminate the call?''

I stared at what I'd dictated, now glowing on the screen. I hated it.

"Mr. Boddekker, shall I terminate this call?''

It might make me feel better, but it wouldn't bring back the idea—a bad one at that. "No, that's all right. I'll take it on handset.'' My line flickered green. I punched the button and put the phone to my ear. "Boddekker here."

"Well, if it ain't the big man on Mad Avenue." I froze. There was no forgetting the coldness of that voice, not even after putting the encounter behind me.

"Ferman?"

"You got it."

I wanted to ask how he'd gotten my number, and then I remembered—*I'd given it to him.*

"Looks to me like you got caught in a lie, big man on Mad Avenue. Looks to me like me and Jet and Nose and Rover and Jimmy Jazz gonna come over and break every bone in your body."

"Caught in a lie?" I asked, trying not to sound to nervous. Or stupid.

"You made a promise to us. Now are you going to tell me that you can't keep it?"

"Of course I didn't forget about my promise." I tried to sound disgusted at the fact that he thought I had, though in truth it had vanished from memory until that voice brought it all back.

"Then why haven't you put us in a commercial yet?"

"Look, Ferman," I said. "You probably don't know a lot about the advertising business, and I don't blame you. Your concerns lie in another area. You need to understand, though, that it can take weeks—sometimes months—between the time a commercial is on the boards and the time it airs."

"But you have to shoot it before it airs. Right?"

"Yes. But that's a process that can take weeks in itself, sometimes longer if the cassie doesn't strike the customer's fancy—"

"Cassie?"

"It's jargon, Ferman. It's a computer-animated simulation that shows what the commercial will look like once it's done."

"But you *are* going to put us in a commercial. Right?"

I quietly sighed and looked at my pathetic attempt for Na-noKleen on my terminal. At this rate, I might as well join the Smilin' Guy in the lobby, selling eternal roses to passersby. "Absolutely," I said.

"Well, when do you think it's going to happen, Boddekker? I mean, it's not for me, you understand. The guys want to know. They suspect you were jackin' us."

I guess what I should have done was given him a date to come in for a shoot and have the police pick them up as they came in the door. It crossed my mind, but the last thing I wanted right now was more complications in my life. Instead, I looked up at my screen and it inspired me to lie.

"I don't think it'll be too long, Ferman. In fact, I was just working on your spot."

"Our spot?" he asked, almost flattered.

"Well, not a spot advertising *you*," I explained. "But using you and your gang to endorse a product."

"Who's it for?"

"I can't tell you right now. All I can say is that it's for something that we think is very exciting." No exaggeration there, I thought. "And it isn't a PSA, and it has nothing to do with hemorrhoids."

There was a momentary silence on the line. "So," Ferman finally said, "I should call you back then in a week or so?"

"Heavens, no," I said. "We'll still be in the negotiation stages by then." I decided that all of the NanoKleen madness would be over within a month, and I told him to call back then. That's when I'd tell them to come in. And I'd have the cops waiting.

"Okay, then," he said.

"And if we need you sooner, I know how to get in touch with you."

"Fine. Oh, one more thing, Boddekker. Me and the guys were wondering, should we maybe look into getting agents for this thing?"

I laughed. Perhaps they should start looking for an attorney instead. "No," I told him, "we'll drive off that bridge when we come to it. Right now we're looking at this as a one-shot deal. If it turns into something bigger, then I'm sure one of the Pembroke Hall agents would be glad to handle you."

"Good," Ferman said. "Good." Another pause, and then, "You ain't lyin' to us, are you, Boddekker?"

"It's the truth, on my mother's grave."

"Fine. 'Cause if you are, the boys and me would have to come over and break every bone in your body."

"This is a sure thing," I said. "Relax. I'll be in touch."

"All right," Ferman said, and then abruptly rang off.

I sat in silence, staring at the phone. Laughter crept up on me. I had outwitted them not once, but twice. And the third time would be the charm. I would see them all in jail. What would Robenstine think of that? It would be a proud moment for me.

The glow of victory quickly dissipated as I looked back at the terminal. I still had to do battle with NanoKleen. "All right," I told the terminal. "Let's wipe everything starting with the video description." The screen flickered and my words mercifully disappeared. "Start with Audio. Narrator says—"

"Mr. Boddekker," the ferret announced. "I'm back with the information you requested on universal human experiences."

I shook my head. "All right," I sighed impatiently. "Let's hear it."

"There's quite a bit," the ferret said. "It'll take quite a while for an aural dump."

"Can't you give me the highlights or something?"

"Things are broken down into categories, Mr. Boddekker, and there are lots of categories. There are your basic primal experiences, which include the birth experience, hunger, pain, discomfort of bladder and bowel—"

"Skip it."

"Ascending scale primal, on a more intellectual level yet still intimately physical, with difficulty of separation—"

"Sounds sexual."

"It is."

I couldn't see tying that to laundry other than in a very oblique way. "Skip it."

"Then there's the tragic influence. This is everything from loss of a loved one to something as simple as getting mugged on the subway—but doesn't include things like loss of body parts, which is in the violation of private space category."

"Where does laundry fit into all of this, ferret?"

"Let me run a quick scan. Laundry—"

Suddenly something clicked. It was the movement of Robenstine and Ferman into the same place at the same time. "Hold it!" I shouted to the ferret, so loudly that the terminal picked up on it and entered it on the screen as the first words spoken by a yet unnamed narrator.

"Yes, Mr. Boddekker?"

"What was the last thing you said—"

" 'Yes, Mr. Boddekker?' "

"No. Before that. Before you said you'd scan for laundry in the universal human experience."

"You must be talking about the tragic influence, which covers loss of a loved one to getting mugged on the sub—"

"Stop right there!" The terminal dutifully recorded it. "Give me subway muggings, ferret. No. Better yet. What does this file say about victimization? The role of the victim as part of the universal human experience? Cross-index that with street gangs."

"Street gangs as part of the—"

"Street gangs as victimizers," I said.

"One moment."

I looked at the terminal, smiling. I told it to erase again.

"Mr. Boddekker? As an adult experience, that is, past the age of twenty-one, statistics indicate that there is a Citizen Affectation Rate of one hundred thirty-four percent. This means that you will be victimized by someone—not necessarily by a member of a gang, although the odds do favor it—one and one-third times during your life. That's at the national rate. The rate for NYC—"

"Is higher," I said, slapping my hands. That was it. Those were the exact statistics that Robenstine had quoted, although I seriously doubt that he realized what a gold mine he was sitting on.

"Do you wish me to continue?"

"Keep the stuff about victimization," I said. "Lose everything else. Then you can go. Oh, and ferret—"

"Yes, Mr. Boddekker?"

"Thank you."

"Merely following my programming."

The ferret popped away. I was busy looking at the screen and laughing. This would be it. The cake. Eating it, too. It would be revenge on Ferman and revenge on Dansiger and revenge on Levine and his brave new advertising world. And if I should end up being fired, I could take what I knew to another agency and use it to make them a fortune.

When I finally stopped laughing, I turned to the screen and started dictating.

"Selling you to the world since 1969"

Offices in Principal Cities: New York - Montreal - Toronto - Sydney - London -
Tokyo - Moskva - Beijing - Chicago - Oslo - Philadelphia - Amarillo

CLIENT: »World Nanotechnologies, Ltd.		PRODUCT: »NanoKleen
WRITER: »Boddekker	TIME: »:60	MEDIA: »Video
TITLE: »*There Were Ten of Them*		
PRODUCTION ORDERS:	»Full copies to Sylvester, Mortonsen, and Deppe for creation of full cassie (pending acceptance)	

AUDIO	VIDEO
SFX: *Kitchen and cooking noises; frying hiss, clanking of pans, beeping of microwave and autocook, etc.*	*A woman dressed in a business suit is working in a modern kitchen, giving orders to the autocook and nuke.*
SFX: *Door opening.*	*The* WIFE *looks up.*
HUSBAND: Honey, I'm home!	WIFE *reacts, smiles at voice. Cut to the* HUSBAND *standing in the doorway. Light forms a sort of halo around him, and he is framed by the open door. The* HUSBAND *looks like he's been through the mill; his clothing (a fancy suit) is filthy, his hair is a mess, and he's got a black eye and assorted cuts and scrapes.*
WIFE: What happened to you, honey? This suit is a *mess!*	*She picks at dirty suit;* HUSBAND *shrugs helplessly.*
HUSBAND: Oh, I had a run-in with a street gang . . .	

HUSBAND: . . . there were at least ten of them . . .

Quick flash to a handful of seedy-looking GANG MEMBERS. *Hold only long enough for the viewer to realize there are only five people there.*

WIFE: Ten?
HUSBAND: Maybe fifteen.

Cut back to the WIFE, *leading her* HUSBAND *through the house. He is undressing as they go, handing clothes to her.*

HUSBAND: I was minding my own business when out of the blue, they surrounded me.

Flash to the HUSBAND, *making a rude gesture at a figure on a park bench. The figure stands up to reveal he is a gang member and towers over the* HUSBAND. *The* HUSBAND *shows alarm.*

WIFE: And what did you do?

The WIFE *is taking clothes from her* HUSBAND *and tossing them into a washing machine.* HUSBAND *gives a cocky smile as he answers.*

HUSBAND: I handled it!

Cut to the HUSBAND *taking a haymaker right on the chin from the* BIG GUY *he was tormenting.*

WIFE: It looks like you handled the clothes, too.

The WIFE *holds up the* HUSBAND's *trousers. There is a greasy footprint square on the seat of the pants.*

HUSBAND: Oh, don't try and save those, honey . . . they're hopeless.

WIFE: Relax, honey! I'm washing them in new NanoKleen!

WIFE's *hand in foreground is turned palm up and gestures to a box of NanoKleen, which fills the rest of the screen (possible slogan—"The micro*

ANNOUNCER: That's right! NanoKleen is the modern wash day miracle that really kicks ass!

ANNOUNCER: And stains? NanoKleen's unique action tracks them down and *yanks* them out by the roots!

ANNOUNCER: In fact, NanoKleen brings *complete submission* to wash day dirt and stains!

WIFE: There you are! All ready for another round!

HUSBAND: Gosh, honey, I've never seen these clothes this clean! Even the old stains are gone! How did you do it?

WIFE: I handled it!

ANNOUNCER: NanoKleen . . . the *modern* wash day miracle! New from World Nanotechnologies, Ltd.!

machines that wash and Kleen!'').

The GANG has the HUSBAND surrounded, and they're taking turns kicking him in the ass.

Two GANG MEMBERS are running down the street, each with one of the HUSBAND's legs tucked under his arm. The HUSBAND has his arms thrown out toward the camera and is trying to dig his fingernails into the concrete in a futile attempt to try to stop from being dragged.

Close-up of the HUSBAND's battered face being pushed into the sidewalk by a heavily booted foot.

Shot of HUSBAND and WIFE. The WIFE waves her arm at her freshly clothed HUSBAND. The HUSBAND picks at his incredibly clean clothes in amazement.

Close-up of WIFE's face. She looks into the camera, winks, and gives us a thumbs-up.

Prominent close-up of the NanoKleen box.

SEVEN

A Day in the Life

"Boddekker, are you out of your ranking mind?"

That was Hotchkiss, and he was looking at the draft of my script that had been sideloaded to his notebook. The two of us were sitting in the Intimate Conference Room on the thirty-ninth floor along with the surviving old men; senior partners Finney, Spenner, and Robenstine; and group leaders Broadbent, Norbert, and Bigelow. The presence of these last three meant that each of the agency's top five creative groups were represented, but even though I was numbered among them, it didn't make what was happening any better.

The occasion was the assessment of creative group scripts for the NanoKleen account. We'd been going through them all morning long, sending them up like clay pigeons for the old men and senior partners to blow apart with a few well-chosen words.

It hadn't been pretty. We'd been through a dozen or so, most of which had been zapped in from the other branches of the agency. But among those casualties were spots from Hotchkiss, Bigelow, and Norbert. Hotchkiss's spot wasn't so much shot down as summarily executed. When it came up on the screen and Levine saw the word *caveman,* his finger came down hard on his notebook's delete key and the script vanished from our screens before we could finish reading. Then he shook his head and said, "You're pretty much a one-note wonder, aren't you son?"

We actually got through Bigelow's spot, which called for a super-retro animation style reminiscent of the stuff I'd seen from the 1960s. A bunch of little men that looked like armored assault vehicles danced around clumps of dirt and blasted them with their cannon snouts, singing to the tune of something that Bigelow called "Hokey Pokey":

> You put your dirty clothes in,
> You pour the NanoKleen out,
> You turn the washer on,
> And it sloshes us about . . .

"Great Scott," was Levine's sole comment. Those were the fewest words I'd ever heard him speak in criticism of a script, and I was trying to figure out whether this was good or bad when the script vanished from my notebook. I swallowed hard, and we moved on.

Norbert's script died a similarly horrible death a few minutes later. A suburban housewife walked to her washing machine with a pile of old moldies and had her hand on a box of the World's Most Popular Brand of laundry soap when a box of NanoKleen began to dance around and cry in a high-pitched voice, "Choose me! Choose me!"

"Who are you?" the woman asked.

The script called for the lid on the box to pop open and reveal a crowd of tiny little men inside. "We're the happy, magical little elves who live in your washing machine!"

Levine and I must read at the same speed. As I got to that line, I heard the *urk!* of a throat involuntarily closing and looked up to see the old man looking aghast at his notebook.

To say the room went silent was an understatement. It was already silent. When the others saw Levine's reaction, ice began forming on the tabletop.

"Number one," Levine said calmly, "these happy, magical little fellows use too many self-descriptive adjectives. Number two, they live in the box of soap, not the washing machine. And number three, send a copy of this to City Metro Hospital because I heard they're running low on syrup of ipecac.'' The script vanished from our screens. ''Next.''

I shivered. My script was up next. I looked down at the screen and closed my eyes, tapping my finger nervously on the SCROLL button so it looked like I was reading something I'd already been over a hundred times. I could hear every sound in the room: the others scrolling through my script, the hissing of air as it passed through their nostrils, the squeak of their chairs under imperceptible shifts in their weight, the moistness of their eyelids as they slid down over the eye and then retracted.

Then, finally, mercifully, the intense silence was broken by Hotchkiss's blurted profanity.

''Boddekker, are you out of your ranking mind?''

The remark's echo died under the roar of the air conditioner, and Hotchkiss looked self-consciously at Harris, Broadbent, and Bigelow. ''Uh, excuse my language, ladies.'' Then back at me. ''Boddekker, what was going through your mind when you wrote this?''

''I'm not sure that I'd want to know,'' Bigelow said with a sour face.

Norbert said something about liking it, which I automatically ignored. I could have imported a hundred random names from the Manhattan Phone Registry Database and served it up as copy and he still would have stood up for it. That was his way, always pushing the edge of what worked and tipping into creativity for the sake of creativeness. He won awards—the reason his group was represented here—but his work moved little product.

I looked at Levine. His eyes were narrow slits as he concentrated on my words.

After another eternity passed, he smiled. ''I rather like it,'' he said. ''It's graphic and disturbing, but you know this is going to get their attention.''

Harris gave him a look of utter disbelief—not surprising since she resented any kind of advertising that didn't get into the nets and replicate itself into the systems of individual users. ''It's violent,'' she said.

''But it's offset by humor,'' Finney said. ''And it gives a graphic representation of what the stuff does without being dull and preachy. This script does what none of the other spots have done—''

Robenstine said, "Excuse me, but isn't that an arbitrary assessment? After all, the purpose of the spot is to *sell* the product, make it move off the shelves, and it hasn't done that yet."

Levine glared at him. "As I recall, Mr. Robenstine, neither has your contribution."

"No," he said, "but I don't think this one is going to sell anything."

"I disagree," said Spenner. "I think we've got something here—"

"Yeah," said Norbert. "The end of Pembroke Hall."

"But this is everything that Levine asked for in his speech," said Finney. "I think this should be the one we send to World Nano."

"You'd have to be out of your ranking minds," Hotchkiss said. "Pardon my Norwegian."

Levine laid his palms flat on the table and rose to gaze at the others. The parade of his stare ended with me. "You'll have to forgive young Hotchkiss," he told me. "The boy moves his lips when he reads." Then, to all of us: "People, we are not stupid. And we did not get Pembroke Hall where it is today by playing it safe. I can tell you right here and now what the competition will give World Nano to introduce NanoKleen to the world. It's going to be caveman professors with sticks pointing at x's and o's on a chalkboard to explain what this stuff does."

Hotchkiss slumped in his seat.

"Call it a sixth sense, but I know in my heart that that's what the other agencies are doing. Their creatives are going to be turning in the same thing, pointy-headed Poindexters going, 'blah, blah, blah, this is how it works.' So if World Nano sees anything remotely different from what's coming in from the rest of the agencies, that's what they're going to run with. This is a case of eat or be eaten."

"No." Harris slammed her notebook shut. "This is a case of eat and then throw it all back up. It's disgusting."

"It's distinctive," said Finney.

"It's never been done," said Bigelow.

"Which is exactly why it *should* be done," said Spenner.

"For the love of ludefisk," said Robenstine. "I can give you a hundred reasons why this spot shouldn't be used, but I shouldn't have to. It's a no-brainer."

"What's number one?" challenged Finney.

Robenstine licked his lips and studied his adversaries; one of the old men and two senior partners. He drew a long breath, but before he could move ahead, Harris spoke.

She said, "The language in it is unacceptable."

"The language," said Levine.

"The *language*?" I asked.

"Advertising has always considered the language used in this script as taboo. I mean, you might hear it all the time on the Animation Channel, but in a *soap* commercial—"

"The language," said Spenner.

"To be specific," said Norbert, "the script uses the word *ass*. Twice."

"But once is in the directions of the script," Finney said. "So it wouldn't be *spoken*."

"No," said Harris. "Just *shown*."

"Besides the point all the way around," said Robenstine. "You can't say *ass* in a spot, Boddekker."

"Why not?" asked Levine. "I've heard *damns* and *hells*."

"Those were for entertainment vids or beer commercials. They're different. Besides, nobody would go for this." He thumped his notebook for emphasis.

"I heard a *bastard* in a spot once," said Finney. "As I recall, that spot was on the air for quite some time."

"Oh yeah," Spenner said. "The one for those contraceptive inserts. It was a very good one, too. All of those sperm cells, lined up and singing that little tune—"

Levine rhythmically drummed his fingertips on the tabletop. "We'll never be your little bastard," he sang. "We'll never show up unannounced and ask you for money."

"That's it," Finney smiled. "That was a Strusel and Strauss spot. One of their best."

"Whatever happened to the writer?" Spenner asked.

"She's now in our Chicago office," Levine said proudly.

"Look, this is all beside the point," Harris said. "The *bastard* had a legitimate place in that spot. It was well within acceptable context. The *ass* in this spot is gratuitous."

"This is a tough street gang," Levine said. "And this is a tough new product. Would you expect either one to say they 'kicked heinie?' "

Harris put her hands over her eyes and shook her head.

Broadbent, who had been silent up to this point, rapped her

knuckles on the tabletop until she had everyone's attention. "Let's say the context isn't there," she said. "What then?"

"Then it's a gratuitously vulgar spot," said Norbert.

"Let's save the editorializing," Broadbent said, "and concentrate for a moment on a series of worst-case scenarios. Shall we?"

I squirmed uneasily in my chair. I didn't know what she was up to, and I wasn't sure I wanted to find out—but on the other hand, whatever she had in mind had to be better than the same kind of bickering I had faced when I'd shown the script to my creative group. "I'm game," I said.

Most of the others nodded in agreement.

"Now, back to my question. Let's say the context isn't there."

"Are you saying it *is* there?" Robenstine asked.

"Let it go," Levine warned. "Let's hear what she has to say."

"All right." The chair squeaked as Robenstine shifted his weight. "If the context isn't there, then the piece is unremittingly worthless, and it stops right here, right now. As well it should."

Broadbent held her hand up. "Now. Without the editorializing, let's say we accept Boddekker's piece and submit to World Nano. Worst-case scenario."

"They laugh us out of their office," Robenstine said. "And odds would be long that we'd ever be invited to do anything for them again."

"All right." She smiled. Broadbent had long teeth that gave her an almost equine look when she smiled, but I didn't notice this time because I was intrigued by her line of questioning. "Now. Say they accept the spot. What happens then, worst case—"

"What's the point of this?" Robenstine demanded.

"It'd never get past the net censors," Norbert said.

I shook my head. "That has *never* been a problem. Since when are commercials screened prior to air time? Except for *Ad Age* previews and perhaps the Commercial Channel, they don't. The trouble comes after the ad campaign hits the streets."

"Well that's the point, then," said Bigelow. "The trouble starts."

Broadbent looked right at her. "What kind of trouble?"

"Fire, flood, and famine," said Finney. Broadbent started to glare, but he raised his hands and said "Relax. I'm on your side. As soon as I figure out what your side is."

"What kind of trouble?" Broadbent asked Bigelow.

"You want the whole drill? First it starts with a public outcry. Then the nets start dropping the spot as if it were shot through with Ebola Atlanta. Then pundits will start asking how such a travesty could actually be released, let alone be accepted as an advertising campaign. That's followed by a full-blown governmental investigation and perhaps persecution under the Calvin Klein Act."

"In the meantime, what happens?"

"We come under fire—"

"No," said Spenner. "The agency never comes under fire. It's always the advertiser who takes the knocks."

"Exactly," said Broadbent.

"And you're willing to bring that all down on World Nano so you can use this *travesty*," said Robenstine.

"Meantime, what happens to World Nano?" Broadbent continued.

Finney said, "Easy. Publicity. *Free* publicity. The kind that money can't buy. Sound bites and vid bits integrated into all of the magazine downloads. Reporters asking questions on the newsnets. Like you said, Bigelow, the pundits asking questions in their columns. World Nano and NanoKleen get the kind of saturation coverage that not even a multitimeshare megabuy could generate."

Broadbent tapped the tip of her finger on the tip of her nose. "There's no such thing as bad publicity," she said. "Which means if you think about it, the worst-case scenario is actually the best thing that could happen."

"If that's the case," Harris said, "then what's the best-case scenario?"

"The spot wins all kinds of awards but stiffs when it comes to selling the product," I said. "As long as you're being contrary."

"And if things go . . . shall we say . . . *normally*?"

"The spot does what it's supposed to, and NanoKleen carves out a healthy niche in the market share for itself."

"So even if the spot stiffs and we win awards for it, the World Nano name will be out there," I said.

Broadbent nodded. "Using this spot puts us in a win-win-win situation."

"No, no, no," said Robenstine. "This thing carries too much weight."

"The only weight this thing carries is your memory of a recent mugging," Levine said.

Robenstine's voice pitched up. "Levine, you're missing the point of this—"

"All right," Broadbent said in a soothing tone. "Suppose you enlighten us. Tell us what's riding on this spot?"

"Pembroke Hall having credibility tomorrow morning," said Robenstine.

"Credibility?" asked Spenner.

"We have a reputation to uphold, and this—this—"

"Excuse me," Levine said, "but what is our reputation, Mr. Robenstine? It seems that for all of our very existence, we have tweaked the noses of conventional advertising wisdom by doing things our own way. The whole business of forming people together into creative groups was unheard of before we did it. Pitting them against one another in company-wide competition to see whose spot went to the client was anathema to the industry. But over the jeers of every one of our competitors, Pembroke Hall became a force to be reckoned with."

"Albeit a bloody-fisted force," Harris said, distantly.

"I still sign your checks," Levine said. Then, to Robenstine, "You may condemn what young Boddekker's spot stands for, but keep one thing in mind. It might be a travesty and it might be trouble from the word *go, but it's business as usual for Pembroke Hall.* I feel this spot is the difference between showing World Nano our best work and turning in something that any other agency in the world could do."

There was selective nodding from around the table; Finney, Spenner, Broadbent.

"So," Levine said, "I call this spot up for a vote."

"Excuse me," said Robenstine, "but we haven't seen what Mez Broadbent's group has to offer."

"Nor have we seen what your offering is," Levine said. "But I'm calling for a vote nonetheless. As for passing over the unexamined spots, well, Mez Broadbent doesn't seem to have a problem with that. Do you, Mez Broadbent?"

Broadbent shook her head.

"But you can't do that!"

"Mr. Robenstine," Levine hissed. "My name is on the company masthead. That means I can do whatever I want. When your name is put on the masthead—providing you leave this meeting

still in our employ—then you, too, may do whatever you want. Are you receiving me?''

Robenstine glowered and nodded.

"A vote has been called to select *There Were Ten of Them* to represent Pembroke Hall in the competition for the World Nanotechnologies, Ltd. account,'' Harris announced. "Let your voices be heard.''

"Creator's abstention,'' I said. The selection meetings followed the same rules as their creative counterparts.

"No,'' Robenstine said. "No way.''

"Mez Broadbent?''

"This piece really speaks to me in an angry sort of way . . . you know?''

"Let's not overanalyze it,'' Harris said. "Your vote?''

"Yes. Yours?''

"No. Mr. Levine?''

"At this point you have to ask?''

"A yes from Mr. Levine,'' Harris said. "That's two for, two against, one creative abstention.''

"Yes,'' said Finney and Spenner, almost together.

"Mez Bigelow?''

"No.''

"Mr. Norbert?''

"No.''

"Four in favor, four against, one creative abstention.'' Harris looked at Hotchkiss. "You are the last voter.''

He stared down into his notebook, avoiding eye contact with everyone.

"Mr. Hotchkiss,'' Levine said, "we need your vote to conclude this matter.''

"No,'' he said.

"No?'' Levine asked. "Are you voting no or are you refusing to vote?''

"I'm voting no,'' he blurted. Then, before I could react, he was saying, "I'm sorry, Boddekker, it's nothing personal. I don't think this script—''

"Mr. Hotchkiss,'' Levine hissed, "you don't have to run your vote into the ground with a protracted explanation. You sound like you're accepting an Oscar.''

Hotchkiss gave a mumbled "Yes sir.''

"The final vote is four in favor, five against. The vote fails.''

A multitude of sighs went up. Harris looked at Levine, somewhat pleased with herself. "The other agencies don't use the democratic process in their creative decisions, either."

Levine shrugged. "Nothing's perfect."

I slumped back in my chair, limp from the tension and glad that it was all over. No—to be honest, I was *telling* myself that I was glad it was over. In all honesty, I was hurt. My ego was sinking its stinger into me over and over again and whispered that inspired as it was, Ferman and his Devils were no better than Hotchkiss's cavemen, than Bigelow's "Hokey Pokey" jingle, or Norbert's flaky talking soap flakes. I tried to tell myself that half of my creative group could quit worrying about what kind of ruin I would bring to them, but it wouldn't come. I had let down the half of the group that had depended on me to come through in the clutch. *Loser,* my battered ego whispered as it plunged its stinger in, again and again. *Loser loser loser.*

I tried to shake it off. My spots had lost before, and I had gone on to bigger and better things. But after Levine's speech about the end of the world and the weight that had been put on the NanoKleen account, I couldn't brush it off as easily as I would have liked.

Still, I kept telling myself: *It's time to get on with my creative life at Pembroke Hall and claim the trophy house in Princeton.*

But first I had to help choose a spot that was *better* than mine—the one that would represent Pembroke Hall at World Nano.

For better or worse, that would be the easy part. It only took a few minutes. The remaining spots were from Robenstine and Broadbent. Robenstine's started with a bass organ note as the scene faded in on a barren African plain. There was a row of washing machines all arranged in a semicircle, chugging away at loads of laundry, and a bunch of apes sat around picking fleas off each other, waiting for the machines to finish. Then a trumpet fanfare began and the apes became excited. Something was attracting their attention and was driving them wild. As the horn fanfare reaches its first crescendo, we see what is causing all of the excitement; a box of NanoKleen at least fifty feet high. As we look up at it from the bottom, the sun is directly overhead, being eclipsed by the moon.

Then something strange happens. The apes all begin to walk upright and they start picking up bones and begin beating on the washing machines. In the background, others are taking business suits out of the washers and are putting them on. Now the whole orchestra comes in and the lead ape, now in a tasteful three-piece pinstripe, takes his bone, and with a toothy smile, throws it up into the air. The camera tracks the bone as it tumbles end over end through the air, then morphs into a box of NanoKleen. It blocks out the eclipsed sun and stars twinkle around it. As the music fades back into a final, extended organ note, a super crawls up the screen: NANOKLEEN—THE NEXT STEP IN WASH DAY EVOLUTION.

"At least it's not *cave*men," Levine grumbled. The script winked out and was replaced by Broadbent's.

"Levine," Robenstine protested.

"We'll come back to it," the old man said preemptively.

Broadbent's spot began with three seconds from the start of another commercial, which was interrupted by a burst of static and a super reading, "SPECIAL BULLETIN." It cut to a breathless news anchor who talked about liberation from wash day and the astonishing new product that was creating it. There were film clips of people walking out of self-service laundries with clean clothes, and a flaky scientist whose chalkboard explanation was cut off by an interview with a woman who had saved so much time from washing that she had taken piano lessons, and began to regale viewers with a fumble fingered rendition of "The Entertainer." The story went back to the anchor, who explained where NanoKleen could be found, then sent us back into the last three seconds of the interrupted commercial.

I liked it. It was compact, succinct, and conveyed an incredible amount of information during its sixty-second life span. I had no trouble voting for it when opinion was called for, and it won handily, seven in favor and two against. The two dissenters were Robenstine, who was annoyed that his spot had been passed over, and Hotchkiss, who did so to vote no on a spot other than mine. I suspected this because he waited until the count on Broadbent's spot was a comfortable five to one before making his opinion known.

"All right, then" Levine said. "I think we've made a good choice, one we can rightly be proud of and one that typifies the kind of work we do here at Pembroke Hall. Mez Broadbent, your group will have until Monday to assemble a full cassie for distribution. The World Nano people require three copies, and of course, we'll require one, plus however many you create for your own archives. To the rest of you, I'd like to thank you one and all for the participation and hard work you've put into this. It would be a real coup for us to capture the World Nano account, and should it happen—I'm sorry—*when* it happens, it will benefit every member of the company." With a nod of his head the meeting was dismissed.

I felt a sharp pang as he left the room. The wounds from my ego were still bleeding. The house in Princeton was getting away from me because I didn't fight hard enough for my spot. I tried reminding myself that Pembroke Hall was the land of opportunity. While my spot hadn't been chosen to go the distance for the World Nano account, I should still be in good shape. The old men knew who I was. I wasn't another of the legions of company copywriters; I had their ear. They had given me one of their pet accounts, although I had no idea what I was supposed to do with it. And I wasn't the magnet for Levine's speculative insults. That distinction fell to perennial award-winner Hotchkiss.

Being chosen for World Nano would have made things happen faster, but I was already on the fast track. Missing out would spare me from the breakneck pace that the agency put you through in times like this. Besides, there were the Devils to consider in all of this, and I could hardly explain to Levine that the spot had been written to apprehend a common street gang, if he was busy using it to bring in a hot new client.

For the time being, things were marvelous.

"Yeah," I said, and then I swore bitterly under my breath. "If I believe that, then I've got a great deal on Electromagnetic Pulse Insurance."

Well, I could always sulk the feeling off in the privacy of my office.

Unfortunately, that was not to be. At some point before getting back to my floor a psychic alert went out, and by the time I arrived, the others were waiting to inundate me with questions.

"Well . . . ?"

"How did it go, Boddekker?"

"Are we going?"

"When do we start on the cassie?"

"When will we hear back from World Nano?"

As if dealing with my own ego hadn't been enough trouble.

"Well, Boddekker? Well?"

It wasn't going to get any easier.

"We're not going to hear back from World Nano," I mumbled.

"What?"

"What?"

"We don't have to start on the cassie because our spot isn't going. The meeting went all right from a Pembroke Hall point of view, but it was lousy for us. I think that covers all of your questions."

Mortonsen swore, a personal insult directed at my lineage. "What happened to this spot you thought was so great, Boddekker? You told us to trust you with it and you screwed us. You turned around and stabbed us in the ranking back."

"Settle your language, Mortonsen," Griswold said. As ever, his expression was unshakable.

"If our spot isn't going," said Harbison, "then which one is?"

"The one from Broadbent's group. It's a nice spot, one that'll do us proud. A commercial that looks like it's being interrupted by a news bulletin."

"Foo," Dansiger said. "That's been done before, unto death."

"It's all right," Deppe said. "We'll nail the next one."

"What if there is no 'next one'?" Sylvester wailed. "I've got things I need to do, important things—"

"You and your treatments," Mortonsen growled. "If you could ever make up your ranking mind about—"

"All *right*!" I shouted. "Look, I feel as bad about this as anybody. I wanted our spot to go as much as—"

"*Our* spot," Harbison hissed. "Your spot. It was *your* stupid spot, Boddekker, that awful, violent thing—"

"Oh, stop it," Griswold said.

"You all read it when he was done," Deppe said. "You all said to go ahead with it."

"With reservations," Harbison said.

"It was an ugly spot," Mortonsen said.

"All right," I said, rising from my chair. "We've gone through this twice before. You all read the spot, you all gave me your opinion on it. And even if you didn't care for it, you all gave me the go-ahead. It was a group decision, and it was wrong, but we've got to live with it, and we'll overcome it."

"But this was World Nano," Sylvester whined.

I shouted, *"I don't care if it was the ranking Beijing Lottery!"* That shocked them into silence, and I went on. "I asked you all to trust me, and you did. I let you all read the spot, and I asked for your blessing to send it on. I got that. Now we didn't get this one—"

"We didn't just not get it," Mortonsen said. "We're not even representing our company."

"Look," I snapped. "I'm not going over this again, not for a third time. We're all in this together and we'll all overcome it and do better things together." Harbison went to speak and I cut her off. "The way I see it, you either let it go and we all move on or you get out of my group. Are you all hearing me on this?"

"This spot—" Mortonsen started.

"I don't want to hear it, Mortie," I shouted, "and I won't put up with it. You want out, you let me know fast. Hotchkiss needs a new AI programmer in his group and I'd be happy to sign the papers for you to make the move." I looked around at the rest of them, taking a moment to make eye contact with each one. "And that goes for anyone else who thinks I've cut them a raw deal. I'll start completely over again if I have to, from scratch, with a whole new team if I have to."

"Boddekker," Dansiger said. "I'm sorry."

My stomach fell at that. If there was anyone who shouldn't be apologizing at the moment, it was her.

"We all had a lot riding on this spot," she continued. "I guess we forgot that you did, too."

"I'm sorry I let you all down," I said.

"Nonsense," said Deppe.

"Hey," said Griswold. "Don't lose the idea. Some other wonderful product can have the distinction of 'kicking ass.' " He nodded at me and then turned and quietly left the room.

"It was our best spot, ever," Deppe said.

"And it was their mistake," Dansiger amended.

They turned and left, one after the other.

Bainbridge looked at me with deep, soulful eyes and said, "Thank you, Boddekker" in barely a whisper. Then she disappeared.

I looked at the three remaining, Harbison, Mortonsen, and Sylvester.

"Well?" I asked. "Is this your notice?"

"No," Sylvester said on the way out the door.

I leaned back in my chair. It squeaked under my weight. I folded my arms and stared at Harbison and Mortonsen until they slowly turned and walked wordlessly out the door.

I let my head fall back and exhaled loudly. Then I swore again, this time in a whisper. I was living the curse of Tantalus, I was certain. Only instead of grapes, I was reaching for the key to a house, one that dangled from the pale, slender arm of a Honniker In Accounting. And as the tips of my fingers connected with plastic, the hand pulled up and a pair of eyes looked away in that flirty manner of Euro Women. In my ears was a throaty giggle, the teasing laugh of Brazilian exotics.

The next objective was to start believing what I had told my own people. That was the hardest thing I would face over the next few days.

But I wouldn't do it today.

"Ferret," I said.

I heard my screen pop as it came to life.

"Yes, Mr. Boddekker?"

I turned off the phone function of my watch. "Amend the time schedule to reflect that I am taking the rest of the day off. Delayed notification so nobody knows until after I'm gone."

"Very good, Mr. Boddekker. The NanoKleen thing didn't go through, did it?"

I sat up fast. "How did you know?"

"High net activity from Mez Broadbent's ferret accessing client information on World Nano. These steps are obviously being taken in preparation for creation of a full cassie."

"Ferret, didn't I tell you specifically not to—"

"Excuse me, Mr. Boddekker, but this information was shareloaded to me from Mez Dansiger's ferret. It was deemed as useful information that I should have."

I closed my eyes and rubbed my temples. "All right, ferret. Thanks."

"Shall I monitor your office, or do you wish to notify me when you are gone?"

"Assume I'm gone as of now, ferret."

"Very good. Have a nice day."

I heard the screen pop as the ferret shut it down. I leaned back in my chair and lolled my head back, moving the massage from my temples to my eyes. Fireworks came as I did, bursts of pale yellow rimmed with red and blue, circle upon circle of rounded rectangles, all spiraling out like cells from the center. I let my mouth fall open and let my breath out in a long hiss, and ended it with a gurgled obscenity.

When I sat up and opened my eyes, Bainbridge was leaning against the door to my office.

"I'm really sorry this didn't work out for you, Boddekker."

"I'm really sorry it didn't work out for *us*," I said.

"Where you going?"

"Going? Me?"

"My ferret says you're calling it a day."

"Really? My ferret must have a big mouth."

She shook her head. "Not really. You simply have to know which parameters you want your ferret to sniff."

"So you've got your ferret sniffing my ferret's behind."

"The way you looked when you came back from seeing the old men, I thought it might be warranted. I didn't expect to get something back so quickly."

"Well," I said. "Call me a quitter."

"No," Bainbridge said. "You're stepping away to recharge. You'll be back tomorrow ready to move on to things bigger and better."

"Is that right?"

Bainbridge nodded.

"You must have remarkable confidence in my recuperative abilities."

She gave a slight shrug. "I thought I'd make sure you got a chance to recuperate."

"How's that?"

"I thought I'd tag along with you."

"Really? Don't you think I should ask you first?"

She ignored the question. "So where're we going?"

"You don't want to come along," I said.

"I don't think you should be alone," she said.

"You think I'm going to do something stupid over a lousy commercial, Bainbridge? Who do you think I am? Hotchkiss?"

"I don't think you're going to do anything stupid."

"That's the nicest thing that anyone's said to me in days," I said.

"All the more reason you shouldn't be alone. Take me with you, Boddekker."

I suppose I could have argued her to a stop, but the mood I was in blinded me to any point there would have been in doing it. In the end I assented, giving Bainbridge one last chance to bail out of the deal. I told her that my plans would take me to the Woodstock Memorial Alternate Lifestyle Extended Care Facility, where I planned to visit my grandmother. That only served to turn the warm glow in her belly even higher, and she told me how wonderful and humane I was to take time out for my family like that. For better or worse, she was spending the rest of the day with me.

We got to the ZepPort around noon, and I booked two seats on a northbound flight, paying for Bainbridge's ticket over her protests. That was done out of the guilt I felt over not being able to tell her to get lost. I would have to work on my courage, I decided as I had the clerk add a gold foil Lunch Stamp to each ticket. If I could handle and outwit the five members of a street gang, I could do something about a girl who insisted on accompanying me on a trip that would only amplify my misery.

The zep ride did its best to compound the basic unpleasantness of the situation. We flew through a spring storm that buffeted and bumped the ship and left most of the passengers feeling uncomfortable, myself included. It didn't faze Bainbridge, who told me unwelcome tales about her own maternal grandmother's adventures right up until the time lunch was served.

The tales continued right through lunch, slabs of sourdough bread hardened to the consistency of granite with packets of some kind of Vegemite-style paste ("Incredible food-like flavor!") to spread over it, and to wash it down, a generously sized bottle of Minute Maid Almost Wine. By the end of the meal, Bainbridge's historical heritage had traced a gumpian path through the biggest historical turning points of the last seventy years. What I will remember most about it all was the piece of reconstituted vegetable and protein matter that rode on one of Bainbridge's incisors during the last dozen years of the narrative.

She retired to the powder room and I returned to my seat, crossing my arms and feigning sleep to reduce the embarrassment she would surely feel after catching sight of the offending food matter in the mirror. The one bit of compassion I had for her, and it worked. I felt the seat shift as she sat down next to me, and I developed that odd prickling sensation that grows on the back of your neck when you know someone is looking at you. She stared at me for three seconds short of forever, then she put a hand to my forehead. After a moment it lifted, the seat shifted, and the sensation vanished. I heard the familiar click of chicklet keys as she sideloaded the zep's in-flight magazine.

We landed at Kingston station, which serves Woodstock and the surrounding communities, and grabbed a bikeshaw that took us to the home itself. The place was laid out like a small college campus on the site of the historical Woodstock gathering. There was a cluster of dormitory-like buildings in the center, which each housed a different group of residents: independent living, assisted living, advanced care, full care, and acid casualties. These were surrounded by administrative buildings and utility centers like maintenance and food services. Scattered around the outskirts were tennis and shuffleboard courts, a swimming pool complex, jogging-walking track, and two souvenir shops—one for modern stuff and the other specializing in retro stuff handmade by some of the abler residents. It really was a beautiful facility, except it turned into a wretched mess when it rained.

On the way in I stopped at the handmade shop to let Bainbridge look around. The charm of the tie-dyed shirts escaped her, but she fell in love with a necklace that was nothing more than a beaded chain from which hung a series of alligator clips. She was about to buy it until I explained the historical significance of the clips, after which she settled on a pair of earrings in the shape of a bird perched on the neck of a guitar.

We walked across the campus to the advanced care facility. As we neared the door, Bainbridge began to slow. I stopped and turned to her.

"Listen," I said, "you don't have to come in. Some people find these places really depressing—"

"It's not that," she said. "I'm concerned about you."

"Me?"

"Are you going to be all right? I mean, with your grandmother in advanced care and all—"

"Bainbridge," I said, "it's okay. It's not full care, right? And it's not the acid casualty ward. She's very comfortable here."

"I guess I don't understand why you came here when—when you need cheering up."

I wanted to say that she was the one who thought I needed cheering up. I had decided to come here on an impulse, largely so I could spend some time alone on the zep and brood about the bad streak of luck that had been handed to me with the World Nano business. But her incessant prattling about family history and that precious bit of vegetable paste stuck to her tooth had succeeded in making me forget all of that.

I said nothing to her. I shrugged and looked away, hoping that she would interpret the gesture in her own way. Her reply to that was, "I've got to learn not to expect instant answers about things like that. Especially when a man is involved."

It was difficult not to cringe at this, a definite *faux paux* on her part, reminding me of the whole male/female thing between us even though she was supposed to simply tag along as a friend. It didn't make sense that she would bring it up, not under the current circumstances. But then, to put a Bainbridgian view on it, I had to learn not to expect things like that to make sense—especially when a woman was involved. *Especially* when the woman was still the better part of a girl, like Bainbridge was.

The Woodstock Memorial Alternate Lifestyle Extended Care Facility's advanced care dormitory is not what you expect. You read back into literature about places that care for the elderly and get descriptions of aisles full of gurneys with people strapped in them, wheelchairs semicircled around vid sets tuned to a channel of mental anesthesia, oldsters reaching out and grabbing at your clothes so you'd stop and talk about *anything*. And there were always references to a smell that created its own miasma of gloom. I don't know if there are any places like that still around. What I do know is that this place was the farthest from those that a person could get. True, Mom and Uncle Kent were each paying a bundle to keep Grandma Missy here, so maybe their guilt at having her packed away explained the reason for putting her somewhere that was so state of the art.

On the other hand, the Woodstock folks know how to take care of people like Missy.

The lobby of the building was bright and cheerful, with an opaque white cover on the ceiling to let filtered sunlight through. Music filled the air, light and bouncy and familiar enough to be maddening when I couldn't name the tune. There were plenty of couches, overstuffed chairs, and terminals for reading magazines; at least two gigantic, well-stocked aquariums; and enough plants to start a small jungle. It all combined to give the place a fresh, life-affirming atmosphere.

Bainbridge followed me to the main desk, where I reported my intent to visit with Melissa Mercheson. After signing in and stylusing our names across a waiver form ("We run a tight ship, but you never know—you just never, never know.''), we took a series of crisscrossing elevators to Grandma Missy's floor. The bouncy music was louder here, and some of the residents who were being wheeled about were humming or mumbling lyrics in time to the string serenade.

''What's a 'radar lover'?'' Bainbridge asked as we walked.

''A what?''

''An old man was singing something about a radar lover being gone.''

I shrugged. ''That music they used to listen to. It was just noise.''

The song gave way to another chugging anthem as we stopped outside of Grandma's room. I rapped on the door frame and called her name. The lights were down inside, but I could see movement from her bed. As I got closer, I could see the odd movements she was making; her right hand was poised above her belly and was scratching at it with something invisible held between her thumb and middle finger. Her left arm was stretched out, bent at the elbow, and her fingers were wiggling.

Bainbridge looked at me. I shrugged again and continued inside.

''Grandma Missy?''

She stopped her motions and looked at me. Her face was one of those that was aging gracefully in spite of the chemical abuse she had put herself through decades earlier. The eyes had an ersatz sparkle that made you think she had more remaining brain capacity than what was actually left. Her smile was of straight, perfect teeth—she still had all of her natural ones, and they had been molded into shape by her post–World War II parents. Her face was framed by long, white hair that fell into perfect place with a few passes from a brush. The room itself was colored in earth tones and smelled of natural pine from the cloned boughs growing out of pots mounted along the wall. The curtains were closed and the vid screen was dark, but the omnipresent music lilted in from speakers mounted in the ceiling.

Grandma's lips turned up into that billion-dollar smile of hers. ''Well, hello. Come on in and let me get a look at you.''

I looked at Bainbridge. ''Looks like she's having a good day,'' I whispered. I walked to the bed and took her hand. ''How you doing, Grammy?''

''Why don't you ever write?'' she asked.

"Write?" I blurted.

"Oh, that's right. You do everything on those little screens now, don't you? Well, I couldn't expect you to write anyway, now could I?"

"Grandma—"

Her voice became low and gravelly. "But the least you could do is stop by once in a while!"

"Grandma, I was here two weeks ago—"

Quick as lightning, her hand slipped from mine and locked onto my wrist. Her nails sunk into my skin and I yelped.

"Don't lie to me!"

"I didn't! Remember, I sat right here and you told me how you and your friends set fire to the—"

Her wrist twisted, pulling the skin of my arm until it burned. "Kent State Mercheson! How many times have I told you not to lie to your mother!"

I turned to Bainbridge. "She thinks I'm her son—"

Grandma followed my gaze and her face lit up. "Sunny! Is that really you? Come here and give your mother a kiss!"

"Don't do it," I whispered, and she jerked my arm so hard that I thought for a moment that she'd dislocated it.

"Don't listen to this miserable wretch," she told Bainbridge. "He told me the other day that he was planning to vote for George Bush!"

Bainbridge took a step forward. I tried to wave her off.

"Mez Mercheson, this isn't your son. It's your *grand*son—"

Grandma's hand dropped my wrist and shot up to grab my ear. "*Listen* to her! Listen to your sister talk like that!" She yanked until the entire side of my face started to burn and I yelped in pain. "You bad, bad children! Have you been in Mommy's stash again? I TOLD YOU NOT TO LICK THOSE STAMPS!" She pulled my head down to bring my ear to her lips. "I TOLD YOU IF YOU WANT SOME OF THAT YOU HAD TO BUY YOUR OWN!"

From the corner of my eye I saw Bainbridge backing toward the door, then she turned and ran.

Grandma screamed. "YELLOW SUNSHINE, YOU COME BACK HERE! BAD LITTLE BOYS AND GIRLS GROW UP TO BE LIKE RICHARD NIXON!"

"Grandma!" I shouted, trying to get her to quit screaming in my ear. "It's me—"

Suddenly Grandma howled and began to double up. The hand holding my ear slid down to her belly, and one of her knees caught me in the temple. Stars exploded in the center of my vision.

"Owwwww-WOOOOAAAAAA!"

"Grammy, what's—"

"I CAN'T REMEMBER!" she bellowed. And then, in almost a whine, "I can't remember, can't remember, can't remember . . ."

"What can't you remember?"

She pulled my head up to face her. " 'A Day in the Life,' " she said.

"A day in the life?"

"I can't remember, Kent. Is it on *Abbey Road*? Or is it on the white album?" Her free hand came up and she began punching herself in the head. "*Abbey Road?* The white album? *Abbey Road?* The white album? *Abbey Road?* The white album—"

There was a clatter from the hall, and a stocky woman came rushing into the room, Bainbridge at her heels.

"What's the problem?"

"She's about to rip my ear—"

The woman stepped around me and looked into my grandmother's eyes. "Melissa, what's the problem?"

"Olivia," Grandma smiled. "Is it *Abbey Road*? Or is it on the white album?"

The woman stroked Grandma's hair with one hand and pulled a fat silver tube from the pocket of her scrub jacket. "What's that, honey?"

" 'A Day in the Life,' " Grandma said. "Is it on *Abbey Road* or the white album?"

"My ear—" I said.

"It's on *Sergeant Pepper's Lonely Hearts Club Band*," Olivia said. "I'm going to give you something to help you remember."

"Okay," Grandma whimpered. "Thank you, Olivia."

She pressed the silver tube against Grandma's neck. There was a click and a hiss. The pressure on my ear eased.

"You can let go of your son's ear, now."

Suddenly free, I pulled away from the bed fast and ended up sprawled on the floor. Bainbridge knelt beside me as I rubbed the feeling back into my face. "I'm her grandson," I complained.

Olivia shook her head, still playing with Grandma's hair.

"She's not the only one. This happens to some of the residents every time a Jimi Hendrix song comes up in the music rotation. I've complained to management about it before."

Bainbridge looked up at Olivia. "Isn't there something you can do about this?"

"She's just having a bad day," I said.

Bainbridge, still looking at Olivia: "I mean, he came all the way from Manhattan to see her—"

Olivia said, "Manhattan's not that far. We have plenty of residents whose—"

"It's all right," I said. "She deserves a bad day, like anyone else."

Olivia smiled and nodded at me. "He's right, you know."

I picked myself up from the floor and tested my mangled ear. "Thanks for helping," I told Olivia.

She nodded and I walked out of the room. It took a few seconds for Bainbridge to realize that I was gone, so I was almost to the elevator by the time she caught up.

"How's the ear?" she asked.

I fingered it. It was tender. "Still attached."

"I feel bad. You came all this way and it turned out like this. Especially after the morning you had."

The hair on the back of my head stood straight up. I knew what was coming. Bainbridge was about to get carried off by a wave of Florence Nightingale syndrome and the unfortunate recipient of same was about to be trapped with her on a zep ride back to NYC. And there I was, without a clue as to how to stop it other than to stand there and ring for the elevator.

"Boddekker . . ."

The slow torture started with her putting her hand on my shoulder. When we left the residence I made a joke to the receptionist about how Grandma had nearly torn my ear off, and the minute we were outside, Bainbridge was carrying on about me trying so hard to keep a brave face.

On the bikeshaw ride back to Kingston station I got the brilliant idea that some alcohol might fog her brain enough to shut her up, and so I had the driver stop at a promising-looking tavern. That was the wrong thing to do, too. She took great delight in telling me that she wasn't planning on drinking, and that it was the worst thing in the world for me to do, given my precarious mental state. I took the better part of valor and swallowed about a half-dozen really great sarcastic remarks.

It only got worse as the day began to fade into evening and the helium-buoyed *Constantinople* lifted us into the air. Half an hour into the trip the stewards brought around more sourdough bread and paste. I turned my nose up at it. After the earlier encounter, I had decided that hunger was a preferable option, although I should have eaten it. The taste would have suited my mood.

But the move made me a target again. Bainbridge watched me return the untouched plate and uh-huhed knowingly.

"Depression," she said.

I looked at her.

"Loss of appetite. A telltale sign of depression."

"Look, Grandma just had a bad day—"

"So did you."

I didn't bother to tell her about her own contribution to the day's rottenness. Not when she was busy patting herself on the back for her perceived insight. And there I was, doomed to relive moments like this over and over and over because I couldn't open my mouth to release the words that would set me free.

Why can't I?

I sneaked a look at Bainbridge. She looked so serious, but lurking underneath it all she was holding back a smile. She was truly happy doing this, following me around on the worst day of my life, being there as a source of comfort. But why was she interested in linguistics and advertising? Why couldn't she have gone into some kind of social work, say finding good homes for kids orphaned during the Norwegian war?

"Boddekker?" she said.

I looked at her face again, trying to make it short so she wouldn't think I was giving her a longing, devoted look. And there was the answer, written on her forehead, and in the corners of her eyes and mouth.

They weren't lines. They were tiny fissures, so small that a nano machine could crawl across them and fasten together the sides using subatomic-sized staples.

What I was seeing was her own personal fragility. If I told her that I wanted out, those fissures would cause her face to shatter and she would explode in tears.

I couldn't deal with tears. And I didn't want to be responsible for ruining her life. Not directly. Not when there had to be another way I could let her down.

In the meantime, I was stuck with Bainbridge and my own cowardice.

"Are you all right, Boddekker?"

I said to her, "I'll get over it. I have lots of days left. Unlike my grandmother."

She nodded. "I know you will." And then she mentioned the word that would become the recurring theme for the rest of the day; "We'll get home and get you a good old-fashioned cure."

I was afraid to ask about the nature of the cure. Knowing Bainbridge it could be anything—she was frighteningly knowledgeable about all of the latest pop culture treatments for you-name-it. I could hear her rummaging through my kitchen cupboard for spices to add to a sludgy poultice that she would spread on my chest with a spatula.

I pretended not to notice.

But not even ignoring the circumstances could detain Bainbridge from the swift completion of her appointed torture. As the trip went on, she took the word *cure* and wielded it like a club, repeatedly clobbering me with it so I'd know for certain that she intended to put me out of my misery.

As the zep put in at Long Island station: "Closer to home, Boddekker. And closer to the cure."

As we waited in a cold drizzle to hail a bikeshaw to take us into Manhattan: "Hang on, Boddekker. The cure will get you all warmed up."

During the initial stage of the bikeshaw ride: "No, Boddekker. We'll go to your place first. And I'll get you all fixed up with the cure."

Dealing with my protests that I should drop her off at her place: "This cure isn't something that can be done by phone."

As we got out of the bikeshaw at my apartment: "I'll handle the fare. You go get ready for the cure."

On the way up the stairs, I hoped that her cure would be lethal.

My apartment was dark as the city by the time I walked in. I turned on one small lamp and then gazed out the window at my view of Manhattan. It was awe-inspiring at night.

Bainbridge walked through the door. "It's been some day," she said, yawning.

"Don't worry. I'm not going to jump."

She laughed. "Before I get you all fixed up, I need to use your bathroom. I won't be long."

"Take your time." I turned my watch back on and it greeted me with a flashing *4*. "I've got messages I need to check." I pointed. "Through the bedroom, on the right."

She vanished into my bedroom and I heard her say, "You're a single man, all right."

I ignored the remark and sat down so I could see the city lights while I called up my phone messages. There was a pleasant chime.

"Boddekker, this is Dansiger. I'm sorry about today. I guess I didn't make that clear to you when we were all mobbed in your office. I stopped by to talk to you later, but Deppe said you'd been dragged off by that little tart Bainbridge—"

I leaned forward to see if Bainbridge was still in the bathroom. She was. I turned the volume down on the watch.

"Anyway, I know how you're feeling. I'm disappointed, too, and I let that color the way I treated you. So I'm sorry. I wanted our spot to go to World Nano, and I know you did, too. You did your best. But we'll get them next time, Tiger. Bye."

Tiger? The thought of hearing that from Dansiger gave me goosebumps. Maybe she hadn't filled the Hotchkiss-sized hole in her life.

Another chime.

"Mr. Boddekker, this is your ferret. I thought you'd want to know that there's been a lot of hi-pri activity in the Pembroke Hall network, and a lot of it has been aimed at your hard storage. I can keep out some of the low-level intruders, but the Tech boys are cracking into it using a Behalf code, and there's nothing I can do to prevent it. I'm forced to use a default protective mode until you tell me otherwise."

I closed my eyes. "What are they trying to access?"

Nothing.

"Ferret?" I opened my eyes and remembered that I'd been talking to a recording.

Chime.

"Boddekker? Hotchkiss. I need to talk to you as soon as you turn your phone back on."

Dansiger calling me Tiger and Hotchkiss with an urgent request to speak with me both on one machine? Perhaps they'd attempted a reconciliation and it had some bizarre side effects.

The next chime came as Bainbridge called my name from the bathroom. I put my watch on hold.

"If you're ready for your cure, I'm ready to administer it."

"It'll be a few minutes yet," I shouted. "I've got a couple of calls to make"—I paused, about to ask what I needed to do for this cure, and in that pause I heard—

Hisst! Hisst!

I fell back in the chair. My head lolled back and my lips parted to whisper a vulgar and wholly appropriate word. Then, quietly, I sat up and peered into my bedroom.

Barely lit from the light of the bathroom, Bainbridge walked to the far side of the bed and threw back the covers. She was naked. In the dim light, I could see that while her figure was fundamentally pleasing, it left something to be desired by current standards. She wasn't lumpy, but a few more pounds between the breasts and hips would have caused the slight curve between them to vanish into parallel lines.

I froze, hoping that the dim light from the lamp wasn't enough to give me away.

She slid between my sheets and laid her head down on my extra pillow.

"Any time you're ready, Boddekker."

I swore again. "Stupid," I whispered. "Why didn't I see that? Stupid, stupid—"

"Boddekker?"

"Still making calls," I said. With a trembling hand I made the watch chime.

"Son? This is Levine."

My heart exploded.

"Something has developed here that will require your immediate attention. I want you to give me a call as soon as you get this message, I don't care what time of day or night it is. I've encoded this with my return number, so climb off that little intern and push the button."

I swore again. Was I the only one in the world who hadn't seen the motive in Bainbridge's moves?

Then I pushed the button.

Levine answered on the third pulse.

"Boddekker," I said, "returning your call."

"Ah, yes!" A dry chuckle. "Son, what's a ten-letter word that means 'casual intercourse'?"

My throat went rock hard and my head instinctively turned toward my bedroom. *B-a-i-n-b-r-i-d-g-e.*

Then he said, "Oh! *Discussion!*" The dry chuckle again and the clatter of his fingers on a keyboard. "These crosswords make me crazy with their ridiculous clues. Guess that's why I love them so much."

In a thin voice I said, "You wanted me to call, sir?"

"Of course. Yes. Boddekker, there were some interesting developments after you the office."

Yes, son. Bainbridge is still underage so now the feds want to prosecute you under the provisions of the Mihaljevic Act.

"Sir?" I croaked.

"Well. Funny thing. After our meeting broke up and I thought we'd all gone our respective little ways, who should show up to see me but Mez Broadbent. And she's coming to tell me that she's concerned that her spot is not the best one that Pembroke Hall could send to World Nanotechnologies, Ltd."

"That happens to all of us, sir. We win the big contest and then start thinking, 'My spot really isn't that good, it was luck.' I've been through it before."

"Well, she was expressing to me that *your* spot should be the one to go. I told her I felt the same way, but we had already voted to a consensus—"

"Good," I said. "Her spot will do us proud."

"—when who should ring into my office but Hotchkiss. He says he's been thinking really hard about this entire situation and he decided that his vote was wrong."

I thought, *But he waited until Broadbent's spot was safely chosen before voting against it.*

"So he changed his vote to a yes. That makes *There Were Ten of Them* the winner, and therefore, the spot which will represent us at World Nano."

"But what about Broadbent's spot—"

"She withdrew it to facilitate your spot's going," Levine said.

My jaw worked open but no words came out. I looked into the bedroom. Bainbridge had turned so her back was toward me.

"Sir—"

"I know you're shocked and surprised and happy all at once. As well you should be. *Congratulations!*"

"I—"

"Now there's a lot to be done in the next week. You and your team have to get a full cassie to us so we can submit them to World Nano.''

"Uh—"

"Son, I can't describe to you how excited I am about all of this. You and your group have really outdone yourselves this time. And I know that nothing but the best will come our way because of it.''

"Well—"

"You're on your way, son! Your rise to group leader was only the beginning! But now? Well, you've taken a giant step—a quantum leap! Nothing is out of your grasp now, young Boddekker. *Nothing!*''

My head turned toward the window. I looked west. And south. Toward Princeton.

Levine repeated his congratulations and then rang off. I sat stunned for a long time. It was all so strange, so sudden. And yet . . .

Dansiger's call. "Tiger." Hotchkiss's call. Urgent.

I brought back one of the messages and hit the dial button. It pulsed and pulsed and pulsed, and finally there was an answer.

"Hello?" asked Dansiger's sleepy voice.

"It's Boddekker," I said.

"Boddekker? Do you know what time it is? Where did that little tart take—"

"What did you say to Hotchkiss?" I asked.

"What did I *say*—"

"What did you *do* to Hotchkiss?"

"Boddekker, are you drunk or something?"

"If I were, I'd have an excuse." I stood and began to pace the floor. "You don't know, then."

"You're in jail. The tart got you in trouble and you need me to come and bail you out."

"Hotchkiss changed his vote," I told her. "On our spot. It's going to World Nano."

I heard shuffling as Dansiger repositioned herself on her bed. "*Our* spot? *There Were Ten of Them?*"

"All ten of them," I said.

"And you thought I—"

"Exerted what influence you had left over Hotchkiss. Forgive me, Dansiger. I overreact to your ambitiousness at times."

"Our spot is *going*?" she asked.

"It's going, Dansiger," I whispered. "We're in the big-time now."

The conversation went on for another half-hour as we made plans to be in early and start work on the cassie. The next week would be hectic, filled with long days, bad food, cheap stimulants, and little sleep.

It was the happiest moment of my life.

I cut the connection and turned to go to bed, but stopped in the doorway.

There was a large lump in my bed, breathing slow and steady. On the inhale it made a soft *zzzzuuuuuk!*

I backed into the living room, turned, and stretched out on the couch.

My last thought before sleep was, *That's two incredible strokes of luck in one short day.*

"Selling you to the world since 1969"

Offices in Principal Cities: New York - Montreal - Toronto - Sydney - London -
Tokyo - Moskva - Beijing - Chicago - Oslo - Philadelphia - Amarillo

CLIENT: »Lovejoy Specialities		PRODUCT: »Love Slave Robotettes (General)
WRITER: »Boddekker	TIME: »:60	MEDIA: »Video
TITLE: »*Tired of the Old Model?*		
PRODUCTION ORDERS:	»Deppe to compose score, arrange music, audition musicians (singers)	

AUDIO	VIDEO
The sound of a cold wind blowing.	*Fade in on a depressing, run down hovel of a home. A grizzled, slightly overweight* MAN *in a stained tank-top T-shirt sits at a battered kitchen table in a dingy kitchen eating what looks like gruel out of a cracked bowl.*
SHRILL WOMAN: [*Voice.*] Henry! Hen-ry! Are you in the kitchen?	*The* MAN *winces as his wife appears, a skinny thing in a housecoat and hair in curlers, her face a wrinkled prune, and nose a sharp, craggy beak. She's this poor guy's worst nightmare.*
SHRILL WOMAN: Hen-ry! Why haven't you taken out the trash? You *know* this is *recycling* day! And the sink is still dripping and the EPA inspector will be	*A series of close-ups of the woman from different angles as she shakes her finger at him and nags and nags and nags and nags and nags.*

here *any time* and if he finds
we're wasting *water*, we're
going to be *out on the street!*
Besides that [*Ad libs, fade
under to favor announcer.*]

ANNOUNCER: Men! Are you tired
of the old model?

MAN *reacts to this, turning from
his nagging wife and nodding
at the camera.*

ANNOUNCER: Then what you
need is a *new* little
woman . . . you need a *Love
Slave Robotette* from Lovejoy
Specialties!

*The fire escape door bursts
open and a whole handful of
men in all colors, shapes, and
sizes come streaming into the
kitchen. The* MAN *looks at them
in astonishment.*

HARD-HAT: C'mon, pal! [*Up
music: the "Love Slave
Robotette Anthem."*]

HARD-HAT *pulls* MAN *out of his
chair as the music starts.*

MEN'S CHORUS: Out with the old
and in with the new,
We'll show you what a woman
can do,
One that you'd be proud to
own,
Once who can make a house
a home—

The group, with the MAN *being
pushed along in the lead,
shoves the harpy* WOMAN *aside
and march straight toward the
camera until it blacks out. Then
it's light again, and the group
is marching away from us
toward a Love Slave Robotette
franchise. Flashing super:
CHECK LISTINGS FOR THE
SHOWROOM NEAREST
YOU!*

MEN'S DUO: You pick the eyes,
the smile, and the bust,
She's your nuclear-powered
bundle of lust!

The HARD-HAT *and a* MAN IN A
BUSINESS SUIT *show the* MAN *the
French Maid model.*

IRISH TENOR: She doesn't get a
headache,
FRENCH BARITONE: And she always
says yes,

*A cop (*TENOR*) and a cook in a
tall white hat (*BARITONE*) show the*
MAN *the swimsuit-clad Miss
February model; the cook gives*

	her a good whack on the bottom and rolls his eyes while delivering his line (the robot should smile appreciatively at this).
TWO OFF-KEY MELODY PARTS: And she doesn't even care If you leave the house a mess!	Two NYC BIKESHAW DRIVERS show the MAN the Cold Warriorette model. She karate chops one of the guys flat; the other guy looks into the camera and winks on "a mess."
MEN'S CHORUS: She's your Love Slave!	The men gather on either side of a chorus-type line of new and recent Robotette models; the MAN is overwhelmed by the choices.
SQUEAKY TENOR: She's my Love Slave!	A little guy in a lab coat tweaks the cheek of the Amazon Goddess model, who stands a full head taller than he does.
BARITONE: Your cute and cuddly,	A guy in pajamas tosses a teddy bear over his shoulder and latches onto the Mez College Co-Ed model.
BASS: Big and bosomy,	A big barrel of a man reclining with his head on the amazingly large bosom of the Forbidden Fruit model.
TWO-PART HARMONY: Sleek and sultry,	Two sailors are playing tug-of-war with the arms of the Shore Leave model.
CRACKING PUBESCENT VOICE: Lean and lovely,	A kid who is not more than sixteen is carrying the Anne O'Rexia model in his arms.

MEN'S CHORUS: Love Slave!
Your Love Slave Robotette!

The men's chorus march in a line toward the MAN in the foreground. The chorus breaks off, alternately passing to the MAN's left and right. Each man has an LSR on his arm.

MEN'S CHORUS: [*Wolf whistle.*]

Shot of the MAN walking past the camera with the Amazon Goddess on one arm and the Cold Warriorette on the other. As they pass out of camera range, we see the wiggling legs of the MAN's original wife sticking out of a recycling wagon.

FORBIDDEN FRUIT MODEL: [*Spoken.*]
Take me home!

Portrait shot of Forbidden Fruit model; she licks her lips as she speaks.

[*Music ends on a final BOT!*]

Blackout.

INQUIRY	RESPONSE
TO: Chesterfield/Legal FROM: Boddekker/Creative	TO: Boddekker/Creative FROM: Chesterfield/Legal

INQUIRY

ENCLOSED A COPY OF THE LSR SPOT FOR LOVEJOY. DO WE HAVE TO PUT IN THE BIT WITH THE ROBOTETTE TALKING? THEIR VOICES AREN'T QUITE RIGHT, AND HAVING THEM TALK ONLY HIGHLIGHTS THE PROBLEM. OVERALL, IT MAKES THE PRODUCT A MUCH TOUGHER SELL.

ALSO, AREN'T WE SUPPOSED TO PUT IN SOMETHING ABOUT THE LIMITED BATTERY LIFE?

—B

RESPONSE

Sorry, Bod. FTC regs state we gotta show the thing talking.

Re: the bit with the batteries. Don't sweat it. Anything with batteries carries an implied caveat. I didn't realize the nuke batteries weren't any better than the chemical ones ("nuclear-powered bundle of lust").

Cool spot, BTW
RMC

PS. You showed a guy carrying one in his arms. You might check, I think these things are too heavy to carry.

EIGHT

Some Adjustments in Orientation

The next week dissolved, vanished into nothing in exactly the way I'd predicted.

I was wakened the next morning as Bainbridge called my name. Remembering that she was naked the last time I'd seen her, I took my time in waking, sitting up, and wiping the sleep from my eyes.

"I'm sorry," she said without apology, "but it's early and I've got to go to my apartment."

Her sour tone gave me the courage to open my eyes. She was fastening the last button of her blouse.

"I need to get a change of clothes. I mean, after all, we wouldn't want people to think we—"

"Our spot is going to World Nano," I interrupted.

"—not that they're going to—" She stopped. "What did you say?"

"One of the messages on my phone was from Levine—"

"One of the old men called *you*?"

"Hotchkiss changed his vote on my spot. Then Broadbent

pulled hers from consideration because she felt my spot was stronger."

Her face peeled into a broad grin, erasing all evidence of her failed seduction. "That's wonderful. No wonder you look awful. You had a late night last night and I kept you out of your bed." She leaned forward and kissed me on the forehead. "In that case you'd better go crawl in now and get some decent sleep."

I shook my head. "I thought I'd go in early. Dansiger's going to be there. We've got a lot to do."

"Then I'm going in early, too."

"You can't." I gestured at her. "Clothes. Remember?"

She looked down at herself and blushed. "Of course. You're absolutely right—"

"Come in at the regular time. The next few days are going to be tight, and chances are good you'll lose your weekend to this."

"I understand. I'll do that." She gathered her purse, started toward the door, then stopped. "You were a gentleman last night, Boddekker. A true gentleman. And if anyone asks, that's what I'll tell them."

"If anyone asks, we'll keep this our little secret."

"Right. You're right, of course." And then she was gone.

If only all of my other problems took care of themselves that way.

True to my prediction, the week was a blur of hard work, back-patting, shouting matches, nights spent on the floor of my office, various chemical productivity enhancers, lunches from Beijing Buddy's, and midnight sandwiches at Ogilvy's. But we didn't lose the entire weekend to production of the cassie. It was completed by three-thirty on Saturday afternoon, at which time I dismissed everyone and tactfully dodged an invitation to Bainbridge's place for a meal of green food. Without a twinge of guilt, I went home and went straight to bed. When I woke, it was four o'clock on Sunday morning and I was ravenous from sleeping off the chemicals. I walked down the street to a Beijing Buddy's and was back in bed by seven. The remainder of the day, I was up only long enough to eat or toilet or turn on the radio to make sure the world hadn't ended.

When I walked into the office on Monday morning, it was evident that everyone else had followed pretty much the same regimen. The members of my group—including Harbison, Mortonsen, and the usually lugubrious Sylvester—were all bright eyed and sharp with the edge given them by winning the corporate sweepstakes. They surprised me with a small ceremony in Dansiger's office, where they gave me a vigorous round of applause before dispatching me upstairs to deliver the cassies to Levine's secretary.

The balance of the day was anticlimactic. By afternoon we were all beginning to slide into our typical postvictory depressions, so I dismissed early and bought my team the first round of drinks at Ogilvy's. I praised them for their support and their ability to put up with me—then put it all in perspective by saying that we had other projects requiring our attention, and that it was time to move on. I knew that most of them thought the major battle lay ahead with the World Nano decision process, but for me it was over. And I wasn't about to rest on my laurels, especially when they could easily be handed to Streusel and Strauss or Mauldin and Kress or McMahon, Tate, and Stevens.

So while we were waiting for World Nano's decision, I tried to get my group to put it out of their minds as completely as I had. We had other advertising worlds to conquer.

Not that we could totally let it go. The wait for the decision had at least one harrowing moment—when the spots were screened for any members of competing agencies who were interested in seeing what had been submitted.

I had chosen not to go, being bogged down with a spot for Lovejoy Specialties—a situation compounded by the misbehavior of the Robotette the company had sent to give us a feel for the product. The problem was that as a floor model, it had no software that bonded it to its owner, leaving it to revert to default behavior. Every time we left the Cold Warriorette alone, it made its way to a computer terminal and tried to hack into our company's database. When we'd catch it, it would beg us to interrogate it, saying "No matter what you do, you'll never make me talk. Never. Ever. *Just try it!*" Then it tried to openly seduce Griswold, which resulted in its getting into a shouting match with Bainbridge, who didn't realize that it was just a toy.

It was all for the best that this had kept me away from the screening. On his return, Deppe could only shake his head and say, "It's close, real close." Hotchkiss's reaction was worse; he took a month off and zepped up to Banff. I didn't know why until I talked to Dansiger. She told me, "Hotchkiss is absolutely sick over this whole thing, Boddekker. The first spot they showed, the one from Streusel and Strauss? It had cavemen in it.''

This motivated me to put the whole thing as far out of mind as I could. To do anything else was to lay awake at night wondering if I'd overdone it at every step of the way, and thinking that perhaps Hotchkiss had been right in always taking the simple, time-honored, well-worn way of doing things.

So, weeks later, when the word finally came down about World Nano's decision, I was one of the last to know.

I was in my office talking to Deppe about an idea he had for a new Lover's Mist spot. While doing some digging through some music archives, he had discovered a musician named Chuck Berry, who had done a song which in essence was thinly veiled description of a sexual marathon.

''It's a really amazing piece of music,'' he was telling me. ''The narrator keeps looking at his watch, and every hour he's doing it in a different room of the house.''

''Sounds interesting,'' I said. I did think it was interesting, but not for the same reason as Deppe.

''The library is transcribing it for me from one of those ancient polyvinyl discs. I'll play it for you when it's ready. I think we could get a great Lover's Mist spot out of it. It seems to fit right in with how we've been pushing them.''

I started to say something when Churchill stuck his head inside my office. ''Hey, Boddekker. I want to know one thing.''

''Dare I ask?''

''What jones are you on? That must've been some heavy duty dose!''

With a laugh, he disappeared.

''What was that all about?'' asked Deppe.

''I have no idea.''

Deppe shrugged. ''Anyway, I was thinking we could obtain the rights and then digitalize his performance from the original master recording—provided it isn't all decomposed, because recording was pretty primitive when he was working. All we'd need to do is drop in the hissing of the squirt bottle as a rhythmic thing—*hiss hiss hiss hiss!* You know, incorporate it as part of the song.''

''Nice idea,'' I said, ''but we need to be careful. I used two squirts in the jingle because that's the standard dose of Lover's Mist. You use four, there may be some problems. Besides, the whole point to Lover's Mist is that it lasts for twelve hours. If we drop it in every time the guy looks at his watch, people will get the wrong idea.''

"True," said Deppe. "But . . ." He trailed off.

"But what?" I followed his gaze to my door. Hotchkiss was standing there. "Yes?"

He gave me a thumbs-up. Then he was gone.

"Is this Weird Day or what?" Deppe asked.

I shrugged.

"Well. As I was saying, if we could feed enough digitalized information on Berry to an emulation program, we could rewrite the song as needed and have him singing the virtues of Lover's Mist. We could even incorporate the directions like you did with your jingle. It'd be a great selling tool, and we'd get the bonus of new music releases by a Chuck Berry emulator, singing all new songs."

"I like it," I said. "It brings income to the agency from two different sources, and it'd be great for targeting the older audience demo, and the ones who are into that classical stuff. Why don't you open a file and report back when the library gets you the transcription? We'll look into who holds rights to Berry's personality and take it from there."

"Great," Deppe said.

"Have you had a chance to listen to that demo of the new SOBs product?" He rolled his eyes. "I know what you're thinking," I said quickly. "Don't say it. What's your evaluation?"

He looked away. "It's awfully derivative, Boddekker. All of their stuff is. They're trying to cash in on what their fathers did." I noticed that Deppe hadn't looked back at me. A glance showed that this time, Upchurch was standing at my door.

"You just missed your little brother," I said.

Upchurch shook his head. "You're out of your mind, you know that, Boddekker? All this house hunting business. Banging Bainbridge. Your mind has gone soft."

I looked at Deppe shrugged.

"Showing some guy taking a beating is not going to sell soap, friend. You ought to enroll in some of Bainbridge's classes to get back in touch with reality before you embarrass yourself and the company." He spun on one heel and left.

Deppe laughed. "Looks like the word has gotten out about our spot."

"About time," I said. "It's been weeks—" I stopped.

Deppe and I stared at each other. The same thought lit our eyes.

"Let's go!" Deppe said, bolting out of the chair.

I scrambled around my desk and followed him into the hall, then passed him as he stuck his head into Griswold's office and said, "Something's up. Get the others and meet us in the conference room." There was a clatter from Griswold's office as I rounded the corner and found myself face to face with Honniker In Accounting.

"Uh," I said, trying to figure out how to negotiate my way around her. "Hello. Excuse me."

"Boddekker." She smiled when she said it. Any other time in my life, I would have been thrilled. "I haven't seen you since Ogilvy's. You really should have stayed."

Deppe came around the corner and bumped into me. A half second later I heard him whisper, "Wow."

"Ah. Listen . . ." I reached out, intending to take her by the shoulders and move her aside, but I looked into her eyes and froze. They were crystal blue today, and served to remind me that this woman was a treasured vase, to be put on a pedestal and admired from a distance. I put a feeble smile on my face. "Excuse me."

"Actually, I was coming to get you," she said.

"Wow," Deppe whispered again.

"Mr. Levine wants to see you right away."

"He does?"

Honniker In Accounting nodded, and shuffled the slates in her hands. "If you'll excuse me," she said, very businesslike, "I have to be going."

"Right," I said. "Thanks."

"I'll see you later, Boddekker."

"Wow," Deppe said as we started walking again. "How do you rate, Boddekker? I mean, she *talked* to you! And 'see you later'? That has to mean some—"

I stopped short and he bumped me again. "Hold it. Change of plans. You and the rest of the group go to the conference room, and I'll meet you there."

"But where are you going?"

I pointed up.

"You're not serious."

"I'm very serious. Why do you think Levine sent someone to ask me upstairs?"

"Honniker In Accounting, no less."

"Why didn't he have his secretary call? Why does Honniker In Accounting always have to be his official messenger? Did you think of that? This is going to be bad, Deppe. But I'm going to live up to my part of the bargain. I'll clear the group of this if I can."

Griswold appeared in the hall. "You're headed the wrong way."

"Boddekker got called upstairs," Deppe said.

Griswold frowned.

"I think we blew it," I said. "I think World Nano shot us down. And I'll bet the old men want to make an example of me."

"We can't have that."

"You're exactly right," Deppe said. "Change of plans. Go tell the others to meet us at the elevators." He turned to me. "We'll go up with you."

"You're crazy," I said. "I told you—"

"We know what you said," Griswold smiled. "But maybe this is one case where a show of solidarity is needed. We've got to prove we can stick together in the face of this NanoKleen mess."

"That's all right—"

"No it isn't," Deppe said, his voice getting loud. "What right do the old men have to pit us against each other? We're all on the same side, aren't we?"

"We all agreed to go with the spot," Griswold said. "Dansiger and her friends all consented to produce the cassie."

"It's better to do it this way," I said. "That way they'll only hang me—"

"What's happening?" asked Bainbridge, a latecomer to the party.

"Boddekker's been called upstairs," said Griswold.

"Honniker In Accounting brought the message," said Deppe. "We think our spot stiffed."

"No," Bainbridge said, paling.

"Yes."

"I'm going with you," she said.

No, I thought.

"We're going too," said Deppe. "Tell the others."

"Of course," Bainbridge said, and turned back down the hall.

In a matter of minutes Griswold and Deppe and I had commandeered an elevator and were holding it, waiting to see who else was coming. And much to my amazement, they all hurried our way; Sylvester, who was showing signs of swelling from her latest hormonal treatments; Dansiger; Harbison; and Bainbridge brought up the rear with Mortonsen in tow.

The elevator doors closed and instantly there was a din.

"What's going on?"

"What's with the spot—"

"—the old men?"

"—get away with this?"

"—who did it?"

"It was the violence," said Sylvester. "I know it was all the violence in the spot."

I looked at Dansiger. "You know what I'm going to ask."

"You want to know if I've done any tacit poking around to find out which spot World Nano was favoring," she said. "What do you think?"

"I think you've been a good girl. I think you know how important this client is and I think you've played this one clean."

She nodded. "You go right on thinking that, Boddekker."

I puffed out my cheeks in a sigh. "Then it's bad. Our best option at this point is damage control—"

This started the questions again, so I recapped what had happened for the benefit of the latecomers. That took us to the lobby of thirty-nine, where I offered the others one last chance to stay behind.

"Never," was the consensus.

"All right, then. At least let me do the talking."

"Wait a minute," said Bainbridge. "Shouldn't we plan a strategy or something?"

"There's no time," said Deppe.

The eight of us swarmed past the receptionist's desk and down the hall toward Levine's office.

"What if they want to fire us?" Bainbridge asked in a whispered wail.

Griswold shook his head. "They won't. We've got a fat lot of talent here, and they'd be fools to cut it all loose at once."

"What if they want to fire you?" Harbison asked me.

"They won't," Dansiger replied. "If they try, they'll lose the rest of us."

"You don't need to—"

Dansiger stared me down from the corner of her eye. "Are we agreed?"

"Agreed," said Griswold and Deppe.

"Agreed," said Mortonsen.

"Agreed," said Harbison.

"This is going to ruin my future," Bainbridge said, "but I agree."

"You're young," snarled Dansiger. "You'll find another one."

"I don't know about this," whined Sylvester. "How am I going to pay for the rest of my Reorientation?"

"If you could make up your mind, you wouldn't have this problem," snapped Mortonsen.

"Oh, all right," she sighed. "I agree."

And thus we continued down the hall, lemmings on the way to professional suicide. I led my squad through the door to Levine's office and we crowded in around his receptionist's desk. She looked up with a certain amount of dismay.

"We're here to see Mr. Levine."

"Who . . . uh . . ." She twisted her head, trying to look at each one of us. "Who should I say is calling?"

"Boddekker. And this is my creative group."

"He's expecting us," added Dansiger.

The receptionist checked her screen, nodded, then picked up a telephone and buzzed Levine for a confirmation. I turned to the others.

"Last chance."

"If nothing else," said Dansiger, "I want to have the pleasure of telling him that the end of the world is *not* as nigh as he would have us think."

"But that was merely his way of saying that the end of an *era* was at hand," Sylvester explained. "Of course, now everything's going to end, with that violent thing Boddekker wrote."

"Shut up," said Mortonsen.

"Well," the receptionist said, sighing with relief. "Mr. Levine will see you . . . *all.*"

"One of the old men!" Bainbridge whispered in awe.

I went to the office door and opened it. It felt strangely right to be doing this. I wasn't scared at all. There truly was safety in numbers.

"Mr. Levine," I said. "Boddekker from creative."

"Boddekker!" Levine, behind his desk, turned toward me and smiled. "Do come in!"

"I'd like to introduce you to the members of my creative group," I said, and I introduced them all by name and job; Dansiger, Griswold, Deppe, Mortonsen, Sylvester, Harbison, and Bainbridge. They all passed in front of me, walked over to the desk and shook with the old man, then stepped back to stand quietly.

"Very nice," Levine smiled. "To what do I owe the honor of the visit?"

"You called for *us,* sir," I smiled politely.

He checked his notebook. "Ah, yes. Of course." He stood and held out his hand. I took it as a cue to leave my position at the door. I shook hands with him and stood in front of the semicircle formed by the others.

"Boddekker, the last few weeks have been tough on the company. I'm sure you're well aware of that. In fact, I'm certain that you know at least one person who has quit in the last two weeks."

"To be honest, no. But I do know someone who's on the verge of a nervous breakdown."

"Side effects," Levine said with a toss of his hand. "Symptoms. Labor pains. To be expected when a new way of doing things is about to be implemented. What you're seeing here in the agency is merely the beginning, my son. What chaff does not sort itself from our ranks will soon be taken care of."

I could hear my troops shifting behind me. They all wanted me to ask the question. I decided to *sort of* ask.

"And, uh, the reason you've brought me—ah, us—here, sir?"

With one bony finger, Levine struck a key on his notebook. He scowled. "Well quite obviously, young Boddekker, I wanted to talk to you about your spot. I've made a serious perusal of the cassie you've produced, and I have the script here before me."

I braced myself.

Levine, still with his scowl, shook his head. "The World Nano people found some very basic flaws in this spot. Frankly, I'm surprised that I didn't see them too when we were going over the scripts. Call it overindulgence in the excitement of the moment."

I nodded.

"But they're fixable."

"Fixable." I think that was Dansiger.

Levine nodded again. "You need to watch your word usage,

Boddekker. You used the word *honey* as an affectionism between the guy and his wife altogether too much in this sixty-second spot. Once is fine. More than enough, in fact. You had it three or four times, and it made them want to puke.''

"All right," I said, trying to sound sufficiently humbled. Still, I couldn't help wondering if the worst was yet to come. "What else, sir?"

Levine studied his screen for a moment. "Now that I look at my notes from the meeting with World Nano, I believe that is it. So you'll make that corrections on the cassie and have it back to me by Thursday at the latest?"

"Sir?"

"Boddekker, the spot has been chosen by World Nanotechnologies, Ltd. to introduce NanoKleen to the world."

Behind me, I could hear the others gasping and laughing in surprise. All I could say was, "Is that right?"

"Absolutely," said Levine, smiling. "And I knew you wouldn't let us down. Your writing was brilliant on that. It was unique. It really was. Every other creative group tried to explain how the stuff worked, with little cartoons and those blasted cavemen doing it and everything else. They were using advertising techniques that hadn't been used in seventy-five years. You know where that sits in my book, don't you? *B-o-r-i-n-g.*"

I looked back at Dansiger. She winked at me and smiled.

"Given the mediocrity of the work turned in by the others, it was a real courageous step not to do the obvious thing. The rest of your group is to be commended for supporting you."

"They're a pretty special group, Mr. Levine."

"This is a pretty special spot, Boddekker. It's a stunning vision . . . and the clarity of the scenes. It's like you've been there, up against a bunch of young hoodlums yourself."

"Well, I was, recently—"

"Yes," Levine almost shouted. "I knew it! I knew it!"

I had a sudden vision of where this happy scene was going to lead, and it turned my stomach into a hard knot. I leaned slightly to ease the sudden stabbing sensation and tried to think of a way to change course. "Of course, *everyone* will be victimized one and a third times during their life—and that rate is higher in—"

"Of course!" Levine said, in jolly spirits. "You've made the appeal of that spot a universal *negative* experience. Do you know how difficult that is? Do you know how many writers will end up leaving this agency because of their inability to do that?"

I had an idea how many already had, but it was beside the point.

"Clarity of vision, Boddekker, clarity of vision. You, of course, based this on your actual encounter with the gang."

"Well—"

"And this cassie is based on the gang that assaulted you, is it not?"

Before I could protest, Bainbridge chimed in. "Of course he did! He spent a lot of time with Mortonsen describing how each member of the gang should look." I could tell from the tone of her voice that she was thrilled to have the attention of one of the old men.

"Then," Levine said, "we must strive to preserve the clarity of your leader's vision. This spot, above all of the others, must be a hundred percent of what Boddekker saw in his mind while writing it. Frame for frame, it must duplicate the look and the feel of that cassie!"

"The cassie wasn't *that* close—"

"He's being modest," Harbison said. "He told Mortonsen and I that it was the closest we'd ever come—"

"Mr. Levine gets the idea," I said.

Levine stood, arms out to the group in general and me in particular. "Boddekker, if you had special people in mind for this spot, this is one instance in which we *must* use them! Now you take your group out to one of your favorite haunts, and you have a great time"—He came around the desk and pressed some quick-cash into my hand—"on the agency. Then I want you to work on getting those people together for the commercial shoot."

"Sir, I patterned them after a gang of kids. I'm sure the right actors could—"

"Nonsense! Think of the publicity value! Pembroke, Hall, Pangborn, Levine, and Harris—masters of the advertisement— and humanitarians! Rehabilitators of vicious street gang members . . . five boys who have been given a future thanks to a benevolent helping hand. So what do you say, Boddekker? What do you say to bringing your vision to life and in turn making your agency the envy of the advertising world?"

It would have been easy enough to say *No, there's another way, and that's how it should be done.* It would have been easy enough to tell Levine that Ferman's Devils were a bloodthirsty lot and that my spot had been written more out of frustration than of wanting to sell a few boxes of laundry soap. I didn't even consider the consequences of breaking my promise to the Devils. That was something Levine didn't need to know.

I was ready to say no when I turned and looked at the others. They were ecstatic. Griswold, whom nothing seemed to shake, had confined his excitement to slapping a grinning Deppe on the back. Harbison and Mortonsen were hugging. Dansiger and Bainbridge had the exact same look on their faces, and it was the joy of being so close to someone who had brought them to genius. And poor Sylvester, I thought she was going to cry. If this spot brought World Nano into the Pembroke Hall fold, the resulting bonuses would certainly mean the answer to her chronic indecision.

I gave a sheepish nod and said, "All right."

A cheer went up in the room. And then there was movement, as we all took turns shaking one another's hands and hugging. Dansiger and Griswold each took one of my arms, and they didn't let go until they had paraded me through the entire creative floor, stopping long enough to get the Ride of the Week key from Hotchkiss. Then it was down in an elevator, past a very confused Smilin' Guy, and over to Ogilvy's, where the revelry began.

It didn't take long for me to slip into a detached mental state. It felt as if I were on the outside of everything that was happening, impartially watching as some kind of strange observer. Maybe that was the Silver Screen effect that Levine had been talking about, or maybe it was something different, some kind of psychological warning that I was being overloaded.

I watched as I led everyone in a victory toast, and we hoisted our mugs in the air in honor of each member of the creative group until we'd drained that first round. Then Ogilvy acted like he merely put up with us because we spent a lot of money there, and ultimately filled our tankards again with his complements. This inspired another victory toast, which made Ogilvy an honorary member of our circle.

After that things started to die down and we drifted apart to talk with others or do things to entertain or blow off steam. Mortonsen and Harbison drifted over to Ogilvy's selection of games to look at the programs and test them out, under the guise of playing them. Bainbridge ended up at a round table with Griswold, of all people, who poured her drinks from a bottle he had bought and filled her head with tales of clients who would not listen to reason. Deppe went into the back room and sat down at a piano used on Ogilvy's jazz nights, and he started to play a song of his own creation, a melancholy piece about unrequited love that surely would have been a hit if only he'd let the agency market it for him. Dansiger took a table near the piano and slowly nursed a drink, eyes closed, swaying to Deppe's melody.

Sylvester and I ended up at opposite ends of the bar. She pulled the umbrella from a drink, crushed it in a fist that hadn't yet been feminized, and stared down into the glass, apparently at her reflection in the ice and liquid. Then she put her face in her hands and slumped.

"Another one?" Ogilvy said to me.

I nodded.

"You know," he said, tilting his head in the general direction of Sylvester, "there's some amazing things that science can do. Especially with this Reorientation stuff and hormones, all of that stuff. But you know what it all comes down to, Boddekker?"

"What's that?" I asked, picking up the topped off glass.

"It all comes down to the way God made you in the first place. You can take a brain out of the 'woman' mode, but you can't take the woman mode out of the brain."

"What, you think Sylvester was originally a woman?" This was a hotly debated topic among members of our group when Sylvester wasn't around.

"The way I see it," he said, winking his eye. "You pour enough liquor into them and the original programming surfaces. It's still there, buried deep."

"So what do you see, Ogilvy?"

"I see a sloppy, weepy drunk. Even when she's a man. Men don't usually do that. There have been cases, of course, but they were Reorientation types. Busy going the other way."

"You could be right about that."

"The way I see it, this Reorientation stuff, it's nothing more than a coat of paint. You start scratching at the paint, you see the original finish underneath."

"Or in her case," I gave a sympathetic look Sylvester's way, "the paint is still wet."

Ogilvy studied the look on my face. "Careful," he said.

I stared into his eye and laughed. "It's tough being a leader," I said. "You have to look out for everyone."

"When you're looking," he said, gesturing at his eye patch, "sometimes less is more."

"You trying to tell me something, Ogilvy?"

"Your weepy friend down at the end of the bar. You want to help her?"

"I suppose I should. I'm in a position of leadership."

"I've been serving drinks to her, and that puts me in a unique position, too."

"Is this something that involves an unspoken trust between client and bartender?"

He nodded. "You try to help her now, you're going to get paint on your hands."

I smiled. "Now I understand."

"On the other hand, you give me the word, and I'll go over to her and say, 'Boddekker wants to know if you'd like me to call a bikeshaw for you.' That keeps you at a safe distance but still maintains your position."

"The word is yours."

I finished my drink while I watched Ogilvy. He walked down to the end of the bar, where Sylvester sat mired in her crisis. He folded his arms on the bar, leaned inches from her ear and spoke, casting a glance my way. She sat up straight and looked at me. I shrugged and gave her a sympathetic look. She smiled and nodded at Ogilvy. I flushed with victory even though it had been all my faithful bartender's doing. He patted Sylvester, disappeared for a few moments to use the telephone, then came back to me as I emptied my glass.

"That," he said, "is how it's done."

"Ogilvy," I said, "why in the world are you running a bar? You could be rich."

"I was once. Hated it."

He filled my glass and I made no effort to question his past any further. After a while the bikeshaw driver came in, rain dripping from his clothes, and he escorted Sylvester out. Victory, I thought. Another little victory for my side. May I get Sylvester's vote the next time I need it.

I finished my latest drink and was in the process of trying to figure out how many I'd had when a hand landed hard between my shoulder blades and Deppe climbed onto the stool next to me.

"Fearless Leader," he said. "What's wrong?"

I sucked a cube of ice into my mouth and crushed it between my molars. "What makes you think that something is wrong?"

Deppe pointed. Dansiger had joined Griswold and Bainbridge at the round table and Harbison and Mortonsen were headed that way with a round of drinks.

"People around here don't usually drink alone."

I shrugged.

"You want to talk about it?"

I sighed. "Wet paint."

Deppe gave me a blank look.

"It's a long story. It means that when you try to help someone, you get your hands dirty. At least, I think that's what it means."

"Your hands look clean to me."

This was sticky. How could I explain that he and Dansiger and the others were the ones who were covered with wet paint? I shook my head. "I don't know, Deppe. Don't you think that we're a little premature with the celebration? Now we have to win the hearts of the entire world on behalf of NanoKleen, and there's a lot that could happen between now and then. We're all a bomb in a pet shop away from oblivion."

"Are you always this cheerful after a victory?"

"I mean it. The least of our problems is this street gang that Levine wants."

"You were the one who wanted them, Boddekker."

"No, I didn't. All I did was use them as a model."

"Yeah. Well now the old man wants to use them as the real thing, and he's not going to be happy unless he gets it."

"They're criminals, Deppe. They almost killed me." I laughed. "In fact they would have if I hadn't . . ." I trailed off.

"Hadn't what?"

"Never mind," I said quickly. "Remind me that tomorrow I've got to go through the talent pool data network and find some actors who fit the description we used in the cassie. Or better yet, I'll turn that over to Dansiger. She's the researcher. She'll have a great time working on that."

Deppe slapped me on the back again. "You know, Boddekker, maybe you're missing the point of this little get-together."

"I give up," I told him. "What is it?"

He waved his hand at the table where the members of our group were assembled. "Look at that. Mortonsen and Dansiger are talking to Bainbridge, and they're not even threatening to kill her. Harbison seems to have forgotten that she hates Griswold. Everyone's having a great time."

"Except Sylvester. I sent her home."

"And you. You've got a seventy-five percent success rate with making your creative group happy. That's not bad. If you'd cheer up, you'd improve your average. Isn't that what it's all about?"

"I don't know. I thought it was about selling the client's product." I waved at Ogilvy and asked him to fill my glass. He gave me one of those sideways looks that meant he thought I'd had enough. I promised that this would be my last. He nodded and honored my request. "You know, none of this matters, Deppe. Really. Not the celebrations, not the awards. It all comes down to moving that stuff off the store shelves."

"Boddekker, why do you always do this? You come up with something that's a killer, a sure-fire hit, and you mope about it. Why don't you be easy on yourself for a change?"

"Why don't you go sing that sad song again? The one about the woman who won't talk back to you?"

"Listen to me. If you're so all-fired geared to sell the customer's product, why aren't you working in retail?"

I squinted at him. Ogilvy had been right about my current state. Or maybe Ogilvy had been wrong about Deppe's condition. "I think you're the one who's drunk."

"Why aren't you in retail, Boddekker?"

"Because I'm good at this. Why haven't you formed a band?"

"We're talking about you. You're good at what?"

"Copywriting."

"But if all you wanted to do was sell something for someone, why didn't you go to work for WorldMart, working directly with the consumer?"

"Are you kidding? What I do here pays better."

"Exactly. What you've written for us, Boddekker, it stands to make the agency a tremendous amount of money. We all want Pembroke Hall to make money because that will line our pockets, too. Because the campaign came from our group, the old men are going to make sure that we reap some of the reward. With the agency raking in billions of dollars, you can bet that we're going to all see a nice chunk of change out of that.

"We stand to make a killing on this NanoKleen thing. And now, my friend, you know why I'm not in a band. The bottom line, Boddekker, is money. *That* is the reason why everyone is so happy.

"So the least you can do for us is not ruin the feeling, because as you've so astutely observed, it may not come through. But for tonight, we're all giants in the Pembroke Hall universe. And if you make yourself a little happier so you won't have to be miserable and drink alone, you'll remember that you took this job to make money, and that'll motivate you to do what you can to give old man Levine the spot he wants.

"The one thing you shouldn't do, Boddekker, is stay on that self-righteous high horse of yours and insist on some kind of standard that no agency in the world can keep. That'll screw things up for the rest of us, because sales and money are inextricably tied together." He slapped me on the back again. "No malice meant, buddy. Merely advice, friend to friend."

He left me at the bar with my half-finished drink, ears ringing and head spinning. What he had said was true, but it seemed somehow incomplete, and I wasn't able to think it through. So I raised my hand and waved to get Ogilvy's attention.

"What can I do for you?"

I smiled at him. Given my current state, it probably looked awful. "This business associate I know is in a situation where he is about to get covered with wet paint. Do you think you could be so kind as to call for a bikeshaw that will take him home?"

"Of course," Ogilvy nodded. "I'll have one for you shortly, Mr. Boddekker."

I finished my last drink of the evening and muscled myself off the stool, walking to where my group was gathered. They broke into spontaneous applause as I approached. It was embarrassing, but I looked at Deppe, who smiled and nodded, and I knew I was doing the right thing. Where would I be without all of these people to think for me?

When I got to the table I put one hand on Griswold's shoulder and the other on Harbison's. It looked like a nice, comradely gesture, but it was also utilitarian. I was holding myself up.

"My friends," I said, "a lot of things have happened today, and a lot of things are going to happen. Some of them will be good, some not so good. And whatever happens, my name is going to be prominently mentioned, as saint or sinner, in direct relation to those things.

"Well, I would like all of you to know something. If I fall, I fall alone. I'm a master of bad judgment. I don't think things out. And I let myself get into ridiculous binds." I was looking right at Bainbridge when I said this, but it went right over her head. She was looking back at me, eyes shining with admiration. "But if I rise, I rise on your shoulders. I rise to greatness because you all have helped me. And I'm not going to forget that. If I rise, I take all of you with me. Because—and I really mean this, my friends—I couldn't have done it without you."

There was more applause, and Griswold said, "Hear, hear." I nodded solemnly and the gesture threw me off balance. I pitched sideways and almost ended up in Harbison's lap. I pulled back to my feet as another rain-soaked bikeshaw driver stumbled into the bar.

"Boddekker," he announced.

"And now, if you'll excuse me, I have a rather pressing appointment I need to keep."

There was more applause as I stumbled away, and Deppe appeared beside me, arm around my shoulders, guiding me toward the door. The bikeshaw driver shook his head as we approached, and he and Deppe eased me out into the cool rain and unceremoniously deposited me in the back of the 'shaw.

The vehicle had its canvas hood up to protect me from the rain, which made a reassuring popping sound as it struck the material. I leaned out the door and let drops hit me in the face while Deppe pressed something into the driver's hand. The driver closed the door, and in a moment we eased out into the street.

I blinked the rain out of my eyes. The coldness of it seemed to clear my thoughts. I was numb from everything I'd had to drink, but I realized that my head was spinning not from the toxins in my blood, but from doubt over Levine's pronouncement about Ferman's Devils. There would be nothing terribly wrong about getting actors to play the parts, but Levine was an old man, and you didn't get to be an old man unless you had the sense and the instinct for what sold and what brought in new accounts. Perhaps he had seen something in my script that I hadn't.

On the other hand, hadn't Levine also found the meaning of life in my spot for Witkins-Marrs? No. But he thought it brilliant. And he'd called some of my embarrassing mistakes brilliant as well. It made me wonder what I was doing with my life.

Somehow, I shook off the haze of the alcohol and looked beyond that. It could have been as simple as the fact that Levine liked me, that he saw good qualities in me, and that he had put me on his own personal list of those on the rise to old manhood. Was there anything so terribly wrong with that? Top it off with the fact that he had personally asked a favor of me—a killer spot for NanoKleen—and I had delivered something that went beyond his best expectations. Or perhaps he hadn't expected anything but genius. And if my spot wasn't genius, then I was willing to simply write it off as a piece with overwhelming inspiration.

Or had he merely chosen the spot because he liked me? That couldn't be the case. Whether genius or inspiration, the spot was good, and it avoided the trap that every other advertising agency in the city had fallen into.

I could live with that. But there was still the idea of bringing in Ferman's Devils. Perhaps they did need a break. Maybe it was a lack of money that kept them on the streets, and if some came their way, then they could use it to get out. That must be the case with Jimmy Jazz, who of all of the Devils looked as if he didn't belong in the group. But Jet? Nose? Ferman himself? And what about Rover? It may not have been right, but I judged them as incorrigible. And I most certainly wanted to distance myself from all of them, even Jimmy Jazz, and I wanted them to stay out of my life, in spite of Levine's demands.

I lolled my head back as the bikeshaw moved, the rain pelting slowly on the canvas overhead. The air was thick with moisture and the tires made a pleasing hiss on the wet pavement. I stuck my hand out, let it get wet, then brought it back in and wiped the rain across my face.

Why should I do it? I thought. *Why should I even bother?*

For Deppe and the others? Perhaps. Deppe had been trying to tell me something at Ogilvy's, hadn't he? Something directly relevant to all of this? I strained to remember.

The bottom line, Boddekker, is money.

All right. I knew that. Money was It. Money was All. Money meant the continued functioning of All Things, including Life As We Know It. Was that what Hotchkiss had been trying to say when he saw the end of the world?

Sales and money are inextricably tied together on this one . . . it stands to make the agency a tremendous amount of money.

Okay. Sales equals money equals money for Pembroke Hall. I

had an understanding of that, but something was missing. I tried to think it out again.

Sales equals money. Money for Pembroke Hall. Money for Deppe. Money for Dansiger and Bainbridge and Griswold and Mortonsen and Harbison and poor Sylvester. And money for me. Deppe had made the point that money was the reason I had joined Pembroke Hall. Money to spend at Ogilvy's and on the Smilin' Guy's exquisite creations fashioned from whatever his archaeologist brother had dug out of last century's landfills. Money to spend on Bainbridge so she could misunderstand my intentions. Money to spend on . . .

It is at this point in stories that lightning usually strikes. This would have been the perfect time in mine, for it would add a real sense of drama. We were riding in a rain storm, after all, and the sense of foreboding would have been magnificent had a blue-white flame arced across the sky, making strange specters of all of the buildings that towered over us. And the thunder could have been a deep, booming voice that brought to me instantly the meaning of life, and why the world wasn't about to end.

Instead, the voice was a nasal, reedy tenor. I had been so lost in thought about useless uses for more money that I hadn't noticed the bikeshaw had stopped, and the slickered driver had opened the canvas door for me. And he said in that voice of thunder, "Here's your stop, sir."

Every thought in my head suddenly stopped, in much the same manner that an overheated engine would seize up. My mouth hanging open, I climbed out, and stared up at the building that loomed over me.

"You don't owe me nothin'. Your friend at the bar paid for you."

Then there was a small flicker of lightning, and the building briefly lit up. But instead of seeing a great beast, I saw a flatulent, corpulent parasite that was feeding off of my paychecks.

"Yes," I said, arms out, staring awestruck at the building that out of necessity I called home. "Yes. I understand now." I nodded. "I understand."

Out of the corner of my eye there was movement—the bikeshaw driver was slowly backing away. I turned, and he froze.

"I'm goin'," he said, frightened.

"What's wrong?" I asked.

"Nothin'." He inched off the curb until one groping hand

found the handlebars of his bike. "What about *you*, mister? *You* okay?"

"Why?" I asked quickly.

"You look like you seen something pretty intense. Your eyes are all wild and lit up, like you just saw God."

"God?" I laughed. "No. Not God. Mammon."

PEMBROKE, HALL, PANGBORN, LEVINE, AND HARRIS

"Selling you to the world since 1969"

Offices in Principal Cities: New York - Montreal - Toronto - Sydney - London - Tokyo - Moskva - Beijing - Chicago - Oslo - Philadelphia - Amarillo

CLIENT: »Seslyn Manufacturing		PRODUCT: »Baby Barely Alive!
WRITER: »Boddekker	TIME: »:60	MEDIA: »Video
TITLE: »*Baby Barely Alive!—Introductory Spot*		
PRODUCTION ORDERS:	»Seslyn to ship 10 units here for use in spots. Harris's granddaughter for cute kid?	

AUDIO	VIDEO
ANNOUNCER: It coughs! [*SFX: Baby coughs.*]	*Close-up of baby doll face wincing as it coughs.*
ANNOUNCER: It limps! BABY DOLL: Ma-ma! Ma-ma! Ma-ma!	*Baby doll walking toward camera, arms out. It has a pronounced limp.*
ANNOUNCER: It spits up blood! CUTE GIRL: Uh-oh! Baby's sick again!	*Baby opens its mouth and vomits a congealed mass on its owner, a cute-looking GIRL of about six. The GIRL doesn't look at all alarmed at this, but smiles and obligingly wipes the baby's mouth.*
ANNOUNCER: Yes, it's Baby Barely Alive!, from Seslyn manufacturing!	*Show a full shot of the baby doll outside of its box. Super: Male or Female doll available!*

It's the phenomenal new baby doll that will bring out the Florence Nightingale in any little nurturing parent!	*The cute little* GIRL *picks the doll up, turns it over, pulls down its diaper, and inserts a thermometer.*
Just plug a disease cartridge into Baby Barely Alive's! back and watch it suffer from any one of more than a dozen modern diseases, including Retro-Parvo Simplex IV, Lyme's Variant, Ebola Atlanta, Korean Measles, Norwegian Blight, and UV burns;	*Hand pulls cartridge out of doll's back and inserts another. Super: (Large) 51 diseases now available!!! (Small) Rabies not available in all areas.*
classic sicknesses like Rabies, Radiation Poisoning, Lead Ingestion, Anaphylactic Shock; or extinct diseases like Tuberculosis, Polio, Chicken Pox, Classic Rubella, and Smallpox!	*Series of cuts showing doll having convulsions; sweating profusely; swollen with hives; with ugly skin lesions; etc.*
Baby Barely Alive! comes with all the things you see here, including a starter disease cartridge and a coupon good for the Biblical Diseases cartridge, which includes Leprosy and Bubonic Plague!	*Show baby doll in hospital gown; disease cartridge; coupon; box that converts to a hospital bed; toy thermometer, stethoscope, nurse's hat and spit-up pan. Super: Power pack not included!*
CUTE GIRL: *My baby has Double Pneumonia!* SECOND GIRL: *Well my baby has Jaundice!*	*The cute* GIRL *and* ANOTHER GIRL, *both clad in nurse hats, hug their dolls as they argue.*
ANNOUNCER: Baby Barely Alive! One sick kid . . . for you to love!	*Medium shot of doll. It winces and coughs and a child's hand comes with a tissue to wipe its nose. Super: (Flashing) Baby Barely Alive!*

NINE

On the Way to Somewhere Else

That next Thursday afternoon found Bainbridge and me in front of the Madison Avenue precinct of the New York Police Department. And I was saying, "All right, remember your job. You're the wide-eyed, wondering intern who is all agog at what I'm doing, and you jot down the information if you can find it."

"But—" She had been protesting the plan since I first explained it to her.

"Bainbridge," I interrupted, "you and I both know that for all intents and purposes you're a professional. All you need to do is get your diploma and you'll be making money at a real, thinking job in the career field of your choice. But you're still here to learn something and I need you dumb. Can you play that for a perfectly harmless half hour?"

"But—"

"I know you want to make good first impressions everywhere you go, but this liaison officer—"

"Sergeant Aramanti," she said, reading off of a slate.

"Sergeant Aramanti. Thank you. Odds are that we're never

going to see this guy again. So try to suppress your intelligence and your sense of outrage for a harmless thirty minutes so we can get this over with."

"You're not making this sound very pleasant," she said.

"If you won't do it for the agency, then do it for me. Please."

"All right," she said, but I could tell she wasn't happy about it.

"Think of the money," I said.

Bainbridge muttered something about prostitution as we started up the steps, but as we pushed through the doors into the station house, she turned flighty.

"Gosh, Mr. Boddekker," she said in a squeaking voice, "you mean there's more to research than telling that cute little ferret program where to go and what to do after he gets there?"

I nodded and warned her under my breath, "Don't overdo it."

With that I looked around, and what I saw shocked me. You see police shows on the vid all the time, and they always show dirty, crowded, and disorganized precinct houses. They're always full of complaining victims and loud arguments, and there are too few uniforms around to hold things together. They always look as if everything were about to explode and go wildly out of control, but somehow the uniforms make do and the big bang never comes.

I never expected that a precinct in the heart of advertising country would look like that. I wasn't surprised at the old precinct house, because a lot of places renovated old buildings to keep the old neighborhood atmosphere. But I thought that the inside would be modern and sleek, lots of glass, a notebook on every desk. I thought the victims would all have a certain amount of dignity and would quietly take their number and wait in line to tell their story. And I thought the criminals themselves would all be well-dressed—albeit sinister-looking—white collar types who could send a shiver through your spine with a slight upward curl of a mustached lip.

It was not to be. Precinct Madison took it's cue straight from the citycop vids. It was bedlam inside. And like on the vids, too few people were coping with keeping the situation under control. I put my arm around Bainbridge, and she took the cue to huddle close to my side as I picked my way through the din. We made our way to a desk where a beleaguered sergeant was trying to sort out a disagreement with a handful of street vendors.

"Excuse me," I said, wiggling in between a pair who smelled strongly of smoked sausage. "I have an appointment with Sergeant Aramanti."

The desk sergeant looked at me as if I were a savior who had failed him at the last minute. He gave me a disgusted look and pointed with a thick finger down a long hall.

"Which door?" I asked.

"Only door," he said.

I took Bainbridge by the hand and started down the hall toward a wooden door into which was set opaque glass. We wove in and out between arguing couples, avoided a bench that was bolted to the floor and to which several toughs had been manacled, and I opened the door and walked through without giving it a thought. I half-expected to see a room full of cluttered desks, with ancient electric typewriters and stacks of actual paper on which to transcribe data.

Fortunately, this room looked like what my expectations of a modern police precinct should be. Newer desks, notebooks everywhere, master screens flashing new information or pictures of known felons. I approached the first desk, behind which sat a heavy-set man with a round face and thinning hair.

"Excuse me, could you please tell us where to find Sergeant Aramanti? I've got an appointment—"

The man smiled and stood, holding out a pudgy hand. "I'm Sergeant Aramanti. And you must be Mr. Bollocker—"

"Boddekker," I corrected. "And this is Mez Bainbridge, an intern with my agency."

"Pleased," he said, taking her hand.

"It's really nice to meet a real, live policeman," Bainbridge gushed. I gave her an evil look out of the corner of my eye.

Aramanti brushed his hands together as if sloughing off something unwanted and circled around his desk. "Now, Mr. Boddekker, I understand that you're interested in taking a look at the PerpNet program as research for a commercial?"

"That's correct. A singles service has hired us to come up with a memorable campaign, and I thought I might take the old law-and-order route."

Aramanti looked at me, not understanding.

"I thought we'd do an ad," I continued, "that shows a woman giving a description to an officer, and the officer is entering it into that computer base of yours—"

"The PerpNet."

"The PerpNet. Exactly."

"The PerpNet hardware is this way," he said, leading us across the large room. "If you don't mind my asking, how is all of this going to tie in to your commercial for a singles service?"

I rubbed my hands as we walked. "Well, I was thinking of showing this woman at a police station, and she's with an officer, and they're going through the PerpNet. And she's describing how this guy looks, and the officer is entering the information. Finally, they get a fix on the guy, and the woman says, 'Yes, that's him.' The officer says, 'What did he do?' and she says, 'Nothing, I want to marry him.' Then the narrator comes in saying, 'There's more than one way to find Mr. Right. Try XYZ Singles Service.' "

"So you need to find out exactly how the PerpNet works."

"Precisely."

"Nice," laughed Aramanti. "Only who is XYZ Singles Service?"

"A hypothetical name," I said. "I can't divulge the actual client right now."

"Oh," he nodded. "Right." He stopped at a terminal connected to a wall-sized vid screen. "Well, Mr. Boddekker, if you and Mez Bainbridge would like to have a seat, we'll get things warmed up and ready to go. Why don't you form a mental description of someone you work with and we'll bring it up on the screen?"

"Heavens," I said. "I couldn't do that. What if he were wanted in Colorado or something? Couldn't I make someone up?

"There are problems with doing that," Aramanti said. "Your mind will shift and you won't give what the computer calls a consistently plausible description."

"How about the man in the restaurant?" suggested Bainbridge.

"Restaurant?" I said.

"You know." She elbowed me in the side. "That awful one who was causing trouble, and they threw him out?" Another elbow.

"Oh!" I exclaimed. "Great idea! Only it wasn't really a man. More of a boy, really."

Aramanti pulled a keyboard into his lap and rattled the keys with his fingers. "Approximate age?"

I shrugged. "Sixteen. Seventeen."

"Why aren't you using a voxlink?" Bainbridge asked.

An elongated oval filled the screen in front of us. "This software confuses very easily," said the sergeant. "We've found it easier to control if we enter data manually. Now." He gestured to a line of characters in the upper left hand corner of the screen. "I've set this up on a citywide net. That means if a perp—excuse me—*alleged* perpetrator is on record anywhere in the nine boroughs, it'll pull him up based on your description. Unless he's from out of town, in which case we can go specifically into different states, or any combination of three states, or the national net, or the international—"

"Can you keep it to this borough?" asked Bainbridge. "I don't think this guy is an international criminal."

Aramanti stroked a few keys. "Manhattan borough, male, all racial categories, ages sixteen to twenty-one."

"Caucasian," I said.

Aramanti nodded. "You're getting the hang of it. Manhattan white males, sixteen to twenty-one."

The screen flickered. ready. Aramanti pushed the keyboard aside and laid his palm on a tracking ball.

"Head shape."

I closed my eyes and brought up an image of Ferman. "Light bulb."

When I opened my eyes, Aramanti was staring at me. "I've been giving demos of this for six years, and I've never heard of someone with a head shaped like a light bulb."

Even Bainbridge was giving me an incredulous look that said, *Who is supposed to be the one hiding his intelligence?*

"From straight on," I said, "his face was skinny. Emaciated. His head looked big, but down around his jaw and chin, it was skinny."

"Skull shaped," Aramanti said. His palm moved the ball. The oval started to swell at the top and cave in at the bottom.

"There!" I said.

Aramanti clicked a button. The shape froze. "That?"

"That."

"Good. Hair color?"

"I couldn't tell."

He looked at Bainbridge, who shrugged and said, "Sorry. I wasn't there."

"Maybe you'd better pick someone from your office."

"No. The reason I couldn't tell was because he had it all shaved off. It was a thin fuzz."

Aramanti worked the program. The top of the oval started to grow hair.

"Hold the length," I said. "A little shorter. There."

"Light colored or dark?"

It was coming back to me now. "Light. And he had scars on his head. A whole bunch of them, crisscrossing. Looked like a map of the subway system."

With one hand he tapped the keyboard until extensive scarring [cranial area] appeared in a lower corner of the screen.

"Forehead topography," he said.

We worked our way from the pimply moonscape of Ferman's forehead to the defoliated forest of whiskers on his chin, and his face slowly took shape, bigger than life, on the screen. When I finally stopped to really look the image over, it took my breath away. It was as if I were still there, lying on the street, looking up into those cold, malevolent eyes.

". . . the boys and me would have to come over and break every bone in your body."

"Impressive, isn't it?" said Aramanti.

"You'll never know how impressive," I said.

"Wait." There were some clicks from Aramanti and the head shrunk and positioned itself toward the top of the screen. Aramanti gave me a heavy black glove with some kind of device fastened to its back. "Now, Mr. Boddekker, I'd like you put this on and walk over to the screen. I want you to look at this gentleman's face very carefully, and I want you to show me with your hand approximately how tall he was."

I rose and stepped to the screen, looking back at the Sergeant.

"Look at the screen," he smiled.

I did. Ferman's head was hovering down by my knees. I looked over at my gloved hand. It was hanging by my side, bathed in a red glow from a tracking laser.

"You've got to be kidding."

I raised my hand over my head. Ferman's head bounded up to the top of the screen.

"I'm not kidding, Mr. Boddekker."

I experimentally waved my hand and watched the disembodied head dance.

"They all have to play with it once they see how it works," Aramanti told Bainbridge.

"Ah," she said. "In the commercial, the woman won't do that, thus giving the impression that she's been through this before."

"Good idea," said Aramanti.

"That's why we came," Bainbridge replied.

"All right," I said, holding my hand below my chin. "This joker came to right about here—"

"Don't think about it too much. This program assumes that you're determining height from the eyes, so it automatically puts them at your hand's level and corrects from there."

I heard him hit a key and Ferman's head locked into place, and a bright red line drawing of a body filled in from the chin down.

"Physical dimensions," he said.

I looked at the image. It had the head of a man, the body of a penguin.

"Skinny. Small boned. Slight." The image changed. "Skinnier," I said. "Skinnier still."

"This guy gave you a hard time?"

"He tried. Is there some way you can make that skinny in proportion to the thinness of his face?"

The image redrew itself.

"Perfect."

"How about his clothes?"

"No shirt. Uh, a military surplus flak jacket."

The image filled in with a camouflage pattern.

"White," I said. "The Norwegian War."

It corrected.

"Pants were, uh, full-length denims, and full-length gangster boots. That's it."

"Thank you. You can sit down."

The image began to waver as I stepped away.

"It's thinking."

I never made it to my chair. Suddenly the image began to correct itself. The head sprouted a familiar network of scars, and the acne on the forehead rearranged itself. The eyes shifted apart slightly, the nose grew straighter, the fuzz on the chin filled out. The gang logo appeared on the flak jacket and oil stains filled out the jeans. And down the left side of the screen, a description appeared.

```
NAME               McKluskey, Francis Herman
AGE                17
RAC                CAUC
HGT                5F2I
WGT                99P
EYECOL             BLU
HAIRCOL            BLN
SEX                MALE
SEXPREF            UNDET [HETERO LEANINGS]
CHARGES            BATTERY I [SUSPECT 23/ACCUSE 11/
                      CONVICTED 3]
                   BATTERY II [9/7/1]
                   BATTERY III [5/2/0]
                   BATTERY IV [2/0/0]
                   ROBBERY I [18/13/2]
                   ROBBERY II [12/6/0]
                   ROBBERY III [4/0/0]
                   BURGLARY [1/1/1]
                   SHOPLIFTING [6/2/0]
                   THEFT BIKESHAW [1/0/0]
                   SALE OF STOLEN GOODS [4/0/0]
                   WEAPON POSSESS I [6/2/0]
                   WEAPON POSSESS II [1/1/0]
                   CRIMINAL MUTILATION [5/2/0]
                   UNDERAGE LIQUOR POSSESS [NA/20/
                      13]
                   GANG MEMBERSHIP [1/1/1]
                   GANG LEADERSHIP [1/1/1]
                   GANG FRANCHISE HOLDER [1/1/1]
                   ATTEMPT RAPE [8/3/1]
                   FORCIBLE RAPE [1/0/0]
                   FORCIBLE ORAL COP [2/2/0]
                   FROTTAGE [SUBWAY] [11/6/2]
                   FROTTAGE [OTHER] [2/2/0]
                   BUY SEX [NA/8/6]
JAILTIME           271 [OUT OF LAST 1000 DAYS]
FINES              $21,464,938.17 [IN LAST 1000 DAYS]
FINESPAID          $00,026,004.26
KNOWN ACCOMPLICES
        DONALD ALBERT ALEXANDER [DECEASED]
        MARTIN MALCOLM GEORGESON
        JAMES JOSEPH JASZCZEK
        RUDOLPH ALAN PIERPONT III
```

PETER RICHARD SWISHER
DREW STANLEY THOMAS [DECEASED]
KEVIN MACKEE YOUNG [DECEASED]
FOR FURTHER INFORMATION SEE CRIMINAL FILE
#FHM160610/221NY-16-1844/MANH.

The sight took my breath away. There was Ferman, life-sized, surrounded by the story of his life.

"Pretty impressive, isn't it?"

"It certainly is," I said. I stared hard at his total fines. I could have bought my house in Princeton with those fines! I felt pangs of jealousy until I realized that this was not his personal fortune. It was his debt to society.

Aramanti was nodding with pride. "It's a really incredible piece of software. Except when it gets interrupted by those stupid intrusive commercials."

"I don't have anything to do with those," I laughed nervously. I looked at Bainbridge, who looked urgently from Aramanti to the screen. I gave her a slight nod and stepped right up to the image and reached out my hand. "This picture is so clear—"

"Don't touch it!"

It worked. Aramanti came out of his seat, almost involuntarily. "Please," he said, almost sheepishly for having shouted. "There are sensors in it for the glove mechanism and some other things."

"Sorry. I didn't mean to panic you." I stepped to the side and he turned away from the screen. I positioned myself between Aramanti and Bainbridge. "Listen, Sergeant, I really appreciate you taking your time to show this to us. I think it's going to *make* this commercial."

"You'll have to send me a copy of the script," he grinned.

"Absolutely," I said. "Without a doubt. And there's something else I'd like you to have . . . a little token, actually . . ." I reached into my pocket and pulled something out. As his eyes fell to my hand, I saw the screen flicker and the display of data changed.

"It's a bubblechip," he said.

"Right," I said. "My agency handles the SOBs, and this is a test recording of their newest album, *Songs We Wish They'd Written*—"

He held up his hand. "That's all right," he said. "Really."

Doesn't anybody like these guys? I thought. "Actually, this is

a rarity. This is a test pressing of the music. There are no subliminals on it and the commercials haven't been inserted between
the songs yet.''

His face brightened. "So it's a collector's item."

"Yeah." Right. For this particular group, maybe in a thousand
years.

"Well." He let me drop the block into his hand. "I might be
able to find some use for it."

"Great." I let him shift the block to his other hand, then
offered mine to shake. "And again, thank you so much. You'll
never know how much you've helped us."

Bainbridge and I parted company with the good sergeant, and
the minute we were out the door and down the steps of the station,
I started in.

"Did you find it? Was it on the next screen?"

Bainbridge kept her eyes straight ahead. "Boddekker, I don't
mind telling you that I've got some doubts about this."

"Don't do this to me. I had doubts too, but—"

"Didn't you see his record? You saw that list! He should be in
jail!"

"But he's not."

"He's a *criminal*—"

"Clarity of vision, Bainbridge. Where were you when Levine
made his speech? This is a chance to rehabilitate—"

"Boddekker, drastic Reorientation wouldn't rehabilitate this
McKluskey guy. He's incorrigible! All of those horrible things—
and he's only a boy! Seventeen years old!"

"Yeah? Well you're no seasoned sage with the wisdom of the
ancients yourself."

"Don't start on me, Boddekker—"

I grabbed her by the arm and pulled her to a stop. "Do you
want Pembroke Hall to be there after you've graduated?"

"Don't use that line on me. There'll always be a Pembroke
Hall."

"Yes, but will it exist as an advertising agency or as some
dinky outfit that makes media buys on satellite radio nets and
places ads between cuts of the next SOBs album? There's a big
difference there, Bainbridge, one that could actually come about.
Do you know how many people have already quit over this one
account?"

She looked right at me with bovine eyes. "I love it when you say my name."

I felt a massive scowl building on my face. I fought to hold it back. "Bainbridge, give me the information," I said. "Bainbridge, it's going to be all right. *Bainbridge, give me that address.*"

She brought up a slate, her notes hand-stylused onto the surface. "He lives in Queens," she said, dreamily.

I grabbed the device out of her hand. "Queens. If there's one thing I hate, it's a criminal who commutes."

We continued down the street and vanished into the first subway entrance we found. When we emerged, we were in a renovated part of Queens, all high-tech and strip malls. Bainbridge emerged from her daze long enough to complain of hunger. My guess is that she wanted to end up at a late, lingering lunch where the lights were low and the conversation was in soft tones. The most I was willing to oblige her was a nearby Beijing Buddy's for a bowl of rice and highly spiced meat. But from the look in her eyes you'd have thought that the two of us were alone in the most elegant restaurant in all of NYC.

From there we caught a bikeshaw that took us into the older part of the borough. There were still rows of identical houses with minuscule artificial turf or stone garden front yards. The occasional skeletal automobile was hollowed out and planted with the latest strains of acid-tolerant flowers; and with the exception of the occasional graffiti, or trash spilling into the gutters, the neighborhood looked well kept. The skies were overcast on this spring day, and there was a smell in the air that I couldn't describe—a chemical sweetness and smoke from outdoor cooking and the sweat of bikeshaw drivers. It all said neighborhood to me.

"How can people live like this?" Bainbridge shivered.

"What do you mean by that?" I asked. "You should have seen this place before."

"Before what?"

"Don't they make you take Retrohistory at the university? This place was a battleground—racial, economic—you name it. All of NYC was at one time."

"Oh," she said bluntly. "Yeah. The Period of Transition. I read about that."

Reading about it, indeed. Of course, it couldn't have meant anything to her. She hadn't been seven years old during the Period of Transition. And her father, fearful that the world was going to lapse into anarchy, hadn't taken her out into the Connecticut woods and taught her how to aim the red dot of a laser sight at a milk carton filled with sand, saying, "Imagine that's some terrorist out to get your mother." And once tiny hands could squeeze a trigger and hit it nine times out of ten, her father hadn't said to her, "There. Now if something happens to me, you can protect your mom and sis."

Before I could turn the sudden upwelling of emotion into a retort, the bikeshaw glided to a halt and the driver said, "Here you are."

I told him to wait and stepped out with Bainbridge right behind me. I was looking at a clonal house, one that had obviously grown from a stray brick that had fallen off of the one next door, and in turn it had dropped a brick from which the house on the other side had grown, and on down the entire block, and the block after that, and the block after that. A nondescript house in a neighborhood of nondescript houses, somebody's red brick dream.

I walked up to a small boy of about ten who was sitting among the sea of front yard stones, driving a toy ATV across the landscape—one that had been successfully launched by Mauldin and Kress. The boy was making fearful noises, no doubt in his mind exterminating great hordes of enemies, and as my shadow fell across the truck, he looked up with a start.

"Hello. Is this the McKluskey residence?"

The boy's eyes widened with fear. His hair was thick and shaggy. His eyes were bright and his face fat. There was no more resemblance between the boy and Ferman than between Ferman and me.

"I'm looking for Ferman." Nothing. Then I realized that perhaps Ferman was a *nom de guerre*. "Uh . . . I mean . . . Francis?"

The boy grabbed his truck and clutched it to his chest.

"Frank? Frankie?"

The boy leapt to his feet and ran screaming into the house.

"Nice going," said Bainbridge.

"What would you have done?"

"Not walk up to a strange kid and engage him in conversation."

"Is this the right house?"

She showed me her notes on the slate. Her number matched the number on the house. The street name matched what she had stylused.

"Let's go straight to the boss," I said.

We walked up four concrete steps to the porch. I raised my fist to knock, and Bainbridge stopped me. She gestured to a brass plate that was part of the doorbell. I nodded and aimed my finger at the button. Bainbridge stopped me again.

"Can't you read?"

I looked at the button plate again. Engraved on it was the name *Zucker*.

"I thought you said this was the right address."

"It's the right *last known address*," she corrected.

"Great. Now you tell me." I looked at the name plate again. "Francis Herman McCluskey Zucker?"

"It doesn't cry momma, does it?"

I shook my head.

"What now?"

I pushed on the doorbell. "We find out what we can from the current resident."

It took two more rings before someone answered the door, a plump, matronly woman with a wrinkled face, the beginnings of gray in her black hair, and eyes which revealed her suspicion by darting quickly between Bainbridge and me. She kept her distance by speaking to us through the screen.

"Yes?"

"Good afternoon," I said. "My name is Boddekker, and I'm a group leader from Pembroke Hall—"

"What do you want," she interrupted, "coming here and scaring my son like that?" From inside the house I could hear the sounds of children playing.

"My associate and I are trying to locate someone," I said. "Perhaps he was a former resident. I was thinking you might be able to help us?"

"Why should I want to help you? Are you from the police?"

"No. Certainly not. We've got a job for someone that could bring quite a bit of money, and we're trying to locate him."

Eyes back to darting, back and forth, back and forth.

"Who?"

"Francis Mc—"

The woman's eyes rolled back in her head as if she was in the throes of a seizure, and a low gargle escaped from her lips. Her hand struck the screen door and popped it open, and her head snaked out. With an evil glare, she spit at my feet, and gave me a hateful look.

"Frankie. You and the whole world are looking for Frankie! He owe you money? You want him to sell your drugs? He pimp you a woman who gave you a disease? The pain in your stones is your curse for knowing him!" She spit again. "I have no son named Francis! Francis is dead, may Satan keep his soul forever! And you . . ." She locked eyes with Bainbridge, and then with me. What I saw was pure freezing cold. "If you know what is best, you will leave him dead. Grave digging—it is a crime in more than one way."

With that, she disappeared inside the house and slammed both doors.

"Well," said Bainbridge, after a moment for the shock to wear off. "That was a cheerful little cupcake—"

From inside the house, the woman's voice shouted. "If I open this door and see you again, I am calling the police."

"I would say, interview over," Bainbridge said.

"I agree."

Bainbridge made it back to the bikeshaw first. Me, I was limping—a psychological limp from being crushed by the jaws of defeat. Bainbridge ordered the driver to take us back to the subway station, and I leaned my head back and closed my eyes, trying to think.

You've just lost your career to a young upstart who slept with your boss. And how do you deal with it? By taking a double strength dose of your favorite forget-it-all formula from Daily—

"Boddekker?"

I opened one eye. Bainbridge was peering down at me.

"What are you going to do now?"

"Think about it." I closed my eye.

It's all too much, isn't it? Your wife has gone off with some Reoriented waiter, your house has been repo'ed by greeners, and the job you thought you trusted wants you to transfer to the Mongol States. You need a getaway—not the kind of temporary escapes that you get from your jones, but a real escape, the kind you can get at TransMind—

"Boddekker?"

I opened my eye again. "Yes?"

"Maybe it worked out better this way, huh? I mean, this Mc-Kluskey character, he was someone that not even his mother loved."

I couldn't decide which point to contend with—that things were better off without Francis Herman McKluskey, or that Ferman's mother probably still *did* love him. I decided not to say anything.

"Really, Boddekker, don't you think that things worked out for the best? Didn't they? Boddekker?"

Sometimes it's a state of mind you're in—sometimes it's something that won't leave you alone, but never, you can never quite put your finger on it. You can sense its effect on you, you know it's something you've been through, but it's never easy to define, not really, not until you're ready to face it head on. It's like the feeling you get when—

"Boddekker?"

This time I popped both eyes open to glare at her. "What now?"

"We're at the subway."

I sheepishly climbed out, paid and tipped the driver, and took Bainbridge down the steps to meet the train. She chattered inanely about something someone had said in a class she had taken: ". . . speaking of Retrohistory, wasn't this terrible and that awful, and do you suppose this or that really happened the way it did?" I said all the right things in all the right places, and it only served to endear me to that girl.

I was not capable of much else. I was starting to develop a thick headache and I was trying to think of those spots that had started to write themselves during the bikeshaw ride. Two of them had completely faded away, but there was a third, something for Witkins-Marrs, perhaps in time to place on *Songs We Wish They'd Written.* Something about confrontation.

My head snapped up from its slump. My headache was gone. I felt Bainbridge squeeze my hand, her fingers interlocked with mine. How long had she been doing that?

"Are you all right?"

"Fine," I said. I could feel my heart pounding in my chest. I knew what I had to do.

"Is everything okay, Boddekker?"

"Fine," I swallowed. "Where are we now?"

"Going under the river. Listen, are you sure everything's okay, Boddekker?"

What was I supposed to say? *I hate it when you say my name.*

"Seriously. All of a sudden your hand went clammy."

I used that as an excuse to break her grip on me. I held it up and looked at it. "Actually, I think I'm in cardiac arrest." Then, before she could speak, "I'm kidding."

She hadn't shrunk away from me yet but it was on her mind.

"Bainbridge, why don't you go ahead and go back to the office? I'm not feeling well, and I thought I'd head back to my apartment."

Was that the wrong thing to say. "If you're feeling that bad, I've got a cure for you that's better than any Heal-O-Mat—"

I winced. Florence Nightingale rides again. "Actually," I said, "I don't feel *that* bad." Maybe I could lose her at the office.

"You do look pale, Boddekker. Maybe we should get out and walk? It's kind of stuffy down here, crowded, hot . . ."

My mind raced with possibilities. There was one, right there, which I'd seen in an old vid. "All right. Next stop."

That came two minutes later. People started lining up to get off. I moved sluggishly, letting part of a crowd form, then rose and got in line with Bainbridge. The doors opened and people began to stream out. As we neared the door, I swore and told her that I'd left my notebook on the seat. I neatly stepped out of line, and the rush of people swept Bainbridge helplessly out of the car, calling "Boddekker! Boddekker!" like some strange mutant bird.

"But you didn't bring your notebook!"

From inside the car, I turned to her as the doors closed. "You're right," I said under my breath.

The train pulled out of the station, leaving her standing on the platform. Her last sight was of me giving her a helpless shrug. Then I sat, stuffed my hands in my pockets, and laughed.

She was probably in a state of alarm by now. No doubt she'd head back to Pembroke Hall and tell everyone that I was lost forever with some kind of nervous breakdown on the subway. She might even go back to Sergeant Aramanti and file a missing persons report. And maybe she'd end up marrying the good sergeant, providing I never returned.

Well. There was always that possibility.

I changed trains and eventually stepped onto a platform that was quickly emptying itself of the commuter crowds. On the way out, I stopped to buy a download of the *Times* and slipped it into my pocket. Not that I was planning on reading it. It was my way of killing time.

It was dark as I walked into Columbus Circle. The few people left on the street were in a hurry to get where they were going and didn't have time to warn the mental case waiting in the street. And this mental case was pondering how the city's personality could change so drastically, from something alive and vital during the day, to something dark and undead at night.

Finally, the last of the surviving street lamps flickered on and the mental case started to walk. I went north from the Circle toward Amsterdam, trying to remember the names of the gangs that Ferman had told me and where they ran. It was useless. All I could remember were the Sluts, who seemed to range south of here, and the infamous Nancy Boys, who seemed to be outcast and ranged wherever it pleased them. I wasn't doing well at this. My only hope was to get where I was going and find the Devils before too much happened. Otherwise, I would be one of the few in my profession who had actually died for his art.

A sense of calm started to wash over me as I approached Amsterdam. This was the place. All I had to do was make my way to sixtieth, sixty-first, and find a place to wait. And when I saw one of the Devils—preferably Jimmy Jazz or Jet—I would pass on the good news. Yes, this was going to work.

I turned the corner and ran headlong into a ghost. I stepped back, screamed, took another step back, and found my back against the side of a building.

The ghost spoke. "Sorry, man," it said.

The ghost approached seven feet tall. Under the dim streetlights I could see a long, pointed head, black, which culminated in a luminescent skull-face with empty sockets for eyes and a gaping hole of a mouth. The skull seemed to bob and weave in the air, then came toward me.

"Hey," it said. "You're a *civilian.*"

I blinked. The image became clearer. The skull was actually attached to something, a body clad in dark clothing. The eye sockets were not empty, and the mouth was actually smiling. "You're—"

"Pinhead," said the ghost, and it managed a courteous bow. "You'd better get out of here right now, buddy. I been on a probe of Devil territory, and—"

"The Devils?" I asked. "They're here?"

The Pinhead cocked his large head. "You're looking—"

Before he could finish, there were cries from Amsterdam. "There he is!"

"He's with another one!"

"Get them!"

The Pinhead grabbed me by the shoulders, spun me around, and started to push me back the way I had come. "Run," he said, "if you know what's good—"

I started to protest but there was a loud crack and the Pinhead stumbled and fell into my arms. I was carried away from the sound by the momentum. I caught him under the arms and lifted, pulling us both against the side of a building.

"It's all right," I said. "I know them. I'll get you safe passage—"

The Pinhead looked at me with sad eyes. He opened his mouth to speak, a spasm passed through him, and a torrent of hot liquid sprayed my chest and arms and face. His head went limp and fell on my shoulder, and in a strange moment of epiphany, I realized that the long point of his head was his own hair, carefully shellacked and painted.

I stepped back, arms limp, and the Pinhead hit the sidewalk with a wet thud. There were footsteps from the corner now, and shadows filled the street in front of me.

"Score one *Pin*head!" one shouted.

"And we got us a civilian to boot!" said another.

"Ferman!" I shouted. "This is Boddekker!" I looked down at myself. I couldn't tell what was covering me in that poor light, but judging from the warmth and the smell of it, I didn't really want to know. "Don't you think this little stupid game of yours has gone far enough?"

"Ferman?" asked one voice. "*Fur* Man?"

One by one, they stepped under a pool of light from one of the street lamps.

"You picked the wrong time of day for *Fur* Man."

They were all anorexic skinny with long blond hair. Sunken pale faces with translucent skin that cried out for sunshine. Their eyes were lined with smudged mascara and their lips were bright with red lipstick. The flesh-tone bandages some of them had on their faces stood out like dark patches. They wore tank tops with brassieres underneath, leather pants and black riding boots, and they carried an assortment of weapons—including a smoking gun—in their immaculately manicured hands.

I swallowed, remembering Ferman's words of warning.

"Sluts?" I asked.

"You wish," laughed one.

"This ain't your night a-tall," laughed another.

Now I was paralyzed. *Nancy Boys.*

It was futile, but I turned and started to run. I heard another crack and waited for the pain of something biting into me but it never came. There was a whoop from behind and the sound of running. I pumped my legs hard, but the fear and the smell were getting to me and I could feel myself weakening. Once again, I had the feeling that my pursuers could have caught me whenever they wanted. I found myself wondering if these guys would fall for the same line I had used on Ferman.

There was another crack as I neared Columbus, and I had the strange sensation that something had whizzed past from in front of me rather than from behind. I tried to blink the tears out of my eyes, tried to look, but it was too overwhelming. What strength that remained ebbed, and I collapsed in the middle of the street.

I had closed my eyes and was waiting to die when something grabbed the collar of my coat and lifted me off of the ground. There was something familiar and reassuring in its strength, but I couldn't bring myself to open my eyes.

"We'll be taking it from here, Mr. Boddekker."

And then, for better or worse, I knew that Ferman's Devils had come to save me.

"Selling you to the world since 1969"

Offices in Principal Cities: New York - Montreal - Toronto - Sydney - London - Tokyo - Moskva - Beijing - Chicago - Oslo - Philadelphia - Amarillo

CLIENT: »Jaluka's Produce		PRODUCT: »Jaluka's Prunes
WRITER: »Boddekker	TIME: »:60	MEDIA: »Audio
TITLE: »*Anchor Jingle*		
PRODUCTION ORDERS:	»See notes below	

CHORUS: *Buy! Jaluka's! Prunes!*

NOTES FOR ANCHOR JINGLE: Deppe to compose a 57-second instrumental jingle emulating the current grind style. At :28.5, the music comes to a complete, cold stop, and the above Chorus (:03 in length) is inserted. Immediately following (at :31.5), the instrumental returns to fill out the :60.

This Anchor jingle is to be used for all flights. After a maximum saturation has been achieved (approximately six months from now), the variant jingles will be introduced.

TEN

Urban Barbecue

The fight was the most beautiful thing I'd ever seen in my life.

Ever so calmly, Jet lowered his arm—he was holding me up with one hand—and set me down on the ground by a large garbage Dumpster. I started to turn as soon as my feet touched down, but he forced me into a sitting position.

"Mr. Boddekker. This time you're lucky we found you."

I instantly understood and flopped down, using the object he had chosen as a shelter.

"This won't take long," he said, then walked into the middle of the street where Ferman and the others were facing off against the Nancy Boys. From my vantage point I could see that one of the NBs was down, sprawled in the street with blood leaking from a neat hole in the middle of his forehead.

"You ranking cowards!" shouted one. "You killed our dog!"

"He got better than he deserved," Ferman shouted back. "Bringing a gun into our zone, spilling a Pinhead here."

"Yeah, I forgot you guys got some kind of treaty with them.

Well, we'll take care of them soon's we take care of you for what you done to Lassie.''

"At least Lassie won't burn with the memory of hosting a street barbecue like you're going to do, Binjii.''

Binjii grabbed his crotch and shook it. ''The pleasure is going to be *mine,* Fur Man, when I inject you full of what I got. Three hard diseases, that's what it is, and you gonna be *begging* them to take your application at Ethical Solutions.''

The two groups were about ten feet apart now, spread across the length of the street. The Devils were outnumbered eight to five, but it didn't seem to bother them since the gun-carrying member of the Nancy Boys was lying dead in the street. Looking back at this particular moment, I wonder why I didn't quietly slip away, making my way back home through Pinhead territory. If I'd brought news to them that one of their own had died saving me from the Nancy Boys, they surely would have given me safe passage. I may have even put them in the NanoKleen commercial. But that never occurred to me as I watched this small storm brew. I couldn't bring myself to leave the scene—and only a small part of it was the possibility that the numerically superior Nancy Boys might win and chase me down again. There was this odd fascination as Ferman moved and taunted them, and the other Devils circled around him in carefully choreographed moves. I was sure I would never see anything like this again.

Ferman locked his hands behind his back, and with chest out, thrust his lower lip at Binjii. He dismissed his opponent's threat with a loud *"Fah!"* and then sneered one of his own. "Another idle threat,'' he said in a masterfully controlled tone. "You couldn't find it with a magnifying glass and tweezers.''

Binjii blinked. I could tell that one had hurt him, which struck me as strange, considering their name and way of dress. "You're going to *bleed* for that one, Fur Man. And for that one I might let you live so you can suffer with what we're gonna do to you.''

Ferman's eyes closed to half-mast and he opened his mouth in a wide, wide yawn, covering it over only when he was halfway through. Then he turned on his heel and stood with his back to the Nancy Boys. "Hey, Jimmy Jazz, is it true that Binjii gets a nose bleed every twenty-eight days?''

Wham! With one deft blow, Binjii had been emasculated—some members of his own gang had laughed at that one. He shrieked at them to stop and then jumped Ferman.

Rather, he *tried* to jump Ferman. By the time Binjii was airborne, Ferman had stepped left and turned, and a sawed-off broomstick had fallen into his hand from beneath his Norwegian White flak jacket. Binjii tried to correct but landed hard, impaling his solar plexus on the end of the stick. His eyes bugged out and his face instantly paled, and he tried to fold in half. Ferman grabbed a double handful of tank top and held him up straight, then reached under the shirt and pulled hard, bringing out a thin, red lace support bra. The other Devils cheered as Ferman stuffed the garment into his pocket. Then Ferman made a rasping sound, blew phlegm into Binjii's face, and pushed him to the ground.

"Supper time, Nose!" he called.

With a shout of glee, Nose pulled a long hunting knife from his boot and leapt to the incapacitated Nancy Boy.

Ferman looked back at the other seven and shook his head sadly. "Is that all the better you can do? My *reader* can outfight you hemorrhoids." He turned from them again and started walking away, saying, "Jimmy Jazz. Finish them off."

Jimmy Jazz gave a confident nod and took a step toward them, adjusting his glasses.

"You won't need to take those off," Ferman said. "There's only seven of them."

"Thanks." Jimmy Jazz took another step and the Nancy Boys line broke, screaming murderously as they threw their weapons down and pounced on the Devils. Jimmy crouched as the first one neared and drove his fist into the attacker's groin. The attacker folded, Jimmy caught him over his shoulder, stood, turned, and dumped him on the asphalt. Then two more were on Jimmy, but suddenly Jet was there. That huge right fist smashed square in the middle of one face and then another, and their owners went limp and collapsed. Rover ran to intercept one wearing a Hateful T-shirt, and was instantly confused by a rapid succession of punches to his face. Rover turned away, and the Nancy Boy jumped on his back, kicking as if he were spurring a horse. Rover reached back, grabbed a handful of hair, and pulled the assailant's head down. He sucked an ear into his mouth, there was a flash of white, and the Nancy Boy screamed, flailing his hands. Rover grabbed one, stuffed fingers into his mouth, and bit down again.

Then Jimmy Jazz shouted, "Treaty violation!" and everyone froze. In that moment I managed a quick tally. Counting the one who had been shot in the head, six were down. Nose was still straddling Binjii, intent on his surgery. The remaining Devils were still standing, none the worse for wear except for Rover, whose face looked seriously bloody. It was debatable, however, whose blood he was wearing.

Only three Nancy Boys were left standing, the ones toward the rear when the fray had started. One of them had picked up the dead man's gun and had leveled it at Ferman.

And Francis Herman McKluskey laughed.

"Jimmy Jazz," he said. "Don't you know the Nancy Boys are ranking amateurs? They don't subscribe to no treaty!"

The Nancy Boy fired. Ferman snapped back and hit the ground. Jet roared and ran toward the three, and they broke and ran. Jet caught up with one and smashed a powerful blow to the back of his neck, dropping him instantly. He paused for a moment, then took a step to run after the remainder, when a voice called him back.

Ferman sat up, creatively cursing and looking at the new hole in his flak vest. He pulled out his bone handle, flicked the blade, and dug out a small lump of metal. "This wouldn'ta killed me if it'd hit me." He shook his head and spit on the ground. "Ranking amateur hemorrhoids."

I slowly stood and walked out into the street, eyes wide with adrenaline. "I guess you won't have to worry about them again."

Ferman looked up at me, smiled, and shook his head. "Nah. They'll be back. They always come back. Someone else will become leader, and he'll say, 'I have this plan to bring down the Devils,' and they'll follow him until we put him under. Worse than ranking vampires. Cut one head off and two more grow in its place."

"Excuse me," Jimmy Jazz said, "but you're thinking of the wrong thing—" He started to elaborate, but was cut off by a cry of victory.

Nose was shouting to the sky, "Barbecue! Barbecue! Barbecue!" and he raised both hands. One held the knife, and the other was a bloody fist.

Ferman looked back at the others. "All right! We got work to do! Let's clean this place up, *now!*"

Rover and Jet and Jimmy Jazz jumped into action. They went from casualty to casualty, expertly feeling necks for a pulse, and shouting out the status of each. With the exception of the Nancy Boys' dog, they were all still alive, including Binjii, who no doubt would live to regret that fact. In moments, the Devils had dragged the fallen Nancy Boys down a dark alley and stacked them like cord wood. Then they salvaged a large mylar sheet out of a Dumpster, wrapped Lassie's body in it, and carefully stowed it out of sight beneath a burgeoning pile of debris.

"We aren't going to vikingize him and the Pinhead?" Jet asked, disappointed.

Ferman shook his head. "Too much to do. Nose's gotta have his barbecue. And Mr. Boddekker and I got some things to discuss." He looked at me with those malevolent eyes. "Don't we, Mr. Boddekker?"

"That depends," I said, "on whether you break every bone in my body."

"I thought about it, really and truly. You gave me a good reason to. I thought for sure you'd done a number on us. But you know how it is. You get busy with other things." He turned and watched as his gang worked. Nose wasn't helping at all; he was impatiently dancing in tight circles, around and around, like a child with a full bladder. "You guys about done?"

"We're secure," shouted Jimmy Jazz.

"Awright," said Ferman. "Back to base." He started to head west toward Columbus, picking up where he'd left off. I fell into step next to him to catch the story.

"Always something to do," Ferman was saying. "We got peace with the Pinheads, but they been running probes into our allotment lately. Can't figure that one out. It's gonna look bad too, one getting spilled here. Instead of vikingizing the Pinhead, I think we're gonna have to load him on a wagon and wheel him into Pinhead country under a truce flag. We'll do that later."

"Vikingize?"

Ferman shook his head again. "*Think,* Boddekker. We can't have bodies showing up in our zone. The wrong people will think we're killing folks."

"But you did. You killed Lassie."

"Beside the point. Parents, they get all mad when their kids join a gang and come home dead. They put screws on the cops to crack down and threaten to sue the cooperative. So we gotta follow procedure."

"Vikingization."

"Pull the teeth," said Jet. "And the eyes. And the tips of the fingers. Throw them in the river to feed the fish."

"Nice try," I started.

"Then we burn the body up, and sink the ashes, too."

"That way," chimed Jimmy Jazz, "anything like bone chips that could give even a residual pattern of DNA is in the sludge with parts of a hundred others. There'd never be a positive ID on remains, and the offending deader's name goes on the list of the missing."

"You seem to have thought of everything, Ferman."

He gave a cynical laugh. "Boddekker, you wouldn't last an hour on the street."

"I'll drink to that," I said. If I had been streetwise, I certainly wouldn't be in the company of a gang with an offer that was going to turn the industry on its ear.

"So," asked Jet. "Are we going to be in a commercial?"

Ferman waved him back. "First things first, Jet," he said. "Let's get to base."

Base was a rotting church building on West End Avenue across from a defoliated DeWitt Clinton Park. The stone of the building was streaked and crumbling from neglect, the windows were long gone, and there were no lights around it.

"The building's less than forty years old," Ferman said. "They built the church, decided they didn't like the neighborhood, they moved out." He smiled. "And of course, what better place for Devils to live!"

"They came, they saw, they left." I walked with them up a long set of steps and through doors that were almost off the hinges. Inside, in the center of the cavernous building, a fire in a barrel provided light, and the smoke drifted more or less straight up to a gaping hole in the roof, where it escaped.

"I bet you've got a nasty draft in the winter," I said, noting what looked like tattered bedrolls scattered through the auditorium.

"We move downstairs, then. Classrooms. My office is down there, too." And then he laughed, a dry cackle that reverberated in that empty building for a long, long time. When he finally stopped, he called my name and tossed me an oblong bundle. It was a packet of EZWipes.

"What's this for?"

"You're a bloody mess."

I looked down at myself and my stomach rolled. He was right.

"I don't allow my boys to get that messy," he said. "Even if they been in the biggest ranking fight you ever seen."

"Thanks." I pulled one of the wipes from the box and turned to watch the other Devils as I cleaned myself.

Jet had closed the front doors and was locking them shut with a heavy beam. Jimmy Jazz finished tidying up around an army surplus cot, then lifted up a battered case, opened it, and with a cloth started polishing something brass. Rover was sitting on a mattress, carefully polishing something dark of his own. And Nose was holding a thin rod of metal over the fire in the barrel, carefully cooking something. Ferman crossed his arms and smiled in satisfaction.

"I love it when things go right. When things work the way you want 'em to. I hate surprises."

"Wouldn't it depend on the kind of surprise?"

He shook his head. "All surprises. No matter what they are, you need to adjust. But I suppose it happens. You adjust." Twisting his head, he gave me a sidelong glance. "Don't think what you're thinking, Mr. Boddekker, because you can't surprise me."

"I can't."

"Nope." He folded his arms and turned to face me. "The way I see it, you're here only for one of three reasons. Well, you've already proven that you're not suicidal. I don't think you're here to become a Devil. I don't think you could handle the requirements." He looked back at Nose.

"He doesn't look too up for them, either."

"Wise up, Mr. Boddekker. It wouldn't do you to hang out with a bunch of wild kids who could be your sons. You'd miss your friends at your big agency and your clean women and your lunches in expensive restaurants. You got clean clothes and clean money in the bank to buy whatever you want. You got a place to live that's got heat and A/C. You can brush your teeth whenever you want and turn on the vid when you're ignorant, and power up the robot whenever you're horny. You buy mixed drinks with ice in them and women in bars look at you like you mean something to them. You got this big world of fantasy because you put messages all over the world to make people buy something they don't need, stuff like your SOBs. You do that and you think you got some kind of absolute power." He stopped to spit on the floor.

"I'll tell you what real power is, Mr. Boddekker." He pulled his knife out and flicked the blade. "Power is when you put this against somebody's throat so they can feel how cold it is, and you can see this flickering inside their eyes because they know what you're going to do. And then you edge the blade and pop that artery, and you've got the warm all over you, and you can see the panic in their eyes as it leaks out and they can't do a ranking thing to stop it. It ain't being God, but it's as close as you're ever going to come."

He had a peculiar smile on his face, and coupled with what I'd learned when I saw his record, something occurred to me. "Of course, you've never done that."

Ferman's eyes flickered. I had surprised him. The bright blade disappeared inside the handle.

"The others don't know that."

He smiled, and I saw twin rows of uneven, stained teeth. "I suppose I owe you one. Maybe you got more street sense than I thought."

Maybe in another universe I'd have been a psychologist. "But you're right," I said. "All of those things you talked about, I'd miss them. Which brings me to the obvious subject, the reason I'm here."

"Yeah," he said. "Understand, it's not for me, Mr. Boddekker. It's for them. What you said that night we collared you, you wouldn't know how much that put into their lives. That was all they would ranking talk about. I got pretty sick of hearing about all the things they were going to do after this commercial happened. Me, I didn't want them to get jacked. I've come a long way with these boys."

"Not to mention the fact that I was a serious threat to your leadership."

Ferman's nostrils flared. "Okay, maybe a little, so I'll give you that one without killing you. What you've got to understand, Boddekker, is that these guys got nothing. They got dirt. They got to have somewhere they can belong to, or it's all over for them."

There was a tremendous shout from the fire barrel. The others had crowded around Nose, who was holding his cooking rod high in the air, grimacing and chewing with great production. The others clapped their hands in cadence and chanted, *"Down down down down down . . ."* Nose firmly set his jaw, lowered his head, and opened his eyes. Then he filled the hall with a high-pitched scream. The other Devils howled with delight and lifted him up on their shoulders. They carted him up to Ferman and set him down. Nose grinned like an embarrassed schoolboy. Juice from the barbecue covered his chin.

Ferman reached over and put his hands on Nose's shoulders. "Peter," he said reverently, "you have completed your last step. You now have the right to wear the badge of the Devils." With that, he grabbed Nose by the ears, pulled him in, and kissed him full on the lips. The other Devils howled. Ferman calmed them with a wave of his hands and looked at the others. "It is now time for the bestowing of gifts," he said. "Who wants to go first?"

Rover muscled his way between Ferman and Nose and held out a shining brass cylinder.

"Excellent choice," Ferman smiled. "Nose, this is the shell casing from the bullet that killed the Nancy Boy in tonight's alteration."

"Altercation," corrected Jimmy Jazz.

"Thank you," Ferman said. "Tonight's *altercation*. Always care for it, Nose, for it contains that dead boy's soul."

Wide-eyed, Nose reverently took it.

Jet stepped forward. "Nose, I would be honored if you would let me paint on your badge."

Nose nodded quickly and removed his battered vest and handed it over.

"But Jimmy Jazz got to help me with the spelling."

"Glad to," Jimmy Jazz said. "And Nose, while Jet is doing that, I'd like to serenade you with that John Coltrane piece I've been working on."

Nose was smiling. There were tears forming in his eyes. "That would be fine, Jimmy Jazz."

"And Nose," Ferman said, reaching into his pocket. "You have had your wish by forever altering our sworn enemy, and the sworn enemy of the order of things, the Nancy Boys."

All of them, including Nose, cheered.

"I would like you to have this token of your double victory." From his pocket he pulled out the red lace brassiere that Binjii had worn into combat.

"The now-leader of the Nancy Boys has fallen hard. Through words we have stripped him of the respect of his men. Through combat we have stripped him of his badge of leadership." He held the garment aloft, and there was more cheering. "And you have forever altered him, and cast him into that zone of his own design, where he may never return to the order of things. He had been outed from—''

''Ousted,'' corrected Jimmy Jazz.

''—ousted from their own order of things. He has been completely stripped of all things, and now his own people will make him bleed. This, Nose, is your victory.'' He handed over the brassiere, and Nose accepted it with a polite nod. Then the five of them together made a kind of victory cry, *yip-yip-yowlllll,* and Nose and Jet and Rover and Jimmy Jazz all scattered to different corners of the auditorium.

''You've witnessed something very special here tonight, Boddekker,'' Ferman said, wiping the barbecue from his lips. ''No civilian has ever seen it.''

''I'm honored. But I feel bad that I didn't bring a gift.''

Ferman looked at me and saw the serious face I'd readied. ''Your being here is gift enough,'' he said, ''if your intentions are honest.''

I watched the other Devils trickle back to the barrel. Nose sat down on a crate and held his vest toward the fire's light, and Jet opened a box of paints and went to work with a tiny set of brushes. In other parts of the building, Rover curled up on a pile of rags and propped his head up to watch the artist at work, and Jimmy Jazz ran to Nose, a battered tenor saxophone strapped to his neck. He struck a pose similar to one I had seen Deppe adopt when playing, licked the reed of the instrument, and began to blow. I could almost pick the melody out of the cacophony of squeaks and missed notes.

''He is improving,'' Ferman said, without looking at me. ''When we met him, all he could play was ranking 'Ode to Joy,' and we used to make him play it until tears were pouring from his eyes.''

''What for?''

''He wasn't a Devil then.'' Ferman moved into the *at ease* stance, and for all the world he looked like a general surveying his troops on the field of battle. ''He was a scared little kid who had to walk through our zone to get to his saxophone lessons.''

''Who would send a kid out at night for—''

''This was in broad daylight, Boddekker. The boys and me, we got so every Wednesday we'd meet him and shake him down for his lesson money. Every Wednesday. Rain or shine. And he'd go anyway, on to the lessons. So we started getting him on the way back, and we'd say, 'Yo-ho, James, what did you learn today?' And we'd make him drop his case and take out that monster thing—it was big as he was when we started—and we'd make him play 'Ode to Joy,' because that was the only song he said he had memorized, and we always scattered his sheet music from here to The Park when we saw him.

"But it was so weird, Boddekker. He never gave up. There he was, the next Wednesday, and the next, and the next and the next and the next. And we'd take his money again. And after the lesson we'd jack him, and we'd stand around him in a circle and make him honk out 'Ode to Joy' until we thought he was going to drown in his own ranking tears. And me and the Devils, we'd laugh ourselves sick. He never gave up.

"And then one day, I was on my way ho—I, uh, was on my way to somewhere else. And I go down in the subway, and somewhere downtown I'm changing trains, and I hear this familiar sound. So I look at this crowd of people, and they're all gathered around this musician whose case is laying open on the platform, and they're throwing him money. It's James, and he's playing that same song, 'Ode to ranking Joy,' and he's playing more beautiful than I ever heard it—Coltrane style, he told me later. See, the first couple weeks we shook him, he charged the lessons, said he'd pay later. But we always, always, always shook him for the money his folks gave him. So he was giving his folks some story about where he was, and played on the subways when he could to get the money to keep going to his lessons. You could imagine how I felt."

"So you made him a Devil."

"Not quite. Jet had to get his badge first. See, Jet came to us from Harlem. Had to quit his gang there, said they wanted to use his sister, and he wouldn't participate. They caught him crying over it, tried to harass him, and he broke the leader's neck. Barely got out alive. So he gave it all up, and started walking.

"And he was still walking, right past this very building at three in the morning, and we happened to be on the way in from a hard night's work, but our edge wasn't quite off. So we thought, hey, shake him, call it a day. And Jet bested us, four of us at the time. In fact, he sort of killed our reader, which kind of made me mad, but Jet was so beautiful and violent to watch. He had some martial arts stuff, I think, not enough to be a weakling about it, but enough to be dangerous. So, looking at my guys and me all broken and bleeding, I did the only thing I could think of to save face. I asked him to join.

"Now he needed to get his badge, and things were kind of quiet. The Nancy Boys hadn't gone on their anti-everything rampage; they were still a bunch of guys who hid in a secret clubhouse and made each other bleed. We'd just pacted with the Pinheads, too, so there wasn't much but the usual thieving and so on, and we didn't want to hurt a civilian. Well, not if we could help it.

"This was after I saw James in the subway playing. I never told the others about it, and still haven't. Jimmy Jazz don't even know that I know.

"So we're busted up except for Jet, and we miss a couple of Wednesday shakes, and by the time we're ready for another rendition of 'Ode to Joy,' it's like we can't find him anymore. Did he find a new route or what? So we stake out where he takes his lessons and see him coming out, and he gets into this bikeshaw with this hemorrhoid merchant that lives in the neighborhood. This is a guy that we happen to know is the local podiatrist, because we seen him on and off coming out of the Nancy Boys' secret clubhouse."

Jimmy Jazz was still busy with his saxophone, so I performed his function. "You mean pederast?" I asked politely.

"Yeah," Ferman nodded. "That's her name. Pederast. Anyway, this guy we knew likes to cultivate his victims first and then set them up, and we're like, hey, he can't do this, because James belongs to us. Not that we're gonna make him bleed, of course, but if we were, that would be our option, not his. So we decided to put a stop to it."

"And that's how Jet earned his Badge."

"Yeah." Ferman gave a toothy smile from the memory of it. "One of the best things we ever did. And we found out then that Jet could paint." He laughed. "You should have seen how the Devil looked before. Like some character from a ranking kiddie show.

"So the merchant sort of leaves the neighborhood in a hurry, and the next thing we know, it's an off night and we're all hungover and three A.M. again, this racket wakes us up. We all stagger out, ready to murder whoever is doing it, and we get out on those front steps right there and it's James playing his Coltraneized *'Ode to Joy.'* He sees us and *finishes.* Not stops, mind you. *Finishes.* Then he yells at us, 'Come on out you ranking cowards, I'll take you on one by one! You want to kill me off, so come out right now. I'm ready to give you a fight.'

"I tell the others to stay back and go down and say, 'You crazy, James? We were trying to save you from this guy.' He's like no, no, there's nothing else. He's got nothing else, he's saying. His parents are getting mad about the money for lessons, mad because he's staying out late—although he never admitted to us what he was doing staying out. Soon there would be no more lessons, and we'd scared off some patron who would've paid for them. He'd arrived at the end of the world."

"I've seen that view," I said.

"I told him to calm down. I come back up the steps and talk to the guys. 'I know he's got both parents,' I say, but rules were made to be broken, and this guy needs us. Maybe he can do something for us.' They agree, so I go down and say, 'James, you got us. We'll pay for your ranking saxophone lessons.' ''

"And he became your reader."

"Exactly." He closed in on me and breathed in my face. "But the others don't know about me paying for those lessons. You got that?"

"Understood."

"I take care of all of my people, each in ways that the others might not know about. Like Nose. The others don't know this, but he came out of the Nancy Boys. He got sucked into them, not like he wanted to join. Then they started their anti period and he decided he was Hetero. Not a good scene."

"And Rover?"

Ferman shook his head. "Don't know much about him. His parents got money, tons of ranking money. Then they got divorced. Lovers in, lovers out, more marriages. Not good. The only other thing, one of the parents kept sending private detectives out to see how he was doing. We disappeared three of them before they caught on to leave him alone. Best dog we ever had.'' He looked out at the dying fire and listened for a moment to the improving melody from Jimmy Jazz's sax. "They each got their needs. But I'm fair. I run a loyal boat here, Boddekker. Other groups, they got turnover, defections, even the Pinheads. And a few Pinheads have asked to join up with me because they see what we got here, and they want to be part of it, too."

"What about you, Ferman?"

He laughed bitterly. "My real dad was Irish. Irish Catholic. My mom, she's Jewish. So from both sides of the family I got like ten thousand years of radioactive guilt to deal with."

"Retroactive," I said.

"Right." He went quiet, looking out at his charges.

I sighed. "Well. If things work out, maybe Jimmy Jazz can pay for his own saxophone lessons. And Jet can get some art lessons, Nose can get himself properly oriented, and Rover . . ."

"He won't want money."

"We'll think of something," I said. "And Ferman, if you want, we can get you into psychoanalysis."

He laughed again, not bitter, but as if the prospect truly amused him. "Tell you what, Boddekker," he said. "If I could get laid on a regular basis, that would make me happy. And not with one of those robots, either."

"That's all any man could ever ask for," I said. I remember thinking, *Heavens, maybe Levine was right, and maybe all these boys need is the right break and things will turn out right for them. Maybe this was all meant to be, and World Nano will be making the world a little bit better place in a way they'd never imagined . . .*

These thoughts, of course, were all wrong. But I didn't know that as I sat down with Ferman and started telling him all about NanoKleen.

PEMBROKE, HALL, PANGBORN, LEVINE, AND HARRIS

"Selling you to the world since 1969"

Offices in Principal Cities: New York - Montreal - Toronto - Sydney - London -
Tokyo - Moskva - Beijing - Chicago - Oslo - Philadelphia - Amarillo

CLIENT: »TransMind Technologies		PRODUCT: »StimWorks
WRITER: »Boddekker	TIME: »:60	MEDIA: »Audio
TITLE: »*The Cold Hard Facts*		
PRODUCTION ORDERS:	»Vid script using audio track to follow. Compress-compensate as needed to fit :60	

ANNOUNCER: Here are the cold, hard facts. If you've got a jones,
there's a one in thirteen thousand chance that something will go
wrong and you'll end up dead, no matter how careful you are.
And how about the *money* you pour into that jones . . . on the
average of one-quarter to one-third of your yearly income! Now
consider StimWorks from TransMind Technologies. StimWorks is a
completely portable cranial brainstimming device that works on the
same principle as those in major psychiatric hospitals. Only
StimWorks is affordable and completely adjustable! Whether
you're into hallucinogenics, stimulants, depressants, pleasure center
jolts, or any combination of the above, simply dial up the effects
you want and lie down while StimWorks goes to work on you!
There are no needles. No pills. No inhalant packages that are
hard to use or dermic patches that give you headaches. Just a
clean, sharp buzz every time! And, a StimWorks can help you
keep your budget in check, because the initial outlay will pay for
itself in only three short years! So don't end up cold, hard, and
dead. Call TransMind Technologies *today* and learn how you can
live life the way it was meant to be lived . . . with StimWorks!

[*SFX: TransMind Technologies Sonic Logo*]

VOICE OF TRANSMIND: At TransMind Technologies . . . we *know*
what the brain likes!

ELEVEN

The Pursuit of Vision

On Wednesday, June 15, we started shooting *There Were Ten of Them* for World Nanotechnologies, Ltd. The commercial was to be lensed in a cavernous old Masonic Lodge, which Deppe told me was once used as a studio to record orchestral music. He went on to mention the warm ambiance of the place and how it would bring out the subtleties in that type of music, but his explanations gradually lost me, and I found refuge by wandering among members of the set crew. They were busy putting the final touches on the home in which my carefully crafted suburban dialogue would take place.

I was beginning to wonder if it would all really come together. I had polished the script as Levine had requested, removing all but one of the offending *honeys*. The group had smoothed over the cassies and had lengthy discussions with Talent over who should be in the spot outside of the Devils themselves (my suggestions here only took the form of basic physical types), along with who should direct the spot. The job had been offered to me, and while I tried to use members of my group where possible, I turned it down, and turned in a list of people who could truly bring the vision to life.

Now it was all coming together in this hall. And if I had anything to say about it, it was going to lead to that house in Princeton, that warm stucco house that had become my secret lover. I had managed to slip back to Princeton no less than three times to stare at it and get to know the neighborhood. As if to try me further, the sign out front kept changing from one diabolically tempting message to another; from FOR SALE! to LICENSED FIREPLACE! to 26 MIL to CALL FOR APP'T TO-DAY!; from 3 BEDROOMS! to IN/OUTLETS GALORE! to A REALLY GREAT N'BORH'D.

The thought of that made me feel suddenly alone, so I walked across the hall, stepping over tangles of cable and wire, to where Dansiger and Bainbridge sat, intently looking at a notebook.

"Your repetition ratio is fine," Dansiger said, tapping the screen with her fingernail in a way that reminded me of Jean and my first visit to The House. "And most of the message is fine, with two exceptions. First, you didn't put in the PRM. No subbie will ever fly without the Positive Reinforcement Message."

"I wondered about that when I was writing it," Bainbridge said, "but I wasn't sure what to use."

"Any one of the Ten Commandments," I said, "and you won't go wrong. Otherwise, the FCC and the FTC won't let it fly."

Bainbridge nodded, and Dansiger continued. "The other is that you absolutely cannot, under any circumstance, come right out and say, 'Buy this product.' The commissions will clamp down so hard that you'll have to close the branch office for turning in a script that way." She handed the notebook to Bainbridge.

"Don't worry," I told her. "There are a million billion ways around that rule."

"Then these rules are made to be broken," Bainbridge smiled.

"Not broken. Bent. With ruthless efficiency."

"Other than that," Dansiger said, "the spot is fine. Why not rework it a little and let Boddekker look at it?"

I traded a withering glance with Dansiger, who smoothed the lines of her suit and said, "On second thought, you can work on it right here. I need to discuss some things with Boddekker." She stood and took my arm and pulled me away from Bainbridge.

"If this has anything to do with Hotchkiss," I started, "I take no re—"

"Relax," Dansiger said, walking quickly. "I have to get away for a while. You know how sometimes people don't catch on to the obvious?"

"Is this going to be a lecture?"

"This is about Bainbridge."

"Like I said."

"She's having a little trouble grasping the basics of the subliminal spot."

"Well, there's always something that's bound to cause a problem."

Dansiger stopped short and looked me straight in the eye. "And speaking of trouble, what are you trying to pull by bringing Charlie Angeles in to direct this thing?"

"Don't be so paranoid, Dansiger." I pulled to get her walking again. "The old men asked me who should direct the spot. I gave them a list. Charlie's name happened to be at the top. It's not like I threatened to quit if they didn't choose him."

"Come on, Boddekker. I know how you feel about his work. And with Levine and the World Nano people insisting on purity of vision . . ."

"That's exactly why they chose him. I recommended him because I thought he would come the closest to putting on vid what I saw when I wrote the spot, our cassie notwithstanding."

"If I didn't know you better I'd swear you were taking advantage of the situation so you could meet your hero."

"Me? Dansiger, would I do something like that?" It was a good line to leave on, so I started to go. Dansiger grabbed my arm and held me back.

"There was one other thing I wanted to ask. Is there an element of revenge in all of this?"

"Revenge?"

"I'm talking about the expense of bringing in Charlie Angeles. He's hardly mister one-take-wonder—"

"What director is?"

"But he's a perfectionist. Besides, there's the matter of Charlie's fee. He's one of the most expensive directors in the business."

"No," I told Dansiger, "he's *the* most expensive director in the business. In fact he's listed as such in the Guinness Databank of—"

"And I understand that Pembroke Hall is eating the cost of his fee on this shoot."

I held up my hands. "That was an arrangement they reached with the World Nano people. They had some ideas of their own that they wanted brought in, and Charlie's fee would have broken the budget. So the old men decided to absorb the cost themselves. Purity of vision, you know."

"And Maxie Spielberg or the Coen cousins couldn't have done it as well? For less money? I smell something funny here, Boddekker, and it smacks of revenge. Unless you're shooting to make the world's most expensive commercial."

"Me?" I insisted, somewhat modestly. "Why would I do something like that?" Then I took her by the shoulders and leaned in close to one ear. "Let's call it insurance instead. If this craters, they'll have something to blame it on other than our group's work."

Dansiger glared at me. "All right. So I was off. A little."

I made a sweeping bow to her. "You're catching on to the way this business works. That tells me I should watch my back around you. Now if you'll excuse me, there's somebody I want to avoid."

I walked off, leaving her with the prospect of critiquing Bainbridge's rewrite.

On my way through the hall I noticed a crew making the final setup on the digitalizer and Media Storage Unit. As a test, they took an image of one of the set carpenters, froze it on the screen, exploded it, and had the component parts crawl back together to reassemble. It was impressive—not quite as impressive as the emulators, which took the personality of their victims and extrapolated, but impressive enough to have it on this shoot nonetheless.

Further exploration was interrupted by Sylvester, who came to me with a slate clutched tightly in white-knuckled hands.

"Boddekker," he said, "We've got a problem. Your friends haven't shown up yet."

"Who? The Devils?"

He nodded and I stared at him. This latest round of change was taking quite nicely. Sylvester had enough facial hair that the skin under his lip and across his chin and throat had developed that masculine bluish tint. I realized what I was doing and quickly broke eye contact so he wouldn't get the wrong idea. The man was mixed up enough as it was.

"Don't worry. They'll be here."

Sylvester looked at his slate. "But I've got them on for a costume call in two minutes."

"Costume call?"

"Gang paraphernalia," he said. "You know, boots, jackets, gloves, the whole bit."

"Sylvester, I appreciate what you're doing, but they won't need a costume call. I asked them to show up in their street colors."

"Great," he sighed. "Down time to clean them—"

"They're a street gang," I said, my voice getting a little too loud. "What do you expect? They're not going to look like a radiant bride on her wedding day."

He jotted figures on his slate and shrugged. "I'm sorry, Boddekker, I didn't mean to take it out on you, but there's a lot of pressure on me all of a sudden. Mr. Drain isn't happy with his choice of costume, and we tried so hard to choose one with a subliminally significant design."

"Wait a minute," I said. "Mr. Drain? As in Norman Drain?"

Sylvester nodded. "The face that's launched a thousand products."

"He's the male talent for this spot?"

"One and the same."

I stepped away from Sylvester. My head fell back and my eyes rolled. That's what Dansiger had been talking about when she mentioned the world's most expensive commercial. No wonder World Nano had wanted us to absorb the cost of Charlie Angeles. His fees were a record, but they were nothing compared to the astronomical amounts commanded by Norman Drain. Needless to say, the salaries would only contribute to what would be happening here. Between Charlie Angeles and his passion for recording take after take after take, and Norman Drain's restless pursuit of his own perfect performance, we were looking at a one-day shoot that could take weeks.

"All right. I can accept that. If they want to pour their money down the drain—pun intended."

"But World Nano wanted him. He's launched some really fine products."

"Right. That list also includes holovision for Sony and those self-surgery kits."

"There were a lot more hits than misses."

"Yeah, right, Sylvester. But have you noticed the guys in the stand-up clubs doing Norman Drain jokes and Norman Drain impersonations? When was the last time they did? That's because Norman Drain has become a pathetic self-parody. He's like the universal prostitute, selling himself to the highest bidder, no matter what the product." I looked at Sylvester. He was giving me this incredulous look like he expected me to suddenly fly out into orbit. I stretched out my arms and shook them. "It's okay, though. It's all right. We'll make it. We'll overcome this. That's why I asked for Charlie Angeles."

"Speaking of asking for people—"

I saw Sylvester's gaze go over my shoulder and he kind of froze, a dreamy look on his face. I wasn't sure if I wanted to turn around or not. It depended on whether or not Sylvester's sexual orientation had been adjusted yet.

Against my better judgment, I turned. Honniker In Accounting was on her way toward us, smiling.

"Let's get out of here," I told Sylvester. "Every time she comes around, I get sent somewhere I don't want to go."

Sylvester wasn't saying anything. The look on his face meant that it didn't matter what his current orientation was.

"Look," I said, starting to walk away like I was harried, "when you get those swatches of material, make sure that Mr. Angeles sees them, and I'll see you—"

A hand fell on my shoulder. Immediately the skin beneath my shirt started to burn. "Boddekker."

There was no denying fate. "Well," I said, turning. "My own personal angel of doom. Nice to see you. I think."

Honniker In Accounting looked vaguely troubled. "I'm sorry. Did I miss something?"

Her look was changing now, mutating and flowing like those liquid metal displays that run the gamut of American presidents. She was not so much troubled as hurt. My heart started to break, and I hated myself for it.

"Nothing," I said in an off-handed way. "I was just saying to Sylvester—you have met my group's art director, haven't you?"

I introduced them and they shook hands. The man or the woman in Sylvester was clearly in love. *Good luck,* I thought, then continued.

"Every time you show up, I end up going somewhere that I don't want to be."

Honniker In Accounting looked down and blushed. The effect was incredible. I would have given up my job to get that look off her face.

"Well," she said, "I suppose it would look that way to you, Boddekker, and for that I apologize. As far as being your personal angel, well—"

I waved my hands like a crushed butterfly. "It was a frippery . . . a *comment.*"

"I happen to report to Levine," she said. Then her eyes drilled right into mine as if to say, *And you'd better get this next bit, loud and clear.* "And I know who you are—or rather, know *of* you, and I've followed your work. So after that first big meeting—"

"Where I made a huge fool of myself—"

"—I heard him mention your name and offered to take you the message. So when your spot had been chosen, I happened to be in the neighborhood, and he said to me in that Levinesque way of his—"

"Would you inform Boddekker that I require his presence right away?" I said, using my best Levine.

She laughed at this, and instantly I felt better. "Verbatim," she smiled, and oh, did that make my day.

"So what brings you here now?"

"I begged off. I told them I wanted to see how a commercial shoot goes, and I thought this would be a good one to see." She looked around the hall with a wide-eyed stare. "But I'm lost. This is so foreign to me."

Out of the corner of my eye, I could see Sylvester doing a slow burn. "Tell you what," I said, "I'm in the middle of things right now, but I'm sure Sylvester would be happy to show you around."

Sylvester took an eager step forward.

Honniker In Accounting managed another beautiful blush. "I'd love to, but I'm afraid I've got some more bad news for you, Boddekker. I've got to send you somewhere that you probably don't want to go." She pointed to the back of the hall where a large line of booths had been erected. "There's an unpleasant little man back there who insists on speaking with the writer of the spot."

Sylvester paled. "That would be Norman Drain." He took this as his cue to fade into the background. "Sorry, Boddekker. I'll show those swatches to Mr. Angeles as soon as he arrives."

I smiled at Honniker In Accounting. "All right. Let's see what the almighty has to say." I led her around cables and past construction crews that, on getting the smallest whiff of her scent as we passed by, slowed in their work long enough to savor the moment, and then returned to normal speed. We approached the line of doors, labeled, respectively, C. ANGELES, SIOBHAN SIOBHAN, PEMBROKE HALL CREW, EXTRAS (DEVILS), and N. DRAIN. Pausing for a moment, I said to Honniker In Accounting, "Remind me to have the word *Extras* on that one door painted over," and to her question I answered, "Because life will be so much easier if we do." Then I rapped on Norman Drain's door with the back of my hand.

"Get lost," said a stern voice from behind the door.

"It's Boddekker from Pembroke Hall," I said, opening the door and stepping forward. I was momentarily stunned by the opulence of the room, all mirrors and chrome, brightly lit and lovingly garnished with thick, green plants. There was also a stunning effect from the nude woman who was kneeling before Norman Drain. Even Honniker In Accounting yelped. I closed the door quickly. "I wrote the spot."

"Come in," said Norman Drain.

Neither of us moved.

"It's all right. Really. I've got her turned off."

"Turned off?" said Honniker In Accounting.

I opened the door and stepped in again. Norman Drain was throwing a sheet over the woman who had been kneeling before him. The woman didn't move.

"You know, I travel a lot, do location shoots, and handwork is part of my repertoire," said Norman Drain. He waved his hands with a flourish. "You know, the close-up of the product in a supremely manicured hand? But it's almost impossible to find a consistent manicure. So I went to the Lovejoy People and had them program one of their Robotettes for me—so all I have to do is open the trunk to get a really great looking set of nails." He stopped to admire the work that had been done on his right hand.

"Shouldn't you—" Honniker In Accounting said tentatively, "buy—her—*it*—some clothes?"

Drain gave that famous toothy *trust me* smile that he had used to launch those thousand products. "What for, sugar britches? She's just a *toy*." He looked right past me and I knew he was doing some mental undressing. Honniker In Accounting moved close to me and slid her arm through mine.

"I understand you have a problem with the script as written," I said, intending to change the subject.

Drain snapped out of his sleazy reverie. "Yeah. Right. I had a question about something, Bonniker." I didn't bother to correct him. I waited while he powered up his notebook.

"Yeah," he said, looking at the screen. "What's my motivation here, Bohecker? You've got me wagging a chunk at some guys who are obviously heavy-duty killer types. I'm not even that stupid in real life. What motivates me to do that? And then why do I lie to my wife about it? Why do I even come up with this big story? I mean, why should I even bother with this thing? Friend, I think this spot is in serious need of a rewrite."

"Well, *friend*—"

That wasn't me. That was Honniker In Accounting, and she jumped into the fray before I had a chance to even open my mouth in my own defense.

"It would seem to me that the only thing in need of a rewrite is your attitude. Or perhaps a Reorientation is more the order of the day."

I almost laughed. I would have, too, had I not been so busy wincing.

"What you've got is a perfectly acceptable script that any schoolchild could figure out, given a few minutes. You lie to your wife to cover up the fact that you made a stupid, stupid mistake and had to suffer the consequences of it. The big story serves a dual purpose. First, it provides your rationalization and makes what happened to you another senseless act of violence, thereby preserving your status as family hero. Second, it provides what we in the industry call 'comic relief,' which happens to be used in this case as a buffer from the violence, and as a device to get attention and sell the product. And as far as the motivation for your making the gesture to the killers, as you put it, I'm sure if you gave it any rational thought at all, the reason would come to you. Or is that little piece of machinery under your blanket programmed to spoon-feed you, too?"

Drain looked at her, his mouth flexing as if the answer was on his lips but refused to leave. Finally he said, "Look, sugar britches, who's the writer here—"

"I am, Mr. Drain," I said. "But my colleague has made the point I would have made. Suffice it to say that you must rise to the level of professionalism that you are being paid for and overcome any obstacles you find. Also, I would appreciate it if you did not call this very intelligent woman—or any of the other women on this set—'sugar britches.' "

"Well," said Norman Drain, still working his mouth.

"Why don't you look at it again?" I suggested. "If you still have a problem by the time the shoot starts, we'll discuss some possible revisions."

Drain's head pivoted in a loose loop and he said, "All right. Fine."

"In the meantime," said Honniker In Accounting, smiling, "you probably ought to have your other hand done. You may end up holding the product."

"Sure," Drain said without certainty. "Right." He closed the door and in a moment, the whirring of gears could be heard.

I turned to Honniker In Accounting and we both said, "Thanks," together, then laughed. There didn't seem to be any explanation necessary, and I found myself staring at her—and she was staring back. It was one of those moments that quickly turns into a dizzying rush, where we were standing close together and our faces instinctively began to draw together like magnets—

"Charlie Angeles is here," said someone. And then it echoed through the hall like a mantra.

"Charlie Angeles is here."

"Charlie Angeles is here."

"Charlie Angeles is here."

"Charlie Angeles is here."

The moment between us vanished at the prospect of my finally getting to meet Charlie Angeles. And I wasn't the only one. Honniker In Accounting's head turned away from me to find the door as well. All eyes in the room had done the same thing to catch the arrival of Charlie Angeles. When he didn't walk right in, a feeling filled the void of that moment between us; it was the sudden realization that you had been in near intimate contact with a person who, for all intents and purposes, was a complete stranger. I think Honniker In Accounting felt it, too, for she tensed up at the same time as I. We broke our grip on one another in time for his entrance.

His arrival wasn't like Moses coming down off the mountain, but it felt like it to me. Charlie Angeles walked into the hall, looking around, nodding with approval at the way the sets looked. He was a short, squat man, with a slight belly that ruined the lines of his shirt, a wrinkled black face and a thick mane of gray hair. I remember being astonished that Charlie looked young—a lot younger than pictures I had seen—and short. It's a natural inclination of mine to think that people I admire are taller than me. I thought for certain that the weathered face and hair belonged to a man who was too late for or had abstained from the usual assortment of longevity enhancers. Now I could see that he had merely grayed early, and the lines in his face were all healthy. He was probably not a day over forty.

"Yes, yes, well yes," he was saying now to Sylvester, patting him on the back. Sylvester turned away, his face transfigured by the compliment Angeles had paid him. It was fascinating to watch the man work. He moved quickly among the workers, sending them smiling back to their tasks with a short word or a nod or a pat on the back.

He made his way through the hall, and at one point he looked up at me and his face lit with recognition. He detoured and walked right over, a big grin on his face.

"You're Boddekker?" he asked.

"Yes, sir," I said in a thin voice. Then I introduced Honniker In Accounting. He gallantly scooped her free hand up and kissed it.

"Pleased, I'm sure." He looked at me. "And what is this 'sir' business? You can call me 'Charlie' like everyone else."

"Thank you," said Honniker In Accounting.

"And Boddekker, I just wanted to say—*nice script.* It's interesting. Challenging. I think we're going to have fun with it. I'm looking forward to lensing it."

I shook his hand and thanked him, then he was off working the crowd again. The man was an amazing presence, and in a few short minutes I learned a tremendous amount about handling people. Honniker In Accounting could feel something, too, for she stood so close I could feel her shiver, and then her hand reached out, locked fingers with mine, and held tight.

Finally, Charlie Angeles made his way to the center of the hall where the Techs worked on the cameras and Image Digitalizers and Media Storage Units. He talked with them for a few moments, using more words with them than he had spoken since walking in. They showed him the test with the exploded carpenter and he nodded, then walked to a clear spot on the floor and stood in silence, hands stuffed deep in his pockets.

Everyone in the hall became deathly quiet.

I was expecting a speech or a manifesto reading, or at the very least a prayer, but Charlie Angeles looked around, and when he seemed satisfied that he had everyone's attention, he said, "All right, people, we've got work to do." That was it. The room was his, and everyone was scrambling to finish what they were doing so things could progress.

As I understood it, Angeles planned on shooting two different versions of the commercial. One of these would be shot in the strict Hollywood sequence, namely, the most difficult shots—in this case, the beating of the Norman Drain character—would be saved until last. The simplest shot, with Drain watching his wife pulling the rejuvenated suit from the washer, would be first. The costumes he would wear during the scenes with his wife, and early in the fight, would have designer dirt and stains placed on them by the costumers, with some help from a computer program, which would layer it on little by little during the fight sequence. This would be the "guaranteed" version, the one that would come out identical to the way I had written it.

The second version would be shot in a strict chronological order, starting with Drain in a clean suit meeting the Devils. They'd go through the beating shots in order, during which time the suit would get genuinely dirty. Then it would be actually washed in NanoKleen and the results filmed. This would be the "genuine" version, and would hopefully be the one that would air, being in strictest compliance with all the usual annoying government rules and regs.

As it turned out, *neither* version would air.

Things started off normally enough. Norman Drain and Siobhan Siobhan were called from their respective rooms: he, wrapped in a towel for the climactic Scene of Discovery; she, dressed in what she would wear for the entire spot, a one-piece form-fitting business-class zip-suit in a stylish dark blue pinstripe.

The first few shots were simple enough. Siobhan looked into the camera and gave a thumbs-up. Take two, she winked. Take three, she combined the two. There were takes of each of them holding the box of NanoKleen, and when Drain caressed it with those beautifully manicured hands of his, I noticed that World Nano had indeed put "The micro machines that wash and kleen" across the front. I was very pleased indeed.

While they were shooting the Scene of Discovery, which is

where Siobhan pulls the miraculously healed garment from the washer, the trouble started. Sylvester hurried to my side and poked me in the ribs. I turned with a start.

"Boddekker, there's a problem. The Devils still haven't shown up."

I looked at my watch. "They're not due until eleven."

"Weren't you listening?" Sylvester said, exasperated. "They had a costume call—"

"We've already discussed that."

"And they're now missing the appointment with the choreographer."

"Choreographer? Why do we need a choreographer?"

"To block the fight sequence."

"Excuse me," I said to Honniker In Accounting, and I threw an arm around Sylvester's shoulder and led him away. "Are you nuts? What's there to block? You show them how to pull their punches. Then you tell Ferman to poke Drain in the mouth. He does it. You tell Nose to kick Drain in the 'nads. He does it. You tell Jet and Rover to take Drain for a scrape around the block. Then Jimmy Jazz urinates on him, and they're done for the day. They collect their checks and get out of my life."

"But the choreographer wants to do something pseudo-martial artsy, with a little ballet thrown in, and some of the darker images from the work of Martha Graham—"

I leaned in on Sylvester and spoke in low, conspiratorial tones. "These kids are in a street gang," I told him. "Do you really think they're going to sit still while some dance historian tells them why they're supposed to pirouette before they stab?"

Sylvester looked back at me. He wasn't following this at all.

"Lose the choreographer. Pay him, her, or it for the day. That part of the job is over. And don't say anything to the Devils about a choreographer having been involved with this."

"If they show up," Sylvester said, and left, not in the best of humor.

I hurried back to Honniker In Accounting. "Did I miss much?"

She rolled her eyes and motioned to the set, where the cameras were trained on Norman and Siobhan. Norman picked at the set of clothing he wore and started to recite my lines in stiff, stentorian tones.

"You *know,* I've *never* seen these *clothes* look *this* clean. *Even* the *stain* . . .'' he trailed off. "The *stains* that were there *be-fore* . . .'' He tossed his hands in the air. "I can't do this.''

Angeles made a waving motion with his hands. A buzzer sounded. Siobhan Siobhan slouched and the crew visibly relaxed. Angeles stuffed his hands in his pockets and walked over to Norman Drain, who was standing sheepishly beside the mockup of a laundry room in a suburban home. He spoke quietly to the actor, but the set was so still that we could hear his words plainly enough.

"Norman, are you having some kind of problem?''

Drain pinched the bridge of his nose with two fingers and looked pained. "Look, I'm really sorry, but—''

"Cut right to it,'' Charlie Angeles said icily.

Now Drain looked a little afraid. He picked up his notebook and brought up the script. "I'm having trouble with the motivation of this character,'' he said.

Honniker In Accounting rolled her eyes.

"I talked to the writer about this, but he insisted that there was nothing wrong. But if you take a look at this—'' He started to hold the notebook up for Angeles to see, but the director sternly brushed it away.

"Mr. Drain,'' he said, "I am well aware of what the script says, and I think the words you have to say are fine words. They do what they're supposed to do because the writer did what he was supposed to do. And now I'm here to do what I'm supposed to do, this crew is doing what they're supposed to do, and the lovely Mez Siobhan is doing what she is supposed to be doing. In fact, Mr. Drain, the only person here who is not doing what he is supposed to be doing is you.''

"But the motivation—''

"You've had six takes to find it,'' Charlie Angeles said, without raising his voice. "And apparently you haven't. So try thinking of how you're going to get through the next month without the credit transfer from this shoot if you can't nail this in the next take.''

"Well,'' Drain said indignantly. "Maybe I don't *want* the paycheck from this shoot.''

Charlie Angeles shrugged. "I'd rather not have the man who launched holovision in one of my spots anyway.'' He turned away and eyed the watching crowd, then pointed at a young man wearing headphones who was assisting with the digitalizer. "Casey, please come here."

Casey obeyed.

Angeles looked from Casey to Drain and back. "You look like the spoiled notebook jockey type that the good folks at Pembroke Hall had in mind. But most important of all"—he took one last comparing glance to make sure—"you have approximately the same dimensions as Mr. Drain." He turned to the actor. "Norman, will you surrender your costume to Casey?"

I never did find out what happened next, because at that moment, Sylvester's hand fell on my shoulder and he said, "Excuse me, Boddekker, but the Devils are here. They'd like to see you."

I excused myself from the company of Honniker In Accounting and started toward the front to meet them. Sylvester caught me again.

"They're waiting for you in the *alley*."

Well, of course. I suppose that made sense in a twisted sort of way. Thanking Sylvester, I made my way around and out the back door.

From what I could see of the sky, it was overcast out and the first spit of rain was starting to fall. Looking up and down the alley I saw nothing, and thought this had been some kind of joke. Then there was a rustling and out of nowhere, Ferman and the boys appeared, walking cautiously toward me, their eyes darting in all directions.

"So. Boddekker," said Ferman. "You're here."

"What did you expect?" I smiled.

"The ranking cops," growled Nose.

I made myself laugh. "No, this is all on the level. This is a shoot, complete with a spoiled actor with an enormously swollen ego . . ." Scanning their faces as I talked, I could see that they didn't appreciate any of this. Except for Ferman, they had the look of a child given an unlimited line of credit at his favorite store. They wanted to see.

"But I don't have to tell you that," I said, holding out my arms. "Come in and see for yourselves." I led them to the door and quietly pulled it open. One of the crew was standing by, and he put his finger to his lips to indicate that the cameras were rolling.

"It'll be a second," I told them. "They're lensing right now."

Ferman grabbed me by the collar. "This better be on the level, Boddekker, or we'll break every bone in your body."

I looked directly into Ferman's eyes, with the same you'd use to stare down an angry dog. "If this isn't on the level," I said, "you *can* break every bone in my body." Then, on the go-ahead from the crewman, I ushered them inside, Jimmy Jazz then Nose then Jet then Rover, and last was Ferman, whose eyes got big when he saw what we had done to the inside of the big hall. Using whispers to explain what was going on, I led them around to where the suburban home set was constructed, and lined them up so they could get a good look at what was going on.

What they saw was Charlie Angeles holding court, his camera crew dutifully waiting for him to say the word. The word was *action,* and it was barely out of Mr. Angeles's mouth before Norman Drain began to jump through hoops. All he was doing was saying "Gosh, I've never seen these clothes this clean! Even the old stains are gone! How did you do it?" while the camera shot him from an Angeles-chosen angle. This was apparently the third or fourth time Drain had done this, and when the word *Cut!* sounded, he made a sweeping bow to the captive audience as if expecting a healthy round of applause.

Ferman leaned toward me and stretched up on his toes to whisper in my ear.

"Who's that guy? Looks familiar."

"Norman Drain," I said. "King of commercials. You're looking at the face that launched a thousand products."

Ferman studied Drain, looking vaguely unsettled. "If he's the king," he said, "then why is he such a maroon?"

"Maroon?" I looked at Ferman.

"Ferman's a connoisseur of twentieth century animation," Jimmy Jazz whispered in my other ear.

I shrugged.

Charlie Angeles called for a break and strolled over to where we stood. He nodded politely at me and said, "Boddekker, why don't you introduce me to these young men?"

I cleared my throat and said, hesitantly, "Mr. Angeles, these young men make up the gang Ferman's Devils. This is their leader, uh . . . Ferman."

Ferman stepped forward and nodded, then shook hands.

"Ferman what?"

"Ferman," he said emphatically.

"Very good," Angeles smiled. "And your friends?"

Ferman held out his hand one by one to introduce the others. "James Jaszczek, only that's kind of hard to say, so we call him Jimmy Jazz. Also cause he plays the saxophone. And this is Nose, and he don't want you to know his real name 'cause he says it sounds like a Nancy Boys' name. Over there is Rudy, only he don't talk much, so he's our dog, and he'll answer to Rover. Finally, our big guy." Ferman made a sweeping bow and held his arm gallantly out toward the biggest of the Devils and sang, "Meet Jet Georgeson." Then he straightened, threw his head back, and began to cackle.

Jet shook with Charlie Angeles and said, "He does that whenever he introduces me. I don't know why, but it must be good. It sure makes him laugh."

"Fine," smiled the director. "Well, I am Charlie Angeles, a person of no great renown, although some people would have you believe otherwise. But I put my pants on one leg at a time just like you boys do. I'm looking forward to working with you, which is what we'll be doing as soon as we finish some of the key interior shots. I figured we'd do the exteriors out where the alley meets the street, and do most of the action bits in the alley itself. It'll give the spot a gritty feel, I'm sure you'll agree."

As one, except for Rover, Ferman's Devils nodded.

"We'll be using a stunt person for Mr. Drain for the more rigorous parts, and then we'll drop his face in using the digitalizer. But we'll be reshooting the interior sequences once you boys have gotten the clothing quite dirty. I hope this will be a fun experience for you."

Four of the five echoed pretty much the same sentiment; sure it will Mr. Angeles, I think so Mr. Angeles, all-right Mr. Angeles, that's great Mr. Angeles. Mr. Angeles shook with them again, whispered something to Jet, who nodded, then walked over to the digitalizer crew to watch a playback.

The Devils buzzed as he left. "This is really gonna happen, isn't it? Old Boddekker, he really came through, maybe we oughta do something for him, maybe we oughta make him a Devil, give him an honorary badge."

Nose tried to veto that idea. He was still too close to the experience of getting his to like the idea of me getting one gratis, but it never got beyond the discussion stage because Norman Drain walked over and planted himself in front of me.

"Well, Mr. Boddekker," he said, too loudly. "This day is turning into a pretty good shoot in spite of some minor complications with the script."

"Don't you need to have your nails done?" I said.

Drain laughed. "What a sense of humor. Actually, I came over to meet the young actors who will be working with me."

"Oh, we're not actors," Nose said, proudly.

I winced. Drain looked right at me.

"What he means," I said, "is that they're members of an authentic street gang, brought in for the purposes of proper atmosphere, but they haven't received their union cards yet."

Drain looked like he was buying it until Ferman said, "Boddekker, you didn't say anything about us having to join a union."

"You don't remember?" Jimmy Jazz said quickly. "I do. Maybe you were busy or something, Ferm, but I distinctly—"

"Cut the crap," Drain said malevolently, pushing Jimmy Jazz out of the way and moving in on me, nose to nose. "What are you trying to pull here, Boddekker? You know how I feel about working with—"

"Hey!" Ferman barked, trying to step between us. "This guy is our friend!"

I looked over at Charlie Angeles and the digitalizer crew. They looked up from the playback and Angeles went right into action, pointing and sending men in different directions to flank the Devils, showing them what he wanted with hand signs.

"I don't care who you think you are," Ferman was saying, "but you lay a finger on him and we'll break—"

"Wind," Drain interrupted, and he grabbed Ferman by the edge of his Norwegian war flak jacket. "I've been doing adverts since before you were a gleam in your mother's eye, kid, and don't think that means I can't take you, because I *can*."

Ferman stepped back and tried to lock onto Norman Drain's lapels, but without breaking his stare, Drain brought his hands up and grabbed Ferman's arms, pushing them back down to the jacket. Then he hooked his thumbs around Ferman's skinny wrists, using his other fingers to latch onto the flak jacket and pull Ferman close.

"See what I mean? Now I'd clean the room with you, only you're so ranking skinny that you'd probably break. So why don't you go home to your mother—"

Drain's words closed my throat. Before I could move,

Ferman's head fell back and his legs bent as if in a swoon. Drain took one step forward under the sudden dead weight. As he went off balance, Ferman suddenly stiffened and his head snapped forward, smashing Norman Drain's nose flat with a sickening crunch. Drain's hands opened wide as he gasped in pain, and Ferman neatly stepped to one side and dropped him by kicking the flat of his foot against the lock of Drain's knee. On the way down, Drain's head impacted with the side of Nose's knee, and the small of his back lashed out against Jet's elbow. As he hit the ground, his solar plexus tried to break Rover's toes.

"No!" I shouted and lunged forward, but something caught me by the shoulder and pulled me back. I spun hard, expecting to see Jimmy Jazz, but I was staring instead into the benevolent face of Charlie Angeles.

"Leave it," he said. "Boys will be boys."

I flailed my arm at the scene. The Devils had picked Drain up off of the ground now, and were taking turns punching him in the stomach. Blood soaked his lips and chin and was making a nasty blotch on the collar of that nice, clean suit.

"Don't you see what—"

Angeles held firmly onto my shoulder as Drain was pitched across the room, skidded on his side, and collided with a coffee urn, which bounced onto its side and proceeded to shower the actor with its steaming contents.

"I see," Angeles said. "And I'm not going to miss a thing."

"What?" I looked at his smile. No, that wasn't benevolence on his face. I could tell now it was something else.

"I've got the cameras running," he said.

"Are you out of your—"

He put a finger to his lips. "There's no way we could have choreographed something like this. It's great stuff, Boddekker. It's real life. It's the spirit of your spot, better than we could have arranged it. Those boys aren't acting, they're emoting, which is something Norman Drain couldn't do with a gun to his head." He paused while something metallic crashed. I never found out what it was. I couldn't bear to look.

"This spot, Boddekker, it's going to be wizard. No, it's going to be better than that. It's going to be killer. Trust me on this one. You'll see."

PEMBROKE, HALL, PANGBORN, LEVINE, AND HARRIS

"Selling you to the world since 1969"

Offices in Principal Cities: New York - Montreal - Toronto - Sydney - London -
Tokyo - Moskva - Beijing - Chicago - Oslo - Philadelphia - Amarillo

CLIENT: »Ethical Solutions		PRODUCT: »Self-Termination Services
WRITER: »Boddekker	TIME: »:60	MEDIA: »Audio
TITLE: »*The Final Solution*		
PRODUCTION ORDERS:	»Use ''Piano Bar Mellow Variant'' jingle. Target placement after newscasts.	

ANNOUNCER #1: [*In slow, even tones.*] The Final Solution may not
always be the *right* solution for you. That's why we at Ethical
Solutions employ a full-time staff of counselors, twenty-four hours a
day, seven days a week, three hundred sixty-five days a year, to
help guide you in your decision. We'll help you study your motiva-
tions. Do you want attention? Revenge? Or do you really and truly
have a deep-seated need to end it all? An Ethical Solutions counselor will talk to you about it for as long as you need—and will
assist you in making the decision that's right for your life. If life is
not in your plans, your Ethical Solutions counselor can help you
choose the death that's right for you. We can also handle those
postmortem details that always arise—from notification of next of
kin in any manner that you deem appropriate—to finding someone
to feed your canary. And, from beginning to end, our services to
you are *free!* That's because we *care* about you! So when you've
decided that it's check-out time . . . make sure your final solution
is an *ethical* one!

ANNOUNCER #2: [*Quickly.*] Applicants must be twenty-one years or
older. Ethical Solutions retains the right to determine final disposi-
tion of mortal remains. Service not available in Utah. Applicants
must pass Hargrove Lucidity drug screening test. Ethical Solutions is
a licensed subsidiary of Allied Organ Brokerage and is in strict
compliance with all FTC rules and regulations.

TWELVE

Tugging the Threads of Reality

In NYC, July 5 is Cantaloupe Day. The city is filled with tourists, most of whom are heading down to Bleecker Street for the evening festivities. I had thought about heading that way myself instead of chasing a round or two at Ogilvy's, but I wasn't certain what kind of ending the day would have.

For this was the day on which *There Were Ten Of Them* would premiere on broadcast vid, introducing the first wholly commercial product from World Nanotechnologies, Ltd.

Things had been hectic since the commercial shoot. After the thrashing he received at the hands of the Devils, Norman Drain wasn't in any shape to finish. This was directly contrary to his wishes, because he insisted that he was a consummate professional who could rise above what had been done to him.

Unfortunately, his loose teeth and bleeding nose and cracked ribs and facial lacerations and crushed testicle all begged to differ, and he collapsed as soon as he finished his epic speech. It was then that he finally received the applause he'd been seeking—but he was in no state to acknowledge it. The Devils stood around, casually dusting off their flak jackets and pointing and laughing at their handiwork.

Charlie Angeles posted one of the crew to sit next to Drain's inert figure so we could be notified if he came to, then called a creative meeting. We huddled in the Pembroke Hall dressing room and discussed the possibilities, then decided on a course of action that consisted of finishing the shoot using Casey as Norman Drain's stand in, getting the appropriate exterior shots, and using the digitalizer to put it all together during the editing process.

It was also decided that we needed to have the suit that Drain wore during his beating for the sake of authenticity, so we took care of that first thing. We had some of the crew strip it off of him while Honniker In Accounting called for an ambulance.

"Hey Boddekker, look at this," Deppe said, bringing me the suit. "It's got some lovely stains on it, but you'll never be able to use it in the redone versions of the final shot. Look at this."

I saw what he meant. Aside from blood and paint and coffee and urine and ground-in dirt, there were also small rips and scuffs and loose threads all over the fabric.

"Oh," said Charlie Angeles, looking at the garment's state. "That's not going to be very camera friendly."

"Could we take some shots of this, front and back," I asked, "and then drop the stains onto the clean suit with the digitalizer?"

Angeles nodded. "To be fair, though, we'll need a shot of the suit after it's been cleaned."

"Absolutely," I said. "We're not here to lie."

By the time the EMTs arrived we had shot different angles of the suit and dropped it in a washer full of NanoKleen. The medical technicians had loads of questions about Norman Drain's state of health, but Honniker In Accounting took care of them. I think she told them that Drain fell down a set of stairs.

Next we put Casey in the duplicate suit and walked through the key scenes that Drain hadn't been able to complete. He did an admirable job of taking Drain's place, and he was thrilled to play a short scene with Siobhan Siobhan as she revealed that the seat of the suit had a large, oily footprint on it. From there, Angeles took the camera into the alley and shot a number of exterior angles, and the Devils and Casey acted out the pun scenes of the commercial, such as where the husband is dragged to indicate that NanoKleen pulls stains out by the roots.

It made for a full day that would end up melting into a full week, during which time I sat with Charlie Angeles and the digitalizer crew in a small editing studio in midtown, carefully watching as Drain's face and expressions were grafted onto Casey's body; listening as Casey's voice was restructured into Drain's; and mapping out contours of the suit at a computer terminal to ensure proper placement of all the authentic stains. Everything seemed to be going without a hitch, although for a day or two Norman Drain had refused to allow us to digitalize his likeness into the parts of the commercial he hadn't been able to finish.

His reasoning was that he had never resorted to that in all of the thousands of commercials he had made, and he didn't feel that it was time to start. On top of that, he was plenty angry about the beating he had received, and Dansiger had called to let me know that the old men had gotten some upsetting legal documents from Drain's attorney. But within a day, a solution had been reached which made everyone happy. Pembroke Hall bought out the law firm that Drain used, along with the shopping mall it was in; and a delegation from the agency went to see the actor in the hospital and convinced him that this situation could be parlayed into a public relations windfall if handled correctly.

"Imagine it," Honniker In Accounting had said to him. "Headlines in the downloads. 'DRAIN GIVES HIS ALL TO HIS ART— SUSTAINS REAL LIFE INJURIES TO PROMOTE NEW MIRACLE PRODUCT.' And you can give an interview saying that demand was taking its toll on you, and you wanted to experiment with digitalization as an alternative to a hectic schedule."

While it was true that the Personality Rights brought to Drain less than what he would have made for finishing the spot, the idea of publicity appealed to his ego. Honniker In Accounting and the others walked out of the hospital with his signature stored on a slate.

But the most remarkable thing that happened involved the product itself. The Saturday after the shoot, as Charlie Angeles was sequestered with the editing crew and I was revising dialogue to reflect changes brought about by the footage we now had, I was approached by a custodian who said there was a man outside who was frantic to talk to me. I thought about having the custodian brush the guy off, but had second thoughts. If it was Ferman or one of the other Devils, we could end up short one janitor. If it was anyone else, there really could be a problem that needed attention.

I went to the door and found Deppe pacing nervously on the sidewalk with a package under his arm. "Boddekker, you've got to see this," he said, and muscled his way inside.

Telling the custodian that things were all right, I led Deppe to the reception area. "What's the problem?"

"Get Charlie Angeles. There's something with the suit."

Great, I thought. Now those little machines eat fabric. That was all we needed. Hadn't the World Nano people tested this stuff?

Within moments, Deppe was looking at the whole group of us, including the custodian, who pretended to be busy fixing a lock on a desk drawer.

"This had better be good," I told Deppe. "It's been an awfully long week."

Deppe spoke, agitated. "Well, Boddekker, you did want me to take over the logistics end of the shoot while you did all this revision stuff—"

"The point," I said.

"The point is, we all forgot something, namely the suit soaking in the NanoKleen. We shot the footage of it to digitalize the stains and then left it soaking in the washing machine until today. A crew came in to strike the set, and this foreman comes up to me and says, 'Hey, did you know that washer's still full of water?' And I'm thinking, 'Oh great, the suit is in there and we all forgot.' "

"Keep going."

"Well," Deppe said. "I think you'd better have a look at this." He slid the package from under his arm and opened it, pulling out a folded bundle. He held it up and with a flick of his wrist, send it tumbling open to full length. It was the suit.

"Nothing wrong there," said Charlie Angeles.

He said that because the suit was clean. Or perhaps I should say *kleen.* The blood and the paint and the ground-in dirt and the myriad other miscellaneous stains and marks were gone. Vanished. I squinted my eyes and looked closer. Not a trace was left behind.

"That's clean," I laughed. "It's really clean. This stuff really works." I looked back at Charlie Angeles, who looked very pleased indeed.

"You're missing it," Deppe said. "Look again."

We did.

"Take a closer look, Boddekker. And think. Think about what kind of shape this suit was in when you last saw it."

From behind me came the most creative outburst of profanity I have ever heard in my life. The source was Charlie Angeles.

"He's right," the director said. "Look at that suit. *Look at it!*"

Then I saw what Deppe was talking about. The tears. The scuffs. The loose threads. They were all gone.

"That's not the same suit," I said.

Deppe threw it into my hands. It was damp. I turned it over to look at the label stitched onto the collar. Embossed on it was DRAIN COSPROP #1—NANOK. SHOOT #336.

"The machines—" I started, feeling lightheaded.

"Fixed it," Charlie Angeles said, running his hand across the fabric. "Those little suckers must have rewoven the damaged areas while it was soaking."

"After it was already clean?"

"Possibly. If they're programmed to detect anomalies in the structure of the host fabric and repair them, why shouldn't that extend to physical damage as well as a stain?"

"I wonder if the World Nano people know about this."

We went to work finishing up the spot, and early the next week I spent hours on the phone with product engineers at World Nano while Charlie shot footage of Casey in the repaired suit and grafted it into the climax of the spot, along with before and after shots of the damage.

As it turned out, the World Nano technicians had speculated that such a repair event might be possible, but they had speculated that it might take place over several washings. But with NanoKleen washings were less frequent, and they decided that any repair capability would be inhibited. Their research—including the experiments to see whether the machines would take their host clothing apart—had all been done with new or relatively undamaged old clothing, and concentrated on the removal of stains. Since NanoKleen tended to eliminate the worst of those stains in an overnight soak, there had been no reason for an extended soak like Norman Drain's suit had gotten.

An emergency conference was held between Pembroke Hall and World Nano, where it was decided to go ahead with the spot with a few minor additions to imply NanoKleen's miraculous healing powers. This would air while the World labs did further research to determine the limits of this phenomenon, and any future spots would reflect that NanoKleen did more than clean.

Accordingly, there was one more rewrite. A round of digitalization was required to alter the narrator's speech and one of Norman Drain's lines, and ten days after the initial day of shooting, *There Were Ten of Them* was turned in for dubbing and distribution to those participating in a multimarket timeshare buy—a virtual all on the big ten cablenets, with maybe a dozen of the minors to pad out the demographics.

I scarcely had time to get back into my normal routine when word came down that it was time for the spot to premiere. It was one of those things that I tried to forget. After all, I had much to do elsewhere, including that spot for Boston Harbor. Besides, the one thing I really hated doing was sitting tight with a stupid smile pasted on my face while everyone I knew sat around watching or listening to one of my spots. It was like sitting naked before the whole agency. In fact, it was worse. I'd have much rather addressed the entire Pembroke Hall staff stitchless than have them view my own work—but one had to play the game.

And so I went, but not to the big meeting hall where most of the others were gathering. Instead I went to my creative group's meeting room, and quietly slipped in at about 4:15—plenty of time to catch the 4:22 commercial break.

The vid set was already on, soundlessly showing the grudge match between the 'Rico Rumrunners and the Moskva Bolsheviks, and the room was sparsely populated. In fact, my creative group was represented more by who was not there than who was. Bainbridge was at Columbia taking the last of her final exams. Harbison and Mortonsen were in the main conference room, there to listen to Levine's pre-premiere speech. Sylvester was on another of the endless series of medical leaves—this time I think it was a hormonal imbalance caused by the constant comings and goings between genders. That left Dansiger and Deppe and Griswold from my group, plus the Church Brothers, who wanted to see the completed spot but wouldn't sit through a Levine speech to do it. Hotchkiss was there, torn between watching the game and pecking something into his notebook. And Honniker In Accounting was there—something that did and didn't surprise me.

I slid into the conspicuously vacant chair beside her and smiled. From the corner of my eye, I could see the Church Brothers doing a slow burn. "You're in the wrong place, aren't you?"

She returned the smile. "What ever makes you say that?"

"What if the old man needs to talk to me?"

Honniker In Accounting laughed. "Then he'll have to come and get you himself. I wanted to be *here* for this."

I'm sure at this point the Church Brothers were ready to explode, but for some reason that fact no longer mattered. I said, "There's nothing to see, really. In a couple of minutes the commercial goes on the air, and everyone watches it while I die the world's slowest death. Then everyone leaves and life gets back to normal."

"It does?" There was no mistaking the look on her face.

"Well," I admitted. "Most of the time."

"And when it doesn't?"

"Then life gets . . . interesting."

That feeling was setting in again, that druggy attraction that's like being pulled in by some slow, hypnotic magnet. And instead of breaking the spell, a kiss would only deepen it.

"Here we go!" Deppe said loudly, and he turned up the volume on the vid in time to hear the score; Rumrunners eight and a half, Bolsheviks thirteen.

The screen winked dark. Then it faded in. A woman programming her kitchen. Siobhan Siobhan going about her business. "Honey, I'm home!" She turns and does a great reaction. Cut to Norman Drain, emerging from the glowing halo of the door. And he looks bad. Really bad. So bad, in fact, that Churchill whistled.

"They really pasted him, didn't they?"

"Quiet," snapped Dansiger.

They didn't even notice the fact that Drain, with all his stains and rips and injuries, had been digitally superimposed over the form of Casey. There were ways that you could tell such a thing by looking, but you had to know what to look for. I could tell because I was there during the editing. Dansiger and Churchill knew too, but they were too engrossed to say anything.

"What happened to you?" asked Siobhan Siobhan. "This suit is a *mess*!"

"Oh," said Casey in Norman Drain's voice, "I had a run-in with a street gang. There were ten of them."

And now the world got its first glance at Ferman's Devils. It was a quick flash that looked like they were posing for a family portrait. But Charlie Angeles, true to the instructions in my script, had made it abundantly clear that the numbers from the husband had been exaggerated.

"Ten?" asked Siobhan.

"Ten or twelve," replied Casey/Drain. "I was minding my own business when they surrounded me . . ."

A series of quick cuts, all fitting together like a cinematic jigsaw puzzle. Casey/Drain making fun of a rumpled figure in an alleyway. The figure gets an angry look on its face. It's Jet. With a massive hand, he grabs his tormentor by the collar.

"And what did you do?"

"I handled it."

Drop-in shot of Jet backhanding Drain. Drain's head snapped back, real blood flowing. That had happened in the studio, but Charlie had superimposed it onto a standing shot of a brick wall lined with overflowing trash barrels.

"It looks like you handled the clothes, too."

"Don't try and save them. Even if you could get the stains out"—A close-up of the stains, and the rips, and the unraveling seams—"these clothes are hopeless!"

"Relax, dear . . . I'm washing them in *NanoKleen!*" Siobhan turns her hand to gesture at the box. Letters are superimposed across the bottom of the screen—"The micromachines that wash and kleen!" Yeah, it was cutesy and maybe a bit too punny when I wrote it. Normally I would have hated it, but something erupted inside my head, something triggered by the sight of that semi-illiterate pun.

Now there's a whole new way to spell clean.

Oh, yes. That was it. That should have been it on this spot. That's what my subconscious had been trying to tell me. It was great. It was perfect. It would be in the next spot—if Pembroke Hall was able to keep the account.

Suddenly Dansiger said, "Ooh," and I snapped out of it. Ferman's Devils were beating the daylights out of Casey/Drain— no . . . it was just Drain this time. This was the beating he had received on the soundstage, superimposed over one of the alley backgrounds. It looked good. Charlie Angeles really was the best at what he did.

Then Deppe swore sharply as the beating went on and the announcer droned on about NanoKleen and the Devils dragged Casey/Drain down the street to show how this revolutionary new soap yanked stains out by the roots. I realized that it wasn't my writing and it wasn't the visual pun and it wasn't the richness of Charlie Angeles's superb digital editing. It was in the jerky motions that resulted when Charlie had turned the camera crews toward the attack on Drain and they had swarmed around the fight like vultures. It gave the sensation of actually being there. The scene even climaxed with them getting Drain down on the floor/ground and continuing the attack, much the way they had done to me on that lost April night that seemed so long ago. And the narrator droned on about NanoKleen bringing complete submission to wash day problems. Oh, yes. Charlie Angeles was a master, all right.

It finished quickly after that. The shots of Drain with the new suit on, and with his actual cuts and bruises edited onto his "before" face, saying how wonderful it looked now that NanoKleen had washed and repaired it. It was inaccurate, I know, but the suit looked as good as new. Charlie had said the suit looked better than new after the soaking, so it was within his right to show merely the new suit in its place. There was another super, this one saying, "Extended soaking required for repairs." Siobhan said, "I handled it!" then delivered a witty retort that I had added at the last minute.

"Now if NanoKleen could do something about your *face*!"

A thumbs-up, a prominent close-up of the box, and the narrator's voice. "Handle it . . . with NanoKleen . . . the *modern* wash day miracle from World Nanotechnologies, Ltd.!"

The screen winked out. The game between the Bolsheviks and the Rumrunners reappeared, strangely silent. Then a voice came in.

"Well. Uh, we're back at San Juan Stadium, where, uh, where the action is continuing. And speaking of action, Tad, how about that commercial?"

Tad's reply was lost as Deppe killed the sound.

"Well," Upchurch said. "That was . . . that was *something*, Boddekker."

"Likewise," said Churchill, rising quickly. "Well, we've got to be getting back."

"Absolutely."

They hurried out of the conference room without any further ado. Hotchkiss watched their retreat and sniffed.

"Well," he said. "I thought the spot was . . . was . . ." He waved his hands as if probing the air would bring the right word to the surface.

"Brilliant." That was Honniker In Accounting. The others looked at her. "It was, you know," she continued. "I'm not creative like you are. All I do is juggle numbers. But I still know the basics. What is an advert supposed to do to its victim? Get their attention. Don't you all agree that that spot held your attention?"

One by one, they all nodded.

"Of course it did! And it should give an impression of the product. In this case it was graphic. NanoKleen beats dirt at its own game. Right?"

"She's right," said Hotchkiss. "You know, the rest of us creative types have been so close to this that we couldn't see it. But she's right. It is brilliant." Hotchkiss started to clap, and the others followed suit. Griswold whistled.

I nodded and smiled and said I couldn't have done it without them, then Deppe cleared his throat and stepped forward with a large package in his hand. The others immediately fell silent.

"What is this?" I asked.

"Well," Deppe said sheepishly, "those of us in your group, including those not here because they're busy politicking—"

Dansiger hissed.

"And a few other principal witnesses to your career"—he motioned at Hotchkiss and Honniker In Accounting—"have all chipped in to get you this little token of thanks for doing such a great job of helping us land this account." With that, he handed the package over. It weighed heavily in my hands. I held it to my ear, as if listening for ticking. They laughed.

"You really didn't have to do this."

"Open it," Dansiger insisted. The rims of her eyes were moist. It was either the moment or the presence of Hotchkiss. For her sake, I turned the package over and tore at the wrapping.

"Gift wrapped, too. This must have cost a fortune."

"We'll make it back," Griswold said confidently.

I got the wrapping off to see a white box with a hot orange sticker in the middle. Printed on it was a stern message in flat black lettering.

WARNING!
Careless handling of this product could result
in lacerations to the extremities.

Ingestion of this product could result in
toxic metals poisoning (Mercury).

Product is flammable! Always store away
from and do not use near open flame.

Store in a cool, dry place. Product may mold
or mildew if wet.

Recycle or dispose of properly! This is a
Class VI pollutant, and all applicable
antipol laws and their penalties apply.

"It *is* a bomb," I said, and they laughed. Pulling off the lid, I looked. Inside were perfect, delicate rectangles of white, hundreds of them, stacked with precision.

"We figured," Dansiger said, "there was only one thing left to give you a common link with the other great writers of the world. Paper. So now you have some."

My face was burning and a lump was forming in my throat. I stammered out some feeble words of thanks, and then laughed at my inability to compose, when I made my living as a wordsmith. Finally I said, "Let me write all of you a thank you on this wonderful stuff," and started to search the box for something to write with.

"Pen," I heard Dansiger say. "A pen? Pencil? He needs something to mark on the paper."

Deppe patted his pockets like he expected to find one there, then held his arms out.

"How about a stylus?" asked Hotchkiss.

"Only works with a slate," said Griswold.

"I'm sorry," Deppe said, embarrassed. "We'll get you one."

"That's all right," I said. "This is plenty, really. You're all too kind."

"Well," Dansiger said, after an awkward moment of silence. "Boddekker, we know you like to be left alone when your spots premiere. And we figure you have a lot on your mind now, so if you'll excuse us—"

Before I could protest, she had risen, and she and Deppe and Griswold and Hotchkiss all left the room, offering polite good-byes and see-you-tomorrows. I felt my heart pounding in frustration. My reputation had preceded me. I usually did want to be left alone after seeing one of my adverts, but this time had been different. It was almost as if I wanted this moment to go on forever.

I realized that I hadn't been completely abandoned. I was alone in the room with Honniker In Accounting.

"So, Boddekker," she smiled, looking at her watch. "It's after five. What are your plans?"

I caught myself staring. I'm afraid my mouth may have been hanging open. It was like I still couldn't trust the reality of it all. Our near miss at the soundstage a few weeks ago had an ethereal, dreamlike quality to it, and I had started to doubt whether it had actually happened.

"Uh . . ." I shrugged. Someone like Honniker In Accounting probably looked down her nose at a plebeian celebration like Cantaloupe Day. Still, it was probably better to tell the truth and get it over with. I managed to stammer out, "I thought I'd wind down after the three-day weekend and go down to Bleecker Street to see what was happening."

Her face lit up. "You know something, Boddekker? I've lived in this city nine years now, and I've never been to the Cantaloupe Day celebration. I've always heard how terrific it is, so it's probably about time that I went. That is, if you wouldn't mind my company."

For once something went right, and one deep breath allowed me to compose myself. "I'd be honored."

On the way out of the building, Smilin' Guy hailed me to talk about the new advert. I stopped for a moment and introduced him to Honniker In Accounting, then let him give his recap of the spot, which as he saw it, was about a someone who got beat up because he used the wrong laundry soap.

"And I really liked the part about ten of them, Mr. Boddekker," he said, "because there was only one of him."

"Thanks," I nodded to him. "We're going to Bleecker Street this evening. Do you want me to bring you a cantaloupe?"

"Naw." He shuffled his feet and looked away. "Our house father, he's taking us there, and I'll see Jenny, her house mother is taking her there, and she likes to dance with me."

"Maybe I'll see you there, then."

"Heavens, no. Not if Jenny's making me dance. I'd be 'barrassed."

"We won't look, then. I promise."

As we walked out and headed for the subway, I noticed that Honniker In Accounting had suddenly become quiet, and her gaze had locked onto the sidewalk. My face started to burn with the sense that something had gone terribly wrong. It was time to do the honorable thing.

"Listen, if this isn't right, or if this isn't in your plans—"

She looked up at me. Her eyes looked as if they were holding back tears, and she clasped my hand. Hard. "Nothing's wrong. I really do want to go."

"But if something's not right—"

She stopped on the sidewalk and wiped her eyes. "There is something wrong, but it's not with you. It's with me. You put me to shame, Boddekker, did you know that?"

"If there's some kind of conflict or something, I'll understand. Really. We all get put into positions—"

"In the years I've worked for Pembroke Hall, I don't know how many times I've walked past that poor man and saw him staring at me and thought he had the most terrible thoughts about me. So I've spent the last couple of years avoiding him. On purpose. And he turned out to be such a charming man—if a person could call him that. He probably didn't think of me any more than as another person to sweep up after." She looked up and down the street helplessly, biting her upper lip. "Take me away from here, Boddekker."

Not being a fool, I hailed a bikeshaw. I tried to sit a platonic distance from Honniker In Accounting, but she closed the distance and picked up my hand again, holding it tight.

The driver let us off a block from Bleecker Street, which was closed at both ends for the big celebration. The street was lined with pushcarts and street merchants, and the stores had all

brought tables out to the streets to sell merchandise. The air was
sharp with the scent of meat and onion and peppers grilling over
charcoal grills, and the yeasty tang of beer. There was music from
a half-dozen places at once, including a garage full of kids playing covers of grind and retropop, a steel drum band, and a dozen
or so guys fronted by an obese accordion player who enticed
people to dance polkas.

As soon as we hit the street, we were accosted by vendors who
pushed free cantaloupes into our hands, and there was nearly a
scuffle over whose melon would have the honor of being carried
by Honniker In Accounting. We settled the matter by quietly slipping out into the middle of the street and cutting through a crowd
of polka-dancing couples, trying to dance our way around while
holding onto our cantaloupes. Before long we both found a vacant
table along the side of the street and collapsed, laughing.

Next we ate too much, trying to sample everything; sausage
and onion, sausage and kraut, ribs and chicken, and that new fish
and soy protein stick that cooks up like a shish kebob. Everyone
had their own brand of beer, darks and lights and greens and reds
and ales and lagers, with any level of alcohol you wanted, and you
could do it without touching any of the national brands. Strangely,
only a few desserts were in sight—some cheese and carrot cakes,
and a few street-cooked donuts—but fresh fruits were everywhere, especially the festival's namesake.

Dinner fast became a blur and before I knew it, we were on the
street dancing again, a little farther down the block, where a small
dark woman in one of those new multiform dresses sang a sensational set of Latin-based ballads. Honniker In Accounting licked
barbecue sauce from my fingers. I kissed her to catch a stray fleck
of mustard on her cheek. Our eyes were tired, our faces dirty, and
our breath smelled of beer. The light vanished and everything was
done to the glow of the street lamps, which added to the intoxica-
tion.

Finally, melons in hand, we walked away from it all. Before
long, we found ourselves standing in front of a small hotel in the
Village. It was one of those regal looking places, and it hadn't
always been a hotel. It had been bought at the turn of the century
and converted to capitalize on the Village tourist trade after Cantaloupe Day had been declared a holiday.

Honniker In Accounting and I stared at the place, the neon

HOTEL bright against the garish color of the brick. Then we looked into each other's eyes. And we knew.

There was a certain amount of abandon to the moment. Everything had been leading up to this. There was even a euphoria as I shelled out twenty-five thousand dollars for the room, money I could have saved toward that still-vacant house in Princeton. But at that particular moment in time, it didn't matter.

The room was small but comfortable, and housed a single brass bed. A small table sported a bowl with a knife and two cantaloupes, and the two I had brought from Bleecker Street joined them. I looked over at the dresser and saw Honniker In Accounting hovering near the vid set.

"Don't even think of it," I said.

"I wouldn't dream of it." She wandered over to the window and opened the blinds. We were looking out across Village rooftops onto the river, over which burst a bright plume of white, followed by red fingers blossoming out into the night sky.

I walked up behind her and started kissing her neck. There was another burst of light over the river, this one purple and silver. She sighed, as did the crowd on the street below. I reached around, still kissing, and started to unbutton her blouse, and she watched the explosions of light and color, softly murmuring something about Cary and Grace that I didn't completely catch.

Then we were sitting on the bed, and I turned away for a moment, going through my clothes, sheepishly wishing that I'd thought to bring along some Lover's Mist. My mind started to work its way out of the mood that had been set, but Honniker In Accounting calmly pulled her satchel from the floor and produced a can, unscented, and pressed it softly into my hand.

The jingle I had written was a million miles away.

I slowly crawled onto the bed where she was waiting, breathing, warm. She took my face in her hands and kissed me and then she said, "Don't worry about me, Boddekker. This one's for you. This one is for you."

I kissed her gently. I wasn't in any mood to argue.

Neither of us had thought to close the blinds, so I was wakened by the first light filtering through the window. I unwrapped myself from Honniker In Accounting's embrace and eased out of bed to correct the problem, but decided that I liked the view of the city and her slim figure in the morning light. So I propped my pillow to keep the light out of her face and sat down at the table, where I cut up and peeled one of the cantaloupes and chewed several slices while I stared out the window.

I glanced back at the sleeping figure in the bed, then across at the mirror. The sight of the vid set reminded me of the NanoKleen spot. For once I'd gotten through the night of a premiere without losing sleep over the Early Reaction to the spot and whether or not there were indications that it was going to sell the product. I went to look at my watch, but it had been abandoned somewhere in the room.

Well, from the light outside, it looked late enough to get something on the Early Reaction from the Pembroke Hall datanet. I went looking for my watch, and when I found it I activated the phone.

Then I stopped.

Did I really want to do this? Especially now? Here?

I had to. I turned the watch on. The number one came up.

One message. Early reaction. I pushed the button to play it back.

A sultry voice came over the watch's tiny speaker. "Boddekker! This is Ringwold over at Mauldin and Kress. Remember me?"

Did I ever. I looked over to make sure that Honniker In Accounting was still asleep.

"Listen, I just saw that piece you did for NanoKleen. Congratulations. That was some piece of work, kid. Makes me glad that you beat us out for the account. And besides"—there was a pregnant pause—"it's about time somebody gave a boot in the groin to that ranking chancre Norman Drain."

There was a musical tone. *End of message.*

Then three more to remind me: *No further messages.*

They hadn't even done an Early Reaction study.

My heart sank as I realized the only possibility. *They didn't do an early reaction study because there was no Early Reaction. The spot stiffed.*

I thought about telling Honniker In Accounting that, but I didn't think she'd appreciate finding out that she'd just slept with a loser.

Too bad, Boddekker.

The phrase haunted me. I heard it in a hundred different

voices; from Hotchkiss, Robenstine, and Norbert. From Honniker In Accounting as she walked out the door and out of my life. From Levine as he deleted my file from the employee database. And from Ferman as he eyed my tibia and slowly swung a baseball bat so it smacked against the palm of his hand.

I turned the phone function off and stared out the window. Out on the horizon, it looked like a storm was headed our way.

PEMBROKE, HALL, PANGBORN, LEVINE, AND HARRIS

"Selling you to the world since 1969"

Offices in Principal Cities: New York - Montreal - Toronto - Sydney - London - Tokyo - Moskva - Beijing - Chicago - Oslo - Philadelphia - Amarillo

CLIENT: »Boston Harbor Tea		PRODUCT: »Name Awareness Campaign
WRITER: »Boddekker	TIME: »:60	MEDIA: »Vid/3-D hybrid
TITLE: »*It's Always Better*		
PRODUCTION ORDERS:	»***IMPORTANT!*** See special instructions as indicated throughout script!	

AUDIO	VIDEO
We hear wind blowing outside a house. We hear a crackling fire.	*Interior shot of a house[1]—a nice house. To our right, midground is a fireplace with a prominently displayed license, and a crackling fire inside. Lying in front of it, right foreground, is a white bearskin rug,[2] on which is a china saucer. Behind all this, in the background, is a big picture window with a classic winter scene—snow on the ground, ice on tree branches, etc.[3] This scene is in a grainy black and white.[4]*

[1] There is a specific house that should be used for the interior on this shot—please see Boddekker for details.

[2] Make sure the viewer can tell it's a polar bear synthate, or those animal terrorists will be setting off bombs in the john.

[3] This will have to be inserted digitally. Mattingly will provide the artwork.

[4] In the version for the Union of Mongol States, this section is in color 2-D.

ANNOUNCER: No matter the time . . .
SFX: The chime of a teacup being placed on the saucer.

Movement and high resolution color at the right side of the screen—a feminine hand with bright red fingernails enters from the right and sets a china cup full of steaming liquid on the saucer. As the steam rises, the room fills with its natural colors in high-resolution mode.[5]

Up music: Soft piano jazz, barely audible.

Cross-fade to a bar scene.[6] In our foreground is a section of a round table with another china saucer. Left fore- and background is a comfortable bar, and in the far back left is a piano. Again, grainy black and white.[7]

ANNOUNCER: . . . no matter the place . . .
SFX: The chime of a cup being placed on a saucer.

Again, a colorized female hand places the cup of tea on the saucer in the center foreground. Steam rises, and hi-res color fills the bar.[8]

SFX: Fireworks, and a crowd oooh-ing and ahhh-ing softly in the background.

Cross-fade to a shot of a small but clean hotel room.[9] Right foreground is a neatly made bed. Left center is a small table with a phone and a china saucer. Center background is an open window with the drapes drawn back. Through the window we see fireworks

[5] In the version for the UMS, the hand and cup are in 3-D, and the steam makes the image slowly fill out into three dimensions.
[6] There is a specific bar that should be used for the interior on this shot—please see Boddekker for details.
[7] See note 4.
[8] See note 5.
[9] There is a specific hotel which should be used for the interior on this shot—please see Boddekker for details.

over a city. Again, all in grainy
black and white.[10]

ANNOUNCER: . . . no matter the
reason . . .
SFX: The chime of a cup being
placed on a saucer.

One more time, the hi-res hand
comes in and places the cup
on the saucer. Color fleshes out
the room.[11]

ANNOUNCER: . . . it's always
better with a cup of Boston
Harbor Tea!

Grainy black and white shot[12]
of teacup on china saucer
looming large center ground.
Right behind it, the product box
of standard Boston Harbor Tea.
Instead of steam, hi-res color
rises from the cup.[13]Crawling
super: WARNING: Tea
contains caffeine, which may
have adverse effects on user.
Prolonged brewing times may
cause caffeine to break down
into tannic acid. May cause
stomach irritation and dental
staining in some individuals.
High serving temperature may
cause burns if handled
improperly or carelessly. Users
should exercise extreme caution
when using this product.[14]

[10] See note 4.
[11] See note 5.
[12] See note 4.
[13] For the UMS version, grainy black-and-white steam does rise from
the cup but it should appear to rise up and out of the set to make a fog
across the viewer's ceiling.
[14] Isn't there some way we can avoid this last bit? It ruins the
atmosphere of the spot.*

*Sorry, Boddekker. FTC Regs again. Now gimme a break and quit whining,
huh?—Chesterfield.

THIRTEEN

There Were Five of Them

Occasionally in this business, an advert comes along that defies the laws of advertising physics. It doesn't behave as it's supposed to as far as selling or informing or entertaining. When that happens the results are disastrous—although occasionally they can be exhilarating.

There Were Ten of Them was one of those spots. The Early Reaction had not exactly pronounced it dead, but it was certainly coughing up blood. My usual response would have been to blame my writing, but in this case I blamed World Nano's insistence on putting Norman Drain in the spot. Drain had been seen everywhere endorsing everything, and I was convinced that his credibility was nonexistent. No wonder people were resistant to this new miracle product. I wouldn't have touched their product with a hack like Drain pushing it.

As the week dragged on, things began to look like a major end of the world. One by one, the members of my group quit talking to me; Mortonsen, Harbison, and Sylvester all in one day, then a few days of respite; then Dansiger, Deppe, and the usually unflappable Griswold. Only Bainbridge kept the lines of communication open, and I'm sure it was a combination of her dogged optimism and crass opportunism. Nothing was ever said between us about the ill-fated Woodstock trip, and so she no doubt felt she had some unfinished business with me. I continued to play it cool—although Dansiger would have said that I was playing it stupid. Whatever worked.

Outside the group, things were worse. When the Church Brothers saw me coming one day, they deliberately acted like they were hiding from me, and when I passed they whispered "Leper! Leper! Unclean! Pariah!" Another time, Upchurch threw his arm around Churchill, pointed his free hand at me, and said in an overly paternal voice, "There, son! *That's* what a *loser* looks like! Make sure you don't turn out like *him*!"

I heard nothing from Hotchkiss, but thought nothing of that. He had probably fallen into a depression of his own, so the last thing I needed was to be around him. I didn't hear anything at all from the other creative group leaders. There were sessions at Ogilvy's during the week, but I wasn't invited to any of them. Again, it was nothing I wanted a part of. Alcohol would have only made things worse for me.

The worst part was that I hadn't heard anything from the old men. If this campaign had Died and Gone to Hell as badly as it seemed, they'd surely be scrambling for position and performing massive acts of damage control. Part of that would naturally be terminating me—but I heard nothing. And I couldn't take Bainbridge's word that no news was good news. The silence immobilized me. It was as if not hearing anything was worse than getting the news that I no longer had a job.

Again, the only person outside our creative group who kept in touch was Honniker In Accounting. Our parting the morning after Cantaloupe Day I had made clumsy by not wanting to talk about the nonexistent early reaction. I took her home in a bikeshaw, and when I waved good-bye I was convinced it would be the last time I would ever see her.

But on Monday morning I walked into my office to find that she had left a gift; a pen to go with the paper the others had given me. And she had taken a piece of that paper and written a note on it; her telephone number along with the words *For your watch.*

I should have been elated. Instead, my shoulders slumped. If things were as bad as I thought, then what relationship we had would soon dissolve in the wake of my failure to sell NanoKleen. I'd soon be standing shoulder to shoulder with Robenstine in the Oslo office, penning sales letters for tinned ludefisk. So I didn't put her number into my watch—not then. I couldn't bear to even look at her, not after she'd been so giving of herself. But I maintained my presence of mind long enough to fold up the paper and hide it my desk drawer under some dusty SOBs bubblechips.

Meantime, it became evident to me that *There Were Ten of Them* wasn't working. When I weighed everything that had happened, I decided that even Oslo was too good for me. There was no doubt about it—I was finished at Pembroke Hall. If I couldn't sell something as miraculous as NanoKleen, then what good was I? When I couldn't talk myself out of the mood, I called up my ferret and asked it to update my résumé and prepare a potential mailing list, telling it to avoid any position that would require me to write and be creative.

The ferret said, "Oh dear, Mr. Boddekker, are you having another bad day over the World Nano account?"—and then the blasted thing tried to talk me out of my actions. I finally relented, but not because I felt like I could stay at Pembroke Hall. I did it to shut that blasted software up.

By the next Monday, I would be glad that I had stayed.

The week started off on the same sour note that had ended the previous Friday, with the early reaction resembling a desert ghost town, our survey researchers finding that people were either unwilling or unable to talk about it.

But as more complete numbers started to come in, something strange happened. When the reaction numbers were collated with sales figures it became clearly evident that the Early Reaction was wrong. *There Were Ten of Them*—and NanoKleen itself—was worming its way into the consciousness of the population.

My first indication of this was so subtle that I almost missed it. I had awakened late on the morning of Boston Harbor's verdict on what I thought would be my last script for Pembroke Hall. Instead of going to fight with the subway crowds, I ran out onto the street and hailed a bikeshaw, explained my predicament to the driver, and offered a large bonus if my deadline was met. She pedaled hard, in and out of the morning traffic, and I was so absorbed in checking data in my notebook that before I knew it, she had pulled to a stop at Pembroke Hall. I paid her the fare, the promised bonus, and some on top of that, thanking her profusely. Panting, she replied with a thumbs-up: "I handled it."

I returned the gesture and started to walk into the lobby. Then I froze. Spinning on my heel, I ran back out to the sidewalk, but she was already pulling back onto the street, another fare in tow.

Had I taken it wrong? It could have been coincidence. A lot of people might say, "I handled it," for a lot of different reasons. It's the perfect thing to say when you're giving someone a thumbs-up.

Right?

Coincidence.

Then the Smilin' Guy met me on the way to the elevator with some kind of glider he had built out of the same material as the roses. He sailed one straight for me, something I wasn't expecting, and I reached out deflect it with my free hand. As it hit my hand, I realized that it was another of his works of art, and tried to keep my fingers from closing too hard, but it was too late. I heard it crackle under my grip and dust filtered to the floor.

"I'm really sorry," I told him. "I didn't mean to break it."

Smilin' Guy took the sight of the disintegrated flyer with his usual cheery aplomb. "That's okay, Mr. Boddekker," he said. "Looks like you handled the clothes, too."

Instinctively, I looked down at my shirt. Then I realized what I'd heard and looked back at Smilin' Guy.

"Something wrong, Mr. Boddekker?"

"What did you say?"

Nervousness overtook his features. "I didn't say nothin' bad, I don't think. If I'd known it was bad I woulda said something else like 'tough break,' only the plane I made, it was easy to break, so that wasn't right."

"But you said—"

He strained to remember—after all, a whole minute had passed. "Uh, I think, 'looks like you handled the clothes, too.' "

"Why did you say that?" I looked at his face, and then reassured him. "You're not in trouble. I think it's an interesting expression."

He sighed and fidgeted. "I got it from my boss. He's mean sometimes, you know. But I was dustin' something in the small lobby, you know, where people come when they're lookin' for work and stuff, and I sort of broke this globe light. And the boss, he was mad, but someone told me he'd been mad all day, and he asked me what happened, and I told him that I was trying to dust the light globe and I sort of slipped but I tried to catch it and it broke into about a zillion pieces on the floor and he looked at it and said, 'Well, it looks like you handled the clothes, too,' only I didn't get no broken glass on my clothes. And Mercy, she's the desk lady in the small lobby where people come when they're looking for work, she told me not to worry because the boss had been saying that to everyone all day long. And he said it to me a couple more times because I wasn't doin' such a good job of anything that day, and so I figured out that maybe it was something you said to someone when you wanted to be mad at them but weren't really. It isn't bad, is it, Mr. Boddekker?''

I shook my head. ''No. It's fine.''

I paid him for the broken plane and hurried onto an elevator with a bunch of clerks heading for Pine, Creedle, and Walsh, the accounting firm on the seventeenth floor.

''So,'' said one, ''think Trilby's married by now?''

''If his feet haven't frozen.''

''Some party last night, huh?''

''It was all right.''

''You did your share.''

''It was nothing.'' There was a blissfully pregnant pause. ''I handled it.''

Scoffing laughter from the other. ''You handled the clothes, too.''

''Get off it.''

''Get off it yourself. I saw you heaving out on Trilby's front lawn.''

No, I thought. *There's no more coincidence.* Something was going on, and *There Were Ten of Them* was directly responsible.

When I got off the elevator at Pembroke Hall I called my group together for a meeting to discuss what had happened. When that meeting was interrupted by outsiders who wanted to describe similar experiences, climaxing with Finney and Spenner, I knew for certain that something was up.

It was as if some great psychic dam had broken. If people weren't aware of what NanoKleen Could Do for You, they were certainly aware of the ad. Even if they were saying things like ''I handled it!'' because they picked it up from someone else, the next time they saw the spot they would realize what was going on—they would become part of the joke, and NanoKleen would be burned forever into their memory.

The meeting gave way to more meetings. Someone from the Analysis department took a six-month sabbatical when he realized that the Early Reaction he had compiled for the spot had been totally off the mark.

"But the numbers were clean," he had protested. "I looked over the sample base personally because I knew this was a big campaign. Everything was run by the book, and the Pembroke Hall machinery ran flawlessly. And I personally supervised the Tally and Breakdown analysis."

Spenner watched the man, scratched his chin, and chose his words carefully. "It looks like you handled the clothes, too."

"Why don't you take some time off?" Finney suggested politely.

I had two minutes to feel sorry for the guy. It wasn't his fault. It was simply bad luck that he was wrong about the spot that was the exception that proved the rule. Then I was caught up in more meetings as Pembroke Hall studied the best way to ride the juggernaut that had been created.

The first thing decided was that we needed to keep Ferman's Devils around. If this got any bigger they were going to come in handy, especially if NanoKleen wanted follow-up spots.

"Bring them in," said Spenner, "and we'll offer them nice contracts. If they're working for someone else, we'll offer them more money. Lots more. Enough to buy a nice house!"

I would have glared had I not remembered that Spenner was a senior partner. "It's not like they're working in a doughnut shop for college money," I said. "They're a street gang. And I doubt they could buy a house with their criminal records."

"Yes," said Finney, innocuously. "But they're *our* street gang. You created them, after all."

It was beyond arguing. The only way that upper management would see the Devils for what they were was to actually bring them in and let them disrupt a meeting in their own, unique way. It would be a pleasure to see that, and it would be an even bigger pleasure to return to the normal pattern of life at Pembroke Hall. I was, after all, a writer, not a meeting man.

So some twelve days after Ferman and company had been introduced to the world, I was walking with them to the elevators of Pembroke Hall. The Smilin' Guy saw that strange group of us, and for better or worse, immediately recognized the Devils. They didn't notice him, of course—they were too awestruck by the lobby of the building—but I could see him watching them carefully, trying to stay hidden behind one of the pillars against the prospect of their turning him into their next victim.

When we stepped off the elevator on a Pembroke Hall floor, we were instantly surrounded by a phalanx of the company's finest, well-wishing and pushing us here and there, and arranging us in front of the corporate logo. They formed a line of us; Ferman and Jet and Jimmy Jazz and Nose and Rover and me, and started aiming cameras. Then they decided that a more layered look was in order, so they put Ferman in front of Jet and staggered me halfway between Nose and Rover.

"That's great, that's great," they said.

"What's all of this for?" I asked, and a split second later we were bathed in laser light and captured on film for everyone to see. I'm sure you've seen that picture of us, especially if you've studied advertising at all. It's become a classic. Ferman looking dour and threatened, Jet looming menacingly over him. Jimmy Jazz trying to politely smile, Nose giving one of those stupid attention-getting smiles that only a teenager can muster. Rover looking disgruntled, like he wants to pull out your heart and eat it, and yours truly looking torn between bewilderment and fright. That's the origin of that dark family snapshot.

From there we were all ushered into the Intimate Conference Room. I was placed in the midst of the Devils and we were flanked by Levine and Harris; Spenner, Finney and Robenstine; the rest of my creative group; Honniker In Accounting, who gave me a hopeful look as she walked into the room; another accountant named McFeeley; two people from Rights and Permissions—Abernathy and a prim-looking woman named Justman; and a man whose smile was as sinister as the Smilin' Guy's was innocent, whose name I would soon forget but whose profession I wouldn't.

"Well," said Spenner, once all of the chairs were filled, "I guess everyone is here, so we can get started. First of all, I am most pleased to announce that we have a new addition to our little family here."

Everyone except the Devils oohed and aahed at the surprise, and most of my group looked over at the man we didn't recognize.

"As of this morning, we have officially hired a graduate of Columbia University as a linguistics expert, a position she was currently already filling, albeit in an unofficial capacity. So please give a warm Pembroke Hall welcome to Cassandra Bainbridge.''

Eager to please, Ferman and the Devils were quick to applaud. It was a good thing, too, because most of the group—myself included—was stunned into momentary inaction by the announcement. None of us had been consulted about her and none of us wanted her. She had permanently filled the vacuum in our department by riding the tide the Devils had created. Ordinarily, she would have been a political asset to me—but in the light of her failed seduction and my perceived relationship with Honniker In Accounting, I couldn't even count on that.

The group quickly rallied and added a smattering of applause to the welcome, as Spenner continued.

''And to introduce the agenda, the senior-most partner of Pembroke, Hall, Pangborn, Levine, and Harris.''

There was scattered applause. The Devils had been caught off guard except for Jimmy Jazz, who clapped until he saw that I had quit. I smiled and nodded at him.

''Thank you,'' Levine said, dusting an imaginary piece of lint from his lapel. ''Gentle persons of the advertising trade, I would like to introduce you to our newest sales sensation, Ferman's Devils.'' And he quickly introduced each by their street name, and then added me in ''as the sixth Devil and creator of this outrageous concept.''

During the applause, Ferman leaned over to me and spoke in quiet tones, ''What's going on here, Boddekker? Am I going to have to feed you your own spleen? You didn't create us. We created you.''

Nobody in the room was more painfully aware of that than I. ''More jargon,'' I told him. ''They have to give me some credit for this. You guys are the ones who will see all of the money and women. I'll be lucky if I can get the time of day from someone like her.'' I gave a slight nod toward Honniker In Accounting, who noticed the gesture and smiled at me.

Ferman raised his eyebrows at me and grinned. ''Put your watch in your pocket and lie, Boddekker.''

I don't have to take my watch off to lie, I thought, and Levine continued.

''Boys,'' he said, and here he was addressing the five Devils directly, because he never referred to anyone in the company as that. ''I have asked Mr. Boddekker to bring you here because we are interested in having you become part—a very special part—of the Pembroke Hall family.''

"Gee, thanks," Ferman said, not aware that Levine's pause had been rhetorical. Most of the Pembroke Hall eyes in the room glared at him, and he went silent.

"We know you're hesitant about the prospect because you're not used to the idea of gainful employment. And frankly, because of your backgrounds, we were not without trepidation at the prospect of making this invitation, but we believe that your talent will bear out our ultimate decision.''

Ferman's jaw trembled and his hand started to jump. He was ready to sign right there and then, but as he watched, he saw that none of the Pembroke Hall people were ready for him to sign. He took a deep breath and tried to ease back in his chair.

"So," Levine continued, "we hope that you will hear us out and consider the offering we are about to put before you, and that you will find it pleasing, and that you will be pleased yourselves to become a part of this family. And so, without further delay, I am going to turn this over to some of my experts, who will discuss terms of the contract with you.''

Ferman and Nose and Jet started to applaud and quit when they saw that nobody else was doing it.

McFeeley from accounting stood, opened his notebook, and waited for its screen to come on. "Gentlemen," he said, "Pembroke, Hall, Pangborn, Levine, and Harris is prepared to offer each of you an exclusivity stipend of two hundred thousand dollars a month—"

My heart stopped when I heard that figure.

"—plus a working salary of an additional two hundred thousand dollars per spot. In other words, you will each collect a weekly issue of fifty thousand dollars in return for which you will *not* consider offers from any other advertising agency. You will be exclusive employees of Pembroke, Hall, Pangborn, Levine, and Harris. This salary should ensure your loyalty to us, and is a guarantee of our loyalty to you.

"In addition to that, every time we use you in a commercial you will each receive two hundred thousand dollars, that being your working fee. You will notice that this is a considerable raise in fee from what you previously received for appearing in *There Were Ten of Them,* which was . . ." McFeeley tapped his screen and looked lost.

"A hundred-fifty thousand dollars," said Honniker In Accounting, from her screen. "For the entire group."

The Devils wowed.

"Plus," McFeeley continued, "you will receive allowances for transportation and housing, at a rate to be determined once housing is found and travel distances are determined. Are there any questions?"

"Excuse me." Bainbridge raised her hand. I cringed. "It occurs to me that these young"—Her upper lip curled into an involuntary sneer—"*young men* quite possibly have, shall we say, a tainted past, with records that would very well prevent them from buying their own homes. That could be a problem."

"Hm," said Levine, fingering his chin with thumb and forefinger. "Any solutions?"

"Let's scratch the housing allowance from the offer," said McFeeley.

"We gotta live somewhere nice if we're gonna be stars," Nose blurted. The room went silent. All eyes were on him. "I mean, if we're these big shots, maybe not like that sucker that we beat up the other day, but I mean, we're gonna be famous, too, right? And we gotta have, like, a place to bring girls."

From Bainbridge I heard a strange sound of disgust, like she was trying to clear her throat and swallow her revulsion at the same time. It was even stranger than her snore.

"I think what Nose is trying to say," Ferman said, in thin tones at first, then increasingly louder as he found his confidence, "is that it wouldn't look right for Pembroke Hill's brightest new stars to be living in a burned-out church."

"Hall," corrected Jimmy Jazz.

"You live in a burned out church?" said Spenner, amazed.

"It seems so," replied Finney.

"What an incredible, romantic image." Spenner made an entry in his notebook. "We've got to use that for our press."

"Now about this housing thing," Levine said. "There is a definite problem here. Romantic as that wild cowboy/lost pilgrim/burned-out church image is, if this thing takes off like we're anticipating, it won't do to have groupies coming and going from some deserted building at all hours and having sycophants and hangers-on camped out on the front sidewalk."

"Of course not," said McFeeley from accounting. "We're going to want to buy that place and turn it around. Charge admission, sell souvenirs inside. Maybe make the place into an advertising museum.''

"The last thing in the world we need right now," said Griswold, "is another advertising museum."

"No matter that," said Levine. "These boys need a decent place to sleep, and with their records, they're not going to get one."

"Well," said Abernathy from Rights and Permissions, "We have had that problem before. And what we've done, we've let the people in question choose their own apartments, and then *we,* that is Pembroke, Hall, Pangborn, Levine, and Harris rent it and then rent it to them for a modest fee that would cover our costs plus administrative expenses—say, fifty thousand dollars a month."

McFeeley tagged a key on his notebook. "Sixty-two thousand, five hundred thirty-four dollars, ninety-one cents, and sixty-four mils." He looked up at us apologetically. "We have to compensate for the New York State Rental Property Income Recovery Tax."

"We could automatically deduct it from their monthly exclusivity salary, prorated to a weekly fee," suggested Honniker In Accounting.

"Sounds good to me," said Levine.

"Cries momma," said Bainbridge.

"Now wait a ranking minute here!" Ferman slapped his palms on the table and stood. "I might be new to this show-business stuff, but I didn't fall off the ranking soycake truck yesterday. You folks might have me grabbing my ankles, but I know the sound of someone unzipping their trou's."

A shocked silence fell across the room.

"I've talked with Boddekker about this." Ferman looked around the room triumphantly. "I want an *agent* to help us negotiate through all of this stuff!"

I stifled a yelp. My impulse was to say that Ferman was lying, but he wasn't. I *had* mentioned that he could get an agent to help negotiate things. But I'd been lying. That was part of the trap I was trying to spring on him.

"Ah," said Levine, after a moment to compose himself. "Yes. Of course." He looked over at Abernathy, who again stood.

"We anticipated this, and we can't say that we blame you," Abernathy said. "So I've brought along my associate, Mez Justman. She has agreed to act as your agent during this process."

Justman stood. "Mr. Ferman," she said politely.

"McKluskey," said Ferman.

"Very well. What is it you're having a problem with, Mr. McKluskey?"

"This housing business." He looked around the room at all of the women. "I don't have to tell you what I think it's a load of. I think you can figure it out for yourself. They think they got us in this situation because we got records and can't buy our own houses—at least, not till we're eighteen and our records clear. So they're going to hit us with this thing where we have to pay to live in their apartments."

"*Au contraire,* Mr. McKluskey," said Justman. "This really is a situation of bonus to you. You see, Pembroke Hall is offering you the opportunity to *choose* your own place of living. They will in turn take care of the technicalities, and the money that comes out of your paycheck is in essence what you would spend on housing anyway. You see, Mr. McKluskey—and other Devils—*most* agencies, when you enter into a talent-exclusive contract such as this, and you have a residential restrictive situation such as the one you're in, give you no choice as to where you can live. You would either live in the agency-owned apartment complex, or you go back to the burned-out church building."

"I'd rather go back to our church," said Jet.

"But you won't have to Mr. Georgeson," said Justman, "because you can choose your own place to live. And you can all live together, if you want, or you can get your own places. It doesn't matter to Pembroke Hall."

"I think I want to live by myself," said Nose.

"Okay." Ferman smiled. "Thanks."

"Any further questions, please don't hesitate to ask Mez Justman," said Levine. "Now, continuing with our offer, here is Mr. Abernathy from Rights and Permissions . . ."

Abernathy nodded. "Thank you. As you may well guess, with the slow-to-rise reaction we received on this spot, we had feared the worst. But now the late returns are in, and NanoKleen is disappearing quickly from store shelves all over the English-speaking world—which is most of it." He snorted a laugh. "Now we seem to have a sort of double-bonus situation, because of the High-Profile, High-Awareness curve put on this product by our friends here. Thus, I think it would be due time for us to seriously consider going into a heretofore unconsidered subphase of this campaign, namely, merchandising the product image.''

''Excuse me,'' said Griswold, looking calm as ever. ''Are you sure it isn't a bit premature? World Nano has committed a sizable investment in this campaign alone. This loop on the Awareness curve may be a passing thing, and this campaign may well have peaked by now as the novelty wears off. To ask World Nano to finance the merchandising phase now would be folly.''

''I don't think so,'' Abernathy said, ''and if you'll all switch your notebooks to the mutual dataload frequency, you'll be able to see the data that heretofore only a few of us have been privy to.''

I flipped up my notebook screen and keyed it into the sideload subchannel. A bold heading appeared at the top of the screen, followed by a long list of names, addresses, and figures preceded by dollar signs. I offered to share the screen with Ferman, who looked away. Jimmy Jazz leaned forward and squinted at the information.

''Again, this is something we weren't expecting. These are offers we have received for merchandising licenses. They started to roll in last Thursday.''

''Remarkable,'' said Griswold.

''Some of the more intriguing ideas include a pair of white pants with a greasy footprint stamped across the buttocks—''

''Oh, for heaven's sake!'' I cried, shaking my head with disgust. ''Why not imprint them with the words 'Ferman's Devils were here' and leave no question about it?''

Finney scowled. ''Don't be crass, Boddekker. And from here on, if you're not going to say something constructive to the progress of this meeting, please refrain from speaking.''

''Lighten up,'' Levine said abruptly. ''Let Boddekker speak his mind. There's nothing wrong with that. Shows he's got a spine. Really, we've got to stop hiring invertebrates at this place. Someone make a note of that.''

Finney reluctantly entered it in his notebook.

Abernathy chuckled. ''Entrepreneurs are having a field day generating ideas from this one. One wants to make this kind of clear plastic shirt for women with openings to expose the breasts. Then he wants to attach eight prosthetic breasts to the shirt itself—he's already been in touch with the Robotette people to see if they could run them for him—and across the back he wants to

put, in that stand-out holo lettering, 'There were ten of them.'
Isn't that delightful?''

"No," said Harbison, before I could. I had been looking at
Honniker In Accounting, and suddenly my face burned and I
looked away in shame. I heard Mortonsen mumble, "Might as
well repeal the ERA while you're at it."

"Well," Abernathy said hesitantly, "this same gentleman has
come up with something rather unusual for the slogan 'I handled
it,' but perhaps I shouldn't say any more."

"Thank you," said Honniker In Accounting.

"But the point remains that those are only two offers out of the
dozen we've gotten in the last two working days. And, as we see
it, it's only the tip of the proverbial iceberg."

"Very fine, indeed," said Levine.

"Wait a minute," Ferman said. "Back to that soycake truck
again. What's in it for me . . . us . . . the Devils?"

"Well," said McFeeley, "the offers we've been discussing are
image specific but not product-specific. In other words, they deal
with the ideas we've put out for NanoKleen, like 'There Were Ten
of Them' and 'I Handled It.' It seems inevitable that a product-
specific merchandising campaign will follow, using the identity of
the NanoKleen box itself. When that happens, you gentlemen will
no doubt be involved. Your image will be required to tie the
identity to the product."

"What are you talking about?" asked Jet Georgeson.

"Our pictures," Jimmy Jazz said, a distant look on his face.

"A quick study, he is," smiled McFeeley.

"He's going to want to put our pictures on stuff, Ferman. Stuff
like holo shirts, pillow cases, lunch boxes, action figures. Possibly
the box of soap itself."

"The possibilities are limitless," said Abernathy. "You could
appear on anything and everything, *with* the box of NanoKleen
closely associated with you."

"Which is something we *must* do in the next vid spot," Levine
said. "Boddekker, please make note of that."

"Done." I pretended to tap it into my notebook.

"And, of course," said Abernathy, "since this ties into the
great financial web of things, we're going to pay you for the
exclusive use of your image."

"Two points of net on Pembroke Hall's NanoKleen-related
profits," said McFeeley.

"Great ranking stuff," Nose and Jet said together, slapping palms.

I happened to glance at Dansiger at that moment. Something was wrong. Her facial features were starting to twist and her hands were shrinking into fists.

"Wait a sec," Ferman said. "You're going to put us everywhere, right?"

"You already are everywhere," said Finney.

"But I mean in places that vid screens don't go. You're talking about putting us on—I don't know. Toothbrushes. Pajamas. Dumb stuff like that . . ."

"And you'll receive remuneration for that."

"Yeah, but I'd like a little control over it. I mean, what if it's a product I don't really like, or is so ranking stupid that even the Nancy Boys would laugh themselves sick. I mean, I wouldn't like it if I was about to play slip 'n' slide with some girl and there was my picture on the ranking condom package. I want a little approval of what goes on."

Justman stood. "I feel that my client has a valid point, Mr. Levine. This is a problem. We need to have some sort of compromise in which my client can maintain some form of moral integrity."

Levine nodded. "And what do you suggest, Mez Justman?"

"I would like the contract with these gentlemen amended to include a right of endorsement refusal on any imaged product that they deem unbecoming or inconsistent with their beliefs or lifestyles."

"Which means—" Ferman asked.

"If you don't like the product featuring your image, you don't have to personally endorse it," explained Levine.

"Is that acceptable to you, Mr. Levine?" asked Justman.

"It is. Consider it done."

Ferman's mouth dropped open, and he looked at Justman with awe.

"Amend the contract to include right of endorsement refusal along with two points of net NanoKleen-related agency profits."

"Done," said Abernathy.

Now breath escaped from between Dansiger's teeth in a hiss. She leaned forward like she was going to stand, then sat back as if she was trying to relax. "Something's not right," she mouthed silently.

"So," Levine said, seeming very pleased with himself. "Mr. Abernathy, if you would please load the amended contracts to the slates for these gentlemen to sign—"

"Wait a second. Something isn't right."

That was Dansiger. She had finally found her nerve, and more important, she now had the attention of the old men. She said, "There's something here that strikes me as being off kilter, gentlemen, and I was wondering if you'd like to address it."

Levine nodded politely. "Why certainly, Mez Dansiger."

Dansiger waved her hands to punctuate her point. "Right now you are doing a lot of talking about compensation for the talent, that is, these boys here, Ferman's Devils. That's going to amount to quite a chunk of change for the meat part of the campaign." She glanced over at the Devils. "Excuse the expression."

"Those rates are within the initial norms for this type of talent," said Abernathy.

"And I don't doubt that you're going to give them what they deserve." She continued after a long pause. "But what about the bones that made the success of the meat possible?"

"You're referring, of course, to the writing talents of Mr. Boddekker," said Levine.

Of course she was. Dansiger might be my fiercest opponent within the creative group, but she had a sense of justice. In this case, however, I thought that sense might have fallen a bit short, so I chimed in, "I think Mez Dansiger is referring to the entire creative group, sir."

"If this campaign works out," Dansiger continued, "Pembroke Hall is going to realize enormous profit. And while I realize that the public's need for the meat needs to be satisfied, that meat would not be possible without the efforts of the creative group."

Levine bowed his head with some of the others for a moment. They murmured and nodded their heads.

"Of course, you're right, Mez Dansiger. It was quite unfair of us to put consideration of the superficial source of the success ahead of the true source. While I can't divulge fully the nature of your individual and group rewards at this time—we were saving them, you see, for the next agency-wide meeting—I can assure you that you will find this initial success reflected in your initial credit download at the end of this week. Additionally, as success follows success, the rewards will become more frequent and proportionately . . . *larger*."

That struck a positive note with the members of my group. I smiled. I was happy for them.

"Oh," continued Levine, "and perhaps this is the appropriate time to mention to you all that a reporter from *Advertising Age* will be here tomorrow to interview Mr. Boddekker about a number of things, including creative group leadership, and how the basic concept of Ferman's Devils came about."

And that went over even better. There were oohs and aahs that dissolved into a round of spontaneous applause. I was one of those applauding, because this heralded the beginning of a series of events that would surely culminate in my triumphantly crossing the threshold of the house in Princeton. Levine seemed happy too, as the founder of this feast.

"Now then, if we have that for the moment appeased, I believe it is time for us to move on to our contract with the Devils."

"By all means," Dansiger grinned.

"Hold it. Something is still not right."

This time it was Jimmy Jazz. He slowly stood and looked about the room accusingly. I'm sure I heard at least three different people draw a guilty breath. I don't recall if I was one of them.

Jimmy Jazz looked directly at Levine. "Do you guys know what you're getting into?"

"Something," said Levine, "that I'm hoping will prove to be a sound business decision."

"Yeah," sneered Jimmy Jazz. "I thought as much. Well we're not knights in shining armor, sir. Our reputations are rather tarnished. Can I be blunt?"

Levine nodded.

"We're criminals."

"Sit down, Jimmy," warned Ferman.

"We're not nice guys, and we're certainly not professionals like that guy we messed up, Norman Drain."

"Jimmy, this is a sweet deal and you're going to rank this out for us—"

"Mr. Ferman," Levine said gently. "Please. Let your associate speak. By all means, we want to get any misgivings out in the open so we can reach an agreement that is equitable for everyone involved." Ferman backed down. "Continue, please, Mr. Jazz."

"Well," Jimmy said, his anger for the moment diffused. "You guys are supposed to be the world's greatest advertising agency, right? And we're like, you know . . . we're scum." He raised his arm and stretched it out toward Honniker In Accounting. "It's like, if she says she wants me to go with her to the prom. Right? And I'm like, thinking, 'Why does someone as nice as that want to be seen with the likes of me?' "

"A valid point," said Levine. "And one that should be addressed. Perhaps I should let it be addressed by the very man who is going to be grappling with this—conflict of image, if you wish to call it that. Are you willing?"

"Sure," said Jimmy Jazz.

"Very well." And Levine introduced him—the man whose name escapes me to this day. He introduced him with that fleeting name and explained that he was Pembroke Hall's terminal rights liaison.

"Excuse me," Sylvester said upon hearing the man introduced. "I'm not feeling at all well." She hurried from the meeting room.

The terminal rights liaison shrugged, as if the departure were an insult that had been lost on him. "Gentlemen," he said, opening his notebook, "and Mr. Jazz especially, what we are looking at is a compounded conflict between the sales image and the actual image. Actually, the two are very close, based on that brilliant spot that you're in. You are in fact a rough-and-tumble street gang. The public perceives you, however, as a rough-and-tough street gang *with a sense of justice,* this emanating from your quite rightly justified pasting of Norman Drain. The true novelty here— that of your being an actual street gang—is too precious a commodity to waste. Why, I'm willing to wager that NanoKleen usership reaches its highest ratio among your surviving victims."

"The Nancy Boys?" questioned Jet.

"A failure to reconcile these two images into a cohesive whole among consumer groups will result in a kind of anomie, which, left unchecked, could result in the bottoming out of the effectiveness of Ferman's Devils as an effective sales tool. The solution?" He looked around to see if anyone had an answer. Naturally, none of us had the faintest idea of what he was talking about.

"The solution," he said, swinging his arms up, placing his palms together, and locking his fingers, "is to link these two images together into one cohesive, easily digestible, morally reconcilable whole. We do that by interfacing images, by injecting a soft interior into those stone-tough boys."

"No drugs," warned Ferman. "I won't let any of my boys have a jones."

The terminal rights liaison laughed. "Relax, Mr. Ferman. It's not that difficult. All we have to do is add something to your image. We like what the public has now. We merely want to polish it a little. We want to take one common ground and unwrap it a wee bit to show the public. What do you suppose we want to reveal to the masses?"

"Our pubic hair?" Nose asked meekly.

"No," said the terminal rights liaison. "What is the one thing that all of you have in common?"

"We're all convicted felons," offered Jet.

"Yes," said the man. "Yes. But more important than that. At the heart, the base, the core of it all, you five boys are all what?"

"Human beings," said Honniker In Accounting.

"Yes! You are all human beings. And that, my friends, is where I come in." He touched his notebook with one finger and a short melody leaked out. His eyes fell to the screen for a short moment. "In Lawrence, Kansas, there is a seven-year-old boy named Timothy Curtis. His life's ambition was to be the tactician for the Boston Privateers, but it doesn't look like that's going to happen. You see, little Timothy has been diagnosed as having Chronic Brain Masses. These tumorlike things start to grow, the doctors shoot Nanos in to check their spread, he's fine for about a year, and then they start growing again. Little by little, he's losing brain capacity. Doctors say that even if the growths quit now, his brain won't be able to mature much beyond the age of twelve. But of course, they won't quit. That's the nature of this beast."

"Well ain't that a trip on the meat-grinder of fate," said Ferman.

Jimmy Jazz darted out his hand and slapped Ferman on the arm. "That's awful," he said. "But what's it got to do with us?"

"Everything," smiled the terminal rights liaison. "You see, once you guys hear that Timothy is your biggest fan, and once you hear of his heart-rending plight, you're going to go and grant him his fondest wish."

"We're going to make him tactician for the Boston Privateers?"

"Better than that. You're going to make him an honorary Devil, complete with Norwegian War surplus flak jackets and those delightfully illiterate badges."

"Hey," said Nose, defensively. "I had to go through a lot to get this." He thumped his Devil with a thumb for emphasis.

"But I thought he wanted to design plays for the Privateers," said Jet.

"It's his dream," said the terminal rights liaison. "And dreams are fungible. Timothy's father is a solid waste management engineer, which puts him way up on the pay scale—but these tumor-containing Nanos are highly specialized, as is anything that you have to send into the brain. It's a constant economic drain. I'm sure that Timothy would have no problem meeting you boys if he knew it was going to ultimately help his family."

"No," said Jimmy Jazz loudly. "No way."

The terminal rights liaison checked his screen. "Maybe that one is a bit too much. I have a twelve-year-old girl who had a diving accident and there were complications when they tried to rewire her spine. No? A fifteen-year-old chronic masturbationist who got into his dad's Stim Works and burned out most of his cerebral cortex. Oh, here's one that'll have you in tears. There's this family of six out of Logan, Utah, and every one of the kids has had this mega-serious bout with Retro-Parvo. Why the pharmaceutical bills on this one alone!"

"Stop it!" Jimmy Jazz shouted. "Just stop it!" He took a deep breath to compose himself. Tears were running out of his eyes. "That's not going to fix anything, and you know it! It's going to be like dressing us all up like Nancy Boys. You're going to image us like something we're not. Well, it's wrong!" He pointed at the other Devils. "You don't know what these guys are like. You don't know what it's like to live in fear of them, day in, day out. But I do. And I'm not going to sit here and let you make them out to be some kind of . . . some kind of patron saints to the terminally miserable." He tore open his vest and threw it to the floor at Ferman's feet. "You can stay here and suck this up if you want, but I'm not. You're poison, Ferman, I've seen it. I could never say it before because you never pushed me far enough, but now I can. And here's something else. I *never* wanted to be a Devil. I don't have to be one anymore." With that, he spit on the crumpled flak jacket and stomped out of the meeting room.

"Well." The terminal rights liaison snorted. "What's with his ranking attitude?"

Ferman chewed a nail. "He can't quit my club," he declared,

and bolted from his seat toward the door. "I'm going to break every bone in his body."

I was out of my seat, right behind him. "One minute," I told the others.

I ran out of the conference room and down the hall in time to see Ferman run up behind Jimmy Jazz and grab his shoulder, arm cocked to throw a punch.

"No!" I shouted.

"It's okay," said Jimmy Jazz, turning to face his pursuer. "Go ahead, *Francis,* if it'll make you feel better."

"You can't do this," Ferman sputtered. "You can't bail out. Nobody quits."

"Right. Nobody quits the Devils. You kill them first."

Ferman surged forward. I caught his fisted hand and yanked back, threw my arm around his chest and pulled him away from Jimmy Jazz.

"You can't say that about Fudd and The Mack. They died righteous, in arms."

"What about Drool, Ferman?" A wry grin crossed his face. "Oh, I forgot. You had to have Jet kill him."

Ferman started to rage, and I pulled him harder. He was surprisingly light, and I had to take care and not toss him across the hall.

"Let him go!" I said. "This isn't the direction he wants to take. Think about it, Ferman. Maybe it isn't the direction you want to take, either. Maybe this is the chance you've been wanting to turn things around." Slowly, I loosed my grip on him. "What do you think?"

He was breathing hard with anger. "He can't quit, Boddekker," he said, moving from foot to foot like a prizefighter about to pounce. "Ain't nobody been through the street barbecue who quit the Devils. Man, that's the point of no return."

Jimmy Jazz laughed. "Is that it?"

"You knew the rules going in, Jimmy."

"Then you and I have no argument."

Ferman grinned at me. "I knew I could talk sense into that brain of his."

"Because I never had the street barbecue."

"Are you out of your ranking mind, Jimmy Jazz? I saw you take them off of one of the Hammerheads."

"Smoked oysters," said Jimmy Jazz. "I shoplifted a can of

smoked oysters and during the fight I sliced my palm with a razor so they'd be bloody. It was slight of hand, Ferman, a magic trick. Nobody got hurt and you guys started to treat me like a normal human being.'' He held up his left hand and pointed at a faint scar across the heel.

"You!" Ferman shouted. "You! You—you—you—"

I nodded as a signal for Jimmy to go, and I took Ferman by the shoulder, turned him around, and started to guide him back toward the conference room.

"I don't believe it! That ranking little weasel! He—he—"

"Give him the last laugh," I advised. "In this case, he deserves it."

Ferman shook his head in disbelief. "What's he gonna do now? Look for ranking work? What a laugh! If I see him honking that horn of his on the subway—"

"You're going to look the other way and you know it." I stopped outside the conference room door. "Now you've got a bigger problem, Ferman. There's a parasite in this room who wants to attach himself to your spine. You need to think about what you're going to do."

"Yeah," said Ferman, staring at the floor. "Smoked oysters. Man. Ain't that the meat-grinder of fate." Then he reached out with surprisingly fast reflexes and caught my hand from opening the door.

"Yes?"

"About Drool. It had to be done. He was the leader, you know? And I was second, I was recruiting all the guys like Jet, you know? I was nothing to him, and he was ruining the Devils. Boddekker, the Devils are everything to me."

"Drool's Devils?" I asked.

"Yeah," he laughed. "Ain't that a lobotomized, synthate name if you ever heard one?"

Inside the conference room, the terminal rights liaison was busy explaining his craft to the others. "—not to mention the *wonders* we've done for some of the major antisocial acts like Killer Without A Conscience, the Marching Morons—"

"But not Ferman's Devils," announced Ferman. "Gentlemen, my organization means too much to me to see its image varnished by the likes of this guy here."

"Tarnished," I quietly corrected.

"So if you will take Rover and Nose and Jet and I as we are, criminal records and all, then, shall we say, you have a deal with the Devils.''

There was commotion in the meeting room, most of which came from the terminal rights liaison, who was protesting this unfortunate turn of luck. The rest was relief from the others, and the businesslike sounds of the old men entering the final points of the contract.

Finally, they handed a long slate to Ferman along with a stylus, asking him to take as much time as he needed to look over the contract before he and the others signed. Ferman looked at the first page quietly glowing on the board, then at the others, then at the stylus. He chewed his lip for a moment, then his face brightened. ''I think,'' he announced, ''that I shall let our agent handle all of the complexities of the business end of things.''

''Why, of course!'' Justman said, delighted. ''I'll take care of these as soon as I get your Power of Attorney.''

''When you do,'' said Ferman, ''maybe you can have him look into fixing this Frottage charge I got hanging over me.''

There was a loud *pop!*, and champagne was flowing, spilling onto the marble tabletop and into tiny, delicate glasses.

From there, the day melted, and soon I found myself sitting on a stool at Ogilvy's while Honniker In Accounting once again led the troops in a rousing version of ''Spit in Your Food,'' punctuated by stray shouts of ''We *are* number one!''

I had achieved a certain pleasant numbness, carefully calculated for a number of reasons. As midnight approached, the date on Ogilvy's magnificent railroad clock would slip and Bainbridge would be another year older—Bainbridge, my new full-time linguist. Another year older, diploma in her hand, a new career and the rest of her life ahead of her. What better way to celebrate than with the man you loved? And because the man you love is oh, so special—

I shook my head. Was I writing another spot or would it be my epitaph?

Neither, I hoped. The plan called for me to be so intoxicated that I could gracefully slither away from Bainbridge's designs without offending Honniker In Accounting.

''Boddekker! Hey, Boddekker!''

I turned to the source of the noise and spilled my drink. Deppe and Dansiger were standing in front of me, faces flushed and their arms around each other.

"You're the creative type," Deppe slurred. "So we have the question of the ages for you to answer."

"The sage will try to answer," I said.

"This new linguistics expert of ours," said Dansiger. "We have a difference of opinion over what she should be called."

"I think she should be called Cassie," Deppe said, "after those vids we turn in that are cheap, artificial substitutes. Things we use until the real thing comes along."

"Ouch," I said, shaking my hand as if it had been stung.

"And I," Dansiger announced proudly, "think she should be called Cassandra, after the prophetess of doom."

The two of them laughed, and the railroad clock began to toll midnight. Another year older for poor Bainbridge. The point of no return. No turning back.

Then it hit me.

"Wait a minute," I said. "You two are taking the wrong direction."

Deppe and Dansiger laughed hysterically. "We knew we could count on you! Let's hear it, Boddekker!"

"She should be *Bainbridge*. Only *Bain* with an *e*. Because she's the *bane* of our existence!"

They began to howl and applaud. As they did, the combination of too much alcohol, too little to eat, the adrenaline leaving my system, and the accumulated stress of the last few weeks conspired against me. Before they could anoint me the Master of Names, my eyes closed and the plane of the room tilted wildly. I was struck by the sensation that I was sliding off of my stool in slow, slow motion.

I was out before I hit the floor.

And when I woke the next morning with my mouth dry and my head throbbing *hard,* there was a strange woman hovering over me.

PEMBROKE, HALL, PANGBORN, LEVINE, AND HARRIS

"Selling you to the world since 1969"

Offices in Principal Cities: New York - Montreal - Toronto - Sydney - London -
Tokyo - Moskva - Beijing - Chicago - Oslo - Philadelphia - Amarillo

CLIENT: »Heal-O-Mat		PRODUCT: »Medical Services
WRITER: »Boddekker	TIME: »:60	MEDIA: »Audio
TITLE: »*To Health with You* (Jingle *w/ donuts)		
PRODUCTION ORDERS:	»Use master cut donut: voice parts in donut will be added later. *Music by Deppe.	

SINGERS: We can make your health care choice a snap for you,
You could be at death's door or you could have the flu,
Nothing else matters when your health is in decline,
When you could drop stone dead while you're waiting in line!

[*DONUT #1.*]
ANNOUNCER: Let's face it . . . you don't always get sick between
the hours of nine and five . . . with that hour off for lunch! You
shouldn't have to spend what could be the rest of your life waiting
to see some government lackey who gets paid whether he cures
you or not! That's why Heal-O-Mat says—

SINGERS: To health, to health—
To health with you!
The professionals at Heal-O-Mat will pull you through!

[*DONUT #2.*]
ANNOUNCER: Heal-O-Mat is the latest concept in deregulated health
care, where physicians confer with the latest in science—not some
government regulation file—to determine your treatment! They
never close, so you can go when you feel the worst! At
Heal-O-Mat you get all the treatment you can afford—and if they
don't cure you—*You don't pay!!!*

SINGERS: You can stop in any hour of the day or night,
Cause Medicine's our practice till we get it right!
That is why we sing,
To health, to health with you!

[DONUT #3.]
ANNOUNCER: Don't wait until you're moribund—set your VitaSign
Monitor Beacon to frequency seven oh one double C—and the
next time you're ill, the MedTrans will take you to the Heal-O-Mat
nearest you!

SINGERS: Let the professionals pull you through!

FOURTEEN

Basking in the Afterburn

The woman had a round, pale face, short dark hair, and deep-set, serious eyes. She wore a black turtleneck that highlighted her paleness, and over one breast were two buttons. One was bright orange and said in glossy black letters: I DIDN'T CLEAN MY PLATE! The other was flat black and was festooned with *ARF!* in holographic letters. Cocking her head, she gave me a quizzical look—the way I felt, it was easy to imagine what I probably looked like, so I didn't hold that one against her—and put her hand to my forehead. For a moment she stared, then looked off to her left and said, too loudly, "He's awake. And alive, I might add."

"Good," came a voice garbled by distance and my illness of overindulgence.

I closed my eyes and tried to come up with a fitting scenario. Kidnapped by the Animal Rights Front because of my association with known canary-keeper Pangborn? I had to admit it didn't seem possible. This woman didn't look like a certified nut. If she wore pointed ears and a Church of Trek button I might have worried more, but as it was I wrote her off as a concerned citizen. When I opened my eyes again the dark, serious woman had been replaced by Honniker In Accounting.

"Hello, Boddekker," she said, brightly but quietly. "I'd ask how you are, but I think that would be a foolish question. Don't you?"

I started to nod or say something in agreement, but she quickly put her hand to my forehead and held me still.

"No. Don't move. Don't do anything. We'll get you taken care of." She glanced down at her wrist and frowned at the time. "Or rather, Mollene will take care of you. I have to go to work."

Work. Great.

"Me, too." I croaked.

"No," Honniker In Accounting insisted. "I can arrange for you to be covered. You deserve it, I think. And Mollene is a good person."

I followed her gaze to my left and saw it connect with the Mollene, who looked at me with a serious nod.

Still, I struggled to get up. The result was nothing but pain.

"You should listen to her," said Mollene. "She's right. There are some things you have to wait on, you know. It's typical of modern science. They can find a cure for the common cold, but they can't seem to do anything about a simple hangover."

"Urgh," I said, embarrassed.

"Don't feel bad," Honniker In Accounting said, planting a painful kiss on my forehead. "You'd be surprised at some of the folks who have had your problem. Much more frequently."

"And worse," added Mollene.

"Thanks," I croaked. I meant it sarcastically, but I'm not sure how it came out.

Honniker In Accounting disappeared from view and her voice floated back with a melodical "Good-bye!" Before I could formulate anything in reply, Mollene answered with, "Good-bye from both of us!," then turned back to study me.

I rolled my eyes around and studied the room. I couldn't tell much. There were obvious feminine touches—the types of curtains and wallhangings—but the place was pretty much blacked out for my comfort. Shifting, I noticed a pillow next to mine, with a conspicuous dent in the middle. Only then did I realize that I was in a double bed that had been slept in on both sides.

"Uh," I said, in an erroneous attempt to diffuse the situation, "you her neighbor?"

Mollene stared. I couldn't tell if she was thinking about it or was merely giving me a guilt-inducing stare.

"Roommate," she said.

"So tell me," I said, "does she always make a person feel this good about feeling bad?"

"Only if she likes you," Mollene said bluntly. "If she doesn't, she has no pity. Take no prisoners. The whole bit."

I tried to lick my lips but my tongue was too dry. Judging from her tone of voice, Mollene was also describing her personal attitude, which was in permanent effect.

"One time," she continued, "she brought home this pathetic case from the agency, somebody from the number-chewing department. He was about as fried as you were, maybe a little worse." She paused to study my face. "Don't give me that whipped puppy look, Mr. Boddekker. Nothing happened."

Caught again.

"She only did it because she pitied the guy. She knew that he'd never make it home on his own and if he did that things would not be good when he tried to explain it to his wife. That's right, Boddekker, his *wife*. So she let him sleep it off here, arranged for one of her underlings, some guy, to call the wife and float this little story about how he was staying in the city to do some extra work.

"The next morning, though, it was a different story. Of course, like I said, she didn't like this guy, only pitied him. I mean, she didn't do the shared bodily warmth trick with him, if you know what I mean." Mollene paused in her story and a smile came with her memory of the event.

"That morning she made the loudest omelet that's ever been made in history. We're talking that she actually got out pots and pans and whanged them together. This guy of course was livid— and I do mean livid—with pain. And she gives him this omelet, he sees it and nearly makes a spew right there, but he manages not to. Waving that thing under his nose, she tells him, 'this better not get misconstrued by anybody as anything more than it is, which is to say, an act of kindness between colleagues. You let one word of this out, one word that I did this for you, and I'll be on the phone to your wife with a big pack of lies and the anatomical details to back them up.' " Mollene laughed. "Consider yourself lucky."

"Sounds like she's got nothing to fear from me."

"She better not. Cause she's a pussycat compared to me."

I was able to laugh. "I believe you." Closing my eyes, I laid my head back, and concentrated on trying to ease the throbbing between my temples. There was rustling as Mollene moved around the room.

"I hear you're pretty hot stuff," she said.

I laid my forearm across my eyes. "I don't know about that."

"You came up with this Ferman thing, didn't you?"

"That, my dear Mollene, was a creative accident."

"And everything else isn't?" More rustling. I couldn't imagine what she was doing. "I mean, I hear that you're even handling a group account now, and up until recently, only the Old Men did them."

"You sure have heard a lot about me," I said, aiming it as a question.

"You're not her exclusive subject," Mollene assured me. "But you're definitely in the top ten."

A grudging acquiescence if ever I'd heard one. "As for the group, well, another accident."

"Who is it?"

Plain and simple, these guys were going to haunt me for the rest of my career at Pembroke Hall. "The SOBs."

"Who are they?"

I lifted my arm, raised my head, and stared at her. "You're kidding. You don't know?"

Mollene shook her head.

"Well." I'd had Dansiger do some research since I'd been assigned the account. It was time to see how much I could impress her with what I'd learned. "The Sons of Beatles," I explained. "Julian Lennon, Zak Starkey, someone named McCartney, and a guy who claims to be George Harrison's love child. They had a couple of hits around the turn of the century—'Hey, John' and 'Baby Baby Baby Baby Baby.' "

Mollene shrugged. "All I listen to is grind."

"Give me some credit," I said. "I don't listen to those old SOBs either."

Mollene laughed. There were some people, I guess, for whom the gag would be new.

"I guess the biggest thing is the Ferman's Devils campaign for

World Nanotechnologies, Ltd., although the total success remains to be seen. But it has gotten me—"

"Gotten you what?"

I had frozen. What I was going to say was, "but it has gotten me into a download of Advertising Age," but it hadn't yet. That was because I hadn't yet been interviewed. And if I stayed here, chattering with Mollene, the interview wouldn't happen, the old men would get mad, and I could kiss that house in Princeton good-bye.

"In trouble," I said quickly. "I've got to get out of here." I threw the sheets back, twisted my legs, and stood up. A brainhammer of a headache started to pound beneath my skull and I sank back down onto the bed as if being yanked by invisible strings. "Oh. This is going to take some doing."

"Big day at work, huh?" Mollene said.

"Yeah," I said, pushing on my eyes with the palms of my hands.

"Well, then," she said nonchalantly, "you might need these." With one smooth motion, she leaned over to retrieve something from the seat of a chair and tossed it into my lap. I looked down. My clothes. "They've been NanoKleened."

I don't know how I avoided terminal embarrassment. Maybe I was too sick, or maybe I realized there was no point in dwelling on the humiliation. Whatever the case, I got dressed, then went into the bathroom and splashed my face with icy water. Honniker In Accounting had left a small glass of water on the side of the sink, and with it some aspirin and vitamins and a couple of other small pills that I took without question. I assumed they were for me and washed them all down, noticing that a tube of men's depilatory cream had been left out. Honniker In Accounting had been *very* thorough.

Not much longer after that I wandered out of the bathroom into the living room. Honniker In Accounting and Mollene shared one of those railroad apartments, where the rooms are all strung together in one long vertical line. The living room ran straight through to the kitchen, where Mollene was tidying up.

"So. Boddekker," she said. "You're going to risk it, huh? Going out into the world in that shape, I mean."

I nodded. "Like you said . . . big day at work."

"Aren't they all?"

I shrugged. Mollene walked out to the couch and began to

gather up what was on it; a sheet, a couple of blankets, a pillow, a comforter. She folded them very precisely and stacked them on the coffee table.

"I hope I didn't inconvenience you," I said, looking around to make sure I wasn't leaving anything behind.

Mollene paused and stared—just for a second—then shrugged. "No," she said, after a moment.

"We're all looking for a better place to live," I said.

"Whatever." She picked up the bedding and carried it into the bedroom.

"Well," I said, loudly so it would carry, "thanks for the hospitality. It was nice to meet you, Mollene." She came back in and I lowered my voice. "Maybe I can return the favor under better circumstances. When I'm at my best, maybe?"

Another laugh, this one almost friendly. She reached out and shook my hand. "All right, Boddekker. I'll hold you to that one." She looked pained for a brief moment, then brought something from behind her back, a small bubblechip that rested comfortably in the palm of her hand. "I want you to look at this." She hesitated. "I hope you don't think I'm imposing, but it's important to me, and I think that maybe you could be of help. It's some of the newest ARF literature. Hasn't been released yet. Kind of in a . . . raw state."

I nodded. "And you think I could come up with some way to jazz it up, right?"

"Something like that."

I slipped it into my pocket. "I'll do that," I said. "There a deadline on this?"

"No," she said. "Uh, no."

I could tell there was but she didn't want to push the matter. "I'll look at it as soon as I can."

"Thanks."

Outside of the apartment it took about a minute to find my bearings. Once I had them, I took the straightest, most direct route in to Pembroke Hall. I made it there by a little after ten, and had to explain to half a dozen people why I was there. More Honniker In Accounting efficiency. After wading through the gauntlet of people who wanted to see me, I finally got to my office, where I plugged Mollene's bubblechip into my desk system and brought the documents up on my screen. The image flickered as a voice came from the speakers.

"Mr. Boddekker?"

"Yes, ferret?"

"You've got an awful lot of electronic equipment at home, don't you?"

I turned to the monitor. "As a matter of fact I do, but—how did you know that?"

It didn't answer my question. Instead it said, "And wouldn't it be a shame if it were all ruined? You know, you don't have to die in a terrorist nuke blast for one to ruin your life. Just *think* what one burst of Electromagnetic Pulse would do to your lifestyle . . ."

I shook my head and called for my real ferret.

"Yes, your ferret program would be gone. The ARF Manifesto document you're working on would be gone. Everything in your system would be fried. But lucky for you, Cincinnati Mutual now has what everyone with a high caliber lifestyle needs—"

"Ferret!" I shouted.

"—Electromagnetic Pulse Protection Insurance! That's right, Mr. Boddekker! Should EMP from a terrorist nuke ruin any of your precious possessions, Cincinnati Mutual will replace each and every one of them!"

I slid over to the interface and hammered a few keys. Nothing happened.

"Our computerized client records are kept right here in Manhattan to ensure that you get the fastest service possible! So why delay? Enter your authorization code right now and sleep with the peace of mind that comes to you from—"

There came from the speaker system a sudden shriek that sounded like something was disintegrating inside the datasys. I wondered if there hadn't been a terrorist nuking, and instinctively, stupidly, looked out the window to see.

The ferret's voice came a moment later. "I'm really sorry about that one, Mr. Boddekker. It's gone now."

I realized what I was doing and turned away from the window. "Is that really you, ferret?"

"Indeed it is. You'll have to forgive me. That one slipped in as a handshake subroutine, and I was sniffing it out when it rewrote my directive coding and had me monitoring the air-conditioning system on the sixty-first floor. I had to complete a diagnostic rewrite before I could get out—and then the environmental monitor didn't want to let me go. Those hardwired types are like that, all ROM and no—''

''Is that all you had for me, ferret?'' I asked impatiently.

''Yes, sir,'' it sighed. ''Except I've received word that some-one from *Ad Age* is here to speak to you. About your subscription, no doubt. Should I show him in?''

''Please do.''

There was nothing surprising or unexpected about the inter-view. It was everything I expected it to be, complete with the interviewer taking one of those holos that never looks right by the time it gets to your reader screen. The questions were all incisive and to the point, and I got to talk at length about my feelings toward my craft and why I had to be coerced into accepting awards and what the saving graces and failings of the industry were. Then, finally, with a few well-placed questions, he tied it all together with the Ferman's Devils campaign—at which point I corrected him, saying that the campaign was actually for World Nanotechnologies, Ltd., and drove home the idea that a slogan or phrase or song or character is useless unless you marry it to the client's product—and that marriage results in sales.

Finally it was over and I shook hands with the interviewer and saw him to the elevator. On the way back to my office, I was given all sorts of grief by members of the creative group, and I prom-ised them that I had mentioned them, by name, and that whether or not they were immortalized in the download depended on the whims of the *Ad Age* editor. They hooted in mock derision and returned to their business.

I sat at my desk, and as the adrenaline from the interview faded, I felt myself go pale, my self-inflicted illness welling up inside of me. I propped my elbows on the desk, put my palms over my eyes, and was swallowed up by the sensation that the room was spinning and jerking.

''Well aren't you the glutton for punishment.''

I didn't bother to look up. It was Honniker In Accounting.

''I can't tell you,'' I said, ''how painful it is to have you see me like this.''

''Do you have an easily bruised ego?'' I could picture her expression in my mind's eye. Smiling, but not too much. Not even the hint of a glare or a sneer. She actually wanted to know how I felt.

''No,'' I said, foregoing the pain of shaking my head. ''As a man I try to set up this ideal image when I'm around you. But my current state is the antithesis of that image.''

Her melodic laugh filled the blackness I was staring through. ''It is ego, then.''

''If you say so. Anyway, this is bad enough. I can only imagine what I was like last night. Before you took me home.''

''You didn't want me to take you home?''

''Not under those circumstances. I doubt it would have worked out, though, not with Mollene there.''

I heard her say, ''Hmm.''

''Which brings me to the question of the week. Maybe even the month.''

''That is . . .''

''Is the door closed?''

''I'd hate to hear your question of the year.'' I heard her feet shuffle against the carpet and the door slid shut. ''I think we're alone now.''

''What is happening to us?''

Silence.

I brought my head up and opened my eyes. Everything was blurry. I fought to focus. ''I mean, we . . . well . . . we have this relationship that's for the most part platonic, mercifully so when you took me home. But when you did, you still . . . well. . . . then there was Cantaloupe Day. I think I'd enjoy this situation a little more if I knew exactly what it was made of.'' Honniker In Accounting was still a blur to me, but I could tell she looked confused. ''Listen to me. I'm starting to sound like Bainbridge.''

''Where,'' she said, ''do you want this relationship to go?''

''Where,'' I replied, ''do *you* want it to go?''

''You first.''

''You already know my answer. Part of that is coming from the fact that I'm at the mercy of my own hormones.'' *And your pheromones,* I thought about adding—but it really wasn't the time. ''Aside from that baser part of it, I think I'd like to behave like a human being toward you. What I've seen of you fascinates me.''

She took the compliment with a smile and a nod. ''What about that baser part?''

''Let's take one item at a time. I'm still trying to figure out Cantaloupe Day.''

"All right," said Honniker In Accounting. "What are you doing for the rest of the day?"

"I was thinking of retiring somewhere and being seriously ill." I rested my head in my hands.

"All right," she said. "I think I can get out of here. I want you to do something for me if you're up to it. Are you game?"

"Depends. I'm at a physical and intellectual ebb right now."

"This will be easy. I want you to take me somewhere."

"Where?"

"That's up to you. I want you to take me somewhere that tells me what you're all about. This is a two-way street, Boddekker. I want to learn something about you, too."

"We go somewhere. Now?"

"That's right."

I raised my head and peered through squinted eyes. "And you'll do the same for me?"

"At some point in the near future, yes. And no trips to the wild places unless it's by mutual consent."

"Cantaloupe Day was mutual consent?"

Honniker In Accounting laughed. Her teeth seemed perfect and bright. "Cantaloupe Day I spit in your food."

"You spit in *my* food? That's a new one." The fog seemed to be lifting from my head, so I stood and pushed my chair in. "You're ready to go then?"

"Ten minutes to clear my desk."

"Meet you at the elevators."

It was twenty minutes before I was able to meet her at the elevators. You know how it is when you're in a hurry—you attract more people with things for you to do. Dansiger once theorized that a person gives off certain pheromones when they were in a hurry, and that other people who weren't as stressed were drawn in by those pheromones. It was one of those brilliant things that people talked about a lot but never tested. Too bad. I suppose that there's a lot of genius in the world gone to waste by taking the form of mere idle talk.

Maybe there was something to that pheromone theory, because as late as I was in getting to the elevators, Honniker In Accounting was later still, which only goes to show that anything can be compounded if you're built from all the right genes in the pool. I took her straight to Grand Central Station, where we tried without luck to get a railpass and ended up on the good zep *Baffin Island,* the midweek, midafternoon flight to Princeton.

I told her nothing the whole time we were in the air. Nor did I divulge any information at the Princeton station, where I hailed a 'shaw to take us into that wonderful neighborhood. When I sensed we were nearing the house, spurred on by please for a clue, I told Honniker In Accounting one thing. I said, "Like anyone else, I'm driven by needs. You're about to see the greatest motivation of my life."

The bikeshaw turned the corner, the force pulling us together.

"Third one on the left," I said, watching the sun gleam from her eyes as she looked down the street.

Her lips parted into a smile. "Boddekker. Oh, Boddekker, this is wonderful! You didn't tell me you had family!"

I didn't have time to respond. Instantly my throat closed, tight, and my heart hammered hard against my ribs. Honniker In Accounting was right. I had a family—at least, she thought it was my family. Assorted nephews and nieces or cousins and cousinettes were out in the yard of my Princeton home, scampering among the rocks, waving their arms for balance, toting Baby Barely Alives! and McMahon, Tate, and Stevens's big claim to advertising fame—the Junior Trooper replicas of the Automultifire Standard Issue Combat Rifle, "The Weapon That Won the Norwegian War!" A heated fire-fight had been interrupted with a dispute over who had killed whom first, and the female troops from each side instantly defected when the civilian baby began to have a rather violent seizure.

"You want me to stop here, sir?" huffed the bikeshaw driver.

I tried to talk, but no words came out of my mouth. Tears were stinging my eyes. I had been betrayed by my own real estate agent. Why hadn't Jean called me?

"Boddekker?"

I shook my head violently and motioned for the driver to keep going, then sank back into the seat, looking away from the House, from Honniker In Accounting, from everything.

"Boddekker, what's wrong? Don't you want me to meet your family?"

Shivering, I whispered, "They're not my family."

One of her hands came to rest on my shoulder. The other was playing, gently, with my hair. "They're not your family, but you brought me all the way out here to show them to me?" Her hands tightened. I had lost my grip on a single, heaving sob.

"No," she said. "It wasn't the family. If it wasn't your family, you could have shown me one anywhere. That's right, isn't it, Boddekker? No. It must have been the neighborhood. More specific. The house. You wanted me to see the house."

I didn't say a word.

"It was the house, wasn't it? It was on the market and—well, I won't restate the obvious. But I know what that house had to have meant to you, Boddekker. It meant getting out of NYC, didn't it? You had it picked out and it was perfect, it was perfect for you, wasn't it? And it meant that you were on the way, because you are, you're on the way, and, oh Boddekker, I'm sorry, I really am sorry for you."

Her arms came around me and tried to pull me in, but I was too hurt and embarrassed to let myself be comforted so easily.

"Excuse me," said the driver, braking for a light. "This is a delicate time, I know, but things ain't gonna get no better for me. Where, ah, where should I take you now? The city limits? Or in circles?"

"Back," I managed.

"No," said Honniker In Accounting. "You fall off the bike, you get right back on and keep riding."

"What?" The driver and I both spoke together.

"This is a setback, Boddekker, a minor setback, one of those damnable, annoying things that makes life miserable for most people. But you're not most people, are you, Boddekker? No. Of course you're not. You're the creator of Ferman's Devils."

"Ferman's Devils?" The driver's face brightened noticeably. "Hey." He flashed us a thumbs-up. "I got it handled." The bikeshaw lurched out into the intersection.

Eventually I recovered enough to swallow and try out my voice. I turned and looked right into her eyes. "I think I'm going to live now."

"Great. So that means we're getting back on the bike and we're going to ride it and we're not going to let a fall stop us. Isn't that right?"

"I understand the metaphor," I said, "but you have to understand that I don't have the time or the wherewithal to start looking for another real estate agent. It's a setback, and yes, I was bitterly disappointed, but it's not the end of the world. I'll find a place—"

And that was the moment when I found out exactly what Honniker In Accounting had been talking about. I had missed the point—but the bikeshaw driver had not. He pulled us right up in front of the house, where the war had dispersed, its participants now trying to guess which cartridge Baby Barely Alive's! owner had slipped into its back.

Honniker In Accounting and the bikeshaw driver both smiled. I knew what was expected of me. I got out and started up the sidewalk.

"I know!" said one budding young diagnostician. "St. Vitus's Dance!"

I looked back, briefly. They were no longer watching me. Instead, it looked like the driver was pointing out directions and distances. Plans.

Well, that was it. With my chest out, I marched up to the door and rang the bell. A man answered, and in short time I explained to him that I was interested in buying the house. "Yes, I realize that you've just moved in, but I'll make it well worth your family's while if you agree." Then I named a price that was extravagant for me, but not too high for the house. It impressed him; "Yes, I'll have to discuss it with my wife, but she won't be in for a while yet because she works in NYC and is still on the incoming zep." I shook his hand and thanked him and left him with a phone card, then walked triumphantly back to the bikeshaw.

"Then it's some kind of slow toxemia," one of the children was saying.

"Well?" asked Honniker In Accounting, even though I knew she could tell how it had gone from the look on my face.

"Nothing definite," I said. "But I hope that Levine's promise of substantial reward was the real thing."

She cried out triumphantly and threw her arms around me. "I knew you could do it!" The bikeshaw lurched and we tumbled together, down into the seat as we whisked through suburban Princeton.

"All right," I told her. "Now it's your turn."

"For what?" she asked softly.

"To take me somewhere that says a lot about you."

"One thing at a time, Boddekker. One thing at a time."

I laughed. "I know. We're running out of day. Let me buy you dinner, then."

She shook her head.

"Come on. I'm not ready to go back to NYC yet."

"Neither am I," she said. "I'm ready for something nicer than NYC."

"What's nicer than NYC?"

"Princeton."

I studied her. "I'm not following you."

"I was going to buy *you* dinner. But I decided on something better. I'm going to buy you room service instead."

The bikeshaw driver braked and wheeled into the parking lot of a large, round hotel. "Here you go," he said.

"And you'll be here for us in the morning?" asked Honniker In Accounting.

"Just call."

I started to fish in my pocket for money to pay him, but he waved me off. "Take care of it tomorrow, Mr. Boddekker," he said. "The guys, when I tell them that I drove the creator of Ferman's Devils, they'll want to kill themselves."

The two of us were giddy, more giddy perhaps than Cantaloupe Day, which had carried a serious, erotic pall over it. Had the clerk who checked us in not known better, she might have taken us for a pair of teenagers checking in for a prom-night stand.

We necked in the elevator on the way up to our floor. As soon as I closed the door and thumbprinted the DO NOT DISTURB keycode, Honniker In Accounting said, "This is for you, Boddekker," and attacked me. It took us an hour to get to the bed, and it was another three before she called room service for the promised meal. After the meal we talked and dozed, and as final drowsiness was setting in and the prospect of mentally pacifying ourselves with a selection from one of the cablenets was starting to look good, she announced that she wanted me to come and inspect the Jacuzzi.

"This is for you, Boddekker."

That was still resonating in my skull when, wrapped in warm white hotel robes, we fell into bed for the last time. Fighting to keep my eyes open, I pulled the sheet up under my chin and turned to face her. Her back was to me, and she was looking out the window, out across the lights of Princeton to a glow in the northeast that might have been NYC. I laid my hand on her bare hip.

"Are you all right, Boddekker?"

"I was more worried about you," I said.

"I'm fine," she said, dreamily.

"Not that—"

"And I make plenty, so you don't need to fret about what this little escapade is doing to my financial plans."

"Not that, either. You've been so—" All right, Boddekker, how do you handle this? You're the one who thinks nothing of batting out masterful copy about sexually oriented products. Let's see how you handle your own intimate relationships. "Giving," I said, hating the sound as soon as I said it.

"Giving?"

"Today. Cantaloupe Day. Don't you—"

I drew a blank. No, I take that back. It wasn't so much that I drew a blank. I had finally reached the point where I refused to sound like one of my own commercials. As fate would have it, that blank was exactly what I needed. Honniker In Accounting rolled over to face me.

"It's all right. Really. You don't think I'd still be here if it weren't?"

I couldn't argue with that. In theory, she could have any man at the agency she wanted.

"Of course not," she answered for me. Then she pulled my face down, kissed my cheek, and laid my head to rest between her breasts. "This is for you, Boddekker."

"Thank you," I whispered.

My eyes started to roll back in my head. Something behind them was trying to click, but it was late, I was exhausted, and I knew I was going to have more than a few sore muscles in the morning.

I'm a lucky guy, I thought, closing my eyes and slowly surrendering to the softness of her breasts. A lucky, creative guy.

I had beat the Devils at their own game. Now instead of being beholden to them, they were prisoners of Pembroke Hall.

I would soon have my house.

I was now the top creative man at Pembroke Hall. Before long it would be "Pembroke, Hall, Pangborn, Levine, Harris, and Boddekker."

And I had Pembroke Hall's most desirable woman.

I had Honniker In Accounting.

Creative. Well.

It wasn't love.

But then these days, what was?

Acknowledgments

Writers work alone, but get on the phone to their support staff when they get stuck or have a problem. My support staff for *Ferman* includes

CHEERLEADERS: Doug and Mary Piero Carey and the fen of Harry, who sat through readings of chapters, never knowing if they'd hear the rest of the story; ditto to Gary and Jackie Reed and "Dancin' " Danny Wright. I should also mention Trish, Mary Ann, and Mark of the EJG, who no doubt think they're in this book. They aren't.

EXPERTS: Anne Lesley Groell for editing and correcting my NYC geography; Kurt Busiek for handy house-hunting tips; my wife, Connie, for her usual ruthless (and inevitably correct) blue penciling; my uncle James Innis, who taught me the difference between *ishta* and *uffda;* and Jeanette Faust, who frightened me with ludefisk at a tender young age (*Just kidding, Mom!*). Any mistakes you find were left there by me, through accident or design.

Special thanks go to Jean F. Merrill for Cantaloupe Day. Consider its appearance here as my way of saying thanks for *The Pushcart War*.

And, of course, a lifetime supply of Couscous Critters to my agent, Joshua Bilmes.

Joe Clifford Faust
Centerbrook Farm, Ohio

About the Author

Like Boddekker's friend Hotchkiss, Joe Clifford Faust has been an award-winning copywriter and has had a broken leg and found one oddly preferable over the other.

He currently lives in a 140-year-old Ohio farmhouse, surrounded by family, dogs, assorted small mammals, and tropical fish. When not writing he can be found in the kitchen, where he is coming ever closer to producing the perfect bowl of chili.

And the chaos continues...

Don't miss any of the further adventures of
Boddekker and Co. in

Boddekker's Demons

Coming in 1997.
Here's a special preview:

When I got to my office, there were a whole handful of messages queued up on my system. Most were interview requests that had come in that morning from the likes of *People, Playboy, Time,* and *TV Guide.* I asked my ferret if they actually wanted to talk to me or to the Devils, but it didn't know. I asked it to filter and file any further requests until I could get word from above on what to do.

There was a lot of good news—Charlie Angeles called and said that he'd been recruited to shoot the Boston Harbor spot, and he'd be getting in touch to look over my suggested locations. Finney said that a profitability index was being run on the first flight of NanoKleen ads to determine the bonus that my creative group would share. And the family who lived in my future Princeton home called to say they were considering the offer and were looking at other houses to see what was available.

I called the ferret up again to take the preliminary numbers from Finney's message and process them into a number—hopefully good—that I could give to the rest of the group. And I was beginning to compose a note to all of them when Dansiger knocked on my door.

"So what are you going to say to the press?"

I kept myself from glaring at her. Her ferret had obviously been sniffing my ferret's behind again. "I'll let the old men sort that out."

She looked troubled. "How can you say that after—"

"After what?"

Her look went from hard to one of disbelief. "You don't know."

Something began to nag at the back of my head. It was the source of my morning dread. There was something I had forgotten to do, and I was starting to get a pretty good idea of what it was.

Dansiger said, "I can't believe you didn't watch the Devils last night."

I said, "I'm not their parent. I can't spend all my time watching them, not when I've got other accounts—"

"But this was a big one, Boddekker."

My stomach rolled. "How big?"

"Deppe was going to record it," she said. "I'll see if he brought it."

I followed Dansiger down the hall toward Deppe's office, delivering under-the-breath curses at my own forgetfulness. Naturally, it wasn't a big deal to me. In one way or another I'd been dealing with them for months. But last night was the first opportunity for the world's buying public to get an up-close and personal look at Francis Herman McKluskey and his cohorts.

As *There Were Ten Of Them* exploded into the consciousness of consumers, they demanded to know all about those five awkward boys who were so delightful in their roles as the gang members who destroyed Norman Drain. And when it was learned that they were *real* gang members—well, that made them all the more mysterious and irresistible.

The old men and the senior partners had gone into a huddle to determine the best course of action to take in introducing the public side of Ferman's Devils to the world. The rush to be the first to show the true Devils created a media frenzy. ABCDisney offered to fire up their Barbara Walters emulator. *60 Minutes* decided to sneak in a camera crew during a policy meeting involving the Devils and had to be chased out of the lobby by the Smilin' Guy. And TimeLifeWarnerAnheuserBusch made a complex multimedia offer that included magazine coverage, a book and film deal, a bubblechip collection consisting of Devil interviews and their favorite songs, and a Devil-centered ride in a chain of amusement parks.

But these and more were all turned away in favor of a simple appearance on *The Tonight Show with Harold Ball*—a venerable old institution which had outlived a handful of hosts and even the cablenet that had started it. This was a true coup, and I wish that placing the Devils there had been my idea.

In truth, it was Sylvester's idea. While on his last medical leave, he had spent a lot of time watching broadcast vid. He noticed that Harold Ball, who had hosted the show for the last decade or so, made some kind of reference to the Devils in ten monologues out of the last fifteen days. The rest was easy to figure out.

The powers that be did some digging and found out that Harold Ball was anxious to book the Devils, so each sent representatives to the arbitrators. Finally, after three weeks, the smoke cleared to reveal the final score: Ferman's Devils would appear on *The Tonight Show* in exchange for the usual modest appearance fee, which would be divided four ways. World Nanotechnologies would agree to buy one third of the available commercial inserts during the week of the Devils appearance, but would not be limited to running *There Were Ten Of Them*. The remainder of the avails would be bought up by Pembroke Hall for their other clients.

In addition to getting the first interview with the Devils, Harold Ball agreed to broadcast the show from NYC since we were all afraid of what would happen if we put them on a zep for a cross-country trip. He also agreed to book two other Pembroke Hall guests on the same show; Roddick Erskine, whose book about the Kennedy Cousins had been published by our imprint and was downloading less briskly than expected; and the group Hateful, who would perform the advance single from their forthcoming album.

It would be one interesting night for Harold Ball.

Naturally, the Pembroke Hallers wanted to turn the Devils' appearance into a major event. I was invited to view the proceedings at no less than three different parties which had sprung up around the broadcast; there was the main party, to be held in the large amphitheater; the creative department party, which was going to be held in our meeting room on the creative floor; and there was Bainbridge's private viewing party "for an audience of two." This was to be held at Ogilvy's until she realized they had no video monitors, whereupon she changed the location to her new apartment.

My plans were to skip out on all of the parties. This was to be my way of asserting to Pembroke Hall what I had asserted to Dansiger—that I was not the designated babysitter for Ferman and the Devils, and that I had an obligation to the other clients on my list—including the SOB's, who were the latest irritant to be stuck in my creative craw. And it was writing for these other clients that was becoming increasingly more difficult as the various aspects of Devils logistics ate into my time.

"So what happened?" I asked as Dansiger came flying out of Deppe's office with Deppe and a bubblechip in tow.

"I can't believe he doesn't know," Deppe said.

"I know," Dansiger said. "I know."

"I really can't believe that he *missed* it . . ."

We ran into a dour-looking Bainbridge on the way to the meeting room.

She said, "What's up?"

Dansiger said, "Boddekker doesn't know."

She said, "I don't believe it."

Deppe said, "I still can't believe he doesn't know."

I said, "What is it you don't believe I don't know?"

Dansiger said, "This is something you really need to see to appreciate."

The four of us trailed into the meeting room, where Griswold sat working in his notebook. He looked up, the question in his eyes. To prevent the repetition of Deppe and Dansiger's new mantra, I jumped in with the news.

"I don't know what happened last night. They're about to show me."

Griswold looked alarmed. "No kidding. This I've gotta see."

"You don't know, either?" Bainbridge asked.

"I know," said Griswold. "I want to see Boddekker's face when he sees the replay."

I took the chair at the head of the table. "Do you want to strap me in?" I asked as Deppe flew to the player.

"I don't think that'll be necessary."

He hit the PLAY button. The lights in the room dimmed, and the pictures vanished from the opposite wall to make room for the image—the tail end of a newscast.

—and up next on The Tonight Show *with Harold Ball,* Ferman's Devils . . . *the actors who play the hoodlums in the world's favorite commercial!*

Then the bouncy *Tonight Show* theme, with Ball sidekick Billy Hind announcing the evening's lineup for the cheering crowd.

—Harold's guests to-NIGHT include author RODDICK ER-SKINE, who will tell us the truth about those ca-RAY-zee Kennedy Cousins! Lukewarm applause. *Grinders* HATEFUL, *with a hot new cut from their album* "YOUNG and STUPID!" Enthusiastic applause. *And . . . the world's most FAY-vo-rit street gang and sellers of soap—FERMAN'S DEVILS!* Wild, hysterical applause.

"Run it forward," Bainbridge said.

Dansiger shook her head. "It's better if he sees it in context."

"She's right," Deppe said. "You really need to see this as it happened."

So I sat there, less than transfixed as Harold Ball came out to thunderous applause and the trademark wolf howls, acknowledged his audience with a wide bow, and then went into his monologue. It was a typical Ball monologue, and tonight he went especially hard on the President, who had been threatening to invade Holland over what he called 'strictly anti-American conspiratorial tendencies.'

—so the President tells them, 'I have no fear of you. I took care of the Norwegians, and I'll handle you like I handled the

clothes.' Oh, boy! Now HE'S expecting another miracle out of NanoKleen!

The audience rewarded the gag with vigorous laugher and applause. I leaned over to Dansiger and whispered.

"Now I know how Doctor Frankenstein felt when his creature started strangling the townsfolk."

She looked at me with wide eyes. "Wait," was all she said.

Ball finished his monologue and recapped the names of the evening's guests and we were into the first commercial break; *There Were Ten Of Them,* and a vid spot for Lover's Mist that we had done two years ago; a montage of women talking right into the camera like you're the guy they're addressing, saying things like, *If I'd known you were such a cad, I'd have never gone home with you; I don't care how embarrassing it is, I'm going to tell all of my friends what you did to me . . . and I'm going to have them tell THEIR friends;* and, *If I have anything to say about it, you'll never get laid in this town again!* I called the piece *Don't Say You're Sorry.* We had moved tons of product with it.

After two minutes of local spots, Ball and his cronies were back, this time with a sketch set in a weird singles bar where men dressed like sperm cells were hitting on one woman dressed like an ovum. Finally Ball and Hind walked into the place dressed like multi-armed robots, and together they carried the woman out. The piece had a lot of old tired gags about human sexuality, and you've probably guessed the punchline, delivered with a shake of the head by the bartender:

—He never shoulda washed his shorts in NanoKleen!

The audience howled, more than they should have, I think. Or maybe that's because I was a writer and saw what was coming from a hundred kilometers away. Then something else occurred to me and I turned to Dansiger again.

"I see what you mean. If this is the kind of public perception that's coming out about NanoKleen, we're going to have a public relations nightmare—"

"Shh," she said with one clipped expulsion of air.

A chill shot up my spine. *That wasn't the problem?*

I said nothing and kept watching. The first guest was Erskine, which I thought was a departure for *The Tonight Show.* On the rare occasions when the authors were on, they were the last to appear, sometimes even after the musical guest. Either Ball was saving the big moment for last, or part of the agreement with

Pembroke Hall called for the Devils to be last on to make sure that everyone stayed through all of the commercials.

Erskine's performance was nothing exceptional, perhaps even sub-par. There was just enough inflection in his voice to keep him from being classified as a monotone, and he droned on and on about the research and the facts in his book, revealing for the few who cared about how some of the Kennedy Cousins would forget to pay their light bills, or would order a pizza in and then not give the driver a tip.

This could have been the fiasco everyone was talking about. Clearly whoever handled Erskine should have hired someone to play him on the talk show circuit, but the way authors were nowadays—especially one who had something on a hot topic like the Kennedy Cousins—that solution was becoming more and more problematic. However, Erskine wasn't one of my clients and therefore was not my problem. Besides, I wasn't sensing from Dansiger that this was the moment I was supposed to be waiting for.

Erskine finished droning and Ball tried to liven things back up with a few loaded questions about Kennedy sexuality. Erskine started to mumble something about one of them going into a shop to try and buy some Lover's Mist—that was a nice plug—but Ball took control and went into a commercial break.

—Whoa! Darn the luck, Roddick, but we're done with you! We're not done with the show, though, and we'll be right back after THIS!

There was only one Pembroke Hall commercial in this group, the test flight of the new *Baby Barely Alive!* spot. That could have been the glitch, too. There weren't going to be a whole lot of kids up at this hour who could look at the spot and then demand one from their parents. Better that it would be placed on a multi-timeshare buy during *The Crash and Burn Show!*, where they'd have the little darlings near hypnotized.

One other national spot, a Streusel and Strauss-er for the AmericaPlus Zep Line; then two more locals and back into the show, where Ball introduced Hateful. The band took the stage and yodeled their way through *Gone*, a grind anthem that I think was supposed to be about loss or alienation or something like that. I couldn't really tell. The only thing interesting about this segment was knowing that my subliminal ad for Couscous Critters would be planted under this and the other songs on the album when the time came for its release.

Four more spots; three locals and *There Were Ten Of Them*. Ball came back with a segment called *Wacky Suicide Notes,* in which employees of places like Ethical Solutions and the Kevorkian Klinics submitted the most nonsensical, idiotic, and grammatically fractured things people put into their final statements.

Then it was time for the Devils.

I could tell this was the moment that Deppe and Dansiger and Bainbridge and Griswold had been waiting for me to see. The atmosphere in the room suddenly became tense and electric. Nobody said a word.

Harold Ball said, "You know, unless you're dead or really stupid or something, there's one commercial you couldn't possibly have missed."

They played *There Were Ten Of Them*. Howls and cheers went up from the audience.

Then, back to Ball: "Ladies and Gentlemen, it's my pleasure to introduce to you the group that made this spot such a treat. Please welcome, for their very first broadcast interview . . . *FERMAN'S DEVILS!*

The crowd went absolutely berserk. The camera panned over to the curtains. Ferman was the first one to emerge, looking cocky and confident. He made a vulgar gesture with his hand. The crowd loved it.

Nose came out next. From the look on his face it was evident that he was merely following his leader. When he looked up and saw the crowd, his mouth dropped open in astonishment. Then Jet emerged. Howls went up again and then changed to a low woof of *"Bro, Bro, Bro, Bro, Bro!"* Jet gave a toothy smile and raised a clenched fist in salute. The chant dissolved into screaming and cheering.

Finally, Rover appeared from behind the curtain, peering from side to side as if he was trying to avoid a police dragnet. He hesitated for a moment, then quickly trotted across the stage and disappeared in Jet's shadow. Hind and Erskine moved down to the far end of the couch. Ferman took the seat next to Ball, who said, "Welcome . . ." but then trailed off because the other three were having trouble figuring out where to sit. Ferman barked an order at them. Jet immediately sat on the couch closest to his leader, followed by Rover. Nose ended up next to Roddick Erskine. As he sat, he said, "Whaddyew lookin' at, Big Nose?"

The crowd roared. Erskine's nose was big, but obviously not as big as Nose's.

"Hey," Nose said, acknowledging the applause. "This is ranking great! We met Hateful back stage!"

"They didn't bleep him," I said.

"Why bother?" said Dansiger.

I shifted my gaze back to the set, where Ball was trying to regain control.

"Welcome to the show, boys," he said. "And I'd like to ask the question that's probably on the minds of most viewers right now—"

Nose stood, and in a loud voice announced all fourteen digits of his phone number. Then he said, "And girls, I just passed my test, if you know what I mean—and I think you do!"

It sounded like the men in the audience reacted to that, but the women didn't.

"Not quite," Ball laughed. "The question is, where is the fifth little Devil?"

"I ain't little," Jet protested.

"There's only four of us," said Ferman.

"I'm talking about the young man with the glasses who contributed so wonderfully to your thrashing of Norman Drain."

"Jimmy Jazz!" Jet blurted. Ferman's hand flew and cracked him in the mouth.

"Oh, *him*!" Ferman acted surprised. "He's . . . Well, he's dead."

My stomach plunged. I leaned forward and spoke just as Harold Ball did.

"What?"

"He is?" Nose asked.

Ferman looked at Ball as if sharing a private joke and rotated his index finger around his ear. "You'll have to forgive Nose. He got hit in the head a couple times too many. Tough, but it comes with the territory."

"I see. Now you referred to him as *Nose*?"

Ferman's head nodded loosely. "Ain't it kinda rankin' obvious?"

Ball's mouth hung open for half a second, enough to tell me that he was less happy with this profanity than the last. "So . . . you *all* have cute nicknames?"

"Cute!" snarled Jet.

"Nicknames!" growled Nose.

"Mister Ball," Ferman said, rising out of his chair and leaning across the desk to go nose-to-nose with the host. "They are our *street names.* They're badges of *honor* and *respect,* carefully chosen by me. And the quicker you get it through that ranking head of yours, the better!''

Ball didn't back down. ''Then,'' he said in a voice that was low but slowly rose in pitch, ''then why don't you ranking *tell* me about it instead of making a fool of yourself in front of most of the civilized world?'' A cheer went up from the crowd.

''Nobody talks to me like that,'' Ferman whispered.

''I just did,'' Ball said.

I held my breath.

Ferman smiled, then eased down into his seat. ''Well, Harold,'' he began—as if he was an old timer at this—''We all got these street names, and they all mean something to me and the owner.''

''So . . .'' Ball looked up at the audience and raised his eyebrows. It was the signal that a Ball Zinger was coming. The audience went dead quiet. ''How did you go about picking your Nose, then?''

Screaming, hysterical laughter. Ferman's knuckles went white as he gripped the arms of the chair.

''Well, Harold . . .'' He licked his lips and swallowed. ''As you can see, it's because of his rather large appendix . . .'' He glanced to one side as if he was looking for Jimmy Jazz. Worry flickered over his face when he realized that his reader was gone.

Ball let the malaprop go. He leaned around to look at Jet. ''And I assume that you are *Jet* because you are jet black?''

Ferman cackled. ''Naww. It's because of this.'' He stood, extending his hand down toward the biggest member of the Devils, and sang in his reedy tenor. *''Meet Jet Georgeson!''* Then he began to laugh hysterically, doubling over and clutching his sides, falling back into the guest chair.

The audience could only murmur.

''Why does he keep saying that?'' Griswold asked.

''Because he's a maroon,'' I said.

''What does that mean?'' asked Bainbridge.

''I don't know. I suspect they're related.''

''. . . why this quiet young man is called Rover,'' Ball was saying.

''Because he's our dog,'' said Ferman.

''Every gang got to have a dog,'' said Jet.

Ball leaned to look at Rover. ''And do you talk at all, Rover?''

Rover made the same vulgar gesture that Ferman had on his entrance. The audience came back to life and cheered.

Ball shrugged. "All right. Now I'd like to get back to the question of what happened to the fifth Devil—"

"There ain't no fifth Devil," Ferman said loudly.

"Jimmy Jazz," said Jet.

"Will you shut up!" Ferman yelled.

"Now Ferman, you said he's *dead*?"

Ferman froze for an instant. He reeled away from his boiling point and sat back in the chair, relaxed again.

"Well, Harold, that comes with the territory. You know, when you're a street gang, you always gotta be watchin' your back, 'cause you never know who's going to be waiting for you, wanting to put the knife in. The cops. The Nancy Boys. Your parents."

"And what position did Jimmy Jazz fill in the gang?"

"He—"

"He was our reader," Nose said, trying to be helpful.

"He means researcher," Ferman said quickly.

"Reader?" Ball leaned to look at Nose. "You mean you guys can't read?"

Nose laughed. "Of course not!"

Ferman was out of his chair again. "Nose, you rankin' idiot, I told you to keep your mouth shut and let me do the talkin'!"

Nose pointed straight into one of the cameras. "But Ferman, we're on the vid! Look!"

"Ferman," Ball said loudly. "About the death of Jimmy Jazz—"

"Yeah," said Nose.

"Jimmy Jazz, Jimmy Jazz," Ferman snarled. "Why do you always gotta ask about Jimmy Jazz? Why the rank don't you ask me about *me*?"

"I was going to," Ball said. "But I'm interested in the tragedy of Jimmy Jazz. And I'm sure my viewers are too, because they see him as their favorite—"

"FAVORITE!" Ferman cleared his throat and blew phlegm onto Ball's desk. "That's what *we* think of Jimmy Jazz."

Ball held up his hands—not defensively, but to show he was shifting gears. "All right. Jimmy Jazz is dead. Why don't you tell us what it was like to work with Norman Drain?"

"We coulda broke every bone in his body," Nose said proudly. "But they stopped us."

"Nose—" Ferman threatened.

"Who stopped you, Nose?" Ball asked.

"Nobody stops the Devils," Ferman said. "And why do you want to talk about Norman Drain anyway? He's just an old Homer."

"Homer?" Ball lifted his eyebrows. "Is that some more of your 'street gang talk?' "

"No!" Ferman spun on his heels. "It's commercial talk! You know! 'Here comes Homer! Homer-sexual!' "

I slapped my hand over my eyes. "Oh, no—"

There was a tug on my arm. Dansiger said, "*Watch,* Boddek-ker!"

"—and interestingly enough," Harold Ball was saying, "that's a Pembroke Hall commercial, too. Now as Pembroke Hall's gang—"

"No!" howled Ferman. "We're not Pembroke Hall's street gang! We're my gang! Mine!"

With one more feral cry of *"Mine!"* Ferman was airborne, neatly sailing over Harold Ball's desk, his hands reaching out and locking onto him. Then his full weight hit the comedian and they tumbled backwards into the backdrop, a twinkling holo of the Manhattan skyline. Nose was on his feet next, bolting to join the fray, but Roddick Erskine grabbed him by the shoulder and pulled him back.

It was a brave, ill-conceived move. Nose threw his elbow back in what clearly was a practiced move, and used it to crush Erskine's nose. Erskine fell back and landed on Billy Hind, who had only started to rise to the situation. Nose gleefully pounced on both of them, only to meet a stunning series of blows from Hind's fists.

Rover hopped up onto the back of the couch, looked left and right, then kicked and leaped into the Nose/Erskine/Hind imbroglio, all fists, teeth, and knees, not seeming to care whether his blows landed on friend or foe. The four fused into a tangled knot and rolled off the edge of the stage to the seats, where screaming audience members scrambled to get out of their way.

In the meantime, Jet calmly got up, bent, and tossed Harold Ball's desk to one side as if it had been made of cardboard. This revealed Ferman sitting on top of Ball, alternately throwing punches at his head and gut, screaming, "Homer! Homer! Homer!" as each blow landed. Jet put his hand to Ferman's shoulder and spoke words that went unheard in the din. Ferman nodded and climbed off of the cowering host.

"Will you look at that," I said.

Too soon.

As soon as Ferman was off, Jet attacked with a series of savage kicks. Then he pulled Ball off the floor, punched him in the face, and turned him to face Ferman, arms pinned back. Ferman walked away, turned, and ran full tilt at Ball, ramming his head into his victim's stomach.

I turned away from the scene. "Why didn't they cut to a commercial?"

"They were three minutes from the break," Griswold said. "If they'd gone early, that would have ruined the billing cycle for the spots."

"Here's the good part," Dansiger said.

I looked back at the vid. A shrill whistle came from the speaker and uniformed men began pouring in from either side of the stage. Jet and Ferman each grabbed one of Ball's arms and catapulted him into three of the oncoming officers, bowling them to the ground. Then they ran toward Erskine/Rover/Hind/Nose and deftly yanked their fellow Devils out of the tangle.

One of the officers fired something at Jet, who neatly pirouetted. Whatever it was struck Erskine in the back, knocking him to the ground and throwing him into violent convulsions.

Above the din, Ferman shouted, "Exit! Stage right!"

The Devils split and ran—Ferman and Rover toward stage right, Jet and Nose toward stage left—straight for a handful of waiting uniforms. At the last minute each of the four pivoted and dove off the stage into the audience, landing more or less on their feet—Jet grabbing Nose by the arm to keep him from going into a complete belly flop. And with several quick steps and a few flying leaps, they vanished into the crowd, which had already broken and was jamming their way toward the exit doors. Then one of the cameras swung back and zoomed in on one of the cops, who shouted something obscene. The sentiment he expressed was one clear to even the most ill-practiced of lip-readers.

"That's it?" I said as Deppe turned the replay off.

"There's about another two minutes of the crowd leaving. The cops do the old 'is there a doctor in the house' bit and one comes down to help until someone from Heal-O-Mat arrives."

"I mean the Devils—they got away?"

"Clean," said Dansiger.

"Fatalities?"

"Harold Ball's ego," said Griswold. "Billy Hind's ability to whistle *Dixie.*"

I sighed and sat back in my chair. "I'm glad I didn't see this last night."

Bainbridge said, "The police are drawing up warrants for the Devils, pending charges from the three victims and the officers injured during the brawl. The Devils are officially out of town until things blow over—"

"*Blow over!*" I shouted. "They could have killed—"

"We know," said Dansiger.

"Let her finish," said Deppe.

"They're not really out of town," Bainbridge continued. "They're here, holed up in our penthouse."

I nodded slowly. "All right. Let me think about this. Let me see what kind of spin can be put on this."

"*Spin!*" shouted Dansiger. "Boddekker, have you lost it?"

"This isn't such a bad thing," I told her. "Outside of damage to NanoKleen's reputation, which we can salvage—"

"He's lost it," Dansiger told Deppe.

"This is a good thing," I insisted. "It's going to take care of our Devils problem for us."

The others stopped and stared at me.

"They're criminals," I continued. "Common scum. Right? Where do they belong?" No answer. "C'mon. They belong in *jail,* right? Of course they do! And they've just committed assault, battery, intent to kill, grievous bodily harm, you name it—*in front of at least a billion witnesses!* By the end of the week, everyone in the whole world will have seen the highlights. They're going to get locked up in a really tiny cell and the keys will be thrown away."

"Boddekker," Bainbridge said. "Are you serious about this?"

I looked right in her eyes. "You've got to believe me. From the time they surrounded me on the street and threatened to kill me, I never wanted anything but to see them all rotting in a jail cell."

She looked away. "I guess I was wrong about you," she said, softly.

"Apology accepted," I said. "But that's not our problem. We should call the others together and brainstorm how we can separate NanoKleen from all of this—"

The conference room door flew open.

"BODDEKKER!"

It was Honniker In Accounting. She was out of breath.

"I hate to be the bearer of bad tidings—again—but have any of you looked out the window lately?"

Griswold moved toward the row of windows and started to open the blinds.

"Not those. The ones looking down on Madison."

"My office," I said, running for the door. I grabbed Honniker In Accounting by the hand and raced down the hall, the others at my heels. Darting into my office, I squeezed past the desk, leaned over the credenza, and told my ferret to de-tint the windows.

"Right away, Mr. Boddekker!"

The windows began to clear. Honniker In Accounting looked down and said, "Oh, my. It's gotten worse."

The others crowded in until there were six of us, pressed up against my window, peering down into the street below.

Deppe said, "Wow."

Dansiger said, "Incredible."

The unshakable Griswold said, "Hmm."

Below us, people had formed a crush around the main doors to our building. There were hundreds of them, spilling into the street, tying up the mid-morning bikeshaw traffic, fisted hands in the air, voices joined in a chant that we were too high up to hear.

"What are they here for?" Bainbridge asked.

"The Devils," replied Honniker In Accounting.

"But nobody knows they're here," Dansiger said.

"That's right."

Looking down at the swarming, seething mass of humanity, I began to chuckle. I stepped back from the window and lost myself to wave after wave of laughter.

Honniker In Accounting turned from the window and gave me a tentative look. "Boddekker?"

"I'm fine," I said, still laughing. "In fact, I couldn't be better." Then I gestured at the window in the direction of the crowd. "People," I announced. "It looks like we're going to be rid of the Ferman problem a lot sooner than I thought."

The mind becomes a deadly place to venture in

Circle of One

by Eric James Fullilove

"Razor-edged details, wicked violence and garish colors,
mixed with lots and lots of caffeine (or is it adrenaline?),
give *Circle of One* a voice and style of its own."
—Kevin J. Anderson

Eric James Fullilove creates an unforgettable protagonist in
Jenny Sixa, whose telepathic talent makes her a valuable asset to
the Los Angeles Police Department, saving her from a life in the
mind-sex meccas of the city. Jenny now serves as a consultant
for the LAPD, for she is able to read the final thoughts of victims to create an image of their killers. Jenny keeps some vital
information from the police, though, when she finds her name
in the final thoughts of three dead women. The remarkable
talent that has earned Jenny a living is the same one that has
placed her in the path of a murderer, and she must race to find
the killer before he strikes again.